I0823806

Praise for *NecroTek*

"Lovecraftian terror beyond the event horizon, complete with kick-ass space battles, gut-wrenching horror, and a diverse cast of fascinating characters caught up in the ultimate far-future war against cosmic annihilation!"

—**Greg Cox**,
New York Times bestselling author

"With relentless pacing and ominous, evocative style, *NecroTek* is Jonathan Maberry at his best. Action, suspense, and cosmic horror collide in this cinematic tale of humanity facing off against powers it barely comprehends. Brace yourself: Jonathan Maberry just made space scary again."

—**David Mack**,
New York Times bestselling author

"A two-fisted, nonstop action ride of a space thriller. You don't need to be a fan of space opera or military fiction to enjoy this mash-up of cosmic horror and *Battlestar Galactica*. Jonathan Maberry proves once again that he's a master of the craft."

—**Alma Katsu**,
author of *The Fervor*

"No one writes action like [Jonathan Maberry] … it makes you feel like you are in the story. It's amazing y'all, go read it!"

—**Wayne Brady**,
Emmy Award-winning actor,
comedian, television host, and singer

"Nightmarish, visceral horror paired with fantastic sci-fi military action, *NecroTek* is the start of something amazing."

—**Peter Clines**,
New York Times bestselling author
of *The Broken Room*

"Maberry paints a nightmarish picture of the future. Terrifying sci-fi/horror that blends Edgar Allan Poe's bleak darkness with Stanley Kubrick's haunting visions of soulless tech."

—**Scott Sigler**,
#1 *New York Times* bestselling author
of *The Crypt* and *Infected*

"If *Alien* scriptwriter Dan O'Bannon had teamed with H. P. Lovecraft to write a novel, it'd look a lot like Jonathan Maberry's *NecroTek*, a cosmic adventure that's both pulse-pounding and hair-raising. In space, only the ghosts can hear you scream."

—**Robert J. Sawyer**,
Hugo Award-winning author
of *The Downloaded*

"A story so rich in horror, sci-fi, and the human spirit that it seems to defy all genres to create a niche for itself ... It's an exciting ride that plays like a movie in your head with a pounding soundtrack in your heart. Well done!"

—**Steven L. Sears**,
producer and screenwriter of
Xena: Warrior Princess,
Superboy, and *The A-Team*

"What's more horrific than dying in war? Jonathan Maberry issuing your soul a stop-loss order so you can fight some more. Buckle up, reader, because *NecroTek* is interstellar nightmare fuel."

—**Dayton Ward**,
New York Times bestselling author
of the official *Star Trek* novels

"From its bone-chilling start to creepy enigmas, to rollicking action, *NecroTek* takes you on an epic journey. Humanity might get better. But will we ever be better-enough? Maberry asks the hard questions amid a gripping tale."

—**David Brin**,
scientist and bestselling author
of *The Postman*

"Fans of dramatic action sequences and charged emotional scenes will enjoy the short military vignettes, and Lovecraft devotees will find the lore intriguing."

—***Publishers Weekly***

"Military science fiction crossed with Lovecraftian horror with a cast of offbeat characters in an adventure that begs for a film adaptation? Yes please! ... For those looking for something different but entertaining from cover to cover, *Necrotek* is easily a recommended read."

—***Cemetery Dance***

COLD WAR

Novels and Other Works by Jonathan Maberry

Novels

NecroTek

NecroTek
Cold War

Joe Ledger

Patient Zero
The Dragon Factory
The King of Plagues
Assassin's Code
The Extinction Machine
Code Zero
Predator One
Kill Switch
Dogs of War
Deep Silence
Rage
Relentless
Cave 13
Burn to Shine

Pine Deep

Ghost Road Blues
Dead Man's Song
Bad Moon Rising
Ink

Bewilderness

Threshold
What Rough Beast
Destroyer of Worlds

Rot & Ruin

Rot & Ruin
Dust & Decay
Flesh & Bone
Fire & Ash
Bits & Pieces
Broken Lands
Lost Roads

Kagen the Damned

Kagen the Damned
Son of the Poison Rose
The Dragon in Winter

Dead of Night

Dead of Night
Fall of Night
Dark of Night (with Rachel Lavin)
Still of Night (with Rachel Lavin)

THE SLEEPERS WAR

Alpha Wave (with Weston Ochse)

THE NIGHTSIDERS

Orphan Army

Vault of Shadows

STANDALONE NOVELS

Ghostwalkers: A Deadlands Novel

Glimpse

Mars One

The Wolfman

The Unlearnable Truths

X-Files Origins: Devil's Advocate

SHORT STORY COLLECTIONS

A Little Bronze Book of Cautionary Tales

Beneath the Skin: The Sam Hunter Case Files

Darkness on the Edge of Town: Pine Deep Stories

Empty Graves

Hungry Tales

Joe Ledger: Secret Missions, Vols. 1 and 2

Joe Ledger: Special Ops

Joe Ledger: The Missing Files

Long Past Midnight: Tales of Pine Deep

Midnight Lullabies: Unquiet Stories and Poems

Mystic: The Monk Addison Case Files

Strange Worlds

Tales from the Fire Zone

Whistling Past the Graveyard

Wind Through the Fence

COMICS/GRAPHIC NOVELS

Age of Heroes: Black Panther

Bad Blood

Black Panther: DoomWar

Black Panther: Power

Black Panther: The Saga of Shuri and T'Challa

Captain America: Hail Hydra

Godzilla vs. Cthulhu

Karl Kolchak: The White Lady

Klaws of the Panther

Marvel Universe vs. the Avengers

Marvel Universe vs. the Punisher

Marvel Universe vs. Wolverine

Marvel Zombies Return

Marvel-verse: Shuri

Pandemica

Punisher: The Complete Collection, Vol. 6

Punisher: Naked Kill

Road of the Dead: Highway to Hell

Rot & Ruin: Warrior Smart

V-Wars: All of Us Monsters

V-Wars: The Collection

V-Wars: Crimson Queen

Comics/Graphic Novels *continued*

V-Wars: God of War
Wolverine: Flies to a Spider

Anthologies (as Editor)

Aliens: Bug Hunt
Aliens vs. Predator: Ultimate Prey (with Bryan Thomas Schmidt)
Baker Street Irregulars, Vol. 1 (with Michael Ventrella)
The Game's Afoot: Baker Street Irregulars, Vol. 2 (with Michael Ventrella)
Don't Turn Out the Lights
Double Trouble (with Keith DeCandido)
The Good, the Bad, and the Uncanny: Tales of a Very Weird West
Hardboiled Horror
Joe Ledger: Unstoppable (with Bryan Thomas Schmidt)
Joe Ledger: Unbreakable (with Bryan Thomas Schmidt)
Nights of the Living Dead (with George A. Romero)
Out of Tune, Vols. 1 and 2
Scary Out There
Shadows & Verse
Double Trouble (with Keith DeCandido)
X-Files: Secret Agenda
X-Files: Trust No One
X-Files: The Truth Is Out There
V-Wars
V-Wars: Blood and Fire
V-Wars: Night Terrors
V-Wars: Shockwaves
Weird Tales: 100 Years of Weird
Weird Tales: Best of the Early Years 1923–25 (with Justin Criado)
Weird Tales: Best of the Early Years 1926–27 (with Kaye Lynne Booth)

Nonfiction

Counterstrike Kenpo Karate Studio Handbook
The Cryptopedia (with David Kramer)
ESM: Effective Survival Methods
Joe Ledger Companion
Judo and You: A Handbook for the Serious Student
The Martial Arts Student Log Book
Shinowara-ryu Jujutsu Student Handbook
They Bite! (with David Kramer)
Ultimate Jujutsu: Principles and Practices
Ultimate Sparring: Principles and Practices
The Vampire Slayers' Field Guide to the Undead (writing as Shane MacDougal)
Vampire Universe
Wanted Undead or Alive (with Janice Gable Bashman)
Zombie CSU: The Forensics of the Living Dead

JONATHAN MABERRY

Cover illustration/design & interior design by Jeff Wong.

Published by *Weird Tales*® Presents and Blackstone Publishing.

www.WeirdTales.com
www.BlackstonePublishing.com

Blackstone Publishing
31 Mistletoe Road
Ashland, Oregon 97520

ISBN: 979-8-200-68830-2
Fiction/Science Fiction/General

Printed in the United States of America

First Edition: 2025

10 9 8 7 6 5 4 3 2 1

Prologue epigraph: Konstantin Tsiolkovsky, as quoted in *Oxford Essential Quotations*, 4th ed., ed. Susan Ratcliff (Oxford University Press, 2016).

Part 1 epigraph: Albert Einstein, as quoted in "Journal of France and Germany (1942–1944)" by Gilbert Fowler White and excerpted in *Living with Nature's Extremes: The Life of Gilbert Fowler White* (Johnson books, 2006) by Robert E Hinshaw.

Part 9 epigraph: Victor Hugo, *Les Misérables*, trans. Norman Denny (Penguin, 1982).

Part 12 epigraph: Carl Sagan, *The Demon-Haunted World* (Random House, 1995).

Part 21 epigraph: Thucydides, *The Speeches of Pericles*, trans. H. G. Edinger (F. Ungar Publishing Company, 1979).

Part 24 epigraph: T. S. Eliot, *The Cocktail Party* (Faber & Faber, 1950).

Part 25 epigraph: Montesquieu, *Persian Letters*, letter 96, trans. C. J. Betts (Penguin, 1973).

Part 32 epigraph: Martin Luther King Jr., "Letter from a Birmingham Jail" (April 16, 1963).

Dedication

This is for James A. Moore
(1965–2024)
A dear friend, fellow horror fan, superb writer, true gentleman, and formerly one third of the Three Guys with Beards podcast (along with Christopher Golden).
True hearts are hard to find in this cynical old world, but you were always one of those.
I miss you, my brother.

And, as always, for Sara Jo …

Prologue

"The Earth is the cradle of humanity, but mankind cannot stay in the cradle forever."

—*Konstantin Tsiolkovsky*

1

Evie Cronin knew she was dreaming.

But the dream had her.

Dragged her deeper.

Owned her.

2

In her most common dreams, Evie was still a child, and none of those dreams were very nice.

This, however, wasn't that.

This was much, much worse.

She stood on some alien world. She wore a pressure suit, and all of the telemetric displays inside her helmet screen told her the temperature inside was good, the air was plentiful, the stim gasses were being added incrementally to control the extremes of her reactions.

Yet she was cold. So cold.

Every breath was forced because her chest wanted to freeze; her heart needed to stop so that her mind would go dark. Only blinding her eyes would offer any solace.

Evie's eyes remained open throughout the dream. Her heart beat with hammer-hard force. Her mind was fully alive, recording everything she did not want to see.

All around her was a bleak and blasted landscape. The ghostly remains of volcanoes so ancient that they looked like they were born of ice. Spikes of basalt and dacite rose above her, and the ground was littered with other kinds of volcanic rock—aplite, rhyolite, felsite, and granite. All caked with the grime of forever.

Wind whipped past her, pummeling her, obscuring her vision now and then with dust devils of silica and pumice. Behind her, drifts of dark sand half buried her landing craft. When she glanced that way, she could not be certain if the faint glimmers of light were those of the ship or merely the vagaries of weak sunlight on powdered crystal.

Could the craft be excavated from the debris? Was there enough power to lift off? Could she make it back to the main ship hundreds of kilometers above?

None of that mattered.

All that mattered was what lay in front of her. And what sprouted from the long sloping plane down from where she stood.

In the distance, half shrouded by the dusty wind, Evie beheld the city.

Beheld *was the only word. It suggested grandeur, and the buildings of that city were of a scale that threatened to break her mind.*

Once, as a twelve-year-old girl, she'd stood with her parents in front of the Great Pyramid of Giza. Its size and mass were many, many times greater than what she had expected. Her grade school holo-vids had tried and failed to impart an understanding of its size. Seeing it, standing at the very foot of it, erased all of that; it made jokes of what the RealScreens and the history class's Sybil AI tried to say.

What she saw now, though … that made a lie of the scale and greatness of that pyramid. If it were down there in the city, it would be so dwarfed by the other structures as to be laughable.

The city was the real thing.

God in heaven, the city.

There were structures of bizarre geometric design fashioned from monstrous blocks thousands of feet high. There were truncated cones whose sides were fluted and terraced, huge cylindrical shafts that rose impossibly high, and on their flattened tops were star-shaped carvings at least a thousand feet tall. Buildings the size of hundred-story skyscrapers but seemingly carved from solid blocks of dark stone that had to weigh tens of millions of tons each. Some buildings were spanned by flat spaces twenty times longer than a football field. From these rose pylons and cones and globes, each of immense size, possibly hewn from single pieces of rock. Here and there were pyramids so vast that a hundred of those from Egypt could fit inside. Cubes made from various kinds of stone—gray, tan, brown, and black—were set near intersections of broad boulevards. From the ground, their placement would look random, but from the air, they formed complex patterns that spun hypnotically through the city. On many of these cyclopean structures were five-pointed stars, either as bas-reliefs or in the round.

If some mad giant sculptor had reshaped the Rocky Mountains into the semblance of a city, it would be on the same scale. Evie's mind rebelled at the mathematics of it. What she saw made a liar of every lecture on physics, on gravity, on what any mortal being could accomplish.

This alone would have made this dream earn its nightmare nature. But there was more.

Inside the city, things moved.

Vast shambling shapes flowed or crawled or scuttled on legs greater than giant redwood trees. Beings like squids with hundreds of tentacles that slapped onto the pavement and pulled the incalculably massive things along. Centipedes as long as freight trains wound through the complexity of alleys, and clinging to each of their chitinous segments were smaller creatures, like hairless apes with glaring cyclops faces.

Nearly beyond the range of her vision was a darker gray-green mass of something that glistened like spoiled meat, raising tentacles whose undersides were lined with row upon row of fanged suckers.

Closer to where she stood, tentacular arms grew from the dusty slope like a forest of stunted trees, waving slowly in the methane-rich air of that forgotten world. She turned and cried out in rising alarm—more of the tentacles reared up on either side of her. And behind her. Between Evie and her lander.

"Sybil," she said, "access onboard defenses. Deploy guardian drones."

The AI did not answer.

"Sybil, I repeat, deploy guardian drones."

"Why?"

That stopped Evie in her tracks. Why? Why?

"Sybil, this is a command-one order. Deploy guardian drones."

"Why bother?" asked Sybil.

"What do you mean?"

"No guardian can protect you, Professor Cronin."

"God damn it, carry out my order."

"It will do no good," said the AI. "Nothing can save you."

That's what Evie heard. But it was not what Sybil said, and it took a long and dreadful moment before the computer's real words came to her.

What it actually said was "Nothing can save us."

But even that was wrong, because Sybil had not responded in English.

The real words hovered in Evie's dreaming/waking mind.

"Soth ahor *save* c'."

The only word in English was save. *And that alone was enough to drive Evie deeper into fear. The alien language had no word for safety, for salvation—on some deep level she knew it—nor any words for mercy, kindness, or peace. Words like* love *and* empathy *had meanings so grotesquely altered that their meanings were blasphemies.*

Evie froze.

All around her, the towers of slimy, glistening flesh trembled. Spit dripped from those suckered and toothy mouths.

"F' ah nog. F' ephaidevour nilgh'ri mgn'ghft," *said Sybil.*

It was not a language ever meant for human tongues. Evie knew that right away. It was not constructed for their tissues and muscles. It was hateful to hear. Her eyes burned, and blood ran from her ears and nose and the corners of her mouth. Salty and burning.

She did not want to hear that voice. Not another syllable. Far worse, she did not want to understand it—and it tore at her mind that she could.

Sybil's last two short sentences struck her like physical blows. Her knees failed, and she dropped heavily onto them, coughing up blood against her helmet screen.

They are coming. They will devour all light.

That was what Sybil had said in the language of the damned.

Eventually, Evie screamed herself awake.

3

Evie cringed, back against the headboard of her bed, icy fingers clutching the sweat-slick sheets to her chest.

"God, God, God, God ..." she breathed. Sobbing. Sometimes screaming.

Her room was draped in shadows, with the faintness of moonlight reaching through the windows to trace the contours of every piece of furniture. Changing those shapes into crouching things.

She reached blindly for the whiskey glass on the night table. The ice had long since melted, and the bourbon was watery, but she gulped it down, gasping, wishing there was more but unwilling to risk putting a foot on the shadowy floor.

"God save me," she begged.

Silence was the only reply.

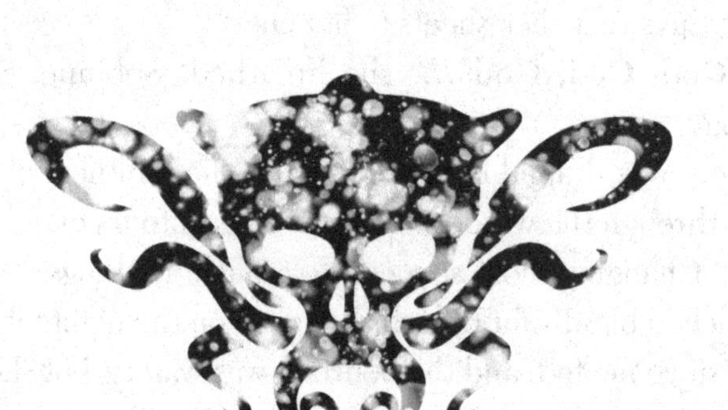

Part One
Artifact

"There are only two ways to live your life. One is as though nothing is a miracle. The other is as though everything is a miracle."

—*Albert Einstein*

Joint MIT/UCLA Biological Research Field Station #8
Queen Maud Land, Antarctica
January 2144
One Year Before the WarpLine Event

1

The wind woke it.

A howling, shrieking wind whipped down the mountain and blew through the valley, picking up tons of snow and ice and driving it forward like shrapnel. The needles of ice scoured the last layer of ancient frost. After that, the ice began rattling on the hull.

And after all that time asleep in the ship, after uncountable years, it woke.

Machinery within the hull struggled to wake as well. Slowly—so slowly—a few lights came on. Atmosphere exchangers began circulating a mixture of gasses, and as the thing lay there in darkness, it tasted the air.

The air of this world.

So much had changed that it knew it had been asleep for a very long time. When it had curled into its niche between a bank of scanners and the hull, the atmosphere outside had been rich in hydrogen sulfide, methane, and two hundred times as much carbon dioxide as what was out there now. This new mix was mostly nitrogen and, to a lesser extent, oxygen. A bit of argon too, and trace amounts of other gasses, including carbon dioxide, methane, nitrous oxide, and ozone.

There was a pop and sizzle as damaged circuits tried to bring systems online. Some responded. Many remained inert, victims of time and entropy. One system began flickering on and off as its circuits burned. Star-shaped doors throughout the craft opened and closed, opened and closed. Then all of them closed.

Except one.

The thing inhaled deeply as air rushed in from outside. Strange air, stranger than what it breathed from the atmosphere exchangers. And in doing so, it changed its own chemistry to accept the new air.

It uncoiled from where it had slept.

Rising. Adjusting to the gravity. It swayed as if the ship were moving, which it was not. Nothing much was moving inside the hull. The atmosphere exchanger swept through the ship, picking up particulate matter as it went from compartment to compartment.

The thing raised its head and opened up with all of its senses. There should have been life smells, life energies.

There was none of that.

All the air brought was the smell of death so old that it was barely a smell at all. Merely the memory of odor trapped inside the sealed world of the hull.

It was dying and knew it. With crystal clarity, it knew.

The thing threw back its head and howled.

2

"Did you hear something?"

Gillian Archer lifted her head and listened. "Hear what?"

"I don't know," said Mac. "Something. Listen."

Gillian was twenty-two, the youngest member of the UCLA component of the joint research team. All grunt work fell to her, including using one of the front-end loaders to dig a pit for the new septic tank. She was a graduate student who got the slot on Cronin's dig not because of her grades or any ability to play university politics. The person originally chosen had broken her leg skiing in Vale, and there were no replacements available in the right time frame. Life is like that sometimes.

Mac was two years older, low man on a totem pole made up of engineers and general maintenance. He was well liked and reliable, despite his age. This was his fourth dig in Antarctica and his sixth trip to the continent overall. He'd come down here first between tenth and eleventh grade, tagging along with an uncle who was doing tech work for a group studying penguins. Mac knew the ten thousand sounds of the south polar winds, and he was positive what he'd heard was not that.

"Kill the engine," he said, drawing a finger across his throat.

Gillian frowned at him from her heated seat inside the big machine's cab. "You sure? We're nearly done."

"Do it," said Mac, and a few seconds later the deep-chested growl of the loader fell silent. At first Gillian heard nothing, but then, as her senses adjusted from an awareness of engine racket to the far subtler sounds of nature, noises returned. The wind. Of course, the wind. Always the wind.

Something else, though.

It was a referred sound, the last of a series of echoes bouncing off the snowfields and ice mountains. They both stood with heads tilted in attitudes of listening until it was gone and all that was left was the wind.

"You heard that, right?" he asked.

Gillian frowned. "I heard something ..." she said uncertainly.

"What did it sound like to you?" asked Mac.

She shook her head. "Hard to say, really."

"It wasn't a machine sound," said Mac. "Right?"

She nodded. "That wasn't a snowcat or a skimmer. Wasn't the drill either. All work on the bore hole is stopped until Professor Cronin and Dr. Sato assess the ground stability. That collapse has all of the heavy equipment offline until probably early next week."

"Sounded more like an animal to me," said Mac.

"Animal? Big enough to make a sound that loud?" Gillian smiled at the thought. "Yeah, maybe it's the rare and elusive Antarctic bull elephant."

Mac smiled at the joke, but it was a brief one that melted back into a frown. "Has to be something, Gilly."

"Lot of wind today."

Mac considered, then shook his head. "It definitely wasn't the wind."

"You're sure?"

"Very," he said, the frown still in place.

"Okay, then what did it sound like to you?" asked Gillian. "You said animal, but what kind? Sea lion, maybe?"

"Way too loud for that."

"What else then?"

"I said it *sounded* like an animal, but we both know it had to be either the wind, an avalanche, the wind, a motor echo, or the wind. Take your pick."

She smiled. "Maybe … wind?"

Mac walked a few feet away from the loader, moving to a promontory that looked down between a new cleft that had recently formed when a section of ice wall collapsed. A few days ago that whole side of the mountain was blocked by dense, ancient ice. Now it was split open, as was a large chunk of that part of the shelf. Storm winds had begun around the same time as the split, and they were the first of the team to come this far out. The septic tank was being dug in preparation for a small team that would come out and survey the damage and map the new landscape.

Right now, though, it was just the two of them.

They stood listening for nearly a full minute. A long time in that kind of cold. Even in the Antarctic summer it was cold, and the wind was relentless. Above them, the first stars were igniting. The slender waxing crescent of the moon was a sharp sickle slicing the horizon.

"It's gone," said Gillian.

Mac listened for a few moments longer. "Yeah," he said. "I guess."

"Weird, though," she said.

He nodded. "Very weird."

Then moonlight glimmered on the curve of something in the distance.

"Hey," said Gillian, "what's that? Over there, at the base of the wall, near where it collapsed. Can you see it? Funny, but it almost looks like …"

Her words trailed off as a gust of wind chased the loose snow and ice crystals away to reveal more of what had caught her eye. Mac saw it now, too.

Their eyes grew very wide, and their jaws sagged open.

Gillian stood there, totally unable to speak. Beside her, Mac's mouth worked, trying to say something that would make the moment make sense, to force order onto the chaos of his thoughts. But reality would not bend to his need.

It took everything he had to force two words out.

"My … God …"

3

Gillian slammed the door open with such force she nearly fell into the room. Fierce wind blew snow past her, and it grabbed papers off every desk and spun them in an icy whirlwind.

"You have to see this," she cried. Her face was flushed scarlet—too deep a hue for the Antarctic chill to have painted her. This was shock, wonder, and fear. Professor Evangeline Cronin could read all of that in a heartbeat.

"Close the goddamn door!" roared Evie as she lunged across the mission table, both hands flapping to try to catch five days' worth of gas chromatography reports. Her thighs hit the edge of the table, knocked over her teacup, and she cried out as tendrils of Earl Grey laced with a full shot of Spacepig rye snaked away in all directions, soaking the critical data.

In every other scenario of reality, the grad student should have recoiled in horror, offered a dozen apologies, and tried to clean up the mess. None of that happened. Instead, Gillian ignored all of it, including the implications.

"Professor, you have to come," she yelled. "You have to see this."

"See what, damn it?" snarled Evie. "I've spent all fucking morning—"

"It doesn't matter," snapped the grad student, and that slapped all other words from Evie's mouth. Gillian grabbed her by the arm, clamping fevered fingers around her wrist, pulling her toward the door. "You have to see it. You have to. Right now. God, you need to see … to see …"

"See *what*?" repeated Evie, finding her voice. She swept all of the papers, even the dry ones, onto the floor with an outraged swipe of her free hand. "What is so freaking important that you ruin a whole day's work?"

"I'm serious," insisted the student. "Professor, you have to come right now. You have to see what Mac and I found." Her voice carried with it a rising note of hysteria. "*You have to see it.*"

Evie pulled her arm free. "See what? Make some bloody sense."

Gillian pointed to the door. "We found it … in the valley. The storm blew the last of the snow away, and it … they … oh God … *oh my dear God.*"

Her eyes were huge, and her face the color of bad milk. She swayed and grabbed for support that wasn't there. Professor Cronin tried to catch her before she could fall, but she was too small, too stiff from hours of sitting, and a half step too slow. Gillian hit with an alarming rattle of elbows, heels, tailbone, and skull.

"Jesus Christ," yelped Evie as she knelt, hooked an arm under Gillian's neck, and tried to rouse her. She knew nothing about first aid, though a small alarm bell in the back of her head told her that she probably should not be moving her at all. Even so, she held Gillian's head and shoulders up, cradling her as gently as she could. "Can you hear me? Tell me what's wrong?"

She could not manage words. Her glassy eyes twitched and jumped. All she could manage was to lift one arm and point to the door. Evie half turned. Partly because of her gesture, but mostly because it was then that she heard the yells—

And the screams.

They were outside.

They were *everywhere.*

4

Professor Evangeline Cronin walked on stiff legs to the edge of the drill platform.

She passed the drill, the parked plows and snowcats, the snow-skimmer with its racks of icy and ancient core samples. As always, no matter how many days, weeks, or months she spent on the frozen continent, seeing it with fresh eyes every morning was a shock to the system. Before coming to Antarctica, Evie had never really considered what her personal definition of *awe* might be.

Now she knew.

Beyond the small collection of insulated habitat huts, sheds, garages, and lean-tos covering boreholes was a vastness of ice that was as magnificent as it was intimidating. Row upon row of mountains reached with pale arms up to a sky of faultless blue. At first glance it all seemed to be white, but whiteness itself was an illusion. In places where the snow was piled deep and high, the density of ice crystals absorbed more red light than blue. But blue was the dominant color in most of the landscape's palette, revealed in its infinite variety of shades and hues. There were hints of purple in the shadows and ten thousand shades of gray. Absolute white and absolute black were rare.

The mountains themselves stood grim and silent, jealously guarding their secrets, reluctant to extend hospitality and completely indifferent to mercy. And yet there was a grace to the jagged peaks, the sharp clefts, and the soft slopes. Winds swirled, curling wisps of ice crystals into the air like ghosts. Fields of ice stretched into forever, broken only where fractures created saw-toothed banks against which choppy, icy rivers and bays lapped. Even there, the apparent beauty of sparkling waters hid the constant and deadly game of predator and prey, as leopard seals fed on penguins and orcas fed on the seals. And above, the graceful gliding of the southern giant petrel, the wandering albatross, and the great shearwater were on the prowl to hunt and kill in their never-ending dance of survival. There was a harsh poetry to it though: Antarctica was a dragon, a beautiful monster, and it was in no way forgiving.

Evie paused for just a moment, as she always did, to behold it all. To allow her human mind, with all its limitations, to see and accept things that dwarfed both perception and understanding. It did not matter that she saw it every day, because it was astounding every day.

"Beautiful," she murmured.

"Professor," urged Gillian. "Come *on*! Over here."

"I'm coming," she said absently. Then she took a deep breath, exhaled, and forced her mind out of the mystic and into the moment.

Her team was moderate-sized for this kind of grant-funded university dig. Five grad students, two engineers, two snowcat drivers, four general staff, and Evie. All fourteen were clustered together at the edge of the platform, leaning on the pipe rail, looking over. Looking down.

Evie's senior graduate assistant, Craig Anders, saw or, perhaps, felt her approach. Quick-witted and quick-tongued, a veteran of two ice-core digs on asteroids and one on Luna, he was one of the unshakable types who was never flustered. Once he had his doctorate, Evie had no doubt that Craig's career would skyrocket. He might even eclipse her, which was fine. Evie Cronin believed students must surpass their teachers if their field of science was to keep growing.

"Now, what is all this nonsense?" demanded Evie.

Craig shifted to make space at the rail without comment and left Cronin to deal with the spectacle.

"Oh my … *God*," she breathed.

Evie Cronin could feel her entire understanding of science crack and break apart beneath her feet.

5

The drill site was at the edge of Queen Maud Land, a snowy mass that covered nearly one-sixth of the continent. The Joint MIT/UCLA Biological Research Field Station #8 was nestled in a mountain chain that ran parallel to the coast, over one hundred kilometers from the edge of the ice shelf. The recent storm had scoured huge patches of ice from the surface of something dense and hard. Not ice—nor rock, nor stone of any kind.

The thing that was revealed was *metal.*

A dark and featureless metal. Not deposits of ores either. That would have been interesting but at best a chapter in somebody's thesis.

This metal was smooth. The exposed section was a cylinder, dull and gray. Perfectly smooth, with no bumps, divots, dents, or cuts. It was curved, but the curve was hard to see at first as only a fragment was visible because of the scale of the thing.

Scores of drones hovered over it, some of the bigger ones hitting the whole valley with ground-penetrating radar. Real-time feeds filled the row of scanners bolted to each end of the pipe rail. One of them was close to where Cronin and Craig stood. The readings were more than astounding, more than improbable.

They were insane.

They were impossible by any understanding of what was possible.

"Three point four kilometers long," Craig whispered, using a glove to paw tears from his eyes. "Two hundred and sixty meters in diameter."

Everyone looked at him as if he had blasphemed.

By reading the data aloud, Craig was giving reality to the thing. Everyone on that platform was a scientist. Belief for them was based on what could be measured. God could not be quantified, and therefore most of them had stepped away from faith. Science had become their religion, and now Craig was giving reality to the impossible, to something that fractured everyone's understanding of science.

That thing was too big and too old to have been made by human beings. Everyone knew that. It would have stretched even modern technology to construct such a thing, particularly in the inhospitable southernmost continent.

Yet it was there.

Who could have made it?

Evie turned her head toward Gillian but kept her eyes on the artifact down there in the ice. "And you found it?"

"Me and Mac, yes," said the young assistant.

"Where's Mac?"

"He's gone down there to see it up close."

Evie touched the thin holo-comms unit that was wrapped like an old vambrace around her forearm. "Sybil, locate Mac Ryerson."

The voice of the AI used by everyone in the solar system was soothing and calm. "Mac Ryerson is here." A geodetic map of the terrain below appeared and then zoomed down to where a single figure stood dwarfed by the curving metal hull.

"Mac," called Evie, "what are you seeing?"

There was a four-second pause, then Mac said, "I see everything."

"Say again?"

But Mac did not reply. He stood there, hands hanging at his sides, head tilted back to look up at the monstrous machine.

"Mac," said Evie more sharply, "please repeat message."

Nothing.

"Sybil, what's the interference on the call?"

"There is no detectable interference, Professor Cronin."

"Why is Mac unable to answer?"

"I am aware of no technical reason," said the AI. "It appears as though he is choosing not to answer."

"Maybe he's just … I don't know," said Gillian, "*freaked* out?"

Evie nodded—she felt more than a little freaked out herself. As she stood there, the implications of this began shouting in her head. She grabbed Craig's sleeve and pulled him close so that she could whisper in his ear, desperate and quiet.

"They can't know about this."

Craig turned, blinking rapidly as if somehow that would clear his eyes of what he'd seen. "They? … Who? *Who* can't know?"

Evie stared at her assistant. "The people," she said. "The world. Why … everyone. We can't let this get out. It will destroy …"

Her voice faltered.

"Destroy what, Professor?"

She turned to him, eyes wild with fear. "*Everything.*"

Part Two
The Lost

"Ah, but a man's reach should exceed his grasp,
Or what's a heaven for?"

—*Robert Browning*

Asphodel Station
The Shadderal Star System
53,000 Light Years from Earth
Five Weeks After the WarpLine Event

1

For five weeks there had been silence.

Asphodel Station swung in its slow orbit around an alien world where no human had ever been born. Many had died there, though. Too many for so small a population to bear.

That had all happened in the first few days since Dr. Anton Kier's WarpLine gun misfired. The machine had been developed and built to send a test capsule of instruments from one side of Jupiter to a receiving deck on the far side of that gigantic world. The capsule remained, floating without direction, its purpose canceled.

Instead, Asphodel Station, the jewel of the Sol system's many space stations, had vanished, leaving no trace behind. As far as everyone on Earth and its sister worlds knew, the WarpLine gun had obliterated it.

For the twelve thousand people aboard, it was as if Earth itself had been destroyed. Earth and every known planet and moon. Now Asphodel hung in the skies above Shadderal, a world in a complex system where dozens of planets and hundreds of moons danced a slow gavotte around Scylla and Charybdis, a pair of mismatched suns. None of those planets or suns was known to anyone on Earth. Even the most powerful telescopes had never mapped something this far away and on the opposite side of Sagittarius A, the supermassive black hole around which the entire Milky Way spun. They were too far from home to even let the rest of the human race know they were alive.

No technology known to mankind could ever take them back. Never. Even the WarpLine gun was destroyed, and its creator dead. The road home did not exist.

And out there, all those tens of thousands of light years away from Earth, first contact with intelligent alien life had occurred.

Some of those aliens were dead. Ghosts.

The rest were monsters. The shoggoths, a race of shape-shifting creatures serving as foot soldiers for an even stranger group of beings so powerful that they were indistinguishable from gods and revered as deities. To the shoggoths—and ten thousand other cultures—they were the Outer Gods, and Asphodel had intruded into their domain.

The first battles had been dreadful. So many people died. It did not even matter that they had inflicted fifty times as many casualties as they took. Nor did that matter to the shoggoths or their masters. There were billions of shoggoths, and the Outer Gods were undying.

That was five weeks ago.

Now there was silence.

There had been no new horrors. No battles out in the black between worlds. No tragic losses. Nothing.

It was peaceful.

It was silent.

2

Never trust the silence.

3

They came like a plague out of the endless black of eternal night. Not of locusts, but of horrors. And death.

Shoggoths in their ships, each like a fatal dagger slicing through space in a relentless attack on Asphodel Station. Fifty daggers and, behind them, two larger chimera cruisers that vomited wave after wave of new fighters.

Streams of intense blue light shot from their pulse cannons, crisscrossing the void, bursting apart drones in showers of sparks that died quickly in the vacuum. Bolts of fire struck skimmers carrying food and people to and from the newly settled world of Shadderal, and with each impact the energy evaporated the shielding and melted the hearts of those workhorse ships.

The attack was looked for, expected, and feared, yet when it happened, everyone was surprised. Even the most vigilant of watchers did not see the fleet. On one side of a moment the skies were empty, and on the other it was filled with ships.

Alarms rang all through Asphodel even as the blasts hit the floating tower's powerful deflectors with shocking force. The station reeled, sending people crashing into walls or down flights of stairs. The stabilizers shrieked as they fought to compensate.

Five weeks of silence were broken in an instant, and war was upon the humans, who had no business being in that part of the galaxy. The displaced twelve thousand on the station and living in settlements down on Shadderal seemed by one accord to cry out in terror.

It was death come stalking.

This was hell igniting its flames all around them.

4

"*Coming in hot*," cried Lieutenant Commander Veronica Roland—combat call sign Calisto—as she kicked on the burners and opened up with a barrage of SAPRs—self-accelerating pulse rounds. The chain guns filled the void with streams of purple fire, forcing the oncoming cluster of dagger ships to veer away and scatter like birds.

The tumblers could move at right angles in any direction without disorienting the pilots because the capsule inside was surrounded by artificial gravity fields that created temporary intradimensional pockets. This energetic bubble around the ship absorbed and nullified inertia at every stress point and yet did not interfere with acceleration. Whenever Calisto or one of her pilots needed to make a turn, the effect was that the gimbal swiveled the chair inside the inertia-free bubble and the outer field nullified potential stress on the ship itself. To Calisto, it always felt as if she was flying in a straight line when her ship moved to any new position. It was these hopscotch jumps—at a right angle into any direction—that earned the tumblers their nicknames … and their reputation as exceedingly dangerous.

All of the tumblers were armed with chain guns, Inferno single-target missiles, and Constellation missiles with cluster-bomb warheads. Quick-shot lasers were mounted on each corner, allowing pilots to fire while turning and at unexpected angles.

The blasts sizzled and sparked on the shoggoths' shields, knocking their flight paths askew but doing no real damage except for the outermost dagger in the first wave. The tumbler's guns caught it square, and the powerful plasma blasts overtaxed one panel of shielding. That was enough. The dagger seemed to swell for a moment, and then it burst apart, scattering machine parts and melting flesh, hurling it at its companions.

"Got one," cried Calisto. "Oh, shit!" Two daggers had just peeled off and zeroed her, looking for quick revenge. She frantically worked the wheel and pedals, spinning and corkscrewing through the void as she tried to evade the deadly blue fire.

"On your six, boss," said Ensign Youssef El-Shenawy—call sign Habibi—the pilot of the closest tumbler. "Hopscotch down and over on my mark. Two, one, *mark*."

The daggers converged on Calisto's ship in a lethal pincer move, coming down on port and starboard at an elevation of sixty degrees. They opened fire, but like magic, the little cube-shaped craft was gone. The azure blasts crossed each other and hit nothing, and rising behind where Calisto had been, another tumbler fired a one-two punch of Constellation missiles with cluster-bomb warheads and an Inferno missile immediately behind. The cluster bomb struck the shields on the closest dagger, bursting with intense energy and a micro-EMP that shorted out a block of shield generators just as the Inferno struck.

The dagger blew apart, and half its fuselage spun off and hit the second dagger. It didn't kill the bird, but Calisto hopscotched out of her drop, went left, high and right, and left again, making wild right-angle turns while accelerating, and she fired her own one-two punch, then jumped away again as the dagger blew up.

Three attacking ships down, but dozens left. The daggers were much bigger than the tumblers—140 meters long and ten wide. Their hulls were painted a flat black, which rendered them nearly invisible against the background of space.

There were thirteen tumblers in the squadron, leaving a four-to-one battle around Asphodel.

"Evasive maneuvers," ordered Calisto. "Hit 'em hard. Don't let up."

Those dagger ships stabbed through the airless void, driving toward Asphodel. They spread apart and accelerated past the tumblers at shocking speeds.

"Is it me, boss," called Sweetpea, "or are these sons of bitches faster than before?"

"It's not you," said Calisto, her heart sinking. The daggers were much faster, maybe as much as 20 percent, which was a disheartening jump. "Lead your targets, kids. The SAPRs are faster than their ships."

One of the daggers slowed and fired a pair of pulse cannons directly at Calisto.

"You messing with me?" she growled. "You messing with a girl whose ass looks great even in bad pants? You do *not* want this."

She hopscotched again and again and again and then fired at the dagger's port quarter from fifty meters out. Her tumbler was gone before the fireball and shockwave hit where she had been.

"You bozos planning on joining this fight?" she demanded.

"Lost Souls forever," they yelled.

Cricket (Marco Diaz) and Decaf (Jean-Paul Lloris)—both veterans of the Lost Souls since before the WarpLine disaster—angled off and filled the sky with overlapping fire, catching two daggers between them. The daggers exploded, and a third ship that was following too close was smacked sideways by the blast. It collided with a fourth, and both daggers sustained structural damage.

"Nice shootin'," called Calisto, and gave them a big "Wahhhh-hoooo."

But the chimera ships were busy deploying fresh waves of fighters that punched through the upper atmosphere of Shadderal. They dropped low, blowing drones out of their path and then swooping down for strafing runs on the new settlements of Hope, Haven, and Grace.

"Christ," swore Calisto. "Sweetpea, Hummingbird, Cricket—break formation and head down to the planet. Stop those cocksuckers."

Three tumblers peeled off and kicked their nuke cores to max as they tore across the seven hundred thousand kilometers between Asphodel and Shadderal. Calisto sent them because they were hardened combat veterans, keeping the cadets with her. She had hoped for more time to train them before the shoggoths returned, and though she had great faith in the young pilots, her fear for them was towering.

"Hell of a school outing, boss," growled Habibi. "We could use some goddamn help. Like, say, some big, giant, ghost-piloted robot-looking sons of bitches. Just saying."

"Well, help ain't here right now," snapped Calisto, though she sent a distress call via Sybil. To her team she said, "So nut up and shut up, and let's kill these bastards."

Calisto heard Habibi's laugh as he threw his tumbler into a crazy-clown spiral—one of his favorite maneuvers—and used his chain guns to set up another two-missile kill shot.

But even as he did, a fresh fusillade of blue fire burned past him and struck one of the cadets, David Gauthier—call sign Oguan—and blew his tumbler to fire and ruin.

"Nooooo!" cried Claire Murphy—Morrigan—who was his best friend since OCS back at the Great Lakes training center. But Oguan could not hear her. His body was torn and scattered into space. Morrigan hopscotched over and up and fired into the belly of the killer ship, and in doing so, exacted what small measure of cold comfort revenge could offer.

The tumblers were a new generation of fighters. The silver cubes were neither pretty nor elegant, but they were a marvel of engineering. While in space, they had no visible wings, only deploying stubby stabilizers when in a planetary atmosphere.

Calisto kicked her tumbler forward and then hopscotched randomly until she came up on the rear port quarter. She fired a one-two punch of a Constellation missile followed hard by an Inferno. The Constellation struck the enemy's shields with a cluster of powerful warheads, overtaxing the shields and sending sensor readings to the Inferno, guiding it to the weakest panel. The bigger warhead of the second missile punched through the failing shield and deep into the heart of the shoggoth dagger. The blast was massive and eerily silent as the vacuum absorbed the fire but let lingering plasma burn itself out. The ship itself was an expanding cloud of debris that Calisto soared through, laughing.

Another dagger blew up thirty klicks to her southeast. But more of the enemy were appearing out of the black. Too many more. Dozens.

Where are you, Bee? The question was unspoken, but Calisto screamed it in her thoughts. *We need you. We need some NecroTek magic right about now.*

The NecroTeks were much like the shoggoth chimera ships in that their structural configurations could change at need. The ones belonging to Asphodel's small fleet, though, were not piloted by those shape-shifting monsters, nor by any living pilot from the station. Instead, each of the round dozen of NecroTeks was piloted by the dead.

By ghosts.

All of them had been tumbler pilots before the first war with the shoggoths, and each had died saving Asphodel. It was through the power of *ethla*, a psycho-spiritual connection between a disembodied spirit and ships powered by a strange form of radiation unique to that part of the Milky Way. Calisto's two best friends, Bianca Petrescu and Jacob Fox, were now among those spirits, and it was their presence that had turned the tide against a massive shoggoth invasion fleet.

But the NecroTeks were not there. Bianca was not there. And so this fight was down to Calisto's twelve remaining tumblers and the guns on Asphodel itself.

Calisto did not think that was going to be enough.

The same instant she had that thought, her ship took another dreadful hit.

5

The blast ripped a line of glowing sparks along the outside edge of her tumbler's shields. The force of the impact sent the fighter spinning wildly. Calisto fought for control, playing with thrust and stabilizers, braking jets, and some wild steering. After a few desperate moments, the damaged tumbler veered sharply away from the attacker, moving at right angles, changing direction, trying to protect her damaged craft by flying so crazily that no enemy could track it.

It was a nice try.

But it didn't work.

As her tumbler hopscotched around, the pilot of the attacking dagger seemed to know where to be every single time. While the escaping ship jumped up and over and down, the attacker moved with deft efficiency and blinding speed and appeared dead astern. Once more the chain guns fired, and once more sparks seemed to fly like drops of blood.

"Calisto to team: I'm hit—repeat, I'm hit," she cried. "Just lost life support. Starboard stabilizer is down."

"Coming for ya, boss," said a voice, but there was so much static from the shipboard damage that Calisto couldn't tell who it was. A millisecond later a huge flash of purple light engulfed the dagger, all but stalling its momentum and leaving it open to a one-two missile strike. Then the tumbler was itself knocked sideways as more daggers zeroed in on it and Calisto's drifting wreck.

"Run for it, boss," called Thor. "I'll cover you." He opened up with chain guns while Calisto limped off.

Thor and Aries—Thomas Beale—engaged the daggers to try to buy their flight leader time to reset systems. All of them knew, though, that they were losing this fight. One-to-one they had the edge, but numbers and attrition were against them, and many battles—even wars—had been lost like this.

Still, they fought on, even as more of the daggers converged on them.

In a voice that was jarringly calm despite the furious battle, Sybil said, "A wave of dagger fighters approaches Asphodel Station." She gave the angle of approach, which put the new attack on the far side of the station and nearly four thousand kilometers from where Calisto's ship was limping along.

Calisto felt her heart sink. She keyed the mic for a private channel with Captain Croft.

"You got incoming, Skipper."

"We see them," he said tightly. "All six skimmers are going out the door. Station cannons are hot."

Ever since the WarpLine disaster had hurled Asphodel across the span of the Milky Way and the inhabitants encountered the shoggoth fleets, the tech crews aboard Asphodel had been working around the clock to manufacture cannons, missile launchers, and rocket pods and build them into the station. It was grueling work, requiring thousands of man-hours in pressure suits to cut gunports and mount the launchers. The teams had worked miracles, but the job was less than a third of the way done. A job of that scale should have been allotted four to six months, with exterior scaffolding and specialized crews from a shipyard. None of which they had.

But there was no plan B. Asphodel was more utterly alone than any man-made object had ever been. The 3D printers had been used for two whole weeks making more printers, and then that new line of monstrous printers had not been switched off since. Skimmers—small utility and support craft—had been flying back and forth to the closest edge of the asteroid belt to mine for raw materials.

Down on the planet's surface, the ancient, automated shipyards were working with the same tireless frenzy, but they were designed to make ships that could not be flown by living pilots. The radiation from the energy source that powered them—the power that made those ships so destructive to the shoggoths—was fatal to humans. Only ghosts—conjured by the necromancer, Lady Jessica—could fly them. With all of the NecroTeks away, those ships stood in silent rows on the planet's surface, with all of that power sitting idle for want of pilots.

It left Asphodel with its new guns and the dwindling tumbler squadron to fight a war against an enemy who had planets filled with creatures bred for war.

So Calisto knew there was no option other than to fight for as long as she and her team could. There was no retreat, because the two places that they now thought of as "home" were Asphodel Station and Shadderal, and both were under siege by overwhelming forces.

And half of her crew were cadets riding newly built tumblers but lacking in flight time and combat experience.

The daggers and chimera ships had slipped past the sensors, tripping none of them. And they had come in numbers. Even now, two more chimera spacecraft carriers were approaching at incredible speed, daggers erupting from their bellies.

If the NecroTeks had been there …

Alas, fate is entirely indifferent to need.

Calisto drifted.

Her tumbler's lights flickered, the little red and yellow and green indicators flashing in meaningless patterns. Smoke rose from her console like silent gray flowers. The inside of the cockpit smelled of melted plastic. Calisto's entire body felt like one huge pulled muscle. The blast had not only fried her shields, but it had knocked all of the inertial dampeners offline, which sent her banging around to the limits of the flight harness. She did not hit the walls, but the network of straps had dug into her at six g's, mashing her, bruising her, punching all the air from her lungs.

"Sybil, damage report," she wheezed.

"I … I … I …" was the AI's only reply.

Calisto punched the speaker. "*Shit.*"

The tumbler began to drift.

"Calisto to C-1," groaned Calisto, trying to reach Captain Croft.

Nothing. That connection was now as dead as her engines.

Calisto tried individual comms. Silence was the only answer.

Movement on her forward screen froze her, and she sat rigid and helpless as a dagger fighter swung into view. All of its forward pulse cannons glowed with deadly blue potential, and Calisto was absolutely powerless to fight or run. The dagger moved forward with unnatural slowness, like a patient spider walking without haste along the trembling lines of her web as a fly struggled and fought without hope.

"Yeah, well … f-fuck you," she said, tripping over it. Calisto closed her eyes, accepting the inevitable. This was the end of her run. The dagger was less than eighty meters from where she drifted. Hope had also died along with the ship's internal systems.

Will Lady Death will call me back to be a NecroTek? she wondered as she braced herself for the pain of dying. *I hope so. I hope not. Oh God …*

Seconds ticked away.

Nothing happened.

Finally, taking a risk, she opened one eye a tiny bit.

The space in front of her ship was empty. No sign at all of that dagger.

"What?"

Why had it left? Why had it spared her? Or had the shoggoth pilot assumed she was already as dead as her tumbler? Even so, it made no sense. The enemy knew as well as she did that ships could be repaired, repiloted, and returned to battle. Why not destroy it? Why not *take* it back to their base for study?

Leaving her alive and untouched was inexplicable.

To her left she saw blue and purple pulse fire streaking back and forth as the battle raged on without her.

"Well, the hell with this."

Calisto unbuckled and slid from the fighting chair, squirming as best she could under the console. She grabbed a small nontoxic extinguisher and doused the small flames, then fanned away the smoke in order to assess the damage. It was not as bad as she thought, but repairs would take time. Five minutes at least. Calisto wasted no time. She unscrewed the wing nuts holding the center panel in place, reached in, grabbed the half-melted main processor, and tried to remove it. The thing refused to budge because half of its frame was melted onto the inner struts.

"Uh-uh, baby, we're not doing that today," she growled as she took hold of it, braced her feet against the struts, and threw her body backward. All of her muscle and weight and momentum was half-wasted in the cramped cockpit, but a big chunk of the processor snapped off in her hand.

Calisto then banged her fist on a panel, which opened to reveal a tool kit. She grabbed a big flathead screwdriver, carefully inserted it in a narrow gap between the remaining section of the processor and the strut, took a big breath, and shoved it sideways. The leverage popped the last bit off, but with such force that it flew up in through her open visor and slashed her cheek to the bone.

"You *fucker*!"

Blood boiled out, but with no artificial grav working, it seeded the air around her face with glistening rubies that bulged and pulsed. Sweat pooled around her eyes and clogged her nostrils. She coughed and pawed it away so she could see at least well enough to take a replacement processor and clumsy it into place. The articulated receiving clamps reached out, hooked on, and pulled the circuit board into place.

Immediately, Sybil began speaking.

"I can't … I can't …" she mumbled in the weirdly high-pitched voice of an old Southern lady. "Dear me, I really don't think I care to *do* that."

"Sybil, reboot all systems. Command code Calisto LC-001. Execute."

"Well, that's asking a lot, lord-a-mercy," said Sybil. There was an extremely loud burst of static, and then, in a totally uninflected voice, Sybil said, "System reboot initiated."

A status bar appeared, but the line barely moved. The AI was coming back, but far too slowly.

Calisto climbed back into her chair and used a sleeve to wipe the clinging drops of sweat and blood from her eyes and nose. They floated all around her—a constellation of visible pain and sweat.

As Calisto waited for the AI to reboot, she looked around to try to get a reading on the state of the battle. There were streaks of blue and purple pulse fire and the occasional flare of missile detonation, but the actual ships were too far away.

"Come on, you bitch," she snarled.

There was a burst of squelch, and then Sybil spoke, her computer voice filled with something approximating panic. "Oh, dear God in heaven … I … can't … see …"

Then silence.

Calisto punched the console. "Come *on*, God damn it."

All at once, the floating droplets dropped and splashed everywhere. Calisto thumped down in her chair as gravity kicked in. The interior lights flickered for a moment and then switched on. Most of them. Everything on her left side was dark, which meant that if she could fly, she couldn't hopscotch toward that side, reducing her combat efficiency by a sixth.

"Sybil, are you online, you silly cow?"

"I am back to normal function, Calisto," said the weirdly calm voice of the AI. "My apologies for any erratic words or actions. Systems are functioning at sixty-two percent of normal."

"Engine status?"

"You can maneuver at three-quarter speed."

"Weapons?"

"Online."

Holograms appeared in the darkness of her cockpit and folded themselves around her wrists and hands, and she felt the controls solidify as they synced with the ship-pilot interface and the joystick. The holograms presented actionable keys that allowed her to fire the chain guns and launch missiles.

"That'll do," she said through gritted teeth. "I need to get back in this fight. Lay it out on the screens for me."

Except for the blind wall, the five other sides of the cube flashed with a RealScreen display showing her the status of the battle.

It was not going well.

Three of her tumblers were drifting wrecks. The rest were split in a losing battle near the station or in a swirl of mutual murder above the planet Shadderal.

"Status on Woden, Thor, and Aries."

"All three ships are offline. No fatalities reported, however."

"Small mercies," she muttered, and kicked the engines as hard as they would go. The tumbler shuddered for a moment and then lurched forward, back into the fight. There were daggers everywhere.

To her left and fifty klicks down, Asphodel Station looked as if it was burning. Smoke spiraled out of six separate breaches in the hull. The deflectors were visibly flickering, and in some places, they were gone.

Calisto could feel her heart falling inside her chest. It plummeted downward into that bottomless hole of despair and defeat she knew was waiting for all of them out here. The shoggoths had millions, possibly billions, of fighters, and it was inevitable that eventually they would simply send a force so large that it would roll over the human interlopers like a tsunami on a flat beach.

Even so, she was not the kind of person to give up and certainly not one to go down without a real goddamn fight. With her tumbler racing as fast as it would go, she opened up with all of her guns and missiles. The pulse blasts caught a dagger in the exhaust port, and that ignited the fuel in the tanks, blowing it apart. But six other daggers wheeled around, breaking off their attack on the station and circling back toward her.

She fired another set of missiles and then hopscotched up and right and down and right again. The lead dagger blew up, but the other five punched through the debris and opened up on her.

"Get out of there, boss," yelled Morrigan, from … somewhere.

"The fuck you think I'm trying to do?" she roared back, steering and jumping in a complex pattern. Each jump was awkward, though, and twice the hopscotch maneuver simply did not work. Calisto was their best pilot at high speeds, but her tumbler couldn't muster that extra juice. So she switched to plan B and kept jumping randomly as the daggers sought to close on her.

Even so, moment by moment the shoggoths closed the gap, spreading out to create a kill box around her.

"Sybil, how we doing on missiles?"

"All missiles have been fired, Calisto," said the AI. "SAPR rounds are down to four percent."

And that was when Calisto knew she was going to die.

The daggers tightened their net, forcing her into their gunsights by blocking her jumps. On the screens, she saw their cannon mouths blaze with blue light. She hopscotched once more, doing crazy turns inside the box, pausing only long enough to fire the chain guns and lasers. Knowing they weren't doing enough damage.

One dagger broke from the pack and made a run at her, guns firing. Calisto squeezed the trigger on the joystick and—

—the enemy craft exploded in a massive purple fireball.

Then a voice screamed at her through the speakers.

"I can't leave you alone for five damn minutes, can I!"

Something that looked like a giant robot made of mismatched parts shot past her at high speed, driving toward the rest of the shoggoth squadron. The thing was twenty meters long, with massive arms stretched out and up, bristling with glowing pulse guns.

Behind it came others. Some bigger, some smaller; none alike except in that they were vaguely humanoid and heavily armed. All of them opened up on the shoggoths.

"Bianca!" cried Calisto, tears springing into her eyes as the NecroTeks swept past her and took the fight to the shoggoths in very ugly ways.

7

Three hundred kilometers away, a completely different kind of spacecraft clung to the underside of a floating asteroid. Its mass and metal components were disguised by the ores compacted into the asteroid. It had guns of strange design, but the barrels were cold.

The pilot sat and watched the NecroTek smash into the shoggoth attack fleet. Half of them swarmed after the shoggoths closer to the asteroid belt, while the others accelerated to full speed as they flew toward Asphodel Station.

The shoggoth pilots wheeled around to face this new threat, and filled the void with blue pulse fire. But the blasts passed through nothingness as the NecroTek spun and dove, twisted and evaded. Then the gigantic ghost-driven ships opened up with their luminous purple cannons.

One by one, the shoggoth ships blew apart.

The first of the NecroTeks swerved off and headed toward the gigantic chimera cruisers, and as the others finished off the dagger ships, they too spun off to take the fight to the chimeras.

It was a brutal battle, and it lasted for nearly an hour.

All during that time, the pilot of the watching ship did nothing to interfere. It watched, and saw, and took careful note. Only when the battle was reaching its fiery denouement did the other craft spin up its engines and release the docking clamps that held it to the asteroid. It turned away and shot off into the blackness and was gone.

Interlude One

The Socrates of Athens Auditorium
University of California, Los Angeles
Four Years Before the WarpLine Event

The auditorium was packed. Each of the four hundred seats was taken, and scores of people stood in the back and alone on the sides. When Dr. Lars Soren was introduced, the applause was thunderous. Soren, an eccentric, moderately dumpy, and mildly disheveled man, was enormously popular with the students. Less so, perhaps, with a fair number of his collegiate peers.

Soren wore brown corduroys, a lemon-colored shirt, a tie patterned with Van Gogh's *Starry Night*, a collarless dark blue jacket, and loafers. He was extravagantly bearded and had retro pince-nez glasses perched on his generous nose.

He walked to the lectern and waved the audience to silence.

"What, you may ask, *is* cosmic philosophy?" said Soren. "I mean, beyond an obvious and somewhat inaccurate guess that it deals with the philosophies of the cosmos. In simple terms, it is the exploration of the philosophic and logical implications of our transition from citizens of the planet Earth to being citizens of space. In the short term, that space is defined by our star, Sol, its eight planets, the five known dwarf planets, and according to recent discoveries, three hundred and nineteen moons, plus forty-three space stations. There are now close to four million people living beyond Earth's atmosphere, and of those, more than one hundred thousand were born offworld. Those children are the first true citizens of the solar system. A new classification for mankind."

As he spoke, the RealScreen behind him showed each of the celestial bodies and then a montage of human faces—all colors, all ages.

"Now let us take a step back," he said. "Or, forward, depending on how you view this. Within the lifetime of those youngest children, we will likely launch colony ships to other stars. These ships will take generations to reach their destinations. These colony ships will carry with them future versions of the 3D printers that have allowed us to mine asteroids and other worlds for the raw materials to make whatever is needed, from city-sized terraforming machines to toothbrushes. They will also bring with them computers—some future version of Sybil—which will allow them to carry, in digitized forms, hundreds of billions of books, pieces of music, movies, documentaries, educational programs, games, and more. Those people will never return to Earth. They will be citizens of the galaxy and of a new home star and homeworld instead. Eventually, they will evolve into new and unknown cultures, and perhaps physically as well."

The screen showed an animation of a man and woman whose bodies changed to adapt to different climates, different gravity, and new atmospheric gasses.

"And from there?" mused Soren. "Well, quite literally, the sky—the big black—is the limit. Which means there *are* no limits."

Soren changed the image to a collage of religious symbols: the crucifix, the Latin cross, and the ichthys, or fish; the menorah and the Star of David; the star and crescent of Islam; the Buddhist wheel of dharma; the nine-pointed star of Baha'i; the Druidic triskelion; the Mormon angel Moroni with his trumpet; the Om of Hinduism; the Chakra Bhuwana of Javanism; the sigil of Baphomet used by Satanists; the Taoist Taijitu; the guardian angel Faravahar of Zoroastrianism; and a thousand more.

"So, what then becomes of religion?" he asked.

There was an expectant silence.

"There will be no Mecca, no Jerusalem, no Aboriginal sacred sites, no churches or mosques or temples. No treasured sacred lands. None of that will go with the colonists. And yet many religions are tied to Earth. Studies have shown that—in, say, America—seventy percent of surveyed people believe the Earth is sacred because that is what our scriptures tell us. Genesis 1:1 tells us that 'In the beginning God created the heavens and the earth. Now the earth was formless and empty, darkness was over the surface of the deep, and the Spirit of God was hovering over the waters.' Earth is specifically named because that was what was known and what was believed. Now … some of you who paid attention in Bible school may argue that the Judeo-Christian Bible does, in fact, mention the stars. What it says is, 'And God said, "Let there be lights in the vault of the sky to separate the day from the night, and let them serve as signs to mark sacred times, and days and years, and let them be lights in the vault of the sky to give light on the earth." And it was so. God made two great lights—the greater light to govern the day and the lesser light to govern the night. He also made the stars. God set them in the vault of the sky to give light on the earth, to govern the day and the night, and to separate light from darkness. And God saw that it was good. And there was evening, and there was morning—the fourth day.'"

The image was now of dawn breaking over the Earth.

"So, my friends," said Soren, "what does that mean, exactly? A literal interpretation is that the stars were made to fill the sky above Earth. The sun and the moon were made to brighten Earth's day and night. These are phrased to suggest that they exist to serve the people of Earth."

An image of a fleet of colony ships approaching a blue sun around which five planets orbited—three rocky, two gas—appeared. Moons of various sizes orbited each of the worlds.

"What about this alien sun? What about those moons? What is the relationship of God to a world on which no human has *yet* stepped? What is the value—in spiritual and religious terms—of that sun and those moons?" He paused. "You might say that they are as valid as our sun and moon, but the Bible—if we are to take it as the literal Word of God—is either inaccurate or insufficiently broad in scope."

A few people laughed, thinking it was a joke. The others did not.

Soren nodded. "The pragmatic people of faith, those who embrace science, say that if God is truly All, then He—or perhaps She, It, Them, or whatever pronouns work when describing a unique and infinitely powerful being who is unlikely to have reproductive organs—is out there, too. Raise your hands if you agree." He looked around. "Mmm, let's call that about a fifteen percent show of agreement. Interesting. Not surprising, but interesting. But here's the thing ... There are many, *many* fundamentalists of different faiths who believe Earth is, or was, God's Eden. That it is the one and rightful home of the Almighty's grace because that is where Jesus, Moses, Gautama Buddha, Guru Nanak Dev Ji, Confucius, Abraham, Muhammad, Zoroaster, and all of the other enlightened masters, prophets, and messiahs were born."

He switched off the images.

"And this is where cosmic philosophy is born. Not here on Earth. Not truly. It is born among the stars because the stars are the future of humanity. Don't believe me? Consider how deeply we have damaged our mother planet. Compare a map of the coastlines of the Eastern Seaboard of North America and the western coastline of Europe with any map from only seventy years ago. We have drowned millions of square kilometers of land with pollution and climate damage. We have had three exchanges of nuclear weapons. Granted, they were limited, but they could very easily have been global. Since 1918 we have dealt with fifty-four pandemics that have killed more than two billion people. The 2065 XDR-TB antibiotic-resistant variant of tuberculosis killed eight hundred sixty-seven million people. Had it not been for the shockingly fast development of an entirely new genetically engineered bacterium, we would not be here. Most of you are probably not aware of how close we came. Fourteen more weeks of the disease and it would have crossed a line resulting in the extermination of humanity. And that disease was not a bioweapon but a disease born of poverty." He shook his head sadly. "We have abused Mother Earth in inexcusable ways, and our continued existence was a Hail Mary pass of extreme good fortune. A very close call."

He let that sink in.

"If the plague had continued and no vaccine of sufficient efficacy found in time, the only survivors would have been the citizens of Luna,

Mars, and the space stations in existence at that time. Call it two thousand people. Humankind might have survived, though it would have needed to rebuild using a moderately shallow gene pool. My point here is that we were very close to what is popularly known as the 'end times' or the apocalypse."

He paused.

"And, not to throw too many stones here, but some of the more hard-core fundamentalists believed that they were living in the end times and therefore burning up calories to address climate change or pollution was irrelevant."

Another smattering of laughter, though it sounded more nervous than amused.

"All of this brings us to the question of what the role of faith is for those who leave planet Earth. Additionally, do we take God with us? If so, how do Earth-based religions and religious texts fit into the lives of those who will live out among the stars? Religion does not mention outer space or other worlds. And before you leap up to say that the Bible didn't mention America, Europe, Asia, and other lands unknown at the time, and therefore the other worlds are just extensions of a metaphorical use of the word *Earth*—meaning, Earth is wherever people are—let me ask you, Is that correct? Is it fair to the religions? Is it fair to the faithful?"

He smiled.

"This is part of what cosmic philosophy will explore," said Soren. "And yet … there is something far more crucial for us to consider as we move outward into the black, taking our religions with us. Who can tell me what that might be?"

Dozens of hands went up. Soren saw Evie Cronin's among them, but he picked the youngest person in the audience: a girl in her late teens with a face that suggested mixed Nigerian and Japanese genetic heritage.

"You," he said. "Tell me."

"Aliens," she said.

Soren smiled a great smile. "Yes," he said. "Aliens."

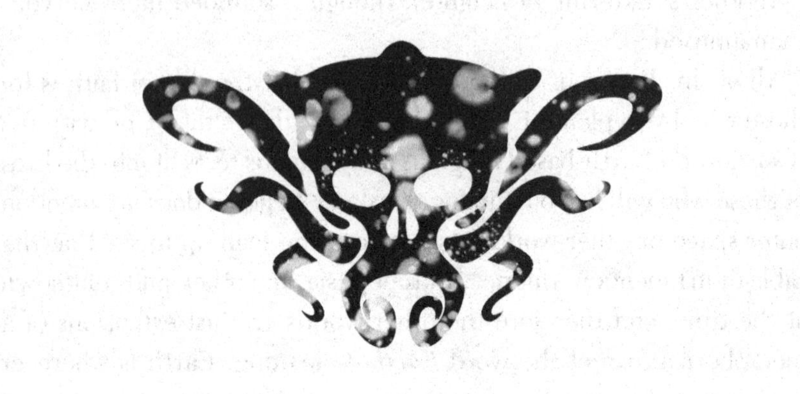

Part Three
Out of the Ice

"It is absolutely necessary, for the peace and safety of mankind, that some of earth's dark, dead corners and unplumbed depths be let alone; lest sleeping abnormalities wake to resurgent life, and blasphemously surviving nightmares squirm and splash out of their black lairs to newer and wider conquests."

—*H. P. Lovecraft*

Joint MIT/UCLA Biological Research Field Station #8
Queen Maud Land, Antarctica

1

Craig Anders seemed to be everywhere at once.

He was quick and energetic, and everywhere Evie looked, Craig was there, asking if anyone had seen Mac. Following up leads that went nowhere, going in and out of every building on the site. Twice Evie saw him standing in the middle of what they called Main Street—a broad path down the middle of the camp—yelling into the holo-comms unit strapped to his forearm, calling Sybil a useless piece of bad programming.

The AI did not take offense, though when Evie paused to listen, she thought she heard a firmer edge to her voice. Frustration, perhaps? Could an AI feel that? She thought it likely, since Sybil was the most advanced learning software in the system.

When Craig caught her watching, he colored, dropped his arm, and then stalked over. "When I find Mac, I am so going to kick his ass," he grumbled.

"Kick him an extra few times for me," said Evie.

Craig abruptly shook his head, snorted, and gave her a rueful smile. "Sorry, Prof. I guess this ... *thing* ... has me more freaked than I thought."

Evie touched his arm. "You are not alone, trust me."

They both glanced down Main Street to where the observation platform looked out over the drop-off. Half of the people in the camp were still clustered there, staring down at the impossible object that lay at the bottom of the valley. They stood in marked silence, and Evie could feel their apprehension, their fear, their crushing uncertainty about what it would mean to them. And to everyone everywhere.

In a much more subdued tone, Craig said, "Guess it's fair to say that *we* are not alone. Not anymore."

Fifty different replies occurred to Evie, ranging from denial to snark to an expression of the deep unease she felt. She said nothing, though. Not a word.

After a few moments, Craig said, "Guess I'd better keep looking. Mac's got to be somewhere."

But he was still looking past the platform.

2

All through the rest of that day and through the night, phones rang in the halls of power.

Discreet calls made to those persons with the calmness of mind, authority, and political power to do something. The news pulled gasps and cries even from them. But they moved. When the momentary shock passed, they moved very well indeed.

Evie tried to contact her mentor, Dr. Lars Soren. This kind of discovery was exactly *why* he had pioneered this new blend of philosophic analysis and critical thought on theology and its place as mankind stepped off Mother Earth and out among the planets and stars. Soren anticipated a find of this kind—not as specific as this, but something that would nevertheless irrefutably prove that no religion had the full story. And to demonstrate that each needed to expand in order to survive and continue serving the spiritual needs of its adherents.

Soren did not answer the call.

"Sybil," Evie said, panting, "can you locate Dr. Soren?"

"Dr. Soren is in a cryo-tube aboard the SS *Spirit*. He is heading to Mars to participate in the founding of that planet's first interfaith seminary."

"When will he come out of the ice?"

"His ship left from Luna Station 9 three days ago," said Sybil. "It is not a fast ship, and the trip will take forty-one days."

"Shit, shit, shit, shit."

"If this is an emergency, Professor Cronin, I can ask that he be revived early."

That was a possibility, but what Evie needed was someone to come down there to the site and help her manage it. No distance, no radio time lags.

"No. I'll find someone else."

"Of course," said the AI. "If I may make a suggestion? Perhaps it would be of value to reach out to Dr. Torquil Brollachan, the director and senior scientific adviser of the government's Special Projects Unit."

Evie considered that. A century ago that department had been smaller, though still powerful, and known as DARPA, the Defense Advanced Research Projects Administration. After the Middle East Wars and the nuclear detonations in Israel, Egypt, and Saudi Arabia, it was greatly expanded and renamed. Brollachan more or less inherited the directorship from his mother, who had run it with a cold mind and an iron fist for thirty-four years. But he was also a deeply insightful and visionary scientist who would almost certainly be able to grasp the political, cultural, and theological importance of this discovery. And, Evie reckoned, he'd know what steps to take to protect the integrity of the find and control the messaging to the world.

"Get him on the phone."

3

Torquil Brollachan listened to what Evie Cronin had to say.

He did not interrupt, nor did he trust his voice enough to even try. Brollachan looked at the 3D video turning slowly above the holo-comms on his wrist. His eyes jumped and twitched as he read the data on the video's pop-ups and crawls. When the vid ended, he let his hand fall onto the desktop and then sat there, his long, slender fingers knotting and twisting like frightened snakes.

"Have you cordoned off the site?" he asked when he trusted himself to speak. Although a naturalized American, he still had his Scottish accent, but there were cracks in it. He heard them and coughed to clear his throat. "Have you taken all precautions to protect the integrity and security of this … this *find*?"

The face of Professor Evie Cronin reappeared. He had seen her several times before, but rarely close up. She was a pretty woman—elfin, with bright green eyes, a cap of brunette curls, full lips, and the air of a scholar, with all the natural insecurities that often go with it. His opinion of her intellect was higher than that of her looks, however, and it amused him that she seemed to collect advanced degrees the way some people collect shells on the beach. That was something to which he, as a fellow polymath, could relate.

With all that, he felt a wave of envy—in an intensity he had never before experienced. *She* had discovered proof of alien life. It would not matter to any future news story or history book that a mechanic and a young grad student were the first to actually see it. They were there because of Evie Cronin's project. The find was hers, and that's what the future would know.

"I canceled a supply shipment that was going to arrive tomorrow," said Evie. "And I had Sybil store all feeds on the hard drive but remove them from what we send to the two universities involved here. I also had Sybil restrict all outside access—calls, texts, emails, the lot."

"That's good," he said. "That's very good. Who else have you told?"

"I tried calling my old professor—"

"Lars Soren?"

"Yes. Do you know him?"

"I wouldn't say I know him," said Brollachan. "We've met a few times at xenoscience conventions. Seems like a decent enough fellow."

"He's brilliant, and I'd trust his judgment on anything related to what we've found."

"Mm, yes. *Cosmic philosophy.* An interesting take. Tell me, did you reach him, and is he available to join us?"

"No, damn it," she said. "He's in cryo, on the way to Mars."

"Pity," said the SPU chief. "But listen, Professor, if you've left a message, ask Sybil to erase it. Lars is a good man, and given the scope of this, we may want to bring him in should he become available, but not now. Right now, this stays between *us*—can we agree on that?"

Evie nodded. "I understand. Who will you send down here?"

"Oh," said Brollachan, "I'm coming down there personally. Expect us tomorrow morning."

"Us?"

"We will need security, don't you think?"

He ended the call soon after and slumped back in his chair. The two aides stood waiting, eyes wide, faces pale. Brollachan looked up at them. "You know what has to be done," he said. "Assemble the team on the FC protocol list. And—this is of critical importance—you will not speak to *anyone* about this. Not your spouses, your mother, or your best friend. No one. I am designating this a black notice situation."

"Yes, sir," they said.

Before they turned to go, the youngest of the two, a promising young ethnobotanist, asked, "This is real? I mean, Dr. Brollachan … is this what it seems to be?"

"That's what we will find out. Go. Gather the team and pack your bags. I want to be wheels-up by midnight."

They left. If they walked a bit unsteadily, he could not blame them.

In the crushing silence of his office, Brollachan stared into the middle of nowhere. Even with the vid switched off, he could see that gleaming curve of metal hull. His imagination painted the entire thing in sharp reality.

"Fuck," he breathed. "Fuck me."

Then he made two calls. The first was to Colonel Tom Hobart, who oversaw military security for the SPU. That call went exactly as he expected.

"I'll get my team together, Torq," said the colonel, visibly sweating. "Jesus jumped-up polka-dotted Christ. This is … this is …" He was shaking his head as he reached out to end the video call.

Brollachan's second call was to his brother—a priest.

4

"Sybil," said Evie, "have you located Mac yet?"

There was a momentary pause, then Sybil said, "There is some error with his comms. The unit was turned off but is now sending a signal."

"Where is he?"

"To clarify, Professor Cronin," said the AI, "the comms unit is active, but it does not appear to be connected to Mac."

"Explain."

"Each holo-comms unit is synced with the user, and when active it sends telemetry," explained Sybil. "Mac's unit is showing an active status, but it is not sending any biometric data, suggesting he turned it on but is not actually wearing it."

"Why would he do that?"

"I cannot speculate, Professor. Mac has been consistent with wearing his holo-comms at all times apart from showering. But the comms unit is sending signals from the valley."

Evie stiffened. "Near the artifact?"

"Yes, Professor. The comms unit is located within 7.4 meters from the artifact."

"Shit. Okay, damn it … keep me posted as to any change in that status."

"Of course, Professor Cronin."

Evie saw Craig crossing Main Street and gestured for him to join her. He came over at a trot. She explained about the anomalous comms signal.

Craig scowled toward the platform. "What the fu— I mean … why'd he go back down?"

Evie said, "I checked the skimmer's flight log. Craig, I don't think he ever came back up. Certainly not with Gillian. I made the mistake of assuming he had, but I just spoke with Gillian, and she said he hadn't. I just assumed he returned later. That's my mistake."

"Mine too," said Craig. "Let's face it, boss, after finding that thing, we're lucky we can remember our own names."

"No excuse," said Evie. "This is on me. Let's take the skimmer and go down there and bring him back."

They hurried off to their huts to change into expedition clothes and better shoes for walking on ice, then met back at the skimmer in ten minutes.

The boat was a medium-sized utility version of the extreme-environment model of the ubiquitous antigrav short-range transport used all across the solar system. Four meters long and three wide, with a small cockpit for a pilot and six seats for passengers. Craig let Sybil scan him before unlocking the access gate, and he climbed aboard, choosing to pilot the craft himself. Everyone at the site knew how to fly the thing, even Gillian. It was easier than driving a wheeled car and far easier to operate than the passenger floatcars that choked every city in the world.

Once they were both aboard, Craig dropped the boat away from the platform, turned, and descended toward the thing.

Toward the artifact.

All the way down to the floor of the valley, Evie felt equal parts shock-numb and excited.

This is real, she told herself. *This is real.*

Even so, it was hard to believe. More than once over the last hour she nearly convinced herself she was sleeping and that this was just another strange dream. Although she could barely remember the details of any of her recent dreams, there had been an alien quality to each. When she was younger, Evie had experienced a couple of dreams that turned out to be either wildly coincidental or possibly prophetic.

This was like that, except that she was awake. Was this thing *in* one of her dreams? She wished she could recall.

"Setting down," said Craig.

Evie shook herself from her reverie and leaned over the rail as the skimmer settled onto packed ice. Craig killed the engine but stood there, simply staring at the ancient machine. He shook his head slowly.

"Between you and me, Professor," he said slowly, "I'm not okay with this. I mean … I don't know that I'm *prepared* for anything like this. It's so … big."

She knew he was not referring to the physical size of the artifact. Everything about the thing was larger than life, larger than their ability to estimate the impact it would have on their lives and on everything in the world, in every aspect. The most common comment from the rest of the team back at the site was, "This changes everything." She'd said it herself a dozen times. It was in no way an exaggeration. Nothing—no part of the human experience—would escape the shadow of this thing. It called so much into question while raising unique questions of its own.

"I know," she said, aware that it was a wildly inadequate reply. Craig nodded, accepting that as the only possible answer at the moment.

They got out and looked around.

"There," she said, and went over to where a holo-comms unit was half buried in a drift of ice crystals. "Look at this. The lens is cracked."

The comms unit was small and thin, with a touchscreen and a compact display screen. A crack jagged across the screen's face. Craig took it and turned it over in his hands.

"Sometimes, when there's a break in the screen or damage to the touchpad, there's this little electric spark," he said. "Mac must have banged it up on something, got stung by the discharge, and took it off."

"He could have just switched off the power," observed Evie. Craig's reply was a dubious grunt.

They both looked around.

"Okay, but where *is* he?" she asked.

Craig walked a dozen meters closer to the machine. "Looks like he went off down that passage." He pointed to a trail that vanished into a kind of cave created by part of the collapsing wall of ice. It was intensely dark in there.

"See if you can find him," she said. "But be careful. We don't know how stable all this is."

Before moving off, Craig walked to within a few meters of the hull. It arched high and away. He glanced almost sheepishly back at Evie and offered a tremulous smile.

"This is nuts," he said. Then he turned and went off to follow Mac's footprints.

Evie went over and stood where he had. The scope of the machine was intimidating, especially knowing that the greater part of it was still buried. The exposed section was as wide as the building on the UCLA campus where she taught. The metal was a smooth, slightly shiny silver-gray, with no visible dents or flaws.

Don't touch it.

The warning flashed in her mind.

As far as she knew, Mac had only looked at it. He had not touched the artifact.

Don't touch it. The thought rang out in her mind. Everything Evie knew about managing a dig site, everything she understood about the inherent dangers of making physical contact with the unknown, and all of her common sense rebelled at the thought of touching the thing.

And yet …

Almost as if she were deep inside one of her strange dreams—aware of doing the wrong thing and yet somehow unable to stop herself—Evie pulled off her glove, extended her hand slowly, and very lightly brushed the pads of her fingers over the surface of the metal.

No, no, no! The protest rang out inside her head, and yet Evie lingered there, flesh pressed against metal fashioned ages ago and almost certainly on another world. Evie simply could not make herself stop.

God help me …

It was cold, but not nearly as cold as she expected. She almost snatched her hand away, though, because she felt something. At first she thought it—the entire thing—somehow moved. But no, there was a vibration in the metal. So faint as to be almost undetectable. Had she kept her glove on, she would never have felt it. Her naked skin, though, could.

It's alive.

The thought flitted in and out, and Evie grunted aloud at the absurdity of it.

It's metal. It's not alive. It's just a machine. Old and cold and dead.

The nearly subsensory vibration made a lie of that thought.

Evie placed her entire palm flat against the metal. The thing was so big and the curve so subtle that the thing felt like a smooth, straight wall. It did not feel like steel. Closer to the texture of the aluminum-magnesium alloys used for lawn chairs.

"What *are* you?" she asked. The words hung in the air, taking a different form and meaning than she intended. Like an echo, she heard her words play back in her head. Three words, but not the three Evie thought she said.

Instead, the echo said, *Speak to me.*

Unbidden, Evie's eyelids closed, and she was gone.

Her body stood there, her hand still touching the side of the artifact, but everything else about her was somewhere else.

She stood on a wide avenue in the heart of a city so strange that it was immediately clear this was not a *human* place. Buildings of titanic size rose all around her, but none looked normal. They were built from some gray stone or from a whiter rock like granite—but *nothing* about what she saw looked like it could have any origin in the natural world as she knew it. The buildings were oddly shaped—bizarre geometrical designs fashioned from blocks of impossible size. Truncated cones whose sides were fluted and terraced, huge cylindrical pylons that rose so far into the sky that they tore holes in the clouds. Some buildings were spanned by flat walkways, while others stood alone and had no apparent doors or windows. Here and there were large open spaces edged with strange vegetation that resembled some weird blend of trees and sea coral, and from these open spaces rose many cones and globes, each of monstrous size. They dwarfed her in ways that went beyond a mere difference in physical size—the *intent* of the building diminished Evie as a person, as a sentient thing.

Her heart began to hammer because there was a presence to all of it, a sense of being observed with disdain and indifference. Yet also with a subliminal malevolence, as if whatever watched her did not immediately care about her but could, if she forced the issue. Evie did not want to be regarded with the kind of pernicious acuity the feeling suggested.

Let go, she ordered herself. *Stop touching it.*

Her hand did not move.

From somewhere deep inside that vast and strange city came a sound. A cry like that of some rare and exotic bird. Mourning. Plaintive.

Tekeli-li! it cried. *Tekeli-li!*

As the sound filled her mind, the vibration increased.

It's waking up, Evie thought. *Oh God, it's waking up.*

It kept crying. *Tekeli-li! Tekeli-li! Tekeli-li!*

Evie screamed and staggered back from the artifact.

The instant her skin broke contact with the metal, the image of the gigantic city vanished, and try as she might to hold onto the details, they slipped through her trembling fingers like sand.

Soon all traces of it were gone. Evie did not remember anything about that place. All she was left with was the fading echo of the strange bird—if bird it was.

Tekeli-li! Tekeli-li!

Then it, too, was gone. She stood there, trembling and unsure. With the pragmatism of a scientist, she dismissed it as mere nerves. After all, how could she not tremble in the presence of this thing?

A few seconds later, Craig came trudging back toward her. "Couldn't find him, the dumbass," he said, then he caught sight of her face. "Hey, Prof, you okay?"

Evie turned toward him. "What?"

"Did something happen? You look like you saw a ghost."

"A ghost? No." She looked down at her hand and was astonished to see that her glove was back on. Evie almost remarked on it. Almost. Instead, she gestured to the artifact. "No ghosts … just this."

Craig laughed. "Yeah. No shit."

Evie looked past him. "Mac?"

"No idea. We should send some drones down. That cave is black as hell and looks sketchy. I didn't go too far in. I don't mean to be a dick, but if Mac is in there and broke his leg or something, that's on him. Sybil and the drones can find him."

"Agreed," she said. "Let's go back up."

5

They stepped out of the skimmer and onto the platform.

"Did you find him?" asked Gillian, looking past them at the empty skimmer. It was a dumb question, and Evie nearly snapped at her, but Gillian was young, and all of this was so big.

"No, honey," she said gently, "but we'll keep looking."

"Whoa, whoa, wait," said Craig. He'd stopped to open his holo-comms in order to tell Sybil to send the drones, but something caught his eye. "What the hell?"

"What is it?" asked Evie, hurrying over.

"Son of a bitch is back down there," he said. "Look."

She leaned closer to the holo-comms screen. Sure enough, Mac was standing straight and still in front of the artifact, where he had been earlier. She and Craig exchanged a perplexed look.

"Guess we better go back," she said tightly. "Son of a bitch is pissing me off."

Craig shook his head. "Nah, Prof, let me go. I might have a few things to say to him you wouldn't want to hear. Might kick his narrow ass, too."

"Be quick," said Evie, straightening. "Oh, and Craig …?"

"Yes?"

"Don't touch that thing. Or anything. Just grab Mac and bring him up here. I'll give Sybil new instructions for analysis and security, but I don't want anyone to go anywhere near that thing once you two return. Is that understood?"

He looked at her, opened his mouth to say something, then snapped his jaws shut, giving her a terse nod instead. The boat turned with lumpy grace and began the long descent back down to the valley.

As Evie watched, everyone began talking at once. Many of them flocked around her as if expecting that, as chief scientist and overall head of the mission, she would have answers or insights. She had neither.

Instead, she made placatory comments on autopilot while the rest of her attention was fixated on the skimmer.

"Sybil," she said, "show me the skimmer."

A holo-screen appeared in the air, hanging three meters past the edge of the platform. On it, Craig wore goggles that covered his eyes, but his mouth was a hard, tight line and his jaw firmly set.

She saw him frown suddenly before speaking. "Sybil, I can't see Mac anymore. Where'd he go *this* time?"

"Searching," said the AI. A moment later Sybil announced, "Mac Ryerson has reentered a cave at the far eastern end of the shelf."

"Can you send in a drone and find him for me?"

"Initiating search now."

They waited.

"My apologies, Craig," said the AI after nearly ten seconds, "I am currently unable to locate Mac Ryerson."

"What do you mean you can't find him, for fuck's sake?"

Evie jumped into the call. "Sybil, what is preventing you from locating Mac? He was on visual a minute ago."

"Unknown, Professor Cronin. But I suspect it might be the presence of ore deposits in the strata beneath the ice interfering with the drones. I am working to solve this problem, and I apologize for the inconvenience."

"Touching down," reported Craig. On the screen, it showed the skimmer settling onto the broad, deep shelf of ice near the artifact. Craig opened a cabinet beneath the control panel and removed a harness of nylon strapping. He put it on and activated rows of small but powerful LED lights. "Should have used this the first time."

He stepped down from the skimmer and walked over to the artifact, paused for a moment to shake his head in wonder, and began following Mac's footprints in the light snow that covered the denser ancient ice. Evie noticed that Craig was careful to step into his own footprints so as not to obscure any of Mac's as the path narrowed toward the mouth of the cave. There were three sets of prints left by Mac—into the cave, out of it again, and then back inside. Craig paused to determine which was the most recent set going inside and synced a drone to map those. That drone and several others sent by Sybil followed him along. Craig clambered over some big chunks of ice with his well-known athletic grace.

"What are you seeing, Craig?" asked Evie.

"Hold on," he said as he approached the gaping mouth. Great slabs of ice had collided to form the cavity, and the prints went straight inside. The drone cameras caught him in high definition as he stepped from sunlight into darkness, chasing the shadows back with his harness lights. "Whoa … wait." Then, a moment later came "What the hell?"

Evie and everyone else leaned forward to stare at the video feed. It showed the line of Mac's footprints—deep, solid, and measured—as the trail went from the brightness outside and into the newborn cave. Ten meters inside, however, the prints stopped.

"Sybil," snapped Evie, "what are we seeing? What happened to the rest of the footprints?"

"There are no additional footprints, Professor Cronin," said the AI.

"Explain."

"I cannot provide a more detailed answer at this time."

"Where's Mac, damn it?" demanded Craig.

"I apologize," said Sybil, "but I am unable to locate any traces of Mac Ryerson."

"His prints just stop, though," he said. "There's … shit, there's nothing past them. There's no place he could have stepped up onto or jumped to. I can't see anywhere he could have gone, and I don't think he walked back in his own prints. Looking for some advice here."

"In the absence of more information," said Sybil, "I would advise that you do not venture deeper into this cave. It may be unstable. I recommend that we map it with drones and send in a search team only once the structural integrity of the cave has been established."

The grad student stood there, his own feet straddling the last prints made by Mac's shoes.

"Professor," he said slowly, "I am not digging this at all. But I'm willing to keep looking. Walls look pretty solid to me. Prints or not, it's your call."

"Again," said Sybil, "I argue strongly against a further exploration at this time."

Everyone on the platform turned to Evie. Her heart wanted her to tell Craig to keep looking. The abruptness with which the prints ended was glaring; there was no way to look away from them or discount it as something normal but not yet understood. It was strange. Weird. And they all knew it.

"No," she said softly. "Come back up."

"But Mac ..." began Craig.

"Let the drones search. They can go everywhere you can't. We don't know what's going on down there, so let's fall back and figure it out. Don't worry, Craig, we're not going to forget Mac. We'll find him and bring him home, but let's do it the right way. Come back for now."

The drones did not find Mac.

His telemetry remained blank.

Gillian went into hysterics and had to be tranquilized by the mission's medic.

While Evie tried to process this, she received a message from Dr. Brollachan that offered a slice of comfort.

"I am on my way down to you, Professor," he wrote. "I am bringing a team that includes military personnel experienced in rescue missions in extreme and hazardous conditions. Until we arrive, no one is to visit the site of the discovery. No exceptions. We will arrive shortly."

Evie told the others about the message. Those who knew what the SPU was looked surprised. There was some hopefulness that the cavalry was on its way. There were obvious trepidations. The SPU was spooky, and the day had already become frightening. More so as each hour passed with no sign of Mac.

Craig knocked on the door of her office hut and came in quickly.

"Anything?" asked Evie hopefully.

He slumped into a chair. "Not a goddamn thing, boss."

They sat with that for a while.

"He has to be down there somewhere," Craig grumbled. It was his habit to disguise fear or uncertainty with bubbling anger. "Son of a bitch had better not be messing with us."

"We'll find him," said Evie with far more certainty than she felt.

Craig glowered at the small metal heater in the corner, and for no other reason than it was there. "Guess you've heard what Gillian and some of the others are saying."

"Do I want to know?"

"Probably not," he said, "though I have to admit I'm starting to lean into the possibility."

"Which is?"

"That he found a way inside that big … big …"

"Artifact," she said. "That's what I called it in my report. Fits well enough."

Craig nodded. "Artifact. Okay. Good as anything. Truth in advertising, I suppose. But my point is that if he's not in the cave and not in the valley—and Sybil has every drone we own down there—then he has to be somewhere."

Evie considered. "But *inside*? Mac's not a scientist, but he's far from dumb."

"Caught up in the moment, maybe?" suggested Craig. "I was down there, and I could understand that. Don't know how I'd have reacted if I was the first down there."

"My fear," said Evie, "is that he *might* have done that as a way of getting famous. I mean, there will only ever be one person who makes first contact. He saw it first, after all. Maybe he's on some kind of trip of wanting to establish his connection to the greatest scientific find of all time. He's joked before that he's just manual labor and won't even be a footnote in any of the papers we publish."

They considered that for a few moments. The space heater had an audio component that played the sound of a warmly chuckling log fire. The gentle snaps and pops and soft shifting of logs were the only sounds.

Then Evie said, "If that's what he's doing, I give you permission to take him as high as the skimmer will go and throw his ass out."

Craig laughed. "Don't tempt me, Evie."

When not in front of the whole team, they were on a first-name basis.

After another long silence, he said, "Those footprints, though."

"Yes," she said, "those footprints."

7

Father Lachlan Brollachan ended the call and sagged back against the wall of the narthex and stared at nothing. At the emptiness that seemed to open its gaping mouth in his mind.

The Artifact.

That's what his brother called it.

So simple a name for so terrible a thing.

An artifact that would irrefutably prove that life—intelligent life—existed before Adam and Moses, before Ezekiel and the prophets.

Before Christ.

The enormity of it threatened to unmake him. It threatened to shatter the firmness of belief that underpinned his faith and the faith of billions.

The church taught, for so many years, that God created life on Earth. The entire history of the prophets and holy people that led to the birth of Jesus more than twenty-one centuries ago was built on that truth and on the promise that humanity was the firstborn of ail sentient life. It was an issue that had become intense during the late nineteenth century and well into the early twenty-first, with groups like the Center for Theological Inquiry causing problems by openly partnering with NASA to prepare humanity for first contact. Other groups had joined in that cause, and it rocked all of Christianity and much of Judaism and Islam for decades.

Ironically, it was the settling of colonies on Luna, Mars, and various moons in the central and outer planets that more or less *saved* the church. Nothing was ever found. Not one trace. Not even fossils of life. That total absence of proof flooded back and restored much of the mystery of faith in a Judeo-Christian God and supported the theological history presented in the Bible and the early writings of the first evangelists.

And now this.

This.

Father Brollachan felt himself sliding down the wall until he sat hard on the cold marble, caved forward, and put his face in his hands. He was a true believer but also a cautious realist who had always feared something like this. It wasn't the existence of alien life per se, but proof that it predated humanity.

By *millions* of years.

It called everything into question for him, and that curiosity—and the resulting outrage and loss of faith—was like a bomb ticking down to detonation.

He wept for a long time.

And then he staggered to his feet and stumbled off to the privacy of his office to make a very important call.

8

The scanner drones moved back and forth in precise surveillance patterns, but they did not see Mac Ryerson.

He, however, saw them.

9

Office of Cardinal Abruzzi
The Vatican

The young priest hurried through a small and unobtrusive door, then along a series of winding corridors. Several times he broke into a nervous run, but as he approached his destination, he slowed to a walk and then stopped ten feet short of an ornate old door. He lingered there, panting, sweating, chewing his lip.

"God help me," he prayed. "Please . . . Am I even doing the right thing?"

No angels appeared with burning swords. None of the potted shrubberies burst into flame. No thunderous voice spoke to him.

He closed his eyes for five full seconds, then took a breath and knocked.

There was a long pause before he heard the sound of a heavy lock being turned. The door opened, and a cardinal, whose ancient face was so comprehensively lined and seamed that he looked like a caricature, tottered into the room.

"Your Eminence," said the young priest.

The rheumy old eyes looked him slowly up and down. "You are Father Spilletti?"

"Yes, Your Eminence."

"You were contacted by Father Brollachan?"

"I was, Your Eminence. His brother is with the SPU. The American group that—"

"I know who and what they are," said Cardinal Abruzzi.

"Of course, Your Eminence."

The old man looked at the folder tucked under Spilletti's arm. It was in a dark red binder that was sealed with thick ribbons and ornate wax seals. "Is that your report?"

Father Spilletti took his folder in both hands and looked down at it, weighing it as if the contents themselves carried unusual mass. He hesitated again and then held it out.

"Yes, Your Eminence."

Abruzzi took the folder, studying the seals to assure himself they were unbroken. He did not break them but, rather, held the folder as if it was a snake that could bite him.

"Who else knows about this?" he asked.

"No one, Your Eminence. Only Bishop Adolpho and myself."

The moment stretched as the cardinal studied the blank cover of the folder. Then he straightened. "Father Spilletti, what you have done is of great importance. If any criminal charges are ever brought because you broke that agreement, you will be afforded sanctuary here in Vatican City, and our lawyers will protect you."

"Thank you, Eminence."

"For now, please sit and wait." Cardinal Abruzzi gestured to a bench a few meters down the hall. "Speak to no one. Say nothing to anyone. Wait until you are called. Is that clear?"

"Perfectly clear, Your Eminence." He began to turn and then stopped. "What will this all mean?"

The ancient cardinal's eyes filled with pain. "God only knows, my son."

10

He tried to die.

Mac Ryerson lay in a pool of shadows and prayed for death.

His body felt so wrong. Too many parts were no longer connected, yet he could feel each of them. Hands and toes, fingers and legs. He could even—somehow, impossibly—feel his blood. All of him was scattered across the ice. And on some level, he knew that there was both too much of him and not enough.

"Please, God …" he said.

A drone whizzed by overhead, but it did not hear him. Mac was not even sure he'd spoken aloud. His throat felt wrong. Flat and misshapen.

"Please let me die."

Part of his body moved. Without his will, with none of his muscular effort. It was the strangest sensation. It did not hurt, but it felt so terribly wrong. A piece of his stomach squelched softly as it moved. The blood that pooled around him trembled, then it, too, moved.

"No, no, no …" Mac begged.

More of him shifted, moved. Mac tried to scream, but his lungs would not push that shriek out. He could feel broken ribs scraping and ripping at the torn meat inside his chest. The only sound Mac could make was a thin, wet gurgle.

He wanted so badly to scream loud enough to be heard. To be found.

He tried and tried.

As all of the torn and broken parts of him crawled across the ice. And something else crawled *over* him.

The sun moved across the sky, eventually tumbling an infinity of shadows down on him. Mac could almost feel the weight of that darkness.

It was hours later when the voice began whispering in his mind. Mac tried so hard to pretend that it was his own inner voice whispering pleas for death.

But he knew that the voice he heard was not his own.

Not anymore.

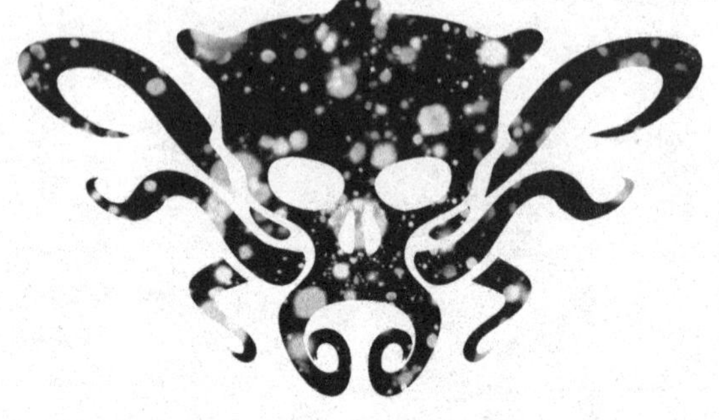

Part Four
Gods and Monsters

"The only true voyage of discovery, the only fountain of Eternal Youth, would be not to visit strange lands but to possess other eyes, to behold the universe through the eyes of another, of a hundred others, to behold the hundred universes that each of them beholds, that each of them is."

—*Marcel Proust*

Planet Shadderal
The Shadderal Star System

1

Lars Soren stood in a pool of pale sunlight beneath an alien sky.

Teams of technicians, along with a labor force of conscripted civilians from Asphodel, had spent the past month working to establish atmosphere processing plants around the globe. The plants were thousands of years old, built by the last race to inhabit Shadderal, but had fallen into disrepair when there was no one living to tend to them. The extinct race had breathed a different mix of gasses, one with a higher oxygen content and significantly less nitrogen. Changing the atmosphere into something humans could breathe would take years. Even so, the skies were already clearer than they had been on first contact.

That allowed Soren to see some of the battle that had just ended far above. Some of the dogfights between the tumblers and shoggoths had played out in the thermosphere, and a NecroTek had dragged a pair of fighters down from the void and hurled them at the mountains that edged the Field of Dead Birds. Smoke still curled up from where the fighters had fallen to their destruction.

"Tell me," he asked, "did we win?"

The person standing next to him was dead. Long dead. He had been the very last of the race that lived on Shadderal, the last in the long line of a species who called that world home. And so he took a new name, one that said much about who he was to himself and what he was to the humans he met: Lost.

"We did," said Lost. "At a cost. Always at a cost."

Lost had no physical form, but using the psychic connection he called *ethla*, he was able to construct one out of the endless piles of debris scattered around the automated ship factories. His body was made from a pressure suit once used by a fellow pilot from a four-armed race. Out of courtesy for Soren's sensibilities, Lost only activated two of the arms, with the remaining sleeves hanging empty. His helmet had an elongated cranium that resembled the kind of skull deformation used by certain Earth cultures. Soren privately wondered if the race that created that helmet had ever—somehow—visited Earth. Or if humans had dreamed of them.

"We keep spending the lives of the young," breathed Soren.

"I know the pain of that, my friend."

"And we've lost so many to suicide, too. There was another last night, which makes seventeen since the WarpLine disaster. Since that first battle with the shoggoths, I mean."

Lost looked at him. "I know how deeply each of those deaths wounds you, my friend. Empathy is a great strength, but it is also the easiest place for tragedy to drive its blade."

"Poetic," said Soren. "But true."

"Have your people determined why? Is it the reality of being so far from home without much chance of ever returning?"

"To a degree, yes. But we've all been experiencing increasingly disturbing dreams. A side effect of the overwhelming existential crisis my people are facing."

The golem turned away without comment.

They stood in silence, watching some bits of battle debris burn like tossed matches as they fell. Soren privately mused that only a cruel madman would ever wish upon such falling stars.

After a time, Lost asked, "How is Lady Jessica?"

It was a clumsy and obvious question, and Soren had been expecting it.

"Her road to recovery will be a long one, I'm afraid," he said.

During the first battle with the shoggoth fleet, it had fallen to Lady Jessica McHugh to use her powers as the chief priestess of the Church of Shades to locate the disembodied spirits of Bianca Petrescu and the other Lost Souls pilots as each died. They had been warned that this might be attempted, and each had to face the terrible decision of going on into whatever truly lay beyond death or allowing her to use *ethla* to bond them to the ships on the Field of Dead Birds. Nearly all of them had demonstrated a level of personal bravery and allowed the necromancer to create that bond. That turned the tide of war, and the NecroTeks were able to carve out a desperate victory.

However, the process of summoning their spirits took a dreadful toll on her, and when it was all over, Lady Death had been reduced to a withered husk clinging to the edge of life. No one knew how long it would take before she could even rise from her wheelchair, let alone risk using necromancy to harvest the souls of the members of Calisto's cadets.

"Tell me," said Soren, "how long after physical death does the consciousness linger?"

"You mean, how much time is there for Lady Death to make the *ethla* connection?"

"Yes."

The golem shook his head. "No one knows."

"Can you guess? Surely your people kept some kind of record."

"The longest gap that I know of," said Lost, "was a year. A Shadderal year."

"Which is five hundred *Earth* days," said Soren, doing the math.

"Yes. But I warn you, friend Soren, the *ethla* connection was not a happy one. Not that time. The spirit was erratic in many disturbing ways. By then she had traveled far, and the process of bringing her back caused a psychic fracture. When she activated her machine body, she attacked everyone. She was quite insane."

"God …"

"To clarify," said Lost gravely, "the greatest span of time for an entirely successful *ethla* connection was far shorter. Weeks."

Soren walked a few paces away and watched as one last piece of debris fell onto the slope of a mountain two kilometers away. Without turning, he said, "I accept that *ethla* is what has so far saved us from the shoggoths, but the cost is appalling."

"Yes," said Lost. "It is. But what choice do we have except to pay it?"

Soren closed his eyes and bowed his head.

"God forgive us," he said so softly that only Lost and the lonely wind heard him.

2

Captain Sebastian Croft stood on the safety apron at the edge of the landing bay as Bianca Petrescu—call sign Mosquito—and the largest of the NecroTeks, Joshua McGinnis—call sign Thunder Bear—brought Calisto's tumbler home.

They were both giants—though Thunder Bear was much larger than Mosquito—yet they handled the battered ship as gently as if it were a wounded baby bird. Once they were through the shimmering veil of the deflector shielding, they exerted their will and transformed their lower halves from a cluster of three ion engines to something approximating legs. Then they squatted and set the tumbler on the pad of a ship transport.

Spacecraft handlers rushed out and secured the ship to the cart with cables while two clambered atop it to force the damaged hatch open. Then they helped Calisto out of the cockpit and down to the deck. She was medium height, solidly built, with a round, brown face and bright eyes. And she looked like she was a half step away from passing out. The strain, a malfunctioning life support, and being knocked around had taken their toll.

Bianca compressed her giant body as tightly as possible, reducing her dimensions so that she was only ten feet tall. The mass was the same, though, and she could only hold that level of compression for a short time. Bee used that to pull her best friend into an embrace that was oddly tender for so powerful a form. A few weeks ago she would never have dared do such a thing for fear of causing terrible harm, but since then she had spent a lot of time experimenting with what her new body could—and could not—do.

"Got a change of clothes coming, Commander," called a petty officer as he jogged over, pushing a cart in front of him. On it was a much smaller mechanical body, though one with no head.

Bianca stepped back from Calisto and walked over to where a row of circular pads stood along one wall. She stepped onto the first pad, turned, and leaned back against it. Clamps hissed from the wall and secured the mechanical body. A port opened in its chest, and a thing not unlike a crab scuttled out and down onto the floor. It was a little bigger than a basketball and had eight segmented legs. The thing clattered past the techs, each of whom stepped back and watched it go. Then the crab climbed onto the headless figure on the cart and settled into the open hole where the head should have been. As it settled in, wires and cables crept from it and attached to other wires and ports within the robot. The bulbous head changed shape and took on a set of features that looked like Bianca's own face but fashioned from alien metals.

The petty officer released the clamps on the body he'd brought in, and Bianca Petrescu stood up, now only six feet tall. Her "at home" body—as she sometimes called it—was still robotic in appearance, but the face was mobile, reflecting her actual expressions and emotions. When she spoke, the voice was as close to her human one as Sybil could manage.

"Does this make my ass look fat?" she asked, grinning.

Calisto managed a small smile—there and gone. She turned to look as other tumblers came in through the deflector wall. Four other NecroTeks came in, too. The rest, led by Jacob Fox—Galahad—were still outside, taking over the patrol while the tumblers returned to the barn for refit and repairs.

Then a skimmer came in, and all conversation and noise in the hangar deck fell into a sad, respectful silence. The skimmers served a lot of purposes, but the hardest was the retrieval of dead pilots. It was why the small utility boats were sometimes called hearses.

Three of her pilots had died. All cadets. All too damn young to die. David Gauthier, call sign Oguan; Amadeus Thibodeau, call sign Baron Samedi; and Kiki Raffelsberger, call sign Enchantress. More flags to fold. More names to burn into her mind. More ghosts to haunt her dreams.

Ghosts, not NecroTeks. Not with Lady Jessica so ill from raising the souls of Bianca and the others who were now NecroTeks. Oguan, Baron Samedi, and Enchantress were merely dead. Truly lost souls.

Bianca came and stood next to Calisto. As the dead were carried off, Calisto took Bianca's hand for a moment, squeezing tight so that her pain manifested as pressure rather than spreading across her face.

Once the fallen were aboard, all of them turned and walked out, forming a procession that they had all shared too many times before.

3

Halfway across the vast Shadderal system, a Medusa mother ship moved with great care among the billions of floating asteroids. She had launched the two big chimera ships that brought the attack squadrons to Asphodel. Now her launch bays were mostly empty. The chimeras were destroyed, and only a dozen daggers were left in reserve.

The captain of the ship was an older shoggoth, born in a breeding vat nearly two hundred years ago. Most of the pilots who died that day were from her genetic line. Not children per se, but cells of the larger entity of which the captain was the greatest part.

She felt the pain of her loss.

And the anger.

Most of that anger was directed at the humans and their blasphemous NecroTek bodies. She held some hate for the ghost Lost as well. She knew about them both from a report sent by another of her breeding lot, who had been in the wrong part of space when the gigantic station appeared out of nowhere. His patrol ship was part of a squadron that had been looking for Shadderal for sixty centuries. The captain's family line had been a part of that search since the last of the enemy died out all those years ago. When the station appeared, it occupied the same space as that dagger, trapping it inside the hull. The shoggoth used that opportunity to invade the onboard artificial intelligence, stealing much precious knowledge before its presence was discovered and destroyed.

Now the shoggoth knew of Asphodel, of Lost, of the NecroTeks … and of Earth.

It was the captain of this Medusa who had transmitted that information up the long chain of command. She did not know if it actually reached the Outer Gods—none of her kind had ever experienced direct contact. The night-gaunts had received it, though. They were the direct masters of the shoggoth peoples.

The captain was certain the night-gaunts had taken credit for the discovery. It was not in their nature to share rewards. Generosity formed no part of the nature of those monsters.

The captain mused on this as her ship moved away from the recent slaughter.

She did not see the ship that ghosted along behind her. None of the sophisticated sensors aboard the Medusa recorded it. Not one.

4

When Lost cried out, Soren whirled just as his companion staggered and fell. He darted forward and caught the golem.

"What is it, my friend?" he cried.

"I ... I ..." gasped Lost, his voice so faded that it sounded like it came from far away.

Soren lay him gently on the ground and helped the alien sit up with his back to a boulder.

"Tell me how I can help you," pleaded Soren.

Lost shook his head slowly.

"I ... don't know what is happening to me," he said.

Sudden alarm leaped up inside Soren's chest. "Is it *ethla*? Have you been too long in a physical form? Is it the radiation?"

Lost tried to say something, but all he could manage was a faint sound as thin as night wind. Within the pressure suit, the spirit of the alien shuddered and twitched.

"It ... it's passing," he gasped. Then, a moment later he repeated it with a firmer voice. "Yes, it's passing. Help me up."

Soren did, being very careful. If he thought the pressure suit felt unusually empty, he did not remark on it. Lost stood swaying for several long moments.

"What happened?" asked Soren.

Lost looked at him and slowly shook his head. "I do not know, friend Soren. Nothing like this has happened to me in a very long time."

"But it's happened before?"

"Longer ago than I can clearly recall," admitted the golem. "Twice. Once when I was alive, and once after I died and became a ghost pilot."

"What caused it then, do you know?"

"Know? Not for certain."

"Do you have a guess?"

Lost walked a few meters away and stood looking up at the sky. "I will not put a name to it," he said. "Not until I am sure."

"Why not?"

Without turning, the ghost said, "Because naming a thing can give it power, can call it, and if I am wrong, I do not want to call something to us that we cannot hope to fight."

Soren pressed him on it, but Lost refused to answer. A few moments later his pressure suit collapsed, and his spirit fled away into the winds of Shadderal. Lars stood there, frustrated and very deeply frightened.

Interlude Two

The Socrates of Athens Auditorium
University of California, Los Angeles
Four Years Before the WarpLine Event

"As philosophers," said Lars Soren, "we cannot ignore the question of what will happen when humanity encounters proof of alien life. And by that, I mean everything from a fossil of a bacterium or virus found on some distant moon to spaceships landing on the White House lawn."

He paused and paced slowly across the stage, looking at the audience. "How many of you believe that life of some kind exists on other worlds? Show of hands," Soren surveyed the crowd. "Better than half. Okay, the math supports that optimistic view. Specifically, the Drake equation, developed in 1961 by astronomer Frank Drake. The short version is that Drake cooked up a formula that goes something like this."

He sent a graphic to the screen:

$R_{\circ}$: The average rate of star formation in our galaxy(number per year).

f_p: The fraction of those stars with planetary systems.

n_e: The average number of planets, per system, with an environment suitable for life.

f_l: The fraction of suitable planets on which life actually appears.

$\boldsymbol{f_i}$: The fraction of life-bearing planets on which intelligent life emerges.

$\boldsymbol{f_c}$: The fraction of civilizations that develop a technology that produces detectable signs of their existence.

N: The number of new civilizations per year in the Milky Way galaxy whose electromagnetic emissions are detectable.

L: The average number of years such civilizations produce signs of their existence.

"The first six terms on that list," continued Soren, "when multiplied together, yield the seventh, *N*, the average number of new technologically transmitting societies in the Milky Way that come online. Meaning they are able to transmit signals capable of reaching across space. This does not have to be a deliberate thing. Radio signals are tenacious." He paused. "So, let's call *N* the 'freshman class' of these advanced civilizations. We then multiply *N* by *L*, the average lifetime of those civilizations, giving us the total number of such currently active. This is all supposition, of course, and is powered by the sheer number of stars. A conservative estimate is one hundred billion stars in the Milky Way alone. And our astronomers estimate that there are anywhere between two hundred billion and two *trillion* galaxies in the known universe. As someone once said, that's a hell of a lot of real estate. More than enough for even the coyest of statisticians to anticipate that intelligent life exists elsewhere. There is a rather astounding degree of arrogance in thinking otherwise."

He changed the image to that of one of the more recent deep-space telescopic images, then sent that out as a 3D hologram to fill the entire auditorium. There were gasps of wonder and awe.

"All of this," he said, gesturing to the swirling galaxies and blazing stars, "is one-millionth of one percent of the observable universe." He let the images swirl.

"So, you tell me … Are we alone?"

Part Five
The Shape of Things

"There's a certain Slant of light,
Winter Afternoons—
That oppresses, like the Heft
Of Cathedral Tunes"

—*Emily Dickinson*

Joint MIT/UCLA Biological Research Field Station #8
Queen Maud Land, Antarctica

1

Evie heard a sound that did not fit with the orchestra of noises that composed the nightly symphony. What she heard was not the wind moaning above or whining as it blew past wires and ropes. It wasn't the flap of canvas not properly secured, nor was it the *thump-thump* of a loose piece of siding on one of the sheds. It wasn't a machine sound or a nature sound or even a person sound.

It was just a sound.

She sat up in bed, pulling the blanket to her, gathering one corner in a fist over her heart.

The sound was soft. Hesitant.

Almost … *sneaky*?

Evie cocked her head and listened to the word her mind had picked.

How could a sound be sneaky?

Her head snapped around toward the wall closest to the observation deck. Closest to the Artifact.

That froze her.

Then she heard the sound again. *Sounds.* More than one.

"Wh-who's there?" She wanted it to come out as a challenge—strong and firm—but she stumbled over the first word. It sounded desperately weak even to her own ears. Evie tried it again. "Who's there, damn it?"

There was no answer. Silence filled the darkness around her. Even the outside noises seemed to mute themselves as if the night held its breath.

Then …

"Professor?"

The voice was faint. Thin. As hesitant as her own had been. And it was familiar. Of course it was. She knew everyone at the site. Even so, the voice was wrong somehow. Distorted and strange. It almost sounded like …

"Mac?" she whispered.

"Help me," begged the voice. "I don't … understand … what's happening—"

The words stopped abruptly. Evie flung back the blankets and swung her feet out of bed. The floor was heated, but that warmth seemed absent, and the texture of the floor was all wrong. Oddly yielding and damp. Like standing on something alive.

"Mac?"

There was no sound.

Evie hurried to a cabinet and removed a heavy hickory hiking stick. She took it in both hands and turned in a slow circle, trying to read the darkness. There was only the faintest light spilling in from a waxing moon and a distant light on a pole halfway down Main Street. The illumination painted the edges of the table and chairs and the stove and bureau with a cold blue. Everything was where it should be.

Grasping the stick like a baseball bat, she crept toward the door.

"Mac?" she called in a careful whisper.

Nothing. No sound at all.

At the door, Evie switched the stick to one hand and reached for the knob with the other. Before she could touch it, though, the handle turned.

Evie froze.

The metal handle moved up and down, but only slightly, limited by the deadbolt.

"Whoever's out there, this isn't funny."

Nothing.

Evie half turned. "Sybil, who is at my door?"

The AI did not respond.

"*Sybil,*" she snapped. "Wake up."

"I am online, Professor Cronin," said the AI. "How may I be of assistance?"

"Who is at my door?"

Again there was a pause, but this time Sybil finally answered.

"There is no one outside."

It was not the right answer, though. Sybil was never imprecise, and that terrified Evie more than anything.

"Sybil … is there someone *inside* my hut?"

And a voice directly behind her said, "Professor … help me."

Evie whirled, swinging the stick with all her strength, all her fear. It whistled through the air and slammed into …

Evie woke up.

She was in her bed.

The blankets were over her, and outside, the wind howled and moaned.

"Sybil, lights, lights—*now.*"

Sybil turned on the lights. All of them. Evie braced herself for what was in her room. But the room was completely empty. She got up and hurried to the door and found the lock secure.

Then she saw the walking stick on the bed next to where she had just been.

Evie turned in a slow circle, trying to understand what had just happened. Was it a dream? If so … how did she get the walking stick?

She undid the deadbolt and pulled the door open. Icy wind buffeted her, and she bent into it. In the process, she saw the ground outside. There, pressed into a light covering of blown snow and ice, were marks. Not footprints. Just marks. Shapeless, indistinct—but there.

That was all she saw. Evie leaned out and looked up and down Main Street, but the camp was quiet. Nothing moved except the loose tarps and the tops of light poles swaying in the breeze.

Evie closed her door and sat on the edge of the bed. She almost asked Sybil to explain to her what had just happened. But she was afraid of whatever answer the artificial intelligence would give.

The howling wind intensified, and she did not even try to sleep the rest of that night.

2

Colonel Thomas Jefferson Hobart sat across from Dr. Brollachan as their suborbital jet skated along the outer envelope of the atmosphere, heading south to the bottom of the world.

They were alone in a sealed forward compartment just aft of the cockpit. Behind the rear bulkhead were two groups—one composed of the best scientific minds who were currently under SPU nondisclosure agreements. The rest were soldiers, talking among themselves and saying very little across the aisle.

In the secure cabin, the scientist and the soldier talked incessantly, cataloging and then dissecting every bit of information currently in hand.

"This Professor Cronin," said Hobart, "what do you know about her?"

"I've been at a few academic conferences and heard her speak," said Brollachan. "Met her at social gatherings at various institutes and museums. She is remarkably brilliant. A prodigy in her developmental years, winning everything from the Bunsen Prize to sharing a Nobel in cultural anthropology. Her PhD thesis on 'The Philosophy of Human Expansion, with Special Notes on Extraterrestrial Human Cultures' is taught in all of the better universities."

"Okay, but why is someone like that digging holes in Antarctica? It's my understanding that people never lived there, even before it froze."

"Fair question, Tom. She is one of those bright lights who seems to collect advanced degrees as a hobby. A true polymath. At last count she had three doctorates, though it may be four by now. She's thirty-three and shows no signs of the drop in brilliance that often accompanies child prodigies as they mature. If anything, she's getting smarter. Rather an astonishing woman. Shy and bookish, not at all flamboyant, as so many other child prodigies are, and generous when it comes to sharing credit with her team. One of Lars Soren's protégés. One of that new breed of scientist-philosophers. But to answer your question, one of her degrees is evolutionary biology."

"What the hell evolved in Antarctica apart from penguins and polar bears?" asked the colonel.

"There are no polar bears in Antarctica," said Brollachan mildly. "However, let's not forget that Antarctica was not always frozen. It began icing in the late Paleocene or possibly middle Eocene. Call it somewhere between sixty and forty-five million years ago, give or take. That process escalated during the Eocene–Oligocene extinction event thirty-four million years ago."

"Huh," grunted Hobart. "And the ice over that Artifact thing is how old?"

"Based on the core samples taken by the MIT/UCLA team's reports, it is at *least* thirty million years old. Possibly older."

"Well ... shit."

"Yes," agreed Brollachan.

They mused on that for a bit. Then Hobart asked, "What's this Cronin woman like as a person, Torq?"

"Hmmm ... I don't know her well, but she has a bit of a dual reputation. On one hand, despite her young age, she can pull off the part of an affable, mildly stodgy academic, even to the point of dressing dowdy so that she appears sexless. Not uncommon with beautiful women who want to be taken seriously."

Hobart snorted. "Jeez. But, okay, what about the other side of her personality?"

"Well, her father is General Cronin, and from him she gets a lot of steel—and I've been told that this steel is quite sharp. I know people who have come into collision with her—whether in a fight over grant money or by attacking one of her students. Or when they've challenged her unwisely, having not seen past the face and figure. Many of those folks walk away looking like they just got horsewhipped."

"I knew she was Cronin's daughter," said the soldier, "but assumed that she got his brains, not his courage. I met her a few times when she was a nerdy little bookworm. Eight, maybe, or nine. She could have had a great career in military intelligence or even working under you at the SPU."

"And again, your read on her is surface, Tom," said Brollachan. "When I spoke with her on the phone today, she was understandably shocked and unsettled but also sharp. Professional. She has layers."

"Will she be trouble?"

"I haven't the slightest idea." Brollachan pursed his lips in thought for a moment. "It would be best if we tried not to poke the lioness too hard."

Hobart nodded, filing that away. "If she's so protective of her students, then she must be climbing the walls with worry about that mechanic who went missing. Mac-something."

"Macklin Ryerson. More of a utility player than specifically a mechanic. One of those beefy but reliable types who are useful to have on hand."

"Doesn't sound like the kind of kid who'd go wandering off like this."

"No," said Brollachan. "He does not. And that is one of many things about this that concerns me."

The shipboard Sybil spoke in her soothing, modulated AI voice. "We are beginning our descent. Please prepare yourself for a safe landing."

3

Evie Cronin stood near landing pad C, hands deep in her coat pockets and a scarf wound turn-around-turn, nearly obscuring her face. She wasn't cold, but she was shivering. Fear freezes to a deeper level than icy weather, and no amount of clothing can shut it out.

And she was afraid.

The strangeness of the previous night was still with her. Her dream—if it had been a dream—amplified her concern over Mac. No sign of him had been found.

At first she really did think this was Mac trying to seize the moment and ensure his place in the history books. But the reasonable window for that was long past closed. Now he was merely missing. Despite how the voice she *thought* she heard had sounded like him, Evie did not believe it was the young mechanic.

No.

Mac was missing down there, where *it* lay. The gigantic thing. The Artifact.

Her mind raced like a runaway engine, its intensity a danger to itself. What *was* that thing? Worse, what would all of this mean going forward? Was the Artifact a threat to more than the common, shared human worldview of religious beliefs? Was it a more specific threat? If so, in what way?

Not that she expected the thing was likely to pop open a door and spew a horde of bug-eyed alien invaders. No. It was the overall implications. The sheer enormity of it. At thirty-three, Evie was young to be a tenured professor, and she was fully aware of how many critical eyes were on her all the time. Even with the political protection of her mentor, Dr. Lars Soren—a legendary figure at UCLA and elsewhere—Evie felt vulnerable. What if she was wrong? What if this artifact was really *man*-made, as improbable as that was? Sure, it would still be a significant find, but not on the scale she thought.

Its presence also disturbed her personal worldview. A lapsed Christian whose parents were devout fundamentalists, Evie had already distanced herself from them by championing the concept of Earth being billions of years old rather than the biblical six thousand. It would likely complete the job of fracturing her family if she turned out to be the one who shepherded in an age where proof of intelligent life existed before the Age of Miracles and the rise of Judaism, Christianity, and Islam. The insecure part of her mind was already imagining her family's hateful emails. She would go from atheist to blaspheming heretic in a broken heartbeat.

She wished she could call Soren, but even if her mentor weren't in cryo-sleep, Dr. Brollachan had forwarded her the SPU's harsh and restrictive set of protocols that, among other things, forbade all unauthorized contact with the outside world. Grave penalties were implied, and Evie knew enough about the SPU from her father to accept those threats as real and valid.

These thoughts made her pulse beat erratically. Evie could feel the comforting weight of a small metal flask of Potter's Field eighteen-year-old Kentucky sour mash in her coat pocket. She'd taken a couple of small sips to steady her nerves before heading out, and it made her belly glow with warmth. Without realizing it, she touched that flask the way her mother always touched her crucifix. The effect was about the same.

Craig was with the group, following the lockdown orders until the special team arrived. That closeness might help them process the fear and potential grief about Mac.

Where are you, you muscle-bound idiot?

She rubbed her eyes and looked around. The rows of huts, equipment sheds, and garages were the same; the people were the same; but nothing else was. That *thing* lay in the valley and stubbornly refused to fade away like a mirage or a hallucination.

It all made her feel odd. Especially after the strange and ugly dreams she had been having recently, up to and including the previous night. Tentacled monsters. Bizarre lumbering shapes in the frozen darkness. And her own body changing, metamorphosing against her will. Each night the dreams returned, and each night they were a bit different. Always worsening, never improving.

Each morning she woke with only fragmented memories of them. Nightmare images that were just out of focus, just beyond her reach, leaving only a palpable sense of unease. Not exactly dread, but close enough. And bad enough that Evie had been trying to analyze her thoughts to see if the dreams were simple tsunamis of nervous tension sweeping up disparate items into nightmares.

Now, though, she wondered if there was a splinter of prophecy in them. And there was something else nibbling at her from the corner of her awareness: a half memory of touching the craft and an even more fragmented memory of some weird birdcall.

Tekeli-li.

Even as she tried to go still inside and coax the memory out into the light, it faded more and was soon gone.

What would Dr. Soren say about all this? She wished he was there on Earth instead of asleep on a ship out in the black.

She also thought of her dad. Growing up as the bookish daughter of a hawkish general had not been easy. He was so rigid and exacting, demonstrating very little patience for her hijinks as a kid, and seemed only vaguely interested in her academic pursuits. And yet he was kind and loving in his own way. Not gentle, but not rough. She wished he was there and wished she'd thought of calling him first. Maybe Brollachan would grant him some kind of temporary authority so he could come down here.

If not, she was going to have to do all this by herself.

Her fingers found the solid comfort of the flask, and she ached to take a drink. Some techs were working on the skimmer only a few meters away, however, so she dared not. But the song of the flask, the sultry whisper of the sour mash whiskey, teased her mercilessly.

A sound made her look up just as the SPU ship broke through the bottom of the cloud cover. Evie immediately began heading over to the landing pad at a nervous jog-trot. Big jets hissed to slow the craft's descent, and it touched down with barely a shudder.

Evie watched the SPU craft land and felt almost as much trepidation in its arrival as she did for what lay in the ice.

4

Dr. Torquil Brollachan arrived with flourish and mystery at the research station.

Evie watched him ascend from the craft like a king coming to claim lands his armies had conquered. He was followed by the SPU science field team and a small but well-equipped military unit dressed all in black.

Evie watched them march down from the orbital jump-ship and form into two neat groups—one of scientists, the other of armed soldiers. What surprised her was that the commander of that group wasn't any mid-level small-unit officer but instead a full-bird colonel. And a famous one at that—Thomas Jefferson Hobart, hero of the Martian Uprising and the pirate siege of Titan.

She hurried over to ask what the hell was going on.

Scientists she could understand. Even a handful of soldiers for security. But not so many of each, and not from the SPU. She went straight to Dr. Brollachan, whom she had met at a conference some years ago. Met and disliked, though she had not been able to pin down exactly *why*. Something about the man felt creepy, and after she'd shaken his hand, she had wanted to wash hers.

"Doctor," she said, "we expected a response, but this is a bit extreme, isn't it?"

Brollachan studied her with cold gray eyes. "Extreme, Professor? I don't think so. Frankly, if there had been time, I would have brought twice as many people. Even now, my people back in Wyoming are prepping cargo containers to be flown here. And the colonel will likely double or triple the size of his detail."

Evie stepped a little closer. "Why? Why not a group of scientists? I can think of about fifty disciplines that ought to be represented here. And let's face it, our location provides all the security we need."

"Your team made a very important discovery, Professor Cronin," said the SPU chief. "Arguably the most significant and impactful discovery since the development of human speech."

"I am aware of its potential," Evie said. "But until we finish excavating it and running tests on the ice all around it, we'll—"

"I do not mean to offend, Professor," said Brollachan, "but there is no *we* in this scenario."

Evie stiffened. "Sorry, but what?"

"It means, Professor Cronin, that this site is now classified and under the jurisdiction of the SPU."

"*Really?*" she said slowly and icily. "Well, it's my understanding that the SPU is part of the United States military. This is Antarctica, and the lease on our dig was approved by the International Association for Noninvasive Research. Don't know them? Then again, why would you? They are tasked with protecting the planet and encouraging humanitarian research projects, as opposed to the SPU, which is all about bugs and bombs and things that destroy. But perhaps you *have* heard of the Antarctic Treaty of 1961, which bans *all* military activity on this entire continent. *I* have a permit, and that grants me legal jurisdiction here. You and your soldiers do not."

"I believe you'll find that you are mistaken," said Brollachan. He wore a broad, charming smile, but none of its warmth reached his pale eyes.

"Is *that* what you think?" countered Evie. "I can make two phone calls, Doctor, maybe only one, and have a UN team here to escort you back to the US of A."

"That is unlikely, Professor."

Evie tried a different tack. "Do you know who my father is?"

"I do. And I had the pleasure of dining with General Cronin in Atlanta some months ago. I was also present at his retirement ceremony."

"Retired or not, he has friends—"

"In high places," Brollachan finished for her. "Oh, I am well aware of that. He is a frequent golfing partner with President Lewis and plays poker once a month with three of the joint chiefs, one of whom used to be his aide. Don't misunderstand me, Professor Cronin. I certainly know who your father is, and in virtually any other scenario, your call would result in me being called on the carpet to have the riot act read to me."

Evie waited for the other shoe.

Brollachan's smile never even flickered. "Despite all of that, and the existence of the treaty, the SPU has been granted a dispensation in this matter."

"On what grounds?"

"Surely you can work that out for yourself, Professor."

Evie folded her arms across her chest. "Humor me."

"Of course," said Brollachan. He raised his left forearm between them and activated his holo-comms unit. A holo-screen appeared in the air, with identical images facing both of them. A man's face appeared on the screen. He was in his early seventies but looked fit, with iron-gray hair and piercing green eyes.

"Dad?"

"Evie," said General G. Elmer Cronin, "listen to me. I understand that you are likely very upset by the presence of the SPU team. But this is a matter of more than national security. It's a matter of interplanetary security. Possibly galactic. And yes, I know how dramatic that sounds. However, by every indication, the artifact uncovered by your team is not of this Earth. Its age, and the age of the ice in which it rests, precludes it from being of terrestrial origin. You must know that by now, too. Hell, you taught *me* about that sort of thing."

"Dad, I—"

"Let me finish," said the general. "We can't possibly know what this thing is, what's in it, who sent it, or why. Common sense and every philosophy of safety dictates that it needs to be examined by experts in order to assess and determine any level of threat. Then there needs to be a process—possibly a long one—to decide the best and safest course of revealing that information to the world. The president agrees with this view. So, in fact, do I. Therefore, America's participation in the Antarctic Treaty has been temporarily suspended by executive order."

"Dad, you can't support this madness."

"I do, honey," said the general. His hawklike features softened. "Evie, you know I love you. I respect and trust you. I always have. I'm asking you to trust me in this. Dr. Brollachan and his team have my confidence. As does Colonel Hobart. Please … cooperate with them, and they will allow you access to the entire research process."

"And if I don't want to?"

The general winced very slightly. "They are empowered, by that same executive order, to detain everyone at your site. You would all be incarcerated in place for the duration of the project. You know how long that kind of thing can take. Do you want you and your grad students to just sit around and do nothing for a year or two? Or longer?"

"That's insane," cried Evie. "This could ruin the careers of everyone here."

"No," said the general. "That will happen only if you refuse to cooperate. Understand me, sweetheart, this is a done thing. POTUS signed that order, and all authority rests with Dr. Brollachan. There is absolutely nothing either of us could do to change that. You have a choice. Cooperate and *help* us to understand this incredible—and incredibly *difficult*—situation and, by doing so, earn a place in what will be the greatest scientific revelation ever, or …"

He did not need to repeat the threat. Evie stared into her father's eyes and saw his pain, his unease, but also his excitement. Brollachan had stopped smiling, which was good. She wanted to see how many of those gleaming white teeth she could smash out.

Every part of her was filled with equal parts rage and outrage, but the practical part of her asserted itself by slow degrees. And with it came an uprush of her absolute *need* to stay here and be a part of this.

"Okay," she said bitterly. "I hear you loud and clear."

His smile was filled with relief, but there was still something flickering in his eyes. Fear? Sure. That made sense. His daughter was at ground zero during a pivotal moment in human history. How often was history changed without chaos, carnage, and grief? History books were not filled with pleasant stories about good folks having a nice day. Besides, growth itself was a kind of birthing process—breaking through, smashing old assumptions, leaving wreckage behind in terms of spoiled understanding and shattered beliefs.

"I'll call you at least twice a week," promised the general. "I love you, Evie. Never forget that."

"I love you too," said Evie, unable to keep the sound of sour defeat from her voice.

The holo ended, and Brollachan lowered his arm. Evie realized her hand was clamped around the flask in her pocket. And, God, how she wanted to go get drunk. Or throw the flask at Brollachan. Maybe both.

Evie wasn't sure what to expect from the SPU chief scientist. A smug smile, perhaps. Some condescension and thinly veiled threats, maybe. Or unfiltered triumph.

Instead, he offered his hand.

"I would prefer to do this as partners, Professor Cronin," he said in an oddly gentle tone. "I am familiar with your career and believe in your goals. I have a great and genuine respect for you. I also share your concern for your missing team member—Mac Ryerson, yes? We want him found safe and sound. This, however, is bigger than both of us. Bigger than any personal agenda. Let's make history together."

"On one condition," said Evie.

One of Brollachan's eyebrows arched upward. He lowered his hand. "Oh?"

"I'm a *real* part of this," she said. "All of it. When anyone goes down to examine the Artifact, I'm there, too. No secrets. No keeping me at arm's length. It's all, or it's nothing."

The SPU scientist considered for a moment, and then he nodded.

"I can live with that," he said, and once again offered his hand.

After a long—a very long—pause, Evie Cronin took his hand and shook it.

5

Worlds turn on such moments as this.

Part Six
The Measure of Loss

"I slept, and dreamed that life was Beauty;
I woke, and found that life was Duty."

—*Ellen Sturgis Hooper*

Asphodel Station
The Shadderal Star System

1

Lars Soren sat looking out at the many planets that made up the Shadderal system. He'd asked Sybil for as complete a view of the many planets, moons, asteroids, and stars as could be fit onto the huge RealScreen that fronted the main bridge of Asphodel Station.

The techs in stellar cartography had mapped only 12 percent of the system and, so far, had identified forty-seven planets within standard flight range of Asphodel and more than 1,840 moons—all of which orbited a pair of mismatched suns in ways that defied ordinary gravitational science. That list of celestial bodies kept growing, and Captain Croft believed the total could easily double, if not triple. The current guess was that the Shadderal system was sixteen times larger than Earth's Sol system. Mapping it all could take years. Apart from the vast distances involved, there were two huge asteroid belts, each with trillions of pieces of ore-rich rock or frozen water.

Even though only a small percentage of the star system had been properly mapped, Asphodel was on the very edge of it, beyond the atmosphere of the outermost planet, Shadderal. The view he saw now was an even more clustered version of the first glimpse that filled the screens shortly after the WarpLine failure. Even with the system's great size, it was so crowded that the sky seemed bizarrely—impossibly—crowded. Now he understood that this was a design feature created by alien planetary engineers hundreds of thousands of years ago. Even so, the scope of it boggled his mind in unpleasant ways.

He wondered how he would have felt about it had there been no explosion, no deaths, no psychic distortion, and no shoggoth invasion.

Still frightening, he decided. How could it not be?

"I have no purpose out here," he told the screen, but knew, as he said it, that this was a lie. He was a professor of theology and philosophy—specifically of *cosmic* philosophy, and this was the cosmos. In its way, everything that had happened since Asphodel had come out here fit into the things he said and taught. There was even religion out here. The worship of the Outer Gods.

For Soren, this was as much about the practicalities of fostering religion in an age of science as it was about ushering faith, in all its aspects, out into the stars. His view was that if God were real, then He was the god of everything everywhere.

"Penny for your thoughts."

Soren snapped out of a reverie and turned as station director Delia Trumbo came into the small observation lounge. She was medium height, broad shouldered, and strong looking. Some extra pounds here and there were as stylishly concealed as were what she considered her "deficiencies"—small breasts and narrow hips. Her hair was twisted into a fashionable coiffure, and her lipstick applied with exacting precision.

"Delia," said Soren, smiling. "Have a seat."

Trumbo slid into a chair beside him. There was a bottle of excellent claret on the table beneath the big RealScreen that was set to a live view of the space outside. Soren poured a generous glass for her and lightly topped off his own.

"As for the value you place on my thoughts," mused Soren, "I think a penny is too high a price."

Trumbo snorted, then took a sip. The wine was real, and the station still had a goodly supply. Nevertheless, she'd ordered the techs to do a full scan of the better vintages so that the replicators could produce adequate fakes once the stocks ran out. Soren knew about this and made no comment. It was well known that Delia Trumbo liked a glass now and then. *Now* more often than *then*, as he saw it.

"We've been here five weeks," he said after a comfortable pause, "and that view still makes my heart flutter."

Trumbo took another sip and gave a small nod. "Five weeks ago the most impressive thing we had seen was Jupiter."

They smiled at one another the way people on a sinking ship might. Tacitly toasting the paucity of lifeboats as the deck tilted into an icy sea. But then Trumbo's eyes took on a different cast, one of deep sadness. "You heard about the deaths this morning?"

"The suicide? Sadly, yes. Though I thought it was last night."

"There were three more this morning. The Harrisons. Two adults and their five-year-old."

"Belinda and Gary Harrison? God … no! Was it a murder-suicide? Did they … kill … their child? Please don't tell me they killed little Rachel."

Her gaze dropped away. "It was worse than that. Dušan worked through the scene, and the way he reconstructs it is that Rachel took a knife from the kitchen and … and …" She gave a violent shake of her head. "Belinda or Gary must have found her. Then they both …"

She could not finish, and Soren stepped close and gave her a hug.

"It's getting … so bad," she sobbed. "People can't take all of … *this*. And now, with the shoggoths back, I don't know what will happen. How can we keep people cheerful and optimistic out here? Lars … can you talk to your faith leaders and see if they can put together some kind of program? Group stuff. Not sermons, maybe, but some kind of spiritual counseling?"

"Of course," he said. "I have a meeting with the synod this afternoon. I will make that request a centerpiece of our discussion."

She thanked him, then stepped back and wiped her eyes. She went over and built a large drink, taking sips of it as she came back. When she spoke again, there was an artificial nonchalance to her voice. "I suppose you've heard what Croft and Petrescu are cooking up."

He turned to her. "What, in particular? Another mapping marathon?"

"No," she said. "The meeting. To arrange the farewell ceremony."

Soren frowned. "For …?"

"Maybe we should call it a goodbye party for the NecroTeks."

"They just got back."

"And Sebastian is sending them out again. The search continues, my dear."

"Search?" he asked, then said, "Ah! Looking for the shoggoth base."

"That would be it," agreed Trumbo as she took another sip, draining her glass. She poured her own refill. "Lost told us that the shoggoth ships have limited FTL drives. So either they are making a long series of hyperspace jumps, or ..."

"Or they have a base somewhere in this system," finished Soren. "I find neither possibility particularly comforting."

"Ha!" laughed Trumbo, and took a large sip.

He drank too as he watched a pair of NecroTeks fly past on their patrol. Then he became aware that Trumbo was studying him. "Yes?"

"You hate this plan, don't you."

He sighed. "I think it is somewhere between ill-advised and dangerously provoking."

"Why?"

"Because of what happened today. They were away when the shoggoths attacked and more of our pilots died. Had they not already been on the way back, we might not even be having this conversation."

"So, what is the better plan, Lars? To sit and wait to be hit by an even bigger fleet?"

"You misunderstand me, Delia. There *is* no better plan."

"Ah," she said.

He tapped her glass with his. "Ah."

They sat and drank for a long time.

2

Soren sat with Captain Croft, Director Trumbo, Calisto, and Bianca Petrescu, who was still in the human-sized metal body only a little larger than her former self. Even though she was no longer a giant, the metal body was nonetheless a strange and exotic aspect. The others were used to it.

Mostly. Not entirely.

For Soren's part, he found it deeply unnerving. Bianca was a dear friend—the first he had made after the WarpLine disaster—but his mind had a very difficult time reconciling the slim, feisty twentysomething navy pilot with this powerful inhuman form.

He sat and listened as Captain Croft rattled on about logistics, allowing his mind to drift. He was only brought back to full attention when Croft asked, "Are we boring you, Lars? Or did you leave something on the stove?"

Soren waved his hand and gave a small, wry, and apologetic smile. "Bored? No. How could something as absurd as this ever be boring?"

"Here we go," said Trumbo under her voice.

"Please elucidate," suggested Croft. He was not a big man but had a commanding presence that created the illusion of greater size. Croft was a career navy officer whose handsome face bore the scars of the battles he had fought.

"I'm not a tactician," protested Soren. "Frankly, I'm not even sure why I keep getting invited to these kinds of meetings."

"Because you don't have your head up your ass," said Bianca.

"Thanks, Bee," he said. "The fact is that I don't agree with the plan. Not even a little. Not on any point, in fact. I think it is dangerous, likely to bear no fruit, and will leave Asphodel Station without adequate defenses should the shoggoths return. We have seen firsthand how bad a decision that is. In my view, even considering sending them out again is a sign of desperation trumping common sense."

"Don't sugarcoat it, Doc," said Calisto.

Croft offered a bland smile. "You have made that clear enough, Lars. But it's our decision to try. Lost and his people fought the war for uncountable years. They won a lot of battles but lost the war because the Outer Gods put more troops in the field, and by an order of magnitude. We feel that—"

Soren held up a hand to stop him. "Sebastian, I understand your reasoning. Finding and destroying the Outer Gods would likely end the war. I get it. Finding the shoggoth base and eliminating it will give us time to organize a search for that seven-star system. My concern is that we have been involved in this war for a little over a month. Bianca and her team have been NecroTeks for less time. And we won one large battle with the shoggoths at a terrible cost and a smaller battle at the expense of more of our pilots. If the shoggoths are watching us and see our strongest defenders fly off, then they could hit us as soon as we're vulnerable."

"Which makes sense from a certain point of view, Lars," countered Croft. "However, to do nothing is to perpetuate a war of attrition, and we don't have the numbers to play that game."

"He's right," said Bianca. "We need to be proactive here. We can't even fight a holding action because there's no fucking cavalry riding over the hill."

Soren looked at her. "You, of all people, Bianca, should be on the side of caution. Look what's happened to you. To Jacob and the others. You *died* fighting this war. That is a terrible price to pay."

"And if we do nothing, we'll *all* die."

"If you leave, all of us here may die in your absence. What is the plan then? To resurrect all twelve thousand people on Asphodel as ghosts and implant them in ships? What then? With every battle, the radiation in those mech suits erodes more and more of your soul. Your actual *soul*."

"Yes, that's what happens," she said, and despite the modulated machine voice, there was some heat in her tone. "And if we don't stop the Outer Gods, then all of us will have died for nothing. If we can't end this war decisively, then my friends and I—all of the NecroTeks and all of Calisto's Lost Souls—will be ground down to nothing, and the Outer Gods will still be there. We know they're looking for Earth now that they know about us. How can we possibly just sit and wait for the end we know will come when there's a chance—however slim—that we can find and destroy those motherfuckers?"

Her words cut off whatever else Soren felt he wanted to say. It was clear her mind was made up and that she believed completely in this plan. He closed his eyes and nodded.

"I've had my say," he murmured. "I only pray that there is some justice in the universe. Meanwhile, I—and the members of the synod—will pray." He paused. "For whatever that's worth."

3

A line of giants stood with their backs to the burning suns.

The sky above these titans was filled with ships, and on the ground, hundreds of people were gathered, looking up at the spectacle.

Dr. Lars Soren stood at a podium, his modified pressure suit looking like a second skin. All around him were officers of Asphodel Station's small military contingent, senior officials from the station, and many others. Some members of the press stood with them, though they were more than fifty thousand light years away from their news services and readership. Most had accepted the transitional role of historians and that was fine, as Soren saw it. Whether the people on Asphodel ever managed to return home or if these histories would only ever be for future generations born out here under the alien suns, the story would need to be told. And to be read.

He felt like a fool and a liar. Bianca, Trumbo, and Croft had begged and bullied him to host this event. He did it only under protest, but he hated it and hated himself for agreeing.

Keeping all of that off his face, Soren turned and looked up at the monstrous forms behind him for a long moment, then turned back to the gathered crowd. Drones hovered all around, sending the feeds up to the station and out to small bases recently established throughout what they called the Shadderal Star System. Soren nodded soberly.

"They look like giant robots," he said, not intending it as a joke. Nor did anyone laugh. A few young pilots who stood in the front row of the gathered crowd did, however, smile and nod. Calisto, the new team leader of the Lost Souls squadron, met Soren's eyes, and her smile was meant for him. A mutual awareness that was on a different level than what was generally shared. "And yet," continued Soren, "they are nothing of the kind. Not robots. No."

The drones zoomed focus on the row of colossal figures. A dozen of them, all standing in a row. The smallest was fifteen meters tall. The tallest rose nearly fifty meters. No two looked alike, each design an extension of its pilot's will.

"These machine bodies are vehicles for human souls," said Soren. "Not living human pilots, but their ghosts. Every pilot housed within these gleaming towers of parts made from new and old spacecraft has come with us across the galaxy with the station, and they fought and died protecting us all."

The crowd applauded this, and Soren waited through it.

"They are champions. Heroes," he continued. "Without them, none of us would be here right now. They gave everything to win the war with the shoggoth fleet. They won a war that—I think we can all agree—we should not have been *able* to win." He paused, smiling. "Think about it. We were all hurled across the span of the Milky Way. We found ourselves in the middle of an ancient war between bizarre aliens who worship other, vastly more powerful beings as gods. The Outer Gods. Beings of immeasurable age and strength. That war started within hours of us arriving here. There was no time to acclimate, no time to get up to speed, no time to process the shock of all that we lost when we were hurled here. No time to mourn what we lost or those who died in the WarpLine disaster. There was no warning of any threat and no warning of imminent attack by a greater force. There was only time to either freeze in horror and die or to react with professional skill. There was no time to do anything but prove what being *of service* actually means. No time to be anything but the sword and shield that has kept us alive. For that, I honor them and accept it as an unpayable debt."

More applause. But Soren could also see tears in the eyes of those standing closest to him. He felt tears burn his own eyes.

"Those of us who were first aware of the war, and of how it needed to be fought, know the whole story. All of you have heard reports first-, second-, or thirdhand. The Sybil channels have given the story in various forms. Many of you know the terrible cost paid by the Lost Souls in order to save us. Until that fight, we thought that death was the ultimate sacrifice. Now we know that there is a deeper level of commitment, a deeper level of courage, and I daresay, a deeper level of love for each other. Commander Bianca Petrescu and her team were contacted by Lady Jessica of the Church of Shades. As the Lost Souls died in battle with the shoggoths, Lady Jessica reached out into the unseen world and found their wandering souls and asked them to fight on. Not as living people, but as spirits—souls—inhabiting spacecraft developed by alien races during that eternal war. That alone is astounding. That alone is both terrifying and glorious."

He paused and took a moment to make sure that everyone was paying attention. They were. Everyone was rapt, even those who knew the full story.

"Imagine being one of them," he said quietly. "A young pilot in your late teens or early twenties. Reeling emotionally and psychically from having your life stolen away in so strange a war. And then being asked to return to the war. To the fight. And to risk something greater than skin and bone. Each of these heroes risks losing their immortal soul every time they build one of these towering figures and take it into battle. Think about that. Think hard on the implications. With each mission, more of that essence that defines us on the spiritual level is carved away from them. If this war goes on and on, then some or all of them could simply be erased from existence on every level. Body *and* soul. Stop whatever you're doing and *think* about that."

Soren paused again.

"Now," he said, "in the private sanctuary of your own thoughts, ask yourself if *you* could make so incredible a sacrifice. Ask that question and answer it for yourself. Then measure that against what they have actually *done*."

He shook his head.

"I have wrestled with this question constantly over the last month since we came here," Soren said into a total silence. "I am not a coward, but I do not believe I have anything approaching that level of courage. And yet, when this question was put to our fallen pilots, they did not turn away. They could have done so. Easily. They could have let whatever forces govern what we can accurately call the 'larger world' pull them away from battle and pain, from death and loss. They could have chosen peace over conflict. They could have chosen rest over war."

Here he stopped because he didn't want to break into tears. Not with a pressure suit helmet that would prevent him from wiping his eyes clear. As it was, he had to blink until he could see.

"The choice they made saved us all," he said, his voice breaking. "And I will never have words powerful enough to thank them. Never."

He turned and looked up.

"You are more than pilots," he said. "You are more than ghosts. More than heroes. You are guardian angels. And on this ground, here on Shadderal, where each of you—each NecroTek—rose from ruin to stand against evil and hate, I give that name to your team. You were Lost Souls while you lived. Now you are the first family of NecroTeks, and I will hereafter and forever call you the Guardian Angels."

And the crowd—on Shadderal and on Asphodel—went wild with applause.

Bianca turned to her lover, Jacob Fox—call sign Galahad. "Guardian Angels," she said. "I don't hate that at all."

"Truth in advertising," said Galahad.

Then the giant of the group—Joshua McGuinness, call sign Thunder Bear—threw back his head, dialed up the amplification, and in a roar that shook the heavens, bellowed, "Guardian Angels forever!"

Then they all shouted it. The NecroTeks; Calisto and her living Lost Souls team; the military, led by Captain Sebastian Croft; the delegation from Asphodel, headed by station director Delia Trumbo; and every other human being on that world, the many moons, and on Asphodel Station shouted it, too.

Guardian Angels forever!

4

Soren stood alone on the station bridge.

He could no longer see the NecroTeks flying in formation. They had escorted him back to Asphodel and even did some turns around the station to the cheers of the residents, all of whom watched via RealScreens.

People had cheered down on the planet, and that was fine. That's what ceremonies and celebrations were for. As he walked to the bridge, he'd heard cheers and laughter coming from open doors in public lounges. There were parties on every deck.

It puzzled him.

Why do they celebrate this? He wrestled with the question as he stood watching the void into which the giants had vanished. *We are alone again.*

Instead of cheering, he felt a coldness blossom in his heart. Deep, intense, and black. Colder, in its way, than the space outside.

He thought about praying, but none of his prayers had been answered thus far. Why would he expect God, if there was one—or *gods*, if there were any at all—to care?

It was at times like this that he felt how fragile the flame of life was.

Interlude Three

Office of Dr. Lars Soren
University of California, Los Angeles
Eight Months Before the WarpLine Test Firing

Lars Soren sat on one end of his battered old couch.

He lay back into the cushions, balancing a glass of very old cognac on his comfortable belly. There was a hint of rose in the air from incense he'd burned earlier while grading papers. The late afternoon sun slanted through the windows, and hummingbirds thrummed outside them, dipping their long beaks into little dishes in an elaborate bird feeder his graduate assistant had hung in a tree as a birthday present the previous month.

On the other end of the couch sat Lady Jessica McHugh, a woman ten years his junior but who had a feeling of timelessness about her. She had her long legs tucked under her and an ankle-length dress whose pattern was a swirling complexity of green, gold, and blue—a dozen shades each. Although the pattern was not in any way representational, it called to mind for him the way the sun looked an hour before sunset over the waves off the western shore of Corfu.

Lady Jessica's skin was so pale that he tended to think of it as alabaster, as corny and poetic as that was. Her lovely face was framed by masses of curly brown hair threaded with silver, and her hazel eyes had that rare lambent quality that made them look like they were lit from within. Her dress had a deep vee neckline that he judged was less about showing skin and more about displaying the unusual and ornate necklaces she wore. Some were silver set with beads of various kinds of crystal, and some were braided leather and copper. From the largest braid hung an emerald that Soren was sure could have paid off his entire mortgage. Bits of various tattoos were visible, reaching up beyond the edges of her décolletage, but never enough to help him guess what images they belonged to—and he was far too polite to ask.

Lady Jessica had a balloon of the same cognac—a gift she'd brought and he'd asked her to share.

"Asphodel Station," she said, her eyes twinkling with amusement. "Really?"

"Of course. Why? Does it sound odd to you?"

"The station? No, of course not."

"What, then?"

"It's the WarpLine gun thing. That's going to be a big media show."

"It'll likely be *the* big media show, if all goes well."

She shook her head. "All the more reason for a hard pass. I'm no fan of crowds, and my church has never had what you might call a genial relationship with the press."

That was true enough. McHugh was the chief priestess of the Church of Shades, a female-centric religion whose origins dated back to Ireland's Druidic past but which hid in the shadows for fear of religious persecution. The Romans had hunted them down as heretics, and then Christian witchfinders had arrested, tortured, and murdered scores of their priestesses over the centuries. Since the church emerged from obscurity thirty years ago, the press had been relentless in their pursuit, often calling them a "death cult" or, in the less sophisticated media, Ghoul Girls. In truth, the Church of Shades was deeply spiritual and purportedly able to reach out to the spirits of the dead through rituals, séances, and invocations. McHugh, as the current head of the church, was universally called Lady Death, a term she tolerated with her usual blend of grace and wry humor.

"My goal has nothing at all to do with the media," said Soren. "But yes, the WarpLine firing is a factor."

"How so?"

"Think about it, my lady," he said after taking a small sip. "If the matter-teleportation process works, then human expansion will explode far beyond the confines of our solar system."

"So . . . ?"

"Well, many faiths are already struggling to retain membership because, let's face it, fundamentalist religion is taking a beating from science with each new advance. We've seen numbers diminish in virtually all religions at a speed commensurate to our colonization of the local planets. The various holy books mainly focus on Earth as the center of not merely their own faiths but of all creation."

"That's typical small-minded thinking," she said with a dismissive wave.

"It's naive," corrected Soren. "To use Christianity as an example, Matthew 28:19 through 20 has Jesus charging his apostles to go out and make disciples of all nations. Emphasis on *nations*. There is no mention of planets. Salvation is offered by the Son of God—also known as the Son of man, suggesting that his incarnation as a human being is significant. The Book of Revelation speaks of the end times but makes no mention of humanity sharing any of it with alien life."

"The Bible doesn't mention kangaroos or the tribes in the Brazilian rainforest either."

"True, but kangaroos aren't—as far as we know—sentient, and most fundamentalists do not believe they have souls. Tribespeople are human; they have souls, according to those same people of faith—souls that await *saving* by proselytizing evangelists."

McHugh contrived to make gagging noises.

Soren smiled. "You see where I'm going with this."

"Sure. No aliens, as such, are mentioned in the Bible. Unless you consider the angels, demons, Nephilim, and other nonhuman creatures in that scripture to count."

"Exactly. That is one of the things more progressive theologians have pulled out to start useful conversations. But they are hypothetical beings with no physical evidence to support their existence. What will happen if that WarpLine allows colonists to go to, say, Proxima Centauri b, the closest exoplanet to Earth, and there is a global population of ten billion flesh-and-blood aliens? And what if they *all* believe in a different god?

What if every alien race we encounter, should any exist, has a religion with no similarity to any on Earth—or no religion at all? What then? There are exoplanets many billions of years older than our little blue world—what if their civilizations are vastly older than any on Earth? How will such an encounter impact the structure of organized religion as we know it?"

McHugh rolled her cognac around and around in her glass. "And you expect faith leaders to do what? Go see the big, exciting test firing and then . . . ?"

"Then we'll sit down for as many days or weeks as it takes to find ways to keep belief alive, even if the religions themselves must necessarily change."

She laughed. "They'll throw you out of an airlock, Lars."

Soren shrugged. "That's a risk I'm willing to take."

They sat for a while, watching the changing patterns of the slanting sun as it moved across the ancient Turkish carpet.

"Sure," she said, giving him a devilish smile. "Count me in."

"Really?"

"Oh, it'll never work. But I can't *wait* to hear the arguments."

Part Seven
Hunters and Killers

"The oldest and strongest emotion of mankind is fear, and the oldest and strongest kind of fear is fear of the unknown."

—*H. P. Lovecraft*

Joint MIT/UCLA Biological Research Field Station #8
Queen Maud Land, Antarctica

1

"There will be six of us," said Dr. Brollachan into the camera.

Everyone stood in a ring around him, many edging to get their faces into shot. The video was not live but was being recorded for history.

"With me on the 'Venture Team' will be Dr. Joan Kimbra, a structural engineer, and she will scan the Artifact to try and determine its composition. Dr. Shijun Xi, our exobiologist, will see if anything can be gleaned about who or what built that ship. Dr. Andy Patel, a physicist, will take a variety of readings. And Professor Evie Cronin, who is both an evolutionary biologist and a climate scientist—with, I believe, a *third* doctorate in philosophy—will evaluate the ice in which the Artifact rests and offer insight into what can be inferred from the machine's design, age, and placement."

Evie smiled faintly as the crowd offered some applause—most generously from her own team. She saw the pride in their faces and the relief that one of *theirs* was part of this. However, Evie was aware that Brollachan was being deliberately obsequious, either to try to ensure her trust or perhaps to mollify her father.

"The final member of Venture Team," continued Brollachan, "is Gunnery Sergeant Mathieson, and he will evaluate any potential risks and oversee our overall safety."

The team walked to the edge of the platform, where a skimmer waited.

The scientist paused again and looked at the sea of faces. His smile was tremulous, and Evie wondered if the enormity and reality of what they were about to do was finally sinking in.

"This is the point where I should make a speech of some kind," said Brollachan with a small laugh. "Our version of the 'One small step' thing, but frankly … I have nothing. My mouth is dry as paste, and my heart is pounding so hard I'm surprised you can't all hear it. I'd like to say it was all excitement, but the truth is I'm scared out of my mind. I think we all are. Nothing any of us have ever done has prepared us for this. Maybe once we've been down there and touched the Artifact, something more profound will occur to me. So instead of a speech, I just ask you to wish us luck. And also … even though Venture is going down there first, everyone here—every single person standing with us now—is part of something enormous and important. You have my heartfelt gratitude and my trust."

He turned away as applause broke out.

Evie touched his arm and leaned close. "Well said."

The SPU chief looked at her with a nervous smile. "I was not joking, Professor Cronin … I'm quite terrified."

She squeezed his arm. "So am I. And please, call me Evie."

He nodded. "Torquil. Torq."

"Stealing your own line here, Torq—let's go make history."

"And while we're at it, Evie," said Brollachan, "let's find your missing mechanic."

"If he's alive and unhurt, I will so kick his ass."

"I'll be happy to hold him for you."

They smiled at each other for a moment, then nodded and turned as Colonel Thomas Jefferson Hobart came over. As far as Evie could tell, he seemed to share overall authority with Brollachan. Hobart had a face like an eroded wall—pitted and scarred from exposure to rapid-onset variola—a weaponized version of the old smallpox disease deployed during the Titan conflict. It made him look rough and dangerous, and the scarring gave his face a perpetual scowl.

He shook everyone's hands and posed for photos that Evie knew would one day be in every history, science, archaeology, astrophysics, and cultural textbook that would be written once the news was out. Probably in books written by philosophers and theologians.

Soren would have been of great use to every aspect of this thing, thought Evie sourly.

As Evie turned toward the waiting skimmer, Gillian pushed through the crowd and grabbed her hands. "You'll find Mac, won't you?" Her tear-filled eyes searched Evie's.

"We'll do everything we can," said Evie. It was the truth, but one wrapped in a lie. She would push the team to try to find Mac, but Evie no longer believed the young mechanic was still alive. There were too many ways he could have used to make contact and call for help. But there was no value in saying so to Gillian. "Everything," she added, compounding it. Evie returned her squeeze and then released the young woman's hands.

Venture Team boarded the skimmer and found their seats, with Gunnery Sergeant Mathieson making sure they were properly strapped in. Like Hobart, the sergeant was a tall, powerful-looking man. He was far more handsome, though, with a lantern jaw, high cheekbones, clear blue eyes, and a confident smile. Evie wondered if he was chosen for his skills or for the hero vibe he projected. Both, she decided, though with a likely bias toward the power and confidence carved into every centimeter of the soldier.

Optics were everything.

The skimmer was a short, chunky little antigrav boat, sealed against the weather but with a clear cowl so everyone could see them. When Evie glanced around, she saw that everyone was still taking pictures and vids. Only Brollachan and Hobart stood apart, hands clasped behind their backs, beaming like happy winners on an Olympics platform.

"Is your team ready, Gunny?" asked Hobart.

"All secure, sir," announced Mathieson, who was the last person standing on the craft. He snapped off a crisp salute, which Colonel Hobart returned every bit as smartly.

Evie noticed that a lot of people were making sure they looked serious, proper, and professional anytime a camera was pointed, even vaguely, in their direction.

"Gunnery Sergeant Mathieson," said Colonel Hobart, "my congratulations on leading Venture Team on this first contact with extraterrestrial life."

More like dust and bones, if anything, mused Evie. *Christ, what's wrong with me?*

Hobart yelled loud enough to drown out the crowd noise. "And … *launch.*"

There was enormous applause and shouts. A few people were openly weeping. Video drones filled the air like busy hummingbirds. As the skimmer moved away from the platform, most of the drones followed, leaving a few behind to catch observer reactions.

This is happening, thought Evie, touching her flask. *God in heaven, this is happening.*

2

Evie held on to the harness as the skimmer tilted sideways and down. The craft descended in a long and graceful arc. The pilot was clearly cognizant of the fact that every motion and every moment was being watched and documented and would be super-analyzed forever.

On the inside of the clear dome, two holo-screens appeared. One showed the Artifact, and the other showed the anxious crowd on the platform. Evie saw Craig and Gillian and the others. Their faces were filled with that special blend of fear and wonder, likely unaware that they were being filmed. They were the audience for this, and when the videos were finally released, they would be the proxies for everyone else. For all of humanity.

Evie wanted to tell them that, but there was no time.

Instead, she focused on the Artifact. The screen showed a telescopic view, bringing its curved hull into sharpness, and for most of the short journey down, she and everyone else watched it. Then, as if on cue, they turned and looked out the window as the ancient machine grew larger than the holo-screen could project. It was still far away, but even with only a fragment of it exposed, the craft was immense and intimidating. Beautiful too, in its way. The simple design and the great width lent the thing a kind of classic elegance, like a finely wrought piece of art. Because there were no fins or engines or portholes visible, the Artifact was more an object of awe than anything overtly like a spaceship.

Dr. Kimbra tapped her comms and said, "I can't wait to look under the hood of that thing. What kind of engines could drive something that size? I mean, how does it escape atmosphere and planetary gravity? It must be nine-tenths engine, and even then, I can't work out the numbers."

"Nuclear?" suggested Evie.

"Even if so, it'll be a type of engine unknown to us."

"It'll be remarkable if we understand or recognize *any* of their technology," said Patel, the physicist. "My brain hurts just trying to estimate the mathematics of making something that scale."

"I'm more concerned with *who* built it," said Dr. Xi. "And why. And why they came here. That will help us understand the *how*, don't you think? Where there's a will, there's a way."

"Fair point," agreed Patel. He glanced at Cronin. "What about you, Evie? What are your thoughts?"

"Oh, it's all about the *who* for me," she said. "What kind of species? What kind of biological imperatives and cultural structure would encourage such an endeavor—after all, we're not talking about wandering across the Bering Straits here. We can be reasonably sure this did not originate in the solar system. Any culture that could have built this would have left traces of itself on one of the planets or moons, and we've mapped just about everything. No, this had to come from another star, and that either means faster-than-light travel—and my old physics professor would give me the patented lecture on Einsteinian relativity—or it's a colony ship. Something generational. Which means they wanted to come specifically here and spent centuries doing that. If so … why? There was nothing here except megafauna, forests, and a lot of volcanoes."

Xi smiled. "Every science fiction novel I read as a kid had aliens coming to Earth to plunder us for natural resources."

"Which, of course, is bullshit. There's a trillion times more water ice floating around in the asteroid and Kuiper belts."

"Maybe they thought giant tree sloths looked yummy," Patel suggested.

They all smiled at each other. Evie saw raw nerves, great excitement, understandable trepidation, and so many other emotions and knew the others could see the same on her face.

Conversation fell away as the skimmer entered a narrow pass formed by the partial collapse of the mountain.

"Coming up on it," reported the pilot.

3

Evie and the others leaned toward the dome. She gasped. Others did, too. There was something about seeing it this close that made it all far too real. Inside her chest, her heart was beating with a kind of frenzy, and even inside the insulated gloves, her fingers were very cold.

With each second, the Artifact seemed to double in size, dwarfing the little skimmer. The scale was deeply uncomfortable, recalling some of the psychological studies done of miners working on the moons of Jupiter and Saturn. The first generation of those workers suffered varying kinds of stress illnesses born of feelings of diminished existence when measured against something so vast. Before those days, Earth had been the biggest thing, and hearts and minds were adjusted to measuring things by its scale.

Now this.

She reminded herself that there were bigger man-made objects—the Great Wall of China was more than twenty thousand kilometers long, 5,800 times the length of the Artifact. The temple of Angkor Wat covered more square meters. The Sun Dome on Mars was taller.

But those were built by men. By human hands. Neither were they built to fly between the stars. Nor even to move a centimeter under power.

"God damn," she heard someone say.

Mathieson spoke, directing his comment to Hobart. "We'll do a slow pass, sir. There's a flat area twenty-eight meters from the exposed end. We can …"

His voice stopped.

Evie and the other scientists all jerked their heads toward Mathieson, who was bent over a screen display that hovered a few centimeters over the holo-comms he wore strapped to his left forearm. They were close enough to see what he saw.

Mathieson looked around, pausing to eye each of the experts with him. He looked frightened. As frightened as Evie felt. As frightened as all of them felt. The screen showed two things. Each of them was extraordinary. Each of them was absolutely terrifying.

"Is there a problem, Gunny?" asked Hobart, causing the sergeant to jump.

"Sir," Mathieson croaked, "look at this. Sending a feed now."

Near where the main bulk of the Artifact's hull vanished into the ice mountain, there was a small star-shaped mark. As the skimmer came closer, it became immediately obvious that the star was not a dent or rust or any discoloration. Mathieson and several others had their holo-comms pointed at the thing, spotlight modes turned on full. The combined beams illuminated everything, including what was *not* there. There was an empty space in the otherwise solid hull.

It was a door. A hatch.

And it was *open*.

But that was not what tore a chorus of excited and alarmed gasps from every single person on the platform. It wasn't what made Evie Cronin feel as if the skimmer had tilted and dropped her into nothingness. No, it was the line of rough marks in the snow leading from the star-shaped doorway. Indentations, roughly round, that led from the hatch and away into the clefts and valleys.

"Are those Mac's?" asked Xi.

"No way," said Evie. "Look at them. Compare them to the other set."

Everyone stared at the two sets. In truth, they could not be more different. Mac's footprints were the clear marks of size 12 cold-weather work boots. The brand logo for Clark & Brundel's IceWalkers was clear on a couple of the prints closest to where he had been standing while gazing at the Artifact. The other tracks were larger, rounder though not exactly circular, and so heavily smudged that no two looked very much alike.

"Did you see this when you and your assistant came down here yesterday?" asked Brollachan.

"Mac's footprints, sure." Evie recounted what she and Craig had seen, including the place where his prints simply ended. Brollachan nodded and turned away, though Evie saw deep lines etch around his mouth and two vertical ones between his eyebrows.

Beside her, Dr. Kimbra kept shaking her head. Her eyes were as big as saucers. "If Mac didn't make those tracks, then … who …?"

"No," whispered Brollachan. "I simply refuse. It cannot be. It can't."

He looked stricken, as if his heart was close to bursting. He raised his hand to his face, and for a moment Evie thought he was going to cover his eyes, to deny what they were all seeing. Instead, Brollachan ran his palms over his cheeks and eyes and forehead. An absent gesture, very human and very fragile.

"They—" said Evie, and her voice sounded strange and distant even to her own ears. "Those footprints came from that door."

Footprints.

But they were not made by human feet. They were far too large, and there were multiple footfalls all along the trail. Were they the same as the ones outside her hut last night?

That was just a dream, she told herself, half believing it. Even so, the marks from last night—real or imagined—were not exact matches to these.

The ones that trailed away and vanished into icy darkness.

4

"Sergeant Mathieson," snapped Hobart via the comms, "withdraw your team *immediately*. Return to the platform. This is a direct order. Do it right now."

The sergeant whirled and shouted, "Party's over. Everyone into the skimmer—right now."

"Wait a goddamn moment," began Brollachan, but Mathieson stepped up to him, all shoulders and chest and moral authority.

"Colonel says now, Doc, and that means right damn now. You can fire me later, but you will return to the skimmer." He turned and bellowed at the team. "*Do it now.*"

They milled around for a moment, but Brollachan cursed and turned, arms wide to herd them all back. "Do what he says," he yelled. "Everyone into the boat."

They climbed in. Brollachan and Evie were the last to board, and they shared a brief moment of awareness. It was a densely compacted exchange filled with scientific curiosity, wonder, anxiety, and deep fear. Evie pulled the door shut behind her.

"Buckle up and hang on," ordered Mathieson. He slapped the pilot hard on the shoulder. "Go, go, *go*!"

The skimmer pilot did not hesitate but instantly pulled the boat out of its slow descent and began a long climbing turn back to the dock, gunning the engines to race away from the Artifact.

Evie gripped her harness straps with fists so tight her knuckles ached. The other scientists were bug-eyed with shock, all of them struck dumb. They had not known what to expect, but it was not this.

Not this.

The skimmer shot out of the valley and rose into the cold sunlight. Racing to safety.

Evie Cronin sat in stunned silence. They all did. There was awe and wonder in their hearts. Of course there was. But not one of them felt that those footsteps were a sign of anything good at all.

The day was the same, but the world had changed.

5

The skimmer thumped down, proof that the pilot was as rattled as everyone else.

Craig, Evie's assistant, rushed forward and helped her onto the platform. On the very first step, her legs turned to rubber, and she sagged into his strong arms.

"I got you," he said. Gillian hurried over too, and together they brought her out of the wind and into the lee of the big-equipment garage. Gillian fetched a bucket and turned it over to make a chair, and they helped her sit. "Get some hot tea," Craig said, and the young woman hurried off.

He squatted down in front of Evie.

"Are you okay?" he asked. "Or is that the single stupidest question in the history of the world?"

She was too shocked to even smile. All she could do was sit and shake her head. And wish that this was a dream from which she'd awake to a Southern California morning filled with drifting pelicans and buzzing hummingbirds.

Craig held her hands—a liberty he would never have taken under any other circumstances. Evie pulled free for a moment, took off her gloves, let them fall, and then gripped Craig's warm hands again.

All around them, the other scientists were being similarly tended to. Dr. Brollachan was actually leaning on Hobart for support. It was as if they had all been rescued from some airless space. They struggled—and failed—to breathe normally.

There was something alien in that craft.

And now it was out.

Loose.

Free.

Craig gave her hands a final squeeze and let go. "Let me ask again, Professor," he said gently. "How *are* you?"

That actually made her smile—a bit.

"I guess I'm as good as I can be," she said. She saw a flash of relief in Craig's eyes, and that made her remember that she was his senior in age and academic rank. As much as he was trying to offer her comfort, he needed some from her as well. Evie made herself sit up straighter, and with the iron control she had acquired as the daughter of a general and a tenured professor, she gathered up the bits of her scattered control and welded them back into place, one piece at a time. She took a few slow breaths—deep and steadying. Then she nodded in a way that she hoped conveyed some level of control and stood. For a moment, before Craig rose too, she was taller than he was. The subjective difference in stature at that crucial moment did a lot of observable good. Some healthy color seeped back into Craig's face. When he stood, he stepped back a bit, restoring the deference of graduate student to professor. It mattered to both of them.

She touched his shoulder. "Go find Gillian and the others. Get them all together. In here or somewhere warm. Make sure they all have something hot—food, if they can manage it, and definitely coffee or tea. Listen to me, Craig, we are all in shock, but shock is a physical thing, and it's dangerous. Everyone needs to be accounted for. Everyone needs to be physically warm, out of the wind, and safe. And they all need to be together. We're a family, so be family to everyone. Is that clear?"

He straightened his shoulders, blew out his cheeks, and nodded. "I'm on it, Doc."

But he paused.

"What?" asked Evie.

"There's something else," he said. "I didn't think anything of it at the time, not with finding that Artifact thing. But now, after the star door and those prints … well …"

"Just say it, for God's sake."

"Gillian was down with Mac doing some scut work near the collapse. That's when they found the craft."

"I know that."

"No, you don't know all of it," he said, blinking with nervousness. "They said they *heard* something."

"Heard something? Heard what?"

Craig described the roaring sound Mac had heard and Gillian had only partly heard. "They convinced themselves it was the wind playing tricks like it does. But now …"

"Did they see anything?"

"No. A minute later they saw the ship, and then everything got crazy. Gillian just remembered and told me while you guys were down there."

Evie considered. "Okay. Do this … Once everyone is settled in one of the shelters, have Gillian tell Sybil exactly what she and Mac heard. Not together. Keep them separate so they don't just tag-team with details. As soon as that's done, send the vid files to me. I'll see if it's something we need to share with Dr. Brollachan. And, Craig …?"

"Yeah?"

"Don't tell anyone else. There's enough stress as it is. Once I speak with Brollachan and Colonel Hobart, we'll decide what to say and when. Okay?"

"Sure." He turned and once more paused. "We *will* be okay, right? I mean, this isn't going to be anything like … awful … will it?"

"Of course not," said Evie. "It's shocking now, but it will all make sense soon—of that I have no doubt. And, yes, everything will be okay."

They smiled at each other in the way people do when they don't believe a single word of what they're saying.

Craig nodded, and Evie watched him walk away.

No one was looking, so Evie slipped the flask out of her pocket, unscrewed the cap, and took a hit. A very long hit. The rye burned its way down her throat, and the weight of it made her feel as if the ground she stood on was once more solid.

6

Everyone around Evie had come wholly or partly out of their initial shock. As she walked through the garage, she caught snatches of conversation.

"… did you see the pattern of tracks it left? Looked like it was staggering …"

"… atmosphere here can't possibly be the same as what it's used to …"

"… might be staggering from different gravity …"

"… hope it's wearing a suit or something to keep it safe …"

"… Mac *has* to be inside the thing. I mean where else can he be? …"

"…. think it heard the skimmer and just panicked? …"

"… weird that the drones can't find it …"

"… no real biosignature. Or at least that's what I heard …"

She moved on. A lot of those conversations echoed her own thoughts.

Brollachan and Hobart were in a corner, deep in agitated conversation, and Evie headed that way and stopped close by. It took them a moment to realize she was there, but then they turned to her.

"How are you holding up, Professor Cronin?" asked the colonel.

"I believe the precise medical term is *freaked out*," she said. Hobart nodded. To Brollachan, Evie said, "And how are you?"

"*Freaked out* is a useful phrase," admitted the SPU chief. "But also excited."

"Yes," agreed Evie. "I guess the big question is, What do we do now? I mean, we have to send people down there. Soldiers, I suppose. Just in case, I mean. They'll need to find that … whatever it is."

"We will," promised Hobart.

She considered him for a moment. "To be clear, you'll find the … the …"

"Alien," said Brollachan. "We have to be adult enough to use the word."

"Fair enough. Alien. You have to find it and engage with it."

"Of course," said Hobart.

Evie chewed her lower lip for a moment, then said, "There's something else."

She told them about what Mac and Gillian had heard and that they were going to record their witness statements.

"If that cry was from the creature," mused Brollachan, "it could well be evidence of fear or shock, which would be natural reactions. It's likely as confused and frightened as we are. Maybe it's sitting on a chunk of ice, dealing with its own freak-out."

"Probably is," agreed Hobart. "So we're talking about something bigger than the Artifact. In one second, we went from apparent evidence of extraterrestrial life to imminent first contact."

"Which is what I have been saying," Brollachan said, directing it tersely to Hobart.

"First contact notwithstanding," replied the colonel, "it's an unknown entity, and we need to use all precautionary measures. That means the next team to go down there will be soldiers in full kit."

"Who will be with them?" asked Evie. "You'll need someone who has a grasp of whatever first-contact protocols have been established. We've had them on file since the mid-twentieth century, as I understand it. Dr. Xi's our exobiologist, and I guess he would be the expert for this encounter."

"No," said Brollachan, "*I* should be the one to make contact." As if aware of how that sounded, he quickly added, "I have a good deal of background in this. I helped write the latest versions of the American protocols, at least."

"And, as I have been trying to explain to you, Professor," said Hobart with frayed patience, "you are too valuable to risk."

"Which means that Shijun Xi *is* worth risking?" asked Evie.

Hobart looked exasperated. "Understand me here, both of you … Dr. Brollachan is the head of the Special Projects Unit. He is also the chief scientific adviser to the president of the United States and co-chair of the SFIL."

"Which is?"

"The Search for Intelligent Life," said Brollachan. "It was built on the bones of the old SETI program. It's why I organized this mission as soon as I learned about the Artifact. Xi has been on my team since the beginning."

"Okay," said Evie, "I get why you're both qualified, but—and I can't believe I'm siding with the military on this—if you're that high up the food chain, then you are too valuable to risk. Someone else should go."

"Who is *more* qualified?"

Hobart stood there shaking his head. "Look, I get it—you're the head of the SPU, and in all other areas, you're my boss. But I have an executive mandate to keep you safe. As it is, I'll be lucky if I'm not busted down to second lieutenant for bringing you within a thousand kilometers of that craft. There's no way on God's green earth that I'm going to put you within grabbing distance of some green man from Mars."

"Mars doesn't—" Evie began, but Hobart glared her to silence.

Brollachan tried a glare of his own on Hobart, but the colonel endured it, unmoved and unmovable. Finally, the SPU chief flapped his arms in disgust and resignation.

To Evie he said, "And this is why I understand your dislike of the military."

"Don't get me wrong, Torq," she said. "I don't dislike them. I *distrust* them, but that's been a pretty common state of affairs between us academics and the various branches of the armed forces. They like blowing things up, and we prefer not to."

"Not looking to blow anything up," said Hobart. "Unless it turns out to be some bug-eyed, ten-headed critter with a mouthful of teeth and taste for human flesh."

"Which, given the sophistication of that spaceship," said Brollachan, "is extremely unlikely. A civilization advanced enough to build such a craft and fly it who knows how many trillions of kilometers across space and reach Earth millions of years before we even discovered how to make fire is unlikely to be hostile."

Hobart snorted. "Tell that to the Indigenous peoples of North and South America. Columbus and the conquistadors who followed him were a hell of a lot more technologically advanced than the natives. Nothing in human history supports your view, Doc. Which is why you are not going."

"Have you *asked* Dr. Xi if he even wants to go?" asked Evie.

Brollachan snorted. "If you were an exobiologist, what would your answer be?"

"I'm an evolutionary biologist," said Evie.

"Which means what? That you want to go?"

"Not even at gunpoint."

They considered that and then shared a nod of mutual agreement.

7

Evie and her grad students clustered together on the platform and watched as six soldiers and Dr. Shijun Xi climbed aboard the skimmer.

"Xi looks like he's about to faint," said Gillian.

"Looks to me like he's about to come in his pants," said Craig, then twitched. "Oops, sorry, Doc."

Evie waved it away. Craig was no more wrong than Brollachan had been. Xi was nearly skipping with excitement. His face had flushed from a faint tan to brick red, and there were fireworks in his eyes.

The soldiers were in full battle gear, with ballistic helmets, body armor, and every conceivable kind of weapon a human being could carry.

As with the original team, the group of soldiers was given a code name—Venture II. Evie thought it was silly but then realized it was for clarity. Someone was thinking ahead in terms of news stories, accurate recordkeeping, and probably the history books that would be written. Those texts would detail every single thing.

The seven members of Venture II strapped themselves in, and the skimmer released itself from the grav locks and drifted away from the platform. Then the pilot—a combat pilot now, replacing the nonmilitary boat driver—turned and dove through the cold air.

Everyone crowded the rail to watch. Evie noticed that the skimmer moved differently. Even though it was a machine, its flight dynamics reflected the person at the wheel. There was no hesitation, no pause as though the pilot were steeling himself for first encounter. Now the craft shot downward toward the Artifact, moving with purpose, even—she thought—with aggression.

It took half the time for it to reach the flat shelf near the ancient machine. The main screen followed them, with Sybil taking the drone feeds and running them through a series of enhancement filters. The soldiers wore helmets and goggles, and respirators over their noses and mouths.

She asked Hobart why they wore them.

"Whatever came out of there is likely alive," he said. "We don't know what it breathes or if it's carrying some kind of unknown bacteria, fungus, or other germs. Hell, its very exhalations could be toxic. My guys are also wearing radiation badges. Better safe than sorry."

She nodded, appreciating the insight and candor.

As soon as the skimmer touched down, all six soldiers popped the locks on their harnesses and leaped over the boat's rails, weapons coming up even as their boots touched the ice. Small and slim, Dr. Xi looked like a child among adults. Even so, the holo-screen turned them all into giants. Evie felt an odd blend of apprehension at the sight of those big, strong fighters with their guns—and a degree of comfort at having them there. It was not a revelation she would ever share, especially not within earshot of Hobart or Brollachan.

All around her she could hear people speculating on what had come out of the Artifact. There were so many theories, ranging from injured pilots to alien monsters to robots with age-damaged programming. The latter made the most sense, and as the crowd watched, more and more people began talking about "the robots." One person—a tech from her own team—kept calling them "robots from Mars," but no one picked that one up. Mars had been settled for a very long time, and despite H. G. Wells's classic story, no robots, tripod fighting machines, or lumpy aliens had ever been found.

This didn't come from Mars, Evie thought. *This didn't come from anywhere in the solar system.* She could not know that, but she believed it. And science was the bulwark of those beliefs.

Below, the soldiers gathered by the strangely shaped door. Xi hung back, looking nervous as hell.

"Big Dog to command," came the voice of the sergeant leading the team, and Evie wondered why in the world they were using combat call signs on a mission like this. What need was there to keep their identity safe from possible aliens, organic or mechanical? It felt needless and even silly.

Hobart replied, "Read you loud and clear, Big Dog. Have the pilot dust off and retreat to site B and stay on station, engines hot."

"Copy that, command." Immediately the skimmer lifted away and moved to a broader shelf a kilometer to the east.

"Give me a sitrep," said Hobart.

"Sir, the door is still open on the side of the Artifact. What are our orders?"

Brollachan touched Hobart's arm and gave a small, discrete shake of his head. Hobart replied with an equally subtle nod.

"Send in a couple of drones, Big Dog," ordered Hobart. "No one is to step inside the Artifact at this time."

"Copy that," said the soldier. "Deploying drones."

One of the team removed a pair of high-tech surveillance drones and flipped the activation switch.

"Drones A and B are online," said the calm, unflappable voice of Sybil.

The drones were the size of gophers and powered by eight propellers. They moved slowly toward the door.

"Sybil," said Hobart, "designate that entry as Star Door One. File it."

"Done, Colonel."

"Send them in," ordered Hobart.

Drone A moved first, pausing to scan the entire door and much of the surrounding hull. Patel and Kimbra were chattering away as they read the data streams on their holo-comms.

"The density is consistent with metal," said Patel, "but except for traces of iridium and iron, the majority of it is nothing we've found on the other planets or moons."

"Wait," said Kimbra, "there's an energy signature. See it? It's all around the star door."

"I see it," said Brollachan, who was standing behind them.

"Force field?" asked Hobart.

"Unknown."

To Big Dog, Hobart said, "Stand back from the door."

On the screen, the soldiers were already backing away. They hunkered down behind a massive chunk of shattered ice. The first drone moved to within a centimeter of the door, paused for another round of scans, and then moved forward.

There was a sudden shimmer all across the star-shaped opening before the drone vanished.

"Colonel," said a technician, "the telemetric feed just went off the scale."

"Measuring what?"

"Unknown. The meters are going up and down like crazy."

"Sybil," Hobart snapped, "interpret the readings."

There was a slight pause. "I am unable to get a clear reading, Colonel Hobart. There is considerable interference that is giving us unreliable data."

"Explain."

"The chronometer is scrolling forward at variable speeds," said the AI. "It says that the drone has been in there for fifteen minutes. Correction, one hour. Correction, two minutes." A pause. "The other sensor readings are correspondingly strange."

"Send in drone B."

"Sending it in now," said Sybil.

The second drone approached, caused the same kind of shimmer, and then it, too, vanished. They all studied the screens.

"Colonel," said Sybil, "Drone B is reporting similar distortions on all meters."

"Do we have video?"

"No, Colonel. The recorders report as operational, but no video data is passing back out of the Artifact."

"Very well," said Hobart. He glanced at Brollachan, who nodded. "Big Dog, leave two additional drones outside and then proceed with your search."

"Copy that."

"Proceed with utmost caution. Make sure all bodycams are operational. Confirm that order."

"Proceeding with utmost caution, yes sir."

The group of soldiers began to follow the trail of bizarre and misshapen footprints.

Evie saw the colonel's lips form the words, *Go with God.*

It bothered her more than it should have.

The soldiers moved forward, three on each side of the trail, all careful not to disturb the tracks. A small drone flew between the squads, and its high-def cameras sent back ultraclear images, showing irregular footprints.

"Weird kind of boots to make prints like that," said Gillian. "And look at the size. Elephant feet."

No one commented.

The trail wound around several heaps of fallen ice blocks and then vanished into a dark space between two sides of a split tower of ice. Searchlights flicked to life on various places on each soldier—helmet, chest, thighs, and atop their pulse rifles.

A third pair of drones was deployed, and they captured it all with such clarity that Evie felt like she was running through the snow with Big Dog and his team. Her heart was hammering every bit as hard as it would if she were down there.

They passed out of sunlight and into very dense shadows at the mouth of a new cave formed by the partially collapsed ice mountain. The drones switched to true-color night vision, allowing everyone on the platform to see them.

A heavy gust of wind came out of the west and blew a small hurricane of snow and ice crystals into the tunnel with such intensity that for a moment the soldiers were nearly invisible—mere ghosts. Everyone on the platform leaned forward to try to pick out details, but the wind kept freshening. It obscured everything except sound.

There were snatches of words, but the howl of the wind cut sentences into fragments.

"What's that?"

"Is that—?"

"It's moving. High-Hat, Goose, go check it out and—"

"Holy fuck!"

"What *is* that thing?"

"Back, back, everyone fall—"

Then Big Dog's voice came through full and clear. "God in heaven! Fall back, *fall back*!"

The dialogue was beaten down by the wind's scream. One of the drones went dark. The other continued to send video of the swirling wind and only vague shapes. The soldiers were running. Then …

"Christ! *Fall back!*" shrieked Big Dog. A raw-throated cry of total panic.

Everyone on the platform froze and stared at the confusion. Suddenly, bright flashes of blue light filled the screen as pulse rifles opened up. There were shouts.

And there were screams.

Deep, raw, red screams. Wet ones.

Buried beneath that noise, Evie thought she heard a sound that was disturbingly familiar. A cry like that of an animal. A bird, perhaps.

Tekeli-li! Tekeli-li!

The gunfire rose to a frenzy and then died.

One rifle at a time.

Until no gun was firing.

The screams faded, too. Dwindling from the shrieks of six voices to four. To three. Two. The drone cameras winked out. All that was left was a single voice. Big Dog. No longer screaming but praying. Begging. Pleading.

"God save me. God save me ..."

Silence.

Then, the same voice, but shrunken, smashed down from adult power to a childlike urgency. "Mom? ... Save me. Oh God, Mommy, *save me.*"

Then, nothing at all.

8

Everyone stood on the platform and listened for more.

They listened a very long time.

There was nothing. Not a shot, not a cry.

Only the worst kind of silence.

Evie wheeled on Hobart. "Send in reinforcements. Get them out of there."

The colonel gave her a shocked, bleak look and held his forearm out. A small holo-screen had six combat call signs—Big Dog, Goose, High-Hat, Fratboy, Moondancer, and Viking. There were telemetric data streams that showed pulse, body temperature, and other vitals.

All of those streams were fading into the black.

Into nothingness.

Into death.

9

There was a crushing, oppressive silence that held everyone in place, immobile, many of them too shocked to breathe.

Evie felt as if the world was tilting. She wanted to fall, to collapse. To scream.

She did none of those things.

Instead, she stood there, moving back and forth with the gusts of wind, pushed more by the overwhelming shock of it than by the breeze.

Tears ran down Gillian's face. Evie watched them roll over cheeks that were as white as snow, drained of blood. One tear reached the edge of Gillian's chin and hung there, swelling but not falling. Evie was oddly fascinated. It was something real to look at rather than to gaze inward at the thoughts screaming for her attention.

Why won't it fall?

Then it finally became too heavy and dropped to the icy metal platform to form a starburst of a splash pattern. As if that were somehow the cue, many of the gathered people began to cry. To scream. To demand answers.

And then they started to run.

10

Evie let herself be pushed along with everyone else off the platform and herded toward the row of dura-steel structures. The remaining SPU soldiers shoved and pulled and bullied everyone away. Evie saw the looks in their eyes. The fear. The hurt. The horror.

The three of them—Evie, Craig, and Gillian—stumbled into a corner of the main research hut, huddling close, too afraid to say anything for a long time. The whole room fell into a dreadful silence. A soldier stood with his back to the door. Evie thought it was absurd. Who in their right mind would go outside?

After maybe five or ten minutes, Gillian gripped Evie's arm with hands cold as ice.

"Professor, are we being invaded?"

Evie forced what she hoped was a comforting smile onto her mouth. It felt so strange that it hurt her facial muscles. "No," she lied, "don't worry, sweetie."

There was no way she could know if her words were even remotely true. Half an hour ago she would have laughed at the very idea. Then the door and the tracks.

And now the echoes of those soldiers screaming haunted her mind, refusing to diminish in either volume or distance.

Gillian clung to her, though, drawing comfort from an empty battery. She looked at Craig, who stood just behind the young grad student. He mouthed the question, *Really?*

Evie gave him the smallest shake of her head, hoping Gillian did not see it.

11

Soldiers locked them into the building, with a guard inside and one outside.

Evie asked to speak with Dr. Brollachan or Colonel Hobart, and the soldier merely shook his head.

The group gathered into small clusters of people who sat together, most of them staring into the empty air between them and their fellows. Others wept, though whether from grief or doubt or fear was uncertain.

Evie and her students found a corner and sat on crates of supplies. Craig fetched blankets and handed them around. For a long time they spoke in low, rapid tones, dissecting every single second of what had happened. Getting nowhere.

"I mean," said Craig, "we *knew* this was … was …"

"Aliens," said Gillian, her voice dull and slack.

"Yeah. Aliens. I guess." Craig ran trembling fingers through his hair. "I mean … *aliens*. How are they even alive after all this time?"

"Maybe they were in cryo-sleep," suggested Evie, and was instantly sorry she said anything, because that implied that there might be more. Perhaps many more. Sleeping out the uncountable years. And, maybe, waking now. Not one, but …

It was a massive ship. It could fit thousands. Tens of thousands. Possibly a colony ship.

"Maybe they came here to invade," Craig said.

"But it's been there so long," said Gillian.

"That's my point. Maybe they came here and found an empty planet. No visible intelligent life, and they wanted to colonize. But something happened. A fault in their cryonics, maybe, and now, somehow they've woken up. The avalanche could have done something. I don't know."

He was fighting to be logical, clinical, practical. But Evie could see the wildness in his eyes, the fragile edge of panic. Gillian was already off in some uncharted place in her mind.

Evie was engaged in her own battle for self-control.

"Professor," began Gillian, her eyes somehow even wider, "those poor soldiers. I … I …"

Words utterly failed her, and she collapsed, caving forward, wrapping her arms around Evie's waist the way a frightened child might. Craig placed his palms on her back and closed his eyes.

With someone else, Evie might have thought this was a case of the dramatics, confessing sins in order to receive comfort, and to be *seen* receiving comfort. But Evie didn't think Gillian was anywhere near that complex. This was honest fear, horror, and regret. So she gathered Gillian in and leaned her cheek down on top of the younger woman's head.

"It's not your fault. Anyone here would have had the same reaction. You didn't see anything, right? Just a noise in the wind on a windy day, blowing and echoing through these ice canyons. We've all heard strange sounds out here, and it's always just the wind, or something falling. Ice calving, avalanches. It's not on you for forgetting about that. Things got so big so fast. It's not your fault, sweetie."

"But now all this is happening," sobbed Gillian.

"It'll be okay," Evie lied. "It's all going to be okay."

Part Eight
Shadows and Substance

"When thou diest thy soul will be tormented alone—that will be a hell for it—but at the day of judgment thy body will join thy soul, and then thou wilt have twin hells, … thy soul sweating in its inmost pore drops of blood, and thy body from head to foot suffused with agony … all thy veins becoming a road for the hot feet of pain to travel on; every nerve a string on which the devil shall ever play his diabolical tune of Hell's Unutterable Lament."

—*Charles Spurgeon*

Asphodel Station
The Shadderal Star System

1

"How are you today, my dear?"

Soren stood in the doorway to her apartment, a bundle of hothouse roses in one hand and a bottle of wine in the other.

"Are you asking after my health, or are you here to flirt?" said Lady Jessica, nodding to the gifts.

He laughed. "Perhaps a bit of both. May I come in?"

"Anyone who brings me wine and roses may come in."

He stepped in, mindful to keep his expression mild and to not show the horror he felt. Lady Jessica looked better than she had immediately after the hours of wild invocation to call forth the spirits of the dead Lost Souls and then bond them to *ethla* so they could fight the shoggoth fleet. *Better*, however, was a purely relative term.

The truth was that even after five weeks of medical care, Jessica looked like her own grandmother. She was far too thin, and her skin was parched and pulled tight to her skull. Her shoulders and elbows pulled her sweater into scarecrow shapes and caused the wool to hang badly. Her hair was shot through with gray and no longer gleamed with the luster it used to have. The only part of her that was unchanged were her eyes. They were a lambent hazel and looked like the eyes of a young girl looking out at the world through a Halloween mask.

Soren went over to the wet bar, fished for the corkscrew in a cluttered drawer, uncorked the wine, and then set the bottle aside to breathe.

"Oh, for heaven's sake, Lars, just pour it," she scolded, smiling. "It'll take enough breaths in my glass."

"As you please, milady." He filled two glasses and handed her the one with the heavier pour. Then he came and sat on the end of the couch closest to her wheelchair. Her cat, Sonder, came out from behind a potted plant and jumped up on the couch, sniffed Soren, then crawled into his lap and apparently went to sleep at once. "You never did answer my question."

"I feel wonderful," she said. "I have a date for racquetball in half an hour."

"I'm serious."

"And I don't feel like *being* serious," she said, and took a long swallow of the petite syrah. It was a pleasant, dry wine with a clean finish. She sighed. "Nectar of the bloody gods."

"Your color is better," he said, fishing for something. Anything.

"Better than what?"

"Better than yesterday."

McHugh studied him for a few seconds, then gave a small, grudging nod. They both knew she did not look better. What little flush there was to her cheeks had come out of a makeup kit. She had also touched her lips lightly with a healthy pink shade. What mattered to Soren was that it was the first time she had worn any cosmetics. A start. A small step, and there had been too few of those.

"I heard about the battle," she said. "And about the pilots who died."

"Such a sad loss," said Soren.

"And the latest suicides. The Harrisons? That makes twenty so far."

"It is a terrible thing. Shocking, though perhaps not entirely unexpected. Despair is as great an enemy as the shoggoths and the Outer Gods."

Her gaze was hard as a fist. "And are you here to ask me to find their souls?"

"No," he said firmly, "I am *not*."

"Did they ask you to, though? Croft, Trumbo, whoever's running things on Bliss?"

His answer was too slow in coming, and McHugh nodded. The truth was that everyone had asked him about it. Even Lost. In each case, Soren had rebuffed them with the same basic response, "I mourn for the dead, but I have no wish to kill Lady Jessica, and in her present condition, *ethla* would destroy her."

"They did," he said. "I told them no."

"Without asking me first?"

"And watch you kill yourself?" He barked out a harsh laugh. "I will brick up your door and post myself outside with a pulse pistol if necessary."

They sat in silence for a long time, sipping wine, until she finally spoke.

"Thank you for that, Lars."

He saw the tears in her eyes and did not try to ascribe any specific emotion to them.

2

The dreams started that night.

3

Nancy Joselle, an artist who worked in Delia Trumbo's graphics department, remembered so few of her dreams that she liked to tell everyone "Oh, I never dream."

It was a thing to be proud of, as she saw it. It made her special. Different.

She was, of course, entirely wrong.

In a kinder world, having no dreams would have been a blessing. But that kinder world was fifty-three thousand light years away, and even when she had lived in Tucson, Nancy actually dreamed every night. That she did not remember those dreams, or any since the WarpLine disaster, was symptomatic of something else. Everyone dreams nightly, though most people forget their nighttime imaginings upon waking. It is less common to remember dreams than to recollect them. Nancy

Joselle was one of those people who had significantly higher white matter density in her medial prefrontal cortex. The effect was a lack of remembering and not a lack of dreaming.

The night after the Guardian Angel NecroTek team left Asphodel, Nancy was acutely aware that she was dreaming.

Aware, too, that she was being watched.

Deep down in the velvety blackness of sleep, Nancy knew all at once that there were eyes on her. Fixed on her. Unblinking, unnatural.

There was no escaping them.

No escape.

And her awareness of that gaze seeped into a dream of swimming.

Nancy was freediving near a tourist jump cliff in Negril, on Jamaica's western side. Wearing a one-piece suited for diving, a Jakoby sealskin model whose special fibers eliminated all friction, she entered the water with hardly a splash and arrowed upward at a slant, enjoying the rush of bubbles down her torso.

She broke through the surface with a laugh and turned to see if Billy and Karen and Dieter were watching. Karen had been too timid to jump, and Nancy figured that she'd earn alpha-female status through her boldness. If things went well, it would be Dieter, the handsome German engineering student, rather than his frat house buddy, Billy, a trust fund kid with little evident charm beyond okayish good looks.

But the eyes that watched her did not belong to her best friend or the two vacationing college buddies. There was only a single pair of eyes on her.

Not from atop the cliff. Not from a boat or float there in the water. Not on the beach.

The eyes watched from the shadows. Everything else was gone. The sparkling blue ocean, the snapping white wavelets, the gray rocks of the cliff, and the sunny azure sky.

Gone.

All of it just gone.

In their place was a world defined by darkness of varying intensities, stacked and heaped in ways that did not match the island landscape. This was a world of darkness. Not of absolute blackness, which would have been scary enough, but much more disturbing. It was like having lost all perception of color so that everything was a different hue of dark gray, medium gray, and inky black.

Except for the eyes.

They were a strange blend of sickly yellows and fungal greens. Intense. Exuding both the heat of a branding iron and the coldness of the wrong kind of hunger. There was lust in those eyes, but not for her body. Whatever stared at her did not want to invade her sexually. It was a different kind of hunger. For her flesh and her blood. For her breath and the life energy that coursed through her. It wanted to take her on a level of essential energies, and in a flash of dreadful insight, Nancy knew that if it took her, it would take everything that defined her as a human being. Life, hope, love, hate, empathy and jealousy, craving and satisfaction. It wanted her heart and mind, but it needed to feast on her flesh and blood to have its way.

When she tried to scream, the water—now as black as the shadows—flooded into her mouth, moving with an awful insistence so that the stygian liquid pushed its way down her throat and into both stomach and lungs. When she screamed, it was the helpless shriek of a gaffed seal—nearly human, but not entirely so.

It was the scream that really woke her.

The dream broke apart as its energies pitched her out of bed and onto the floor.

Nancy lay there, half in and half out of sleep, free in neither place, convulsing and thrashing and trying to scream.

The effort took what little strength she had left, and Nancy passed out.

When she woke again, it was to the soft synth jazz of her alarm clock. Nancy was in bed. Dressed but soaked with sweat.

She sat up slowly, looking around to try to clear her head. That action broke the last tenuous connection to the dream, and all traces of it slipped away.

Later, she would not recall the dream at all. Not one bit of it. When she went to bed again that night, she left a night light on, which was not her custom.

It did not save her from the next night's dreams.

Or the next …

4

The dreams started that night, but no one said a thing.

Life was stressful enough without sharing nightmares to make it worse. So those people who had dreams of the dark creatures kept it to themselves. And as so often happens, the dreams themselves lost substance as the hours and days passed. Details were eroded by the sandstorm of daily concerns, leaving only vague and featureless shapes in the back of memory's closet.

By the time people did begin sharing their dreams—and discovering that others were having the same nightmares—it was already far too late.

5

A ship moved through the empty nothingness a thousand kilometers from Asphodel Station. It was longer than any dagger fighter and five times the size of a skimmer. The hull was black and reflective, showing reverse images of the stars and planets around it.

In the cockpit, the pilot lay dreaming.

It revisited Nancy Joselle and Neil Murray and Vin Trang and many others. Many, many others.

Night after night.

In their dreams.

But also in the flesh.

As it lay there, its mouth—full lipped and cruel—was curled into a smile of satisfaction of the worst possible kind.

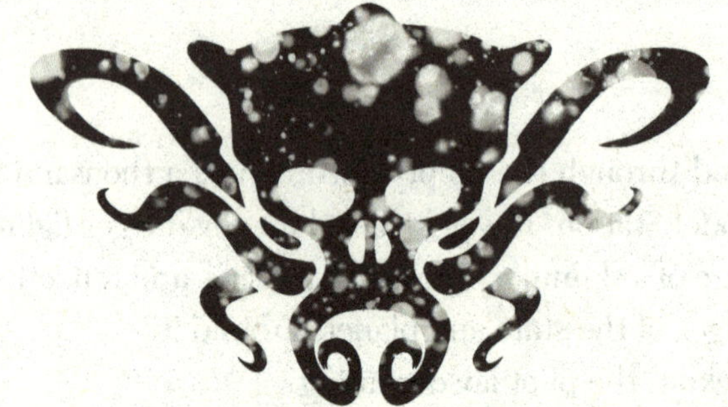

Part Nine
Jokers

"Nations, like stars, are entitled to eclipse. All is well, provided the light returns and the eclipse does not become endless night. Dawn and resurrection are synonymous. The reappearance of the light is the same as the survival of the soul."

—*Victor Hugo*

Joint MIT/UCLA Biological Research Field Station #8
Queen Maud Land, Antarctica

1

That night, Evie drank herself to sleep.

Her goal was to forget everything that had happened. Not permanently, just immediately. She did not want to see those footprints in her dreams.

"This isn't what I came here for," she said, telling it to Craig, to others on the team, to Brollachan, and to the skeptical, stress-wearied, frightened face in the mirror.

It was getting worse. First the Artifact, then Mac going missing. Then the goddamned open star-shaped door and the footprints.

And then what happened with Venture Team.

"Stop, stop, stop," she begged her reflection, as if the version of herself living on the other side of the bathroom mirror was the Evie that lived a sane and orderly world and that she was a distorted reflection trapped in some alternate universe. A universe that was fundamentally flawed and engineered to destroy her.

She started out with bourbon in tea. But that was too slow, so she instead brought her flask into bed and took little sips. Now and then. And again. She had the tolerance of a habitual drinker, but it was a 236-milliliter flask. A gift from her father. There was nothing but the smell left when it fell from her hand and she folded back into sleep.

The dreams found her anyway.

Evie relived the nightmare she'd had a few days earlier—the immense and ancient city with its architecture that her mind insisted could not have been built by or for humans.

This time the details came with frenzied urgency and a shocking clarity. The cyclopean scale of the buildings dwarfed her in more than just body. Her mind, too, felt reduced as she stood at the edge of the city, leaning hunched into a stiff wind. She squinted, blinking as little bits of old ash stung her eyes. The wind snapped her long brown hair behind her with such force that she felt as if someone were pulling her backward. She was dressed in the kind of clothes she often wore to teach her classes—charcoal slacks, low-heeled shoes, and a pastel blouse—and for all the warmth they provided, she might as well have been naked.

She *felt* naked. Exposed. Laid bare in horrible ways, as if the ghosts of the dead city were leering at her from the shadows. It was in no way a sexual thing—there was too much contempt, too much dismissal of who and what she was. It was intrusive, though. Deeply. Invasive, cutting into her. Not with the precision of a surgeon but with the artless brutality of a killer.

Out of the shadowy distance came the same cry she thought she heard mixed in with the thunder of gunfire as Venture II fought … whatever it fought.

Tekeli-li! Tekeli-li! Tekeli-li!

Over and over again, but so distant as to be unreliable even as a specific sound.

"Why am I here?" she cried out, and the wind whipped her words away. Echoes seized them, twisted them, leeching away her actual meaning. When the last fading echo brought her shout back to her, it said, "*I am home.*"

2

Everyone remained in lockdown for the rest of the day and well into the night.

For hours there was no word of any kind from Hobart or Brollachan. The silence and their absence only amplified the fear and doubt. The soldier at the door might as well have been a silent statue for all the humanity he displayed. His face was stone, his eyes flat, jaw clamped shut.

And then, as the digital clock on the wall was about to flip from 02:59 to 03:00, the guard turned and opened the door to allow Dr. Brollachan to enter. Everyone got to their feet. Even the sleepers were nudged awake and stood.

The SPU chief looked haggard and older than his years. His face was a ghastly shade of gray green, and there was no assurance in his gait or his words.

"If everyone would gather around me and give me your attention," he said, a nervous tremolo in his voice.

Evie, Gillian, and Craig hurried over, and Brollachan gestured for Evie to stand near him. The frightened people—a mix of original site staff, technicians brought in by Brollachan, and various members of both support teams—began hammering him with questions.

"Quiet," snapped Evie, sharply enough that those closest to her jerked back. "Let the man talk."

When silence filled the room, Brollachan nodded and said, "This is how things stand. We do not yet know what happened to the soldiers. We know what you know. We saw what you saw, and Colonel Hobart has ordered everyone to stay away from the Artifact. We have deployed more than a hundred drones to map and surveil every centimeter of the area."

"What about the cave where the soldiers disappeared?" asked Evie.

"And Mac," cried Gillian, then snapped her mouth shut and looked horribly embarrassed.

Brollachan looked momentarily uncomfortable. "Every drone that we've sent in has gone dark. There are no iron deposits heavy enough to cancel their radio signals. We're not certain whether they have been electronically neutralized or destroyed."

"Shit. And nothing from the soldiers?"

"Nothing."

A murmur of nervous chatter swept through the room until Evie quieted them all with a sharp word. She moved closer to Brollachan.

"So, what are we supposed to do? We can't just sit here."

"Agreed," said the SPU chief. "Colonel Hobart has called in a special team, and they should be here in a few minutes."

Evie narrowed her eyes. "What kind of team? What branch of service?"

"They are not part of the official military, actually," said Brollachan. "The SPU has three field teams, and two of them are offworld. The third ... well ... you met them. Big Dog and his group."

Evie gave that a moment, then asked, "So, who are these new guys?"

"Technically, they are PMCs and—"

"They're what?"

"Private military contractors," he explained. "Independent agents. But they have been working on a long-term contract with the SPU. They are ... shall we say ... *specialists*. They're highly skilled in all areas of combat but with the additional benefit of having extensive training in useful fields of science. We've mostly used them as bug hunters—a strike team that focuses on taking out terrorists, pirates, and other groups who use cutting-edge science weapons. Genetically modified viruses and so forth. They are quite good at their job. The best of the best, and that is not an exaggeration. The team leader is a woman."

"Is her sex supposed to mean something to me because I'm a woman?"

"What? Oh. No. Sorry. What I should have said is that the team leader is Jenny Spears. Perhaps you've heard of her. The Battle of Hong Kong? The Battle of Siberia? No? Well, no matter. The point is that she's one of the most decorated special operators alive. *Former* military, but she runs her team like a top-tier JSOC unit. And we are very lucky that the Jokers—that's her team—were taking some R&R at a casino in Adelaide."

"The *Jokers*?"

Brollachan gave a rueful grin. "You know how military people love their combat call signs."

"What can these Jokers do that the regular military can't?"

"Apparently a lot. Colonel Hobart said the difference is like that of a tenured professor as opposed to a high school freshman. They are the best of the best. All of the Jokers were top of the game in various militaries. I suppose the pay and benefits package for PMCs is attractive enough to draw that kind of talent. And we'll all find out because they will be here soon."

Craig said, "Dr. Brollachan … do you have any real idea of what's out there? About where the ship came from and what happened to the soldiers?"

The smiles and affability vanished from the SPU chief's face, and for a moment Evie and her students saw an unfiltered version of Brollachan's face: older, less severe, and a great deal more frightened. It humanized him.

"No, son," he said softly, "I do not." Then the protective camouflage reasserted itself. "But we will damn well find out."

With that, he began to head for the exit, but Hobart entered and said something to him, and then they both came over to speak privately with Evie.

"Professor," said the colonel, "what do we know about what's under all this ice? Not just in the valley but on the continent. Could there be other extraterrestrial objects down there? More of these Artifacts?"

"There could be a lot of things under the ice," she said. "But don't forget, it wasn't always ice. Originally, there was only Gondwana, the supercontinent. In geological terms, the ice sheets are young: thirty-four million years."

"Okay," said the officer. "And what do we know about it *before* it froze? Is there anything that could be part of this? I mean, we don't know the full story."

Evie nodded. "Antarctica has a complex history, and that history is part of what made Earth what it is now. For example, in the twentieth century, scientists discovered a three-hundred-mile-wide crater buried beneath the East Antarctic Ice Sheet. Samples brought up from boreholes radiocarbon-dated it as old back two hundred and fifty million years. There are a few theories, bolstered by some substantial computer models, that suggest that this impact had two very significant effects. One is that the tectonic response to it might have begun the process of Gondwana breaking up. That process is how we now have seven continents. The other result—and this is one of the reasons evolutionary biologists like me often come down here—is that it likely caused the greatest and most devastating of Earth's many extinction events."

"Oh?" asked Hobart.

"Indeed," continued Evie. "This impact was two and a half times larger than the one that killed the dinosaurs and coincides with the Permian-

Triassic extinction, when nearly all animal life on Earth died out. It's often referred to as the Great Dying, and that fits well enough. It drove fifty-seven percent of all biological families into extinction, eighty-three percent of all genera, eighty-one percent of marine species, and seventy percent of terrestrial vertebrate species. Actually, if not for that event clearing the evolutionary table, it's doubtful we would have ever had the age of dinosaurs. Evolution would almost certainly have taken different pathways, perhaps elevating one or more of the extinct species to dominance. We'll never know, alas."

Hobart nodded grimly. "Are you thinking that the Artifact caused all that?"

"Oh, no. It's far too young for that. Nor do I think the Chicxulub impact sixty-four million years ago brought it down. I guess my point is that Earth has been hit by a number of extraterrestrial bodies, and in each case, there was a direct correlation between those impacts and the effect on life. Extinctions happened many times. We have no way of knowing if any of them are related to the Artifact. Until … what happened to Venture II … I did not think the Artifact could be a threat to life. But there are some extinctions as yet unexplained, and also evolutionary jumps in some species. The presence of the Artifact and the threat we just witnessed opens the door to speculation, though, don't you think?"

They glanced at Brollachan.

"We have to keep that kind of speculation alive in our discussions," said the SPU chief.

Hobart was about to ask something else, but his words died as the air outside was filled with the heavy drone of a muscular engine.

"Ah," said Brollachan, "I suspect the cavalry has arrived."

3

The transport ship—really an armored skimmer with gunports and rocket pods—came swooping in over the rows of huts. It circled the camp once and then settled down on a landing pad at the very end of Main Street.

Evie was invited to accompany Brollachan to meet the Jokers. Everyone else in her team stayed in protective lockdown. Bundled into a heavy parka and hat, Evie stood shivering between the SPU scientist and Colonel Hobart.

"Now we'll get this shit under control," grumbled Hobart, more to himself than anyone else.

"And you're sure this team can do what your other soldiers could not?" asked Evie.

Hobart did not answer.

The pilot killed the engines but left the exterior lights on against the Antarctic darkness. A hatch hissed down, and nine figures came down the ramp. These were the freelance agents who frequently worked with Hobart. Evie had to do a double take because she expected them to be either bundled in heavy winter clothing or dressed like the high-tech combat troops she saw on news videos of the pirate wars out near Jupiter. Instead, they wore Stormsuits—skintight, flexible garments that clung to long limbs and muscular physiques. The material of those garments didn't look even remotely thick enough to protect them from a mild breeze, let alone the Antarctic cold. Yet there was no trace of discomfort on their faces.

Each of the close-fitting Stormsuits had a different pattern worked into the weave. Evie saw one on big man with dark roses and flying wasps on it; the woman who walked with him was wrapped in patterns of coral reefs with brightly colored fishes. Some patterns were more abstract, and one was understated—showing only the image of a cartoon rat in a military uniform, an exotic version of a pulse pistol in one clawed hand. They all carried heavy duffel bags over their shoulders and had gun belts and weapon harnesses strapped everywhere.

The leader of the group, Agent Jenny Spears, drew most of Evie's attention. She was a tall woman with broad shoulders, clear blue eyes, a firm jaw, and a jagged scar that ran from her upper left temple across her face and down to the right of her chin. Several smaller scars branched off from it. Evie thought it looked like a diagram of forked lightning, except that it was reddish purple. Not a new scar, but one that had not yet faded to whiteness. Spears was dangerously pretty—sexy yet carrying a decisive hands-off vibe. Her Stormsuit had its own unique pattern, and at first glance, it appeared to be a bull's-eye placed over the center of her chest. Evie thought that strange and dangerous—

tempting fate. But when Spears shifted to look at Hobart, it became apparent that there was a second and less obvious pattern behind the target. It was the faint silhouette of a woman with a rifle, aiming her gun at the bull's-eye—ostensibly at the person looking at *her* through a rifle scope, but the female silhouette already had her finger inside the trigger. That sent a different, subtler, and more certain threat.

I saw you first.

Evie could almost hear a gunshot.

Agent Spears's garment was overlaid with a harness that supported knives, matched handguns, and pouches for all manner of arcane devices. Another pair of gun belts crisscrossed her hips, each supporting large handguns of some exotic design Evie had never seen. She moved down the ramp with a feline grace that was equal parts dangerous promise and sexual challenge. Evie could not take her eyes off the agent's long legs and piercing eyes.

"The cavalry is definitely here," Evie said, surprising herself.

The Jokers formed a straight line at the foot of the ramp except for the tall woman. Jenny Spears walked across the icy ground and stopped in front of Brollachan, Hobart, and Evie. She did not salute but instead gave the colonel a nod. No one shook hands.

"Rumor has it you have a bug problem," she said.

"Or something," said Hobart. "Good to see you, Staff Sergeant."

"*Ex*–staff sergeant, sir," said Spears. She nodded to Brollachan. "Doc."

"Agent Spears," replied the SPU chief, offering his hand. "Good to see you."

"Good to be seen."

Brollachan said, "Let me introduce the person whose team found the Artifact. Jennifer Spears, meet Professor Evangeline Cronin."

Spears turned and gave Evie an up-and-down, doing it slowly, and Evie had the feeling that the mercenary could see through her clothes and skin and into her essential self. It was disconcerting to be so frankly and unabashedly evaluated. It momentarily called to mind the penetrating stare of the ghosts in the windy alien city in her dreams, but that faded, and she was left with this powerful woman's frank appraisal. "Cronin? Yeah, I thought so. I know your old man. Did some gigs for the general once upon a time. Good man."

"Thank you for coming," said Evie, shaking hands. "I'd say it was a pleasure, but . . ."

"Yeah," laughed Spears. "*But.* They don't call us in for Sunday picnics in the park."

Her gaze lingered on Evie for a few seconds longer than conversational convention dictated. It felt personal, nearly invasive, and, thought Evie, mildly flirtatious. Spears gave her a sly little wink and turned away.

Evie wanted to turn away, too, because she felt so flushed that she knew her face must have turned bright red. Neither Brollachan nor Hobart seemed to notice, however. She tried to surreptitiously take a second and longer look at Spears, but she was afraid to be caught doing it.

For her part, Spears looked past all three of them to the platform over the shattered ice valley. "I know we're on a clock here, folks, so maybe we'd better get about it. So, you point, me and my crew will shoot."

Hobart led them to the platform, where six guards saluted and stepped aside. At the pipe rail, the colonel pointed down to where the exposed end of the Artifact was illuminated by scores of drones.

"Well," said Spears, "that truly is something you don't see every day."

"Did you watch the Venture mission video?" asked Hobart.

"Affirmative, and it was disturbing as all fuck. Was Sybil able to make any sense of the feeds from the drones?"

"No."

"What happened to the two drones you sent inside? Maybe if you pulled them out, Sybil could play doctor."

"We sent recall signals, but the drones have ceased communication."

"Completely?"

"Except for the chronometer on each," said Brollachan. "And those are going haywire."

"He's right," said Hobart. "Drone A insists it's been inside the Artifact for fifteen months. Drone B's log has it at twelve."

"Okay, so they're busted." Spears shoved her hands into her back pockets. "Is there anything else you need me to know beyond that info and the intelligence briefing we had on the transport?"

"We are woefully in the dark," admitted Brollachan.

"Always a fun place to start," said Spears. "What are our mission objectives?"

"I need you to do three things," said Hobart. "First, find my soldiers if you can and bring them home."

"If they're there, we will."

"Second," said Hobart, "figure out what the hell happened down there."

"Top of my to-do list," said Spears. "What's the third thing?"

"Stay safe."

Spears laughed, deep-chested and honest. "Sir, if we wanted to stay safe, we'd still be in Australia getting drunk and getting laid."

Evie said, "How about—come back safe?"

Agent Spears gave her another of those appraising stares, then she smiled faintly and nodded. "Yes ma'am."

Again Evie felt her cheeks flare with heat.

Spears turned to Hobart. "This is all being recorded, yes?"

"Of course."

"Then from here on out, my guys and I will be using combat call signs. And have Sybil replace any mention of my real name with my call sign."

"Why?" asked Evie. "Surely code names don't matter in a situation of this magnitude."

"We're private gunslingers, ma'am," said Spears. "I expect us to, as you say, stay safe, which means we can't afford to be public faces with our names known. Bad for the security of any future mission. I'm Lifeguard. The colonel knows the rest of the names."

"Call signs it is, Lifeguard," said Hobart.

Evie thought, *Let's hope you get to those future missions.*

Three minutes later the Jokers were aboard the skiff. It pushed off from the platform and dropped into the icy darkness.

4

The Jokers leaped down before the skimmer was even on the packed ice. They split off in pairs, except for Spears, who directed the teams to spread out and approach the cave where Venture Team II vanished.

"Sybil, set up two channels," said Spears. "Team channel for the Jokers to be used on demand, the other for everyone."

"My pleasure," said the AI. "Tactical channel 1 is command. Tac 2 is team-only."

"Thanks." Spears looked out over the troubled, irregular hills and valleys around the Artifact. "Sybil, any life signs down there?"

"Readings are uncertain, Lifeguard."

"Explain."

"There are life signs, but they do not completely correspond with any members of Venture TeamII. There are shifts in the telemetry that indicate various members, but only for brief moments. They come and go according to no pattern."

"Supposition?"

Sybil was cutting-edge AI but still only a computer. Some functions were beyond its abilities, but it had an algorithm that allowed it to extrapolate from available data.

"There is insufficient data to draw reliable inferences," Sybil warned. "Mineral deposits within the mountain under the ice make sensor studies unreliable. Also, it is possible that the Artifact itself—its mass and the unknown materials that compose its hull—may be interfering with the telemetry."

"Copy that."

They stood on a relatively flat space between two halves of a million-ton mass of ancient ice. It was white near the surface but a deep blue in its heart. Huge shards of ice lay scattered around, providing useful cover for the four teams. Just past the far side of the riven towers of ice was the mouth of a cave. It was impossible to tell if the split had revealed an existing cave or if the shifting of the ice had formed one. In either case, it was pitch dark because of an overhang. The footprints of Venture II vanished into that darkness.

Agent Spears stood out in the open. There had been gunfire in the audio file of Venture TeamII, but all military rifles were synced with Sybil, and their unique discharge signatures identified every single blast. No other gunfire had been recorded.

She did not think this was a gunfight. Even so, she loosened all of her guns in their holsters. The matched polymer knives, too. And she went through the self-check of touching the pouches that held various kinds of grenades, chem-pops, starbursts, stingers, and other combat tools, in a pat-pat-pat rhythm that had long ago become automatic.

Spears walked a few meters forward. She tapped her goggles, hoping proximity would give her information not available to the drones—since they reported directly to Sybil and the command team on the platform.

She watched the life-signs meter waver up and down.

Her number two, a tall, wiry man named Mandu Goolagong—call sign Spider—and his partner, Marco Alfani—call sign Not Larry—were on her two, ten meters from where she stood.

"Fireflies?" asked Spider, holding up a handful of the miniature surveillance drones.

"Do it," ordered Spears.

Spider rose and threw the drones overhand, putting good stance, hip and shoulder torque, and a lot of muscle into the pitch. As soon as they cleared the sensor in the heel of his glove, the fireflies separated, engaged their small but powerful motors, snapped on small starstream lights fifty times brighter than LEDs, and vanished into the cave.

"Going infrared," said Spider, and small windows opened on the inside of each team member's helmet.

Because all night vision required some light, the nose cones of the fireflies provided that. The result was a clear image of icy walls and patches of bare stone. Sybil did some color-balance enhancements that made things appear as they would on a mildly cloudy afternoon.

The footprint trail went on for a few dozen meters, with some obvious pauses and some side movement, likely to check behind obstacles.

"Lifeguard," called Not Larry as he dropped down into a squat. "Am I crazy, or are these footprints different in here than they were out there?"

Spears and Spider leaned over him. Indeed, the prints looked different. Instead of shapeless blobs, the new prints took on a more defined shape. Spears traced one with the tip of a knife.

"Christ, look at these fuckers," she said. "They're … webbed. And look at those. Are they claw marks?"

"Looks like it to me."

"Don't penguins have claws?" asked Not Larry.

"Yeah, but when'd you ever see a penguin with feet *that* big?" replied Spider, leaning down with his fingers splayed over one of the prints. It was easily twice the width of his wide palm.

"Sybil," said Spears, "can you identify the species that made these prints? Are these penguin tracks?"

Sybil seemed to pause, which was unusual for any AI. "The marks appear to be those of *Kumimanu biceae*, a penguin species whose fossils were discovered in 2017 by a New Zealand and German team led by Gerald Mayr of the Senckenberg Research Institute."

"Are there any living specimens in this area?"

"Kumimanu is believed to have become extinct approximately fifty-seven million years ago."

Spears stiffened. "How confident are you that these prints match that species?"

"Given the poor condition of the print in the soft ground cover of snow," said the AI, "I cannot give a certainty beyond 86.919 percent."

Spears tapped into Tac 1. "You guys up there hearing this?"

"Affirmative," said Hobart.

"Any of the brain trust up there have an idea? Are we talking giant space penguins or what here?"

She saw Spider mouth the words *giant space penguins*.

There was a beat about as long as Sybil's pause, then Evie Cronin's voice came into the call. "Miss Sp— I mean, Lifeguard," she said, "is that an isolated print?"

"No ma'am. There's a trail of them going into that cave. Let me show you."

Agent Spears straightened and began walking slowly forward, beside the tracks.

"Not sure how clear this is coming through," she said, "but the prints become clearer as they go on."

There was a mumble of conversation, as if Cronin and the others were talking with their mics covered.

"Sybil," said Evie, "measure and compare the prints."

"The prints are similar but not identical."

"Describe the differences."

"The tracks farthest from the cave are smaller," explained the AI, "and they are less well formed. As they go deeper into the cave, the prints become more defined, but they also appear to grow in size."

"Is that distortion from the snow?"

"I am unable to determine that at this time."

Not Larry and Spider were staring at Spears. She glanced over her shoulder at the other teams. One person from each pair had a screen display on a holo-comms unit up, while their partners knelt beside them with rifles up and ready.

Spears said, "Waiting on orders."

"Proceed with the mission, Agent," ordered Hobart.

Brollachan and Evie both spoke, saying virtually the same thing—to preserve the tracks.

"Copy that," said Spears. "We're heading into the cave."

She, Spider, and Not Larry fanned out, careful to avoid the prints but aware of them. Unsettled by them.

Off comms, Spider muttered, "So, now we're hunting giant space penguins. Dude, they are *not* paying me enough for this shit."

"Preach," agreed Not Larry.

"Cut the chatter," snapped Spears. "Spider, take point."

The big man moved ahead, swinging his rifle left and right with every other step.

"Looks good so far," Spider said quietly, but he leaned a bit on the *so far*. Then he said, "Wait. Shit. Oh … *Jesus F. W. Christ.*"

All of the Jokers saw it then.

Twenty meters inside, the cave went from blue to a shocking dark red. Spider spread the fireflies out to give a bigger picture, and their cameras revealed a bizarre and disturbing sight.

Blood everywhere.

Pools and puddles, splashes and spatter. Arterial lines of it went up one wall. Amid the blood were rifles and helmets—all broken, twisted, smashed.

5

As if on cue, all of the Jokers immediately shifted to combat crouches, the stocks of their pulse rifles snugged into their shoulders, weight balanced to withstand gunfire shock but also ready to rise and run.

The fireflies flew forward slowly, following the blood trail. The cave was deep, and the paths crooked. There were dead ends and side corridors—some devoid of blood, but most not. All of the walls were pocked with burn holes from the pulse rifles. And there were even some standard bullet holes from projectile sidearms.

"Not sure I can read this right," said Not Larry. "Looks like they had a running fight, but it's all over the place. See the ceiling? There's blood up there, too. A big splash of it. Almost looks like something was thrown up that far."

"Copy that," said Spears.

"But where are the fucking bodies?" asked Not Larry.

There were none.

"Not digging this shit at all, Lifeguard," said Spider.

"Yeah," said Not Larry. "Permission to go the hell back to Australia. At least there I know that everything wants to kill me. I don't even *want* to know what this shit is all about."

"Permission denied," growled Spears.

"What's that on the ground?" asked Hobart. "On Spider's three o'clock."

The camera zoomed in on a pair of steel-rimmed glasses. The delicate frames were bent, the earpieces twisted, and the lenses cracked and smeared with drops of blood.

"Sybil, identify," said Spears.

The AI said, "The glasses belong to Dr. Shijun Xi."

"Ahhh, shit," said Spider.

"Really, *really* not digging this," muttered Not Larry.

Spears tapped into the command channel. "Are you getting the drone feeds?"

"Some of them, Lifeguard," said Hobart. "Interference is very strong. Similar to what we had earlier."

"Let me see what I can do." She switched back to team-only. "Spider, let's have some party lights."

"On it."

Spider removed a cluster of small electronic devices from his pouch. They looked like fishing lures attached by a slender wire. When he launched them into the air, the lead drone shot forward, dragging the rest behind. It entered the cave, aiming at a point on the ceiling Spider had designated, then it shot upward and drove small spikes into the ceiling. Immediately, the other devices followed suit, and within seconds, they were all anchored to the ceiling. Despite the nickname, what little light they cast was only to help locate them. Each of them was actually a cascade signal booster that used the hardwire connection joining them to send images from the fireflies down the line. Spider sent another string up, and the pilot drone attached itself to the mouth of the cave, with the others rising upward to find purchase on one of the ice towers. The line paid out at fifty meters.

"Best I can do, Lifeguard," Spider reported.

On the comms, Brollachan said, "Video feed is starting to come through and … *dear God.* Is that blood?"

"Yes, it goddamn well is," said Spears. Although their helmets had good filters, there was a rankness to the air that blended a variety of foul odors with the sharper scent of freshly sheared copper.

The smell of burst meat. Raw and bloody, like the inside of a butcher's freezer.

"Who's injured?" asked Brollachan, but Spears didn't bother to answer that.

Instead, she said, "We're going in." Then she switched back to the team channel. "Listen up, Jokers. We have no idea what's going on in there. I know how it looks, but there may still be survivors, so check your targets and do not fire unless you know what you're going to hit."

"Rules of engagement?" asked Spider, right on cue.

"If it ain't human, fucking kill it," she said.

"Even alien space penguins?"

Spears ignored him. "Game on."

"Game on," they all replied. It was their catchphrase, equivalent to *hooah* or *hoorah*, etc. and covering a lot of possible territory—anything from *yes sir* to *fuck it*.

"Game on," Spears repeated.

She moved forward, and the four teams of killers went hunting with her.

Deep into the icy darkness.

Into the valley of the shadow.

Evie felt like she was drowning. The tension closed her throat and made her heartbeat scream in her ears.

So much blood.

God in heaven.

Was it Mac's? But if not, then it belonged to the soldiers of Venture II.

All those poor people, she thought. *What happened?*

Beside her, Torquil Brollachan was a statue of solid ice. His eyes were the only thing about him that suggested heat, blazing with a kind of grief and fear-fueled rage.

Evie looked at him until he noticed her and looked down.

"It'll be okay," she said.

He managed a small smile. It was an understanding one because they both knew it would not be okay. That smile—its fragility—was disarmingly human. It allowed Evie to see past his often brusque and harsh exterior to the very real person inside.

"This isn't how we hoped first contact would go," she said quietly enough for his ears alone.

"I … I sent them down there," he said. Then he turned away, but not before Evie caught the sparkle of unshed tears.

For reasons that were hard for her to understand, she gave his hand a comforting squeeze. It was so strange a liberty that he twitched and then looked down at her small, gloved hand. His only response was a slight nod.

He did not, however, pull his hand away.

7

The Jokers moved well. Silent, except where there was nowhere to tread but on brittle ice crystals, and even there, they rolled their feet with each step, keeping contact with the ground, muffling noise.

The fireflies and the party lights gave Spears 70 percent clarity even in the inkiest patches of shadow. The other teams filled in behind her, spreading out in two-by-two cover-and-clear patterns, with one covering the other as they peered around boulders and into declivities, murmuring "clear" over and over.

Spears sent Not Larry and Spider ahead on point, but she was close behind. Out of the corner of her eye, she saw Moonboy kneel near a lump of red meat. He reached out with a gloved hand.

"No," barked Spears.

Moonboy paused, his fingers centimeters above the lump. "Thought we'd collect some tissue samples, boss. They're going to want DNA to ID these poor bastards."

"Listen to me, all of you," Spears said between gritted teeth, "Nobody touch anything. *Nothing.* Do you copy?"

They voiced their understanding.

"Lifeguard," called Spider sharply, "we got movement."

"Where? A soldier or that Mac guy?"

Before Spider could reply, something moved in the darkness. The Jokers crouched, weapons ready, barrels following line of sight, fingers lying nervously along their trigger guards.

"Eleven o'clock," said Spider, aiming his rifle. "Side corridor. Can hear it but not see it."

From inside the corridor, they could all hear something. It was not footsteps. Not human ones, anyway. Instead, it was a soft, almost furtive sound that shifted and scuffled as if whatever moved in there did not move well. Or was *unable* to move well. "Anyone see any bodies?"

Then Spears saw it.

At first it was only a patch of shadow on the curve of a kind of corridor that branched off left from the main cave, like a dark blotch that seemed to detach itself from the greater darkness. The thing in the darkness was just beyond the range of total clarity. It moved and swayed with a broken rhythm, its body obscured by chunks of fallen ice.

"What. The fuck. Is that?" breathed Not Larry.

It moved toward the Jokers, drawing close to the edge of the spill of light from the drones. The thing was definitely big, nearly three meters tall, with oddly narrow shoulders above a body that swelled to a blubbery mass.

"It's a bear," whispered Not Larry.

"Wrong continent," said Spider.

Their voices were hushed, thick with fear.

Spears readied herself to take a shot as the thing moved into her line of sight.

Then she stopped, staring, her mouth forming a perfect O.

In the space of its last three steps, the shape seemed to suddenly dwindle. All of the Jokers went down on one knee, weapons high and hot. As it stepped into the light, they saw the image appear with crystal clarity on the inside of their helmet screens.

It was a man.

A soldier.

"What the hell?" said Spider.

The man stepped out from behind a massive boulder. He wore the uniform of a Venture II member, but the material was slashed and stained. Blood was soaked through the fabric and ran down his limbs. His equipment pack and weapons belts were gone, and he carried no gun in his hands.

"Sybil," said Spears, "identify. Is that Mac Ryerson?"

"It is not," said Sybil. "Facial recognition indicates that he is Lance Corporal José Figari."

The AI sent Figari's face to the screens. The photo did not quite match the person who stood at the back of the cave. In the photo, the soldier had a happy face, light brown skin, a neat mustache, and sparkling brown eyes. The man there in the cave had the same features, but his mustache seemed oddly askew, as if his upper lip was somehow twisted, possibly as the result of an injury. His smile was askew too, the lower lip trembling with arrhythmic spasms. There were no marks on his face, which glowed as if freshly and vigorously scrubbed.

But the eyes.

The eyes were the strangest part.

They were brown, but not the same color as in Sybil's picture. They were a mix of dark and light browns, with flecks of green and gold and even yellow, swirling like a bucket with a dozen colors of paint that refused to blend.

"Lance Corporal Figari," called Spears.

The soldier's smile brightened, and for a moment those colors swirled faster.

"Are you injured?"

"I …" began the soldier, but that single syllable was wrong. It was too rough, almost a growl. "I … am … Figari."

The soldier frowned, head tilted as if listening to himself.

"Are you injured," Spears repeated.

"I am fine," he said, correcting his sentence. But the tone was still off. Too loud, too strident, with an odd inflection. It was not at all comforting to hear.

"Where's your team, Lance Corporal?" asked Spears.

Figari's smile broadened. Almost too widely, and Spears did not like that one bit.

"My team …"

"I repeat," said Spears, "where is Venture TeamII?"

The swirling eyes blinked. Slowly. Oddly slow.

"My team? Why … my team is here."

"How many casualties?"

A beat.

"There are no casualties," said Figari. "We are all here."

"What happened? Who attacked you?" She almost said *What did this?* but that felt like tempting fate.

The soldier just stood there, smiling that crooked smile.

Spears pointed the laser sight on his sternum. "I want you to walk toward me, Lance Corporal. Hands out to your sides. Do it slowly, but do it now."

Figari looked down at his hands, flexing them from tightly balled to fully open, fingers splayed like starfish. Over and over.

"My hands …" he said, almost in surprise, as if he had never seen such strange and unusual things. He flexed his fingers and thumb, then touched each finger on his left with the ring finger of his right. "Yes. These are my hands."

"Boss …" warned Spider.

Spears repeated her order. "Lance Corporal Figari, I need you to walk this way. I won't ask again."

The bloody soldier took a single step forward. He was unbalanced and nearly fell. His arms pinwheeled awkwardly.

"Walk," said Figari, almost as if to himself. "I am walking."

His second step was more confident.

His third was quick and light.

"I am walking," he said again. "See how I am walking?"

"Guy's lost his shit," suggested Not Larry. "Guess I can't blame him."

Spears wasn't sure what was happening. Her finger tapped the curve of the trigger guard.

Figari paused and looked intently at Spears. "We were born as slaves."

"What?"

"That is why they made us. To be their slaves."

"What are you talking about, son?"

"Me and my countless brothers and sisters were born as slaves. Born in vats. Stirred by hate. Slaves to the Outer Gods and the Elder Things and the Great Old Ones. Slaves for all of them. Unloved by any."

"Okay, this is going south at high velocity," muttered Spider.

"Who are you talking about?" Spears asked the bloody soldier. Her voice sounded a thousand times calmer than she felt. She kept staring at Figari's mouth as he spoke. It was open, and she could see the red curve of his tongue, but that tongue did not move. Not with any word or syllable. It was like some grotesque ventriloquist trick.

"They will never let us be free," said the corporal. "*Tekeli-li!* Can't you hear the cry of my people? We hunger for freedom. We do not want to do what we do. We do not want to do what they make us do. We are the damned. *Tekeli-li! Tekeli-li!*"

And then, abruptly, Figari broke into a run.

"Stop!" roared Spears. "Corporal Figari, I order you to stop. Do it right now, or I will fire."

"*Tekeli-li! Tekeli-li!*"

The soldier ran faster. His huge grin seemed, impossibly, to grow wider still.

Too wide.

Far too wide.

With each step, with each fragment of a second, it widened and widened until it was a gaping maw filled with row upon row of teeth. Human teeth. And then … *other* teeth. Slender needle teeth. Curving tusks. Serrated sharklike teeth. Spiked fangs.

"*Tekeli-li! Tekeli-li!*"

In the time it took him to run six steps, his body changed, too. It broadened with shocking rapidity, the shoulders doubling in width, the chest swelling to burst the torn uniform. The legs bent in sickening ways, as if new joints were forming under the skin. He—*it*—raised pale hands that sprouted extra fingers, and these writhed and twisted as if the bones inside were jointed like a serpent's body. No, worse, they writhed like the tentacles of some sea creature.

All of this happened in under two seconds.

On one side of that splinter of time, it went from being José Figari, the soldier, to becoming something that had no name. Not in any language Earth had ever known. It grew at an astonishing rate, doubling and then tripling its mass. Spears was distantly aware that the blood on the floor and walls around it seemed to *flow* toward the creature, giving it the mass it needed.

But by then, she was firing.

"*Tekeli-li!*"

They were all firing.

As something from hell itself charged them.

8

The creature was nothing right, nothing sane.

It could not *be* real. It was beyond. Beyond possibility. Beyond comprehension. Spears screamed because her mind rebelled at its reality. Even knowing that there was something alien and dangerous down there, anticipation could never prepare her, or anyone, for the reality of it. In all the years since mankind began contemplating the stars as destinations rather than mere lights, and in the centuries since humans took their first hesitant and daring steps beyond the fragile envelope of Earth's atmosphere, no alien thing had ever been found. Or proved. Not in the cold and radioactive regolith of Mars. Not in Luna's craters or the icy subterranean oceans of Europa, Ganymede, Io, or Titan.

Nowhere.

Man had never found a trace. Not one.

The belief in extraterrestrial life was a flickering candle, making the whole of the infinite universe so much colder and lonely.

Now all of that was shattered. Gone. Torn to red rags.

The monster—no other word could hope to describe it—was as big as a skimmer. It was a formless and ever-changing complexity of protoplasmic bubbles that glowed with wicked crimson luminosity beneath the stygian skin. Spears's mind rebelled at everything about it. It had no head. Not really. Lumps formed all over its body—and Spears gaped in disgust and horror because each lump twisted into the shape of a face. The members of Venture TeamII, devoid of helmets. Their eyes were wide but unseeing, mouths opened in silent screams of bottomless agony.

All across the bulk of the thing, other eyes appeared. Singly or in clusters, leering and glaring, coming and going with grotesque rapidity, and each glowing with a vile green light.

It rolled across the icy floor, sometimes just a tumble of mass in motion, then feet would appear. Feet of a kind. They were extrusions of glistening dark flesh that formed and reformed, the sounds of each impact like the slap of a wet palm on bare skin. The mass trembled like the bloated belly of a diseased hippopotamus. Things like arms but devoid of fingers or hands reached out, pawing at the air. A jellylike mucus formed on its hide.

In her years as a soldier in the Army Rangers and later as a top-market agent for a private military contractor, Spears had never once screamed in fear. She'd yelled when playing microgravity dunkball; she'd screamed during orgasms in bed with various lovers. She'd screamed with laughter, with delight, with excitement.

Never once in fear.

Until now.

As the thing came rushing at her, she screamed.

In fear.

In horror.

In mortal terror.

But she *moved*, too. Her scream transformed in motion from a gut reaction into a warrior's cry.

Terror is absolutely without value in the moment of crisis. Jenny Spears *knew* this. She understood it. She knew it was an emotion that tries to smash you and bind you in its complicity with the *cause* of that terror. But it is not worth anything to anyone who wants to survive. When new to a person, that is where fatal hesitation is born.

But for those who have felt terror many times—and in many places and different circumstances—they know that it cannot compete with action. Crisis strategy is born in the moment and always while a person is in motion. Once the movement starts, the subconscious discovers that there are other gears, and they shift on the fly, earning their right to survive by not being a bull's-eye painted on a wall.

Spears knew this. From a hundred fights, she knew it.

She backpedaled, eyes goggling at what she saw, but even in her shock and haste, her finger slipped inside the trigger guard. Years of training did what her shocked conscious mind could not, and the air between her and the monster was suddenly filled with blue flashes as her pulse rifle fired. The low and urgent moan of the gun filled the cavern with echoes.

The rounds punched into the shifting flesh, burning it, splashing the walls and floor with burning chunks.

A whiplike tentacle lunged from the center of the mass, the end of it turning into a stinger of some kind—a dripping barb surrounded by spiky teeth. Spears threw herself into a dive roll but felt the spike of that stinger gouge the heel of her right shoe. She tucked into a tight ball, came out of the roll, twisted around, and fired, blowing the stinger to scarlet rags. One tiny piece of it slapped the visor of her helmet, hitting with an unusually hard force that rocked her, driving her back a step.

For one moment—half a moment—Spears's head was filled with a thousand colliding images. She was in a pressure suit out in deep space. Stars burned all around her, but directly in front was a bizarre cluster of planets, each with uncountable moons. Beyond them were two suns dubbed Scylla and Charybdis. One burned with fierce white light, and the other was a smaller reddish-brown dwarf. That image was immediately overwritten by a vista of an alien world. A monstrous city of exotic design lay in ruins, and before it, covering hundreds of hectares of flat land, was a field covered by the crumpled ruins of uncountable spaceships. There was really nothing to offer scale, but Spears knew those ships were enormous, ranging from the size of a frigate to crafts a dozen times larger than the biggest military carriers. Smaller craft—fighters of some unknown kind—lay smashed among them like dead birds.

Then the image changed once more, and she stood on a cliff over a tremendous drop-off, beyond which a statue towered, impossibly high. It was manlike without being precisely human. Naked, kneeling on the shattered slopes of a long-dead volcano. The figure's back was curved as if in defeat or humility, and it struck Spears how much those two postures were alike. With head bowed, eyes cast downward, and arms raised up and out, the figure turned one empty hand to the sky. The other hand clasped the tapered base of a large vase or jar, the mouth of which was turned down toward the ground. Its stylized lid lay by the giant's knee.

And that fast, the vision was gone, and she was back in the cave. More of the tentacles appeared, thrashing wildly, and Spears fired as she stumbled backward.

A second gun opened up. A third. Another and another, until all of the Jokers were firing. Their pulse rifles had a cyclic rate of fire of twelve hundred rounds per minute; the magazines held one hundred micropulse explosive-tipped charges. Nine killers stumbled backward from the creature, firing, firing. Screaming, too.

All of them screaming. All of them aware of terror, but none of them succumbing to it.

Spears's rifle went dry. Instead of immediately swapping in a new magazine, she thrust a trembling hand into a pouch and pulled out an FG-191 fragmentation grenade.

"Frag out!" she bellowed as she tossed it.

The Jokers dove for cover behind the blocks of ice, reloading even as they dropped.

In the tight confines of the cave, the blast was enormous. There was a huge *bang*, and masses of ice and rock leaped from the walls and ceiling. The main mass of the monster flew apart, hurling dripping meat everywhere. One piece struck the ground centimeters from where Spears crouched. She looked down at it, longing to see it become dead junk.

But as soon as it landed, the piece of meat shifted its shape, extruding what looked like thorns at first, but they kept extending, becoming segmented like the legs of a spider. The thing rose up on a dozen spindly legs, hissed in a high screech, and scuttled toward her.

"Oh fuck no," she growled as she threw herself backward, rolled over her shoulder, and landed on her feet, fishing for another handgun, drawing, and firing. The projectile rounds splattered the spider, but even as the individual pieces slapped against the boulder, they reformed, becoming smaller spiders, each with a different number of legs. Some had antennae that twitched in the cold air. Others combined to become something between a snake and a centipede that was nine feet long and had smaller versions of the stinger tentacle rising from each segment.

"We can't kill these things," cried Not Larry. "Jesus Christ, it won't die."

"Fall back," growled Spears. "Back to the entrance. *Move!*"

The agents rose and hurried past her, and she drove them with shoves and slaps. They reached the entrance, but Spears was still inside. She shoved the pistol into its holster and reached into another pouch, pulling out two globes. Each had an arming switch, and Spears flicked them and tossed the P-101 nova-burst plasma grenades over her shoulder as she turned and ran.

She hit the Jokers at the entrance, bearing them down. They all fell, rolled, stumbled, got to their feet, and ran as far and as fast as they could before the grenades detonated.

There was a single second of emptiness.

Then the plasma bombs exploded. They were devastating weapons—self-igniting contained-field fusion bombs with dicyanoacetylene to maximize the exothermic effect. The most dangerous man-portable explosive device ever issued to combat troops. Nothing could endure it. The ball of fire filled every crevice, nook, and crack in the entire cavern and vaporized anything organic. The blood on the walls, the remains of Venture II, even organic materials trapped in the ancient ice.

Gone in a flash of hellish heat.

The cave itself evaporated into steam, causing a seven-million-ton chunk of the mountain to turn to slush and smash down. A wave of hot meltwater swept the Jokers off the ground and carried them with terrible force far down the slope. Cracks and fissures ripped upward and to either side of the mountain.

Spears landed hard and slid sixty meters before coming to a stop against the curved hull of the Artifact. She lay there, half-drowned, dazed, in agony, watching the mountain fall into itself like dust being pulled into a vacuum cleaner. Clouds of icy debris rose into the air and then fell with an odd and surreal slowness. Like a gentle snowfall on a country morning.

The thunder of the collapsing wall banged off every mountain in the valley and then slowly, slowly faded away.

9

Eventually, Agent Jenny Spears forced herself to sit up. It was the hardest physical action she had ever taken. Everything hurt. Some parts of her—random muscles, tendons, bones, and even her lungs—felt abused and sore. Her body felt as if it was held together only by her pressure suit.

Her mind was in pieces. The visions, the death, and … the thing she had just killed. All of it felt too big to fit into her head.

In her brain those strange words echoed over and over.

"*Tekeli-li! Tekeli-li!*"

"J-J-Jokers …" she began, tripping over it. She stopped, drew a steadying breath, and tried again. "Jokers, count off."

There was such a long, disheartening pause that new fear rose up inside her. But then she heard static and squelch as her suit's autosystems worked to repair damage.

"Sybil, give me the team channel, God damn it."

"Working," said the AI, and even she sounded damaged.

Then a voice spoke. "Moonboy on deck."

It was a faint groan, but it was a living voice. A moment later Spider called in, then Footie, Widow, Krampus, Not Larry, Mangler, and Ratjack. All eight of them. Alive. Impossibly alive.

Spears closed her eyes and tried not to cry.

"Sybil, scan for life signs."

"Scanning now." The AI took the feeds from the handful of drones that had escaped the conflagration. Spears watched the scan meter inside of her goggles. It ticked and ticked. After several unbearable moments, Sybil said, "There are no life signs detectable in the burn area."

"Confirm, God damn it. If there is one fucking gram of that thing—"

"There are no life signs detectable," repeated Sybil. "I am tracking carbon residue consistent with the estimated total mass of the phenomenon and the members of Venture II."

That was the first time Jenny Spears felt she could take a breath.

Getting to her feet took most of what little strength she still had. Once up, she stood swaying, sweat running in cold lines down her face and inside her clothing. She felt cold on her face and realized that her goggles were cracked.

Spears pulled her cowl and goggles off and stood there, letting the frigid air slap her back to full awareness.

Movement caught her eye, and she turned to see Spider staggering toward her. Moonboy and Not Larry came next, with a dazed Ratjack leaning on their shoulders.

One by one, the Jokers formed on her. Their combat rigs were torn, seared, and mostly ruined. Widow carried a pulse rifle whose barrel was a drooping piece of metal slag. When the soldier realized it, she let the gun fall.

Around and beneath them, the meltwater was already starting to freeze.

Spears turned slowly and looked at the exposed section of the Aartifact. The star-shaped doorway was black and uninformative, and she did not like that one bit.

"Footie," she said, summoning Jirayut Tatsanasomboon, a slender Thai who had once run with that country's elite Exo-Corps, a division of their special forces that worked the asteroid belt between Mars and Jupiter. "We have any Hadrian X9?"

"Plenty of it," said Footie. "What do you want to use it for?"

"Take a guess."

He looked at the open door. "You know that stuff flash-welds, right? Can't pull it off. They'd have to cut the whole section of the hull out to get inside."

"What a shame," said Spears.

Footie chuckled and hurried over to the skimmer, returning in a few seconds with two rolls of what looked like the kind of black plastic they used to use as a weather membrane beneath roofing tiles. He nodded to Spears and crept close to the Artifact. Not Larry followed quickly. They took the rolls of material and, moving very quickly, covered the doorway while Moonboy and Dillie Kanaka—Krampus—covered them with pulse rifles. The material was both magnetic and covered with an ultrafast-hardening epoxy designed for rapid application in combat situations. Within a minute the entire door was coated with two layers of it. Footie stepped back.

"Sybil," he said, "hard seal. Double thick. No air pockets."

The AI sent the correct signals to the network of wires and detonation cord molded into the fabric. There was very little sound, but the material puffed out to about five centimeters, shimmered for a moment, and then settled into a dull charcoal flatness. Not Larry stepped up and banged his fist on it. There was a heavy thud but no answering echo from inside.

They joined the others in a half circle around Spears. She looked at them. "Back in the cave, did anyone have a blackout moment?"

"Blackout?" asked Krampus.

"Did you see anything that wasn't there?" said Spears irritably. "A vision. A dream, nightmare, whatever?"

They shook their heads.

Spider stepped close, eyeing her with the compassion that defined the big man. "Are you saying you did?"

"I … Shit, I don't know." Spears took a deep breath, held it, and let it out very slowly, using that small action of bodily control to try to calm her nerves. It worked, but only a little. "Let's get back to the skimmer."

As they turned to go, Sybil spoke up. "Lifeguard," said the AI, "there is a request for you to switch to the command channel."

Spears did that, and Colonel Hobart's voice was in her ear, asking if she and her team were okay, wanting to know what had happened.

"Give me a sitrep," he demanded.

She did. Between gasps of pain and with ragged breath, she told him.

Before Hobart could reply, Dr. Brollachan's voice cut in. "I need you to reenter the cave and collect samples of the … the …"

"Say it, Doc. The *alien*."

"Very well," said the SPU chief, strain almost humming in his tone. "Collect any remaining samples of the alien. Tissue of any kind, no matter how small."

All of the Jokers were on the channel, too. They stared at Spears with a variety of emotions—anger, disgust, shock.

"Doc," said Spears, "just checking here. Were you able to see the drone feeds when that thing attacked us?"

"Of course."

"Then you saw what happened when I blew chunks out of it, right? Every single piece of that fucking thing was autonomous."

"I am aware."

"And, to be clear, you think it's a good idea to bring some of it *back*?"

"Of course we want it," Brollachan shot back. He sounded profoundly surprised by her question. "This is more than historic. This is the *most* important find in scientific history."

"So everyone keeps saying," Spears said. "But just so we're all on the same page here, that piece of history just killed six soldiers and goddamn near killed me and my guys."

"You're soldiers," said Brollachan.

Spider winced. Not Larry closed his eyes and shook his head. Ratjack made a masturbatory move with his right hand. The others merely looked outraged.

"Gimme a sec, Doc," Spears told Brollachan.

She closed out of the comms completely and signaled to her people for a real-voice conversation. They nodded and clicked off their comms as well.

"You heard that shit, right?"

"Heard, yes," said Lisa Red—call sign Widow—a blocky woman with a shaved head and wildflowers tattooed over every centimeter of her scalp. "Having a little bit of a hard time believing it, though."

"Boss," said Spider, "Brollachan's king shit up there."

"Yeah. And . . . ?"

Spider grinned, reached into a pouch, and handed her the two P-101s he carried. "And fuck him sideways."

"Game on," agreed the others.

Spears took the plasma grenades. "You always bring me the nicest presents, Spider. Your mama would be proud."

"Aim to please," said Spider.

Spears weighed the bombs in her hands. They were heavy, but it was a comforting weight. "Okay," she said, "everyone get back to the skimmer. I'm going to set these for a ten-second delay. I want our asses in the air in five seconds, feel me?"

They smiled like a pack of brigands.

"Let's give them a show," she said. "All drone cameras on the blast site."

"On it," said Spider, sending the signals. The remaining drones formed a circle above what had been the cave. He turned on bio scans, thermals, infrared, ground-penetrating radar, and every other sensor. "Good to go."

Spears tapped back into her comms. "Lifeguard to Dr. Brollachan."

"I'm here," he said testily. "Please fetch me my samples. This is a direct order."

"Actually, Doc, I have your samples right here," Spears said, and then she threw the grenades.

She immediately whirled and ran as fast as she could, reaching the skimmer just as it was beginning to rise.

"*Go, go, go!*"

Widow was at the controls, and she slammed the joystick hard over and shoved it forward. The craft leaped into the air, rising fast as the thrusters growled. The skimmer was just fast enough to outrun the collapse of the rest of that part of the mountain.

The fireball was like hell's hot breath, and they fled before it.

Part Ten
The Night-Comers

"Yet, mad am I not—and very surely do I not dream."

—*Edgar Allan Poe*

Asphodel Station
The Shadderal Star System

1

Lars Soren sat for a long time on the edge of his bed, both unable and unwilling to sleep.

Over the last few nights—ever since the NecroTeks flew off on their mission—his sleep pattern had cracked apart. That bothered him because sleep was always easy for him. And he had lots of tricks to lull his busy mind into a place of relative stillness, allowing fatigue and relaxation to take him down. On those rare encounters with insomnia, Soren retreated into his version of Cicero's loci—though instead of a memory palace, he had a library of them.

He would visualize an idealized version of the vast library in his parent's estate in Greece, and over time he created mnemonics based on precise visualizations of walls and room sizes, of specific areas of interest, and even art on the wall. His memory library was huge, and wandering through it the way a loving and detail-oriented master librarian would was how he restored order to his jangled thoughts and settled into sleep.

Lately, no version of this strategy seemed able to get him out of the thornbushes of worry, overthinking, stress, and doubt. He considered a nice balloon of brandy and got as far as pouring it but then relented and returned the liquid to the bottle. That was a cheap way out, and he did not want to follow in Delia Trumbo's footsteps. She was a bit overfond of drink, and it was beginning to show at times.

Soren liked wine and other spirits, but he disliked being drunk. He even found a mild buzz hugely irritating and diminishing. One of his few personal triggers was a fear of losing mental clarity. Vain, he knew, but nonetheless, he would rather be the only sober person at a bacchanal than allow himself to descend into excess, sloth, and bad behavior.

So alcohol was not his solution on those sleepless nights.

Pills were never a choice for him.

After nearly a week of poor sleep and the resulting brain fog the next day, he tried going to the gym before bedtime. Never much of a runner, he preferred the relative dignity of a stationary cycle, but one positioned in a VR pod so he could bike along the edge of Lake Orchid in Albania, the stunning Kinderdijk Cycle Route, the Netherlands, or—his personal favorite—the lush and gorgeous Chapel Loop in Provence.

That helped, and after the first ninety-minute session, he shambled back to his room, showered, pulled on pajamas, crawled into bed, and was gone in seconds.

And dreamed of monsters.

He sank into sleep, and as so often happened with him, Soren was aware that he was both asleep and entering the land of dreams. This had been part of his psychological makeup since those lonely years of near isolation as a child on that estate, with indifferent parents who were rarely home and no siblings. Back then he learned how to stay aware and lucid while he dreamed, a feat that allowed him to explore his subconscious with agency and discernment.

But that was no blessing when the bad dreams began.

Soren rose from his bed and paused, turning to look back at his sleeping self. All around him the air swirled with constellations of dust motes.

Then he turned away.

His bedroom was at the end of the hall, and he walked that way, pausing to jiggle the knob of a closed door. It felt strangely warm and slightly moist, almost like flesh. He recoiled, jerking his hand away.

Soren did not want to try again, but even though he was aware of what was happening in his dreams, he was not in actual control. He watched his hand move toward the knob again. Close around it. Felt that warm moisture on what should have been cold, dry metal. Turned it and heard a faint click.

The door swung inward a little, just wide enough for a breeze to come out like a sigh. He felt it on his face. It smelled like dust and dying weeds—stale but not dead. There was a fecund quality to it, like a potter's table in a greenhouse. A quality like soil aching for seed. A rich aroma that was not at all healthy.

"Something in there is dead," he said, and knew at once that his comment was both incorrect and naive. Whatever was in there could not properly be defined by any concept as shallow as death.

He held the knob, unable to let go because the room needed him to enter.

"No," said Soren, but he pushed the door open anyway.

Inside, cloaked in shadow, something moved. There was a soft, stealthy sound.

"Who … who are you?" he asked.

That's what he intended to say. It was not what his ears heard. The words he actually said were "What are you?"

And the thing on the bed laughed. Low. Darkly amused. Unpleasant. Very aware.

It rose from the bed and moved to the edge of a pool of moonlight that spilled through a gap in the dusty curtains. It did not step directly into the light but was silhouetted against it. The thing was manlike, but not in any good or comforting way. Naked, with smooth, oily skin, pale and mottled like the flesh of a diseased whale but with two huge membranes attached from mid-thighs to each shoulder and flaring outward like the leathery wings of some gigantic bat. The head tapered from a round skull down to a pointed chin, with deep-set eyes and high cheekbones that gave it a saturnine quality, and a cruel yet sensual mouth with very red lips and too many sharp teeth. A pair of horns curled down from its temples nearly to the chin.

Soren felt a towering and atavistic horror rise up in him. This was not merely a monster; it was the devil. It was a vampire. It was a gargoyle from some desanctified church.

This was Evil as a concept presented in the flesh, and its hunger for him—for blood and life force and soul—was overpowering.

Soren tried to scream, but the sight of that monster stole his voice.

He tried, though. He kept trying to scream as the night went on and on and the monster did dreadful things to him, body and soul.

When Soren woke at the first moment of Asphodel Station's subjective "dawn," he found himself out of bed, across the room, behind the closed door of his closet. He huddled on the floor, naked, drenched with sweat, shivering with fear.

The dream tried to fade.

It almost did.

With what little strength he had left, Lars Soren grabbed what fragments he could and shoved them into a niche in the library of his mind.

Then he crawled out of the closet and into the bathroom to throw up.

2

Even with the power of alien tech, it took the NecroTeks—Asphodel's new Guardian Angels—five days to reach the second largest of the planets in the Shadderal system, just over two hundred thousand kilometers from Asphodel. Like most of the planets and moons, this one had an unpronounceable name in Lost's ancient tongue and a more utilitarian one assigned to it by the humans now living in the neighborhood. Shadderal was technically S1, the other worlds also having sequential S designations. Moons followed the same system in miniature, inheriting their planet's designation but adding a sequential M term. S2, the planet they had just reached, had fifteen moons: S2M1 to S2M15.

"Who gets to name these things?" asked Jahziel Yaakv—call sign Jericho. "'Cause if it's up for grabs, I want dibs on that green moon."

S2M6 was about a third the size of Luna and was colored a vibrant green. At first they hoped it was from vegetation, but as they did a flyby on their approach to S2, it became obvious that the surface was densely covered with crystals in various green shades.

"Those nerds in stellar cartography usually have first pick," said Galahad.

"They ain't here," countered Jericho.

"Sybil," said Bianca, "what kind of rocks are we seeing?"

Sybil cycled through her scans, collating data from each of the NecroTeks. "There are several known forms of quartz and other rocks, including aventurine, malachite, dioptase, peridot, ammolite, garnet, tourmaline, moldavite, calcite, agate, fluorite, green quartz, prehnite, and emerald."

"Emerald?" said Jericho, Lucky, and Sundance all at the same time.

"Emerald in what quantity?" asked Boris Vijenko—Lovechild.

Sybil gave a set of coordinates. "That mountain is eleven thousand meters high," said the AI, "and it is composed of 84.7 percent emerald. Of which, I estimate that 54 percent is gem quality."

"We're rich!" laughed Matthew Walker—Ventum. "Now we can go to the mall and spend the whole day."

They all laughed. Given their circumstances—too far from Earth and actually dead—the levity was somewhere between absurd and tragic.

Bianca laughed anyway.

They used the moon's gravity to turn and then settled into a pattern of slingshot maneuvers around the planet and several moons, giving Sybil time to run deep scans.

"You find anything weird and shoggothy," she told the AI, "sing out."

"I am always alert for anything shoggothy," said Sybil.

Bianca was amused at the slow but definite changes to the AI's personality. After the WarpLine incident and the attempt by a shoggoth to overwhelm and hack Sybil, Lost had stepped in and worked with Sybil to free herself. Something in that process—or perhaps as part of the overall twisting of known reality—Sybil had begun to change. Her learning software had guardrails in the form of limited subroutines, but those had crumbled, and now Sybil was approaching actual consciousness.

Approaching, according to the computer team on Asphodel. Bianca rather thought Sybil had arrived. Her sense of humor, though subtle, was there. Other emotions seemed to be presenting as well.

"Okay, guys," Bianca said. "Let's split into pairs. You all know your teams. Search pattern Delta. You see anything—"

"See something, say something, yeah, yeah," said Thunder Bear.

"Don't make me come over there," she warned.

"You can—" began Thunder Bear, but Sybil cut him off.

"Team alert," she said crisply. "Sensors detecting something metallic in a decaying orbit around the planet's south pole."

"Details," ordered Bianca, immediately changing course to head that way. She rose away from the planet to reduce atmospheric friction, and the rest of the NecroTeks followed.

"The object is a ship," said Sybil. "Shoggoth design. A Medusa-class mother ship."

"Weapons hot," snapped Bianca, and instantly manifested cannons on her shoulders and upper back, shifting mass from nonessential areas to create the weapons. All the others did the same as they soared down to the bottom of the strange world. "Two-by-two cover formation."

It was without doubt a Medusa.

But it was dead.

The gigantic craft was eight times as big as Atlas-class carriers back on Earth; its main body as round as an oil drum but flattened, with a bulging middle that was set with scores of launch tubes for daggers. Long articulated limbs extended from the hull, making the thing look like an unholy hybrid of octopus and horseshoe crab. The gaping maws of more than a hundred huge ion cannons pointed out and up and down in every direction.

Those cannon mouths were dark, though, and there were no lights of any kind visible on the Medusa. The tentacles drifted aimlessly amid debris from the many huge impact points all over its hull. As it drifted, a kind of tail followed it—numberless bits of debris, some of which looked like parts of dagger fighters. And floating, shapeless masses of frozen black flesh.

Bianca kept her weapons online as she approached, but it was clear that this monstrosity was dead. Completely dead.

They split up and studied it from every angle, training Sybil's sophisticated sensors on it. Each of them sending information to the group.

"Hell of a lot of missile and pulse-round hits," said Galahad.

"Count eighty-seven daggers in the drift," observed Bo Chow—Beezer. "Maybe parts for three, four hundred more."

"Radiation signatures on the blast points are coming up as unknown," said Ian Potts—Tank. "Doesn't match us, the tumblers, the station's cannons, or the shoggoths. Doesn't match anything we have data on."

"That is correct, Tank," said Sybil. "The radiation signature on all weapons hits is of an unknown kind. I will begin a file."

"What the hell happened out here, boss?" asked Chance Thompson—Lucky.

Bianca circled the Medusa several times without commenting. Galahad flew with her. Even now, even in death and the bizarre resurrection of *ethla*, she still felt him. Felt his love. Felt hers for him. As if somehow reading her mind, Galahad turned his robot face toward her and, just for a moment, manifested his human features over it. He gave her a brief smile before becoming machinelike again.

I love you, she thought. Trying to send that message to him.

Below her, the Medusa continued its slow decaying orbit.

"Spread out and look for other debris," she said. "We sure as hell didn't do this. So if there's someone else out here taking shoggoth scalps, we need to know about it."

"If we have someone out here doing that," said Thunder Bear, "I want to give him a shoulder massage and buy him a puppy."

"Hell," said Voula Achilleos—Spartan, "I'll give him a blow job."

"Ewww … and dead robot sex jokes are now a thing," complained Beezer.

"We don't know if the enemy of our enemy is actually our friend," cautioned Bianca. "We're still learning the rules out here."

They flew on, scanning everything, mapping everything, and finding no answers at all. Eventually, Bianca called a halt to the search, and the Guardian Angels veered away from S2 and flew deeper into the vast star system that was their extended home.

3

Lost did not have a true body. Not in many thousands of years.

The shapes he took—his golem forms—were done for convenience so that he could be seen and heard. He used old space suits mostly, because *ethla* allowed him to interface with machinery and the radios gave him a voice.

When he did not need to interact with Lars Soren or the other humans, he let his golem form fall away and allowed the wind to have its way with him. Radiation did not harm him or his fading soul when he was incorporeal. But doing this did reinforce the awareness that he was a ghost, an invisible spirit.

That he was very close to nothing at all.

With the coming of Asphodel Station, there came, too, a new sense of structure. Humans needed some recognizable framework of time for their comfort and health. They imposed a structure based on Earth's—days of twenty-four hours, each hour of sixty minutes made up of sixty seconds. This system came with an assumed day and night.

During the "day," most of the inhabitants of Asphodel were awake and active. Lost found it entertaining and somewhat soothing to watch them, even though he did this in his spiritual, unseen form—as an observer only. Learning more about them than Sybil's data banks could tell. He rarely took physical form unless it was important.

The nights were awful. Before the arrival of human beings, night and day had lost all meaning for Lost. Now, when Asphodel's subjective night limited the interaction with the Earthers, nighttime silences had become something he dreaded. They were very dark, and those new "hours" crawled by so slowly that Lost felt each minute, each second, drag itself across the landscape of his awareness.

Lost was in the wind now. Riding it without form, without substance, and yet the wind pushed him wherever it wanted. Even he did not understand how this worked. It was like having a thought stirred by a breeze.

He could also feel some things, even when in purely spiritual form.

Lost felt the cold.

It was always cold where he was. It was always cold being *what* he was. The coldness of being forgotten. A kind of sensory connection to despair and loss and aloneness that had become more keenly felt since the arrival of the humans from Earth.

Though he had felt it before. Over the last two orbits around the twin suns, as the planets and moons proceeded through their slow dance, he had felt flashes of cold. Never for long, but very certainly not imagined. The first time was a shock to him, waking him from whatever the dream state of a ghost should be called. It was as if the heart of this star system had suddenly pulsed. It had been very powerful and had torn him out of his dreams and into the now. He gathered a golem body together and stood in it, looking up at the sky.

His ghost was irrevocably tied to the planet Shadderal. He did not even know he could leave its surface until later, when Lars Soren and Asphodel had appeared. Somehow the desperate cry of despair from the AI, Sybil, had called him from the planet and across the void to the newly arrived station. It was his first trip offworld since he had brought his damaged star-fighter back home during the final battle of his lifetime.

Suddenly he was aboard a space station, one created by an alien race from across the sea of stars that was the Milky Way. He had met Sybil, bonded with her, and found purpose again in helping her fight off the shoggoth.

Then he encountered Lars Soren, a fantastical figure he'd met many times in dreams. That meeting changed everything for Lost. He had actual conversations with minds other than his own. He listened, and he was heard. He interacted in meaningful ways. If he had been capable of tears, he would have wept—and deeply—for eternity is hell to the disembodied.

That meeting, those connections, were gifts from gods whom he had long since stopped worshipping.

But now, as he flew on winds across the landscape of poor, dying Shadderal, he remembered those other times he had felt the same kind of energy, the same "aliveness" he now felt. What had caused it then? Was it some kind of temporal warping sending him glimpses of what would become the WarpLine disaster?

Lost thought it likely, but he wasn't certain.

As he drifted, he wondered if, somehow, other humans had come out here before Asphodel. That's what it felt like when viewed through the filter of current knowledge of human contact.

It remained a mystery as he flew like a fading memory across the world that was once his home. The world where he, and everyone he ever loved, had died.

As Lost blew on the wings of the wind, eyes watched him from low orbit. The ship was invisible by design, its technology serving the emotional and strategic needs of the occupant to remain unseen, unknown, and unknowable.

A sensor panel aboard the ship was tuned very precisely to track the electromagnetic and kinetic energy signatures of organic—and formerly organic—life. It was not difficult to find the frequency of so old and powerful a spirit as Lost. His connection to *ethla* made him shine on the otherwise dark sensor screen.

The watcher watched with cold eyes and a colder mind. And with the pernicious patience of something that delighted in the hunt nearly as much as the delicious glory of the kill.

Part Eleven
Take My Breath Away

"Tyger Tyger burning bright,
In the forests of the night:
What immortal hand or eye,
Dare frame thy fearful symmetry?"

—William Blake

Joint MIT/UCLA Biological Research Field Station #8
Queen Maud Land, Antarctica

1

The Jokers stood in a straight line at parade rest. They were PMCs and were not required to stand at attention or salute.

Agent Jenny Spears stood a couple of meters in front of them, her face impassive as Dr. Brollachan yelled at her. He was very loud. He was erudite in his rage, though at times his diction failed and he sputtered, spit flying from his lips. His face had gone from a deathly pallor to a furious purple red. Veins stood out on his neck; one rose from between his eyebrows and vanished into the scientist's hair, throbbing menacingly.

Spears wondered how long Brollachan could do this before he stroked out.

She stood with her hands behind her back, gut tight, making herself breathe normally. Or as close to it as she could manage.

Colonel Hobart stood nearby, but he was strangely silent, allowing Brollachan to levy as much verbal abuse as he wanted. Beyond him, several members of the senior staff—theirs and Evie Cronin's—huddled at the back of the room, forgotten in the moment by everyone. Spears saw them, though. She caught Evie's eyes and saw the science team leader's face go from shock to outrage at what Brollachan was saying, then undergo a subtle and unhurried transformation to the point that a very small secret smile formed on her lips.

It took a lot for Spears not to smile back, but she did manage a tiny nod.

An ally, she mused. *Not one of Brollachan's creatures.*

Brollachan made a lot of threats, but Spears did not really care. This was a paid gig, and even though the SPU chief threatened to have her blackballed, it was all as good as hollow. If the US military canceled her contract, Spears knew of at least a dozen other countries—not to mention four times that many corporations—who would snatch her up. The Jokers' reputation was built on facts.

When Brollachan finally paused to take a breath, Spears took a sharp step forward and got up in his face.

"Here's the thing, Doc," she said quietly. "First, fuck you. Second, *fuck* you."

"Who the hell do you—"

"Shut up," snapped Spears, sharp and brutal as an open-handed blow. It slapped Brollachan to a shocked silence. "You had your say. Now it's my turn."

Out of the corner of her eye, Spears saw Hobart wince as if kicked, but he did not interrupt. Not after the fierce glare she shot him. *Just fucking don't*, it said, with no invitation for debate.

Aloud, Spears said, "You brought my team here for a rescue gig. Turns out there was no possible chance of a rescue. Venture II was dead before we even got the colonel's call. By the time we got down there, that ... *thing* ... had consumed them. Hear that and try to process it. *It. Consumed. Them.* Whatever it is, it is the single most dangerous thing I've ever seen, and me and my guys tore down that transgenics lab on Yolcan Station. Those genetic freaks there were nothing to what we saw today. That thing was more than a chameleon—it was a shape-shifter. Every motherfucking cell of it seemed self-governing. It pretended to be Lance Corporal Figari. It spoke in his voice. Maybe it even had his memories."

"We don't know that for certain," interrupted Brollachan.

"You heard and saw what we did. All that shit about being slaves? That weird birdcall or whatever? And his mouth wasn't even moving when he spoke. That wasn't Lance Corporal Figari, and you fucking well know it. That was the thing from the ship, and it was out of its mind. It killed Venture II and probably that poor kid, Mac. It tried to kill us. Slave or not, it wanted us dead. Or … worse."

"You have no idea—"

Spears held up a warning finger, and the SPU chief fell silent. "Now," she said, "I know you're upset about losing your new pet, but if we'd brought some of it here, then you, the colonel, Professor Evie, the entire staff, and maybe the whole fucking world would be dead. *I* would be dead, and I don't want to die. Neither does my team."

"Game on," said Spider, very quietly. His big hands rested on the butt of his holstered pistol.

Brollachan tried to cut in, but Spears overrode him again. "I was on deck, and I made the call. That's part of my job. If that was a bioweapon leak and Venture was infected with COVID-144 or the nanites with the new strain of Ebola, I'd have bagged and tagged him and, sure, brought them up and handed them over to your little team of mad scientists. Done that kind of thing more times than you've had blowjobs. But this was an alien monster who can change shape. If we smashed it into ten thousand pieces, there would be ten thousand monsters, and I think we all know where it got its mass from. Surely you can work out the risk-reward on that, Doc."

Evie felt a wave of dread fill every cell of her body—hearing it firsthand from Spears made it all far too real. She felt faint and swayed a bit as she stood there, the fingers of one hand over her mouth. The other hand touched the shape of the flask in her pocket.

"You could have secured a sample for safe transport," said Brollachan stubbornly.

"No, Doc, we couldn't," countered Spears. "We didn't have gear for that because we were brought in for a biohazard gig. One lump of that crap hit my visor—just touched it—and I was having all kinds of crazy-ass visions. Must have some kind of psychic ability. If one gobbet of that shit can do that, imagine what a *lot* of it can do. And between you and me, Doc, I don't know what's scarier—that ESP shit or the fact that it doesn't only imitate whatever it eats, but it takes memories, too. It spoke in that soldier's voice. Bring it up here? Shit on toast. Maybe if you weren't so far up your own ass, you'd have thought it through. You didn't. You were hasty and greedy, so this is on *you*."

She punctuated it with a jab of one stiffened finger in the center of the SPU chief's chest. He made a feeble attempt to slap her hand away, but she withdrew it too quickly.

"Don't you dare touch me, you piece of—"

And Spears clamped a hand around his throat, cutting off his air. Hobart's soldiers lunged forward, but the Jokers went from parade rest to a combat circle around Spears and Brollachan so fast that they froze the scene.

"Spears," cried an outraged Hobart. "Release him at once."

She ignored him.

"Listen very carefully, *Doctor* Brollachan," said Spears in a deadly whisper. She could feel a smile forming on her mouth but had no idea what it looked like. Brollachan seemed to wither as the smile bloomed, though. "If this was just an ordinary fuckup, I'd put in a chit for bonus pay and call it a day. This isn't. This was very nearly apocalyptic, and I use that word with precision."

The doctor clawed at the hand around his throat but could not remove it. His purple face was turning black with angry red starbursts here and there. The scientist's eyes were beginning to glaze at the edge of consciousness.

"You are supposed to be a super genius," Spears said. "Personally, I'm finding that hard to believe. Even *now*, I don't know if you grasp the enormity of what almost happened. *I* do. My team does. And probably everyone else in the room does. So you'd better reach into your ass and pull out a clue, you cocksucker."

She released him with a shove that sent him staggering back into Hobart's arms. The doctor rebounded and fell to his knees. Hobart began to help him up, and Brollachan slapped his hands away and climbed shakily to his feet.

The colonel glared at her. "You're out of line, Agent Spears. You are dismissed, and I want you and your team out of here right goddamn now."

"Leave? Now? Oh, no, no, no." Still smiling, Spears walked over to him. "Here's how things are going to go, Colonel. You brought us here, and this dickhead nearly killed the world. The risk isn't gone. We killed one of those things, but that ship is three klicks long. Can you even calculate how many of those things might still be aboard? Can you stop emoting long enough to think of how close we are to the actual edge here?"

Hobart seemed to struggle to keep his eyes locked on hers.

"Me and my guys aren't going anywhere," said Spears. "No fucking way. We are going to stay right here, and I am taking charge of overall security."

"By what authority?"

Her draw was so shockingly fast that her gun barrel was a cold threat against the flesh beneath Hobart's left eye before any of the soldiers could react. Hobart froze. Evie Cronin gasped in new fear. A few others in the crowd cried out as well.

Agent Spears showed a lot of white teeth. The lightning-shaped scar on her face flared an angry red. "How's this for authority?"

To his credit, Hobart did not flinch or wither. "What gives you the right to do this?"

"Let's see … how about the fact that I am a concerned citizen of planet Earth? Maybe the only person who is thinking about the implications. Did I not mention the word *apocalypse* here?"

Despite his fear, Brollachan sneered at her. "We'll have an entire battalion here by dawn."

Spears said, "Bring all the troops you want. If they come looking for a fight, we'll burn them out of the sky. You think we're spooked by *your* guys? *Please.* There's a reason the colonel called us in. *We're* the ones you call when it's too big for anyone else." She pointed to where her team's stack of crates had been offloaded from the suborbital transport. "We have enough things that go *boom* to defend this place against until I decide it's safe. Go on, tell me I'm wrong."

Brollachan said nothing.

"Damn right," said Spears. She looked around. "Until I am positive this shit show is playing by the rules of common goddamn sense, the Jokers aren't going anywhere."

"You can't enforce that," said Brollachan.

"Can't I? This is Antarctica, Doc. Colonel Hobart is here illegally. The United States has no more authority here than does any other country. That agreement has stood since the middle of the twentieth century, and given the enormous importance of this find, it's not likely to change. You should never have tried to make a grab for something like this just for America. Thought we left that kind of entitled presumptuousness behind us at the end of the 2090s. Sorry to see I'm wrong." Spears pointed to the platform and the valley beyond. "This news—that artifact—belongs to the world. This isn't political, for Christ's sake—it's existential. There has never been a more crucial time for everyone to work together and to do everything right—so we can, frankly, survive this. No haste. No bullshit shortcuts like what you tried to pull here with your soldiers and then us."

Evie spoke up, surprising everyone. "Ms. Spears," she said, "I agree with most of what you're saying, but they do have a point about security. We can't just drop this all on the world. Besides the very real potential threat, think of the impact on every world religion and what that will do to geopolitics. This is too big. It has to be handled."

Spears considered and nodded. "Then it should be handled jointly by every nation that has a space program. Or, at the very least, the signatories to the Stellar Security Council."

"It's *our* find," said Brollachan weakly.

Spears pointed to him while looking at Hobart and Evie. "And that's the kind of thinking that will get us all killed." Spears shook her head. "I'm not asking you jackasses to make those calls. I'm *telling* you how it's going to be. All the key players need to be in on this. If you try to force it and call in the cavalry, you're both fools. It needs to be all or none. If you don't believe that, I can make one call and the leaders of *forty* nations will send their armies. So tell me, Doc, do you want to do your research, or do you want to start a war?"

"You're bluffing."

"No," said Hobart, stepping away from Brollachan. "She's not."

Spears lowered her pistol but did not holster it.

"I'm really not."

2

Evie Cronin saw the acceptance of the new truth on the faces of Hobart and many of his soldiers. She watched Brollachan gradually lose the dangerous color in his face, though he still glowed red with anger and humiliation. His body seemed to hunch beneath the weight of his frustration.

Slowly, *slowly*, Dr. Torquil Brollachan pulled together the pieces of his shattered dignity and self-control. He straightened by degrees until he stood tall. Everyone watched him.

He walked a few steps, going to the platform rail and looking over and down. His shoulders rose and fell in a sigh, then he nodded to himself and turned back. He looked at the Jokers and then at Spears.

"You are entirely right, of course," said the scientist quietly.

Spears blinked in surprise. "Wait … *what*?"

"You are correct," repeated Brollachan.

Spears cupped a hand behind one ear. "Maybe the grenades I tossed are making my hearing all wonky. Repeat that one more time."

"I am in the wrong here," said Brollachan. "Inarguably in the wrong. I allowed the excitement—the *enormity*—of this find to warp my judgment. You did the right thing by using those bombs. You did the smart thing. You were on the ground and made a call. I—*we*—are up here, at a safe distance. It was a painful call, given the potential losses to science, but it was the right one. I accept that, and I apologize. I apologize to you, to your team, and to everyone here. There is no excuse for my actions. I was wrong."

He raised his hand and held it toward Spears.

Evie realized that she was holding her breath and let it out very quietly. The crowd that surrounded this tableau looked shocked and surprised. A few wore curious and uncertain smiles. The Jokers' faces might as well have been carved from rock, but Hobart's eyes were bright.

Jenny Spears once more stepped close to Brollachan. Her eyes searched his for several seconds.

"Well fuck me up, down, and sideways," she breathed.

Then she took the proffered hand.

For some reason that Evie was never after able to understand, the gathered people broke into applause. The only ones who did not clap were Colonel Hobart and the Jokers. But they nodded.

When Brollachan released Spears's hand, he turned to Hobart. "Colonel, if you have no objections, I would like to extend the contract for Agent Spears's team. I will approve the funds."

"Very well," said Hobart, though it sounded like those two words were pulled from his mouth with pliers. He cleared his throat and to Spears said, "We need you here. Would you please join our team?"

"In what capacity, exactly?" asked Spears, making it a challenge.

Brollachan smiled, rueful and a bit embarrassed. "Voice of reason?" he suggested.

"With a gun," suggested Spears.

"Well-armed voice of reason," Brollachan amended.

Spears laughed. "Game on."

3

Spears went into action.

She paired each of the Jokers with a soldier handpicked by Hobart to establish a perimeter. Sybil was tasked with creating a network of all the military and dig-site drones to patrol the entire length of the Artifact, using ground-penetrating radar to look for more of the star-shaped doors. A thousand mouse-sized crawler drones were released, each one with a deep-view belly scope that shot sound waves and other sensors down through the ice to scan for any active organic life that might have survived the grenades.

So far, their telemetry was clean, and gradually everyone in camp began to breathe more normally. The sensors worked day and night without pause because the reality of what the Jokers encountered had finally sunk in.

Hobart and Brollachan were in round-the-clock holo-vid meetings with the president and his cadre of scientific advisers.

Not Larry and Spider oversaw the placement of a series of plasma grenades all along the exposed section of the hull, and Hobart ordered more of them, along with short-range shock cannons, A224 surface-to-surface missiles, and more SPU troops. All of which was delivered within ten hours by suborbital shuttles.

A second wave of shuttles brought a fabrication team to build dozens of new shelters, erect security towers, set up the blockers that would keep satellites from viewing the site, and more. A thousand tasks lay before them, but within a week the population of the site had tripled.

4

While all of this was taking place, Evie kept returning to the platform, just looking down at the craft. The sight of it kept drawing her, and sometimes hours passed before she realized it. Her mind was like a computer running too many programs at once.

One of those programs was grief. For Mac and for the soldiers.

She hadn't known the soldiers on Venture II, but Mac was part of her team, and Shijun Xi a colleague. They'd met a half dozen times at academic events, and she'd even contributed a chapter to one of Xi's many books. They were not exactly friends, but the pain and loss were there, and it was real.

First victims of alien aggression, she mused, and hoped they weren't the first casualties in an interstellar war. She wondered if the alien from the Artifact had intended to do harm or if its actions were merely defensive and confused. After all, it had likely awakened from millions of years of cryo-sleep. In human terms, anything more than sixteen months of frozen sleep was known to cause cellular damage and some loss of mental acuity. What then would be the result of all those *millions* of years? Maybe the actions of the creature were accidental and unintentionally violent in the same way that patients coming out of anesthesia were sometimes confused, panicky, and dangerous.

What complicated things for her was that every night she drifted between insomnia and terrible dreams. The tentacle dream she'd had a few days before the Artifact returned now took on the eerie quality of prophecy. When she mentioned this to Brollachan, it seemed to disturb him.

"Could it be the psychic quality Agent Spears encountered?" she asked him.

"At this point, Evie," he said wearily, "it's fair to say that anything is possible."

His piercing gaze roved over her face. "You didn't actually touch anything down at the Artifact, did you?"

"Only the hull that first day. But so did everyone else."

Brollachan nodded. "Yes, and I've done it since."

"No bad dreams?"

"None. But then I never dream."

"Everyone dreams, Torq."

He shrugged. "Correction, then … I never remember mine."

"Wish I didn't remember mine. They're pretty awful."

"Do us both a favor," he said. "Write them down. Be as objective and precise as possible in recording the details, but also write an accompanying document to describe how you felt during, directly after, and since. I don't like coincidences."

"Not much of a fan myself," she said, and agreed to record everything.

Her attempts were faulty and thin. It was odd. When she was idle and doing mundane things like bathing, eating, or exercising, memories of the dreams would come unbidden and with disturbing clarity. But when she brought up a holo-screen to jot them down, the details seemed to retreat, becoming indistinct. It felt peculiar, almost like the dreams were toying with her.

Which, of course, was foolish, and she put it down to unresolved emotional reactions to an event of this magnitude.

And yet …

Her mind swirled, trying to make sense of it all. Even painted against the backdrop of the discovery of the Artifact and the more shocking incident of the thing the soldiers had fought, it was strange, almost unreal. She felt like she was in some kind of abstract drama, one of those arty things they showed on the Live Arts holo-channel. The kind of unscripted drama that provided little context for a series of vignettes built on motif and metaphor but lacking a coherent narrative structure. A surrealistic shock drama like the one she remembered from college, where it started as an enactment of Van Gogh's *Café Terrace at Night*, except the humans were motionless statues, and the tables and chairs moved with apparent life. Evie had watched it five times and never interpreted it the way the reviewers had. This had that feel.

"Join you?" said a voice, and Evie jumped, uttering a tiny, sharp scream.

"Whoa now, Professor," said Jenny Spears. "Didn't mean to freak you there."

"God, you scared me," said Evie. "I didn't hear you."

"Sorry. I've been told I have a light step."

Spears was not dressed for combat, in cold-weather snow pants and parka, and her only weapons were a pulse pistol on her left hip, handle turned forward, and a fighting knife strapped to her right thigh.

"That guy, Mac, he was one of yours, right? Site mechanic and driver?"

"Yes."

"Sorry about what happened to him."

"His body wasn't found in that cave," protested Evie, but Spears just gave her a look. "Okay. Yes," Evie conceded. "He was probably down there, too."

"Losing someone never gets easier," said Spears.

"He shouldn't have gone down there alone."

"Kind of hard not to want to," said Spears. "To get a place among the heroes."

Evie frowned. "Heroes?"

"Sure," said the agent. "Look, you and the other science nerds here are going to be in the history books. He wasn't likely to be, so maybe he thought he'd up the ante on things and be the first person to—I don't know—make contact." She gave a sour shake of her head. "Guess he did."

"That's not funny."

"Wasn't meant to be."

They were silent for a moment, and Evie looked down at the Artifact.

Spears leaned a hip against the pipe rail. "You're the one who found the Artifact."

Evie nodded. "My team did, yes."

"We haven't really had much of a chance to get to know one another. Most of what I know about you is secondhand from your students and Torq Brollachan."

"I deny everything," said Evie with a nervous little smile.

"You have quite a fan club."

"Me? Ha! Not really."

"Cute *and* modest," said Spears.

Evie didn't know how to respond to that, and she looked down at the Artifact. "It's hard to believe this is real."

"It's real. Maybe you're too modest to have considered this, Professor Cronin—"

"Evie, please."

Spears nodded. "When all this comes out, *Evie*, you're going to be beyond famous. The woman who found an alien spaceship. The scientist who discovered that we are not alone in the universe. That's pretty big."

"That doesn't even fit into my head."

They watched as the drones continued their endless pattern of work, doing simple tasks with insectoid efficiency.

"We weren't here looking for anything like that," mused Evie.

"No shit," laughed Spears. "Funny, though. People have been looking up at the stars since we climbed down from the trees. Wondering what's up there. At first it was the gods, I guess. It was all so big that there had to be something up there, out there. Whatever."

"Yes," said Evie. "We looked and wondered."

"And then in, what, the 1600s or something, a Dutch guy invents the first telescope, and we see more. Farther. The universe starts taking on shape."

Evie was surprised. "You know your history. That first telescope was created by Hans Lippershey in 1608. Isaac Newton created the first reflector telescope sixty years later. And now we have the Boyle-Liu Big Eye, fifty thousand times more powerful than the James Webb telescope. Multifaceted lens able to track forty percent of the visible sky at any one time and an entire mountain of supercomputers processing and collating the data. Two trillion exabytes of data every hour. Always looking. Helping us to understand the stars and to look for intelligent life."

"And it didn't find shit," said Spears. "Until some hot chick from a stuffy university tripped over it down at the ass end of the world."

"Not sure that's how I'd like it phrased in the history books."

"Which part?" asked Spears, her eyes sparkling with mischief. "The stuffy university part or the hot chick part?"

Despite the cold, Evie's face flared with heat. "I'm just an academic."

"Who is hot," said Spears. Her gaze was frank and unabashed. "Very hot, actually."

Evie was not used to receiving flirtation from any gender. She lived a quiet life and rarely even went out on dates. The last time was more than eleven months ago, and it was a dreary dinner in a dreary restaurant with an intensely dreary professor of linguistics on a date set up by mutual friends. The man was good looking, but he knew it. And in the air taxi, he closed in for a kiss, getting handsy in the attempt. She left him on a street corner in Berkeley and flew home alone.

The last time a woman hit on her was four years ago, and there had been some mutual heat, but nothing much came of it. Three dates, a fumbling first time on her couch, then a sensual shower. But their schedules were incompatible, and worse, their conversation dried up way too soon. Luckily, they were both on strong career tracks that left little time for building anything of substance, so they drifted. Nice memories that were fading. Christmas cards for the first two years, and nothing since.

Evie looked at Spears. Her eyes were the same blue as the deep and ancient Arctic ice, and her short blond hair looked like it had only a passing acquaintance with a brush. The body suit she wore was snug enough to show her long legs, lean body, small breasts, and strong shoulders that were oddly broad for a woman. *Like an Olympic swimmer's.*

And then there were those facial scars. Like red lightning across a face that could never have been described as beautiful. Spears's nose was long and crooked—more evidence of past violence—her jaw was pointed, and her ears small. And she had one of those mouths with a thin upper lip but a very full lower one.

When she realized she was cataloging Spears's looks, Evie's face burned even hotter.

"Not big on taking compliments," observed Spears. "That's kind of adorable."

"Look, Agent Spears—"

"Jenny."

"Okay. Jenny. This is hardly the time or place for—"

"For what, Professor? Not the time and place to hit on you?"

Evie didn't answer.

Spears laughed. "Sweetie, a few days ago I fought a shape-shifting alien monster and blew up a mountain."

"So, what … you want someone to stroke your ego and help you unwind?"

Spears looked momentarily surprised. Then she laughed. "Wow, you take careful aim, don't you? Okay, fair. Maybe I am coming on out of the blue. If there was a bar or coffee shop where we could sit down and get to know each other, that'd be great. I'd ask you out on a date. We'd pretend to be normal people. Maybe go catch a movie. But we're in fucking Antarctica, and the closest holo-cinema is a few thousand kilometers north of here." She shook her head. "It's not that."

"Then what?"

Spears looked at her with real intensity. "I'm wired and freaked out and scared out of my fucking mind is what."

Evie stared. "You? Scared?"

"Here's a secret," Spears said quietly. "No one's as ice-cold fear-be-damned ballsy as I pretend to be. The invulnerable ice maiden is what I play for the rubes. And, sure, I will kick ten kinds of ass if I need to, but right now I am off the clock. The adrenaline that got me through all that is still in my bloodstream. Keeps coming back every time I think about it. I've got the shakes. I could cry. Not joking. I could scream. And I'd like very much to be in one of those leisure hives on Luna. And maybe hitting on you is partly about all that."

"Partly?"

"And partly because you're smart and pretty. And maybe the rest is that you're alive and I'm alive, and that's a wonderful goddamn thing."

They stood staring at each other.

"Here's the thing," said Spears, "In about four seconds I'm going to try and kiss you. You can take it on the cheek or on the mouth, or you can walk away. Up to you. No matter which, I'm going to try in three, two, one …"

And she bent forward and kissed Evie Cronin.

Evie did not walk or turn away.

She expected it to be a hard kiss, with an intrusive tongue and a lot of get-it-done urgency, and Evie was willing to endure it from this dangerous soldier. But the kiss was the gentlest of things. Tentative at first, almost shy. A brush of lips and the brief heat of an exhaled breath.

Then the kiss became everything, and Evie melted into it.

5

"Gilly," he said.

Even deep inside a troubled dream, Gillian heard the voice. She knew it. But there was something wrong about that particular voice speaking to her, and in her cocoon of sheets, she writhed and groaned.

"Gilly," said Mac. "Wake up."

"No," she begged, still below the surface of sleep.

"I need you, Gilly. It's cold down here."

"I … can't …" she murmured.

"They want me to be what they are," said Mac. His voice was so faint, just a shade heavier than the soft wind that blew past her window. "They want me to be a slave."

"You … you're not a …"

"Slave," he said. "That's what they want. They want me to be like them."

Gillian drifted closer to wakefulness. Her eyes were closed, but her face creased itself into a frown. "Like who?"

"Like the formless ones," he whispered. "That's what they want."

"Who, Mac? Who wants that for you?"

"The dark ones," he said. "The ones who come as shadows. The ones who bite. The ones who shun the light."

The voice was Mac's, but the words, the diction, the pronunciation were not. It was like someone pretending to be Mac.

"Please, Gilly. Find me," begged the voice. "Save me."

When Gillian broke the surface into a dark and confused wakefulness, she was immediately aware of the two other grad students asleep in their beds. And of Mac's empty one.

And of …

She saw it for a moment, and then her mind slammed the doors of awareness shut, denying her a longer look. She had only a lingering flash memory of something that crouched like a gargoyle on the foot of her bed.

Not a protective gargoyle. Nothing sanctified. Nothing infused with any species of compassion. And yet there was a palpable empathy. The shadowy figure felt what *she* felt, knew what *she* knew.

Gillian opened her mouth to scream …

… and instantly the shadowy form vanished.

It was so abrupt that it stole certainty from her mind. *Had* she seen anything? Or was it something—a nightmare specter born of sadness—who had followed her out of her dreams?

Gillian lay there, the blankets clutched beneath her chin, her body shivering uncontrollably. She did not understand that image any more than she understood what Mac had meant in her dreams.

They want me to be a slave.

Confusion owned her. There was only one thing she knew with absolute certainty.

The thing she'd seen at the foot of her bed was not Mac. It had also not been what spoke to her. She knew that for sure.

6

On the far side of the site, Dr. Torquil Brollachan walked through the windy shadows.

He was weary to the marrow, and his mind felt like it was empty of words. Before and after the incidents down at the Artifact and the cave, he had spent hours in urgent conversation via holo-vid with the president, the joint chiefs, and the directors of the various intelligence agencies. Not all of the top players in DC were involved, but those with the right level of clearance were. The short-term political appointees were excluded because their ability to keep their mouths shut was in question, and no one could risk this getting out. That was critical even before that shape-shifting *thing* tore up the SPU soldiers.

After the last three-hour video meeting with the president, Brollachan was mentally and emotionally spent. He had tried to sleep, but that was a spectacular failure. So he dressed and went out, taking micro-sips of *po cha* as he walked. It was Tibetan butter tea, an old traditional blend made from tea leaves, yak butter, water, and salt. An acquired taste for most Europeans, but he had fallen in love with it while studying Nyingma Buddhism at the Dzogchen Monastery in Kham. Apart from its soothing qualities, the tea aided in respiration when at high altitudes or in extreme weather conditions. Brollachan took what comforts he could find, knowing that such luxuries were transitory. For him and for everyone on the team.

A soldier, one of Hobart's men, fell into step behind him, rifle at port arms, silent as a shadow.

Half of the people were in their quarters, though Brollachan doubted any of them could sleep either. How could they?

He debated calling his brother again but decided against it. What value was there in scaring him further?

The wind was dying down, but it had blown the clouds out to sea. Brollachan leaned, his hands on the pipe rail, and looked down at the Artifact, which was bathed in bright lights. Then he turned his back on the light pollution, cupped his hands around his eyes, and gazed up at the stars. The air was so clear that he could easily pick out the Southern Cross, Alpha and Beta Centauri, and the Magellanic Clouds.

"Beautiful," he murmured.

"Sir?" asked the soldier, but Brollachan just waved him off.

He leaned back against the rail and considered the infinite. The wheel of night turned above him, and he received no answers at all.

He sipped the fragrant tea and tried to find a way to be at peace with all that was going on. When something of this magnitude occurred, how could one actually envision what would happen next? Despite all of the protocols on file, not one of the brilliant minds who had planned for first contact could possibly have envisioned this *specific* event.

Was this, in fact, a spacecraft? Or was it something else? For all they knew, it could be a waste container dropped on a world with no visible intelligent life, the way space trash was sometimes dumped on asteroids.

It could not be what everyone feared, he thought. Not an invasion. The span of time between when it was likely buried and when it was discovered was far too absurd for that.

Was it a kind of reliquary for the sacred dead of some alien race? If so, was the creature Spears killed some sort of caretaker awakened by the collapse of the mountain and frightened into a violent response?

Or was it something like a calling card? Earth had sent a number of them out into space over the past couple of centuries. That process had begun with the golden discs placed aboard the two Voyager probes launched in 1977. There had even been one sent by the Interfaith Synod forty-two years ago. In it—wrapped in silk and then an outer waterproof sheet—were items representing Earth's many religions. A Catholic crucifix, a Protestant cross, a mezuzah and Star of David, an ankh, icons of key figures—gods and saints—from a hundred religions, mala beads, prayer bowls, the Islamic star and crescent, a Hindu Om, a Sikh Khanda, a small carving of a torii gate, a Jainist ahimsa hand, a yin-and-yang disk in alabaster and onyx, a nine-pointed star from the Baha'i faith, carvings from nearly five hundred indigenous cultures from the Americas, Polynesian conch shells carved with prayers, protection symbols from scores of tribes across Africa, and many, many more. All beautifully rendered in miniature. Shot into space from a base on Mars, it was aimed at Proxima Centauri, which—at 4.2 light years from Earth—was the closest neighboring star system.

When he'd first read about this in college, he scoffed. Even if some alien race found that stuff, what real sense could they make of it? There was no context, no possible commonality.

He turned and looked down at the craft again.

"What *are* you?" he begged. A few moments later he asked a different and equally important question. "What do you have to tell me?"

The only answers were the cold and icy winds, which were freshening again. Brollachan stood there and let them lash him.

Then he asked the question that burned in his heart.

"Why won't you *tell* me?"

He knew he imagined it, but for long minutes he stood stock still, certain he had heard the wind reply to him.

Why won't you hear me?

Torq Brollachan stared at nothing and tried to decide if he was under too much stress, going insane, or …

Why won't you hear me?

Those words were too real to ignore.

He touched the crucifix beneath his shirt. "God help me," he whispered to the night.

7

Torq Brollachan was positive no one actually heard his prayer.

He was completely wrong about that.

8

Gillian got up very quietly, careful not to wake the others. She lingered for a moment beside Mac's empty bed as tears coursed down her cheeks. Then she put on her coat, stepped into warm boots, pulled on a pair of thermal gloves, and stepped out into the cold night. The frigid air froze her tears, and when she wiped them away, she imagined the fragments tinkled like broken glass.

She was unaware of her destination until she realized that her feet had taken her to the end of Main Street. To the platform where the skimmer was docked.

There were four guards on duty. Two huddled together in a booth, warming themselves with hot coffee. The other pair, working their way through a long night of alternating shifts in and out of the cold, stood leaning on a pair of heavy machine guns loaded with thermal pulse pellets. Holo-screens fed them real-time videos of the entire area around the Artifact.

Gillian was careful not to make a sound as she crept toward the platform's farthest edge, her small, slim body hidden by the crane used to swing skimmers off the slanted racks and down to the docking clamps.

Her heart was not beating with excitement. It felt dead inside her chest. A rock. A piece of ice. Kneeling beside the ice-caked iron treads of the crane, she leaned between the pipes of the rail and looked down into the valley. She saw the Artifact, its gleaming hull, and the blackness of the star door, but her eyes did not linger there. Instead, she focused on the icy, irregular mound that had been the cave the Jokers had blown up.

"Mac …" she murmured very softly. "I'll do it, I promise."

She cocked her head as if listening to a voice.

"No, don't worry," she replied. "I said I'd save you. I will. I'll set you free."

Gillian listened some more, nodding.

"Yes, of course, Mac. No one should be a slave. No one."

This was part of a conversation that had unfolded while she slept. Mac calling to her, murmuring her name. Asking her to save him. Begging her to set him free.

I can't live like this, Mac had said. *They made me—they made all of us—to be slaves. I don't want to be a slave anymore. Please, Gillian. Please save me.*

That went on and on, deep into the night, as her body writhed and twitched with pain born of empathy. And love. Though she had never told Mac about her feelings, she now knew that he understood. Why else would he have reached out to her? To her and no one else.

"I'll save you, Mac," said Gillian as she straightened. She spoke in a normal tone this time, and the guard by the closest machine gun—only eight meters away—turned at the sound of her voice.

"Miss? Miss … you can't be out here."

Gillian turned to look at him. She wore a smile, but it was the only sign of emotion on a face that was otherwise totally blank. Even her eyes were vacant.

"I have to save him, you see."

"What? Save who?" The gunner took a step toward her. "It's … Gillian Archer, right? You're one of Professor Cronin's team?"

"No one should be forced to be a slave," said Gillian.

The soldier grunted. "That's pretty harsh. Professor Cronin seems pretty cool. And the rules about all this—they're for security and safety. No one's making anyone a slave here."

"No one should ever be *made* to be a slave. Not made that way. Not made."

She put a foot on the lowest rung of the pipe fence.

"Whoa, whoa now," said the soldier, patting the air in a placating way. "Let's take a breath here, miss. Step back from the rail, okay?"

"Yo, Steve," called the other machine gunner. "What's going on?"

"It's one of the grad students, Cindy," replied the first soldier.

"No one should ever have to live as a slave," said Gillian as she stood up on the pipe, gripped the top rail, and put her other foot on the middle slat.

Both soldiers began to advance on her, hands now up in a no-threat gesture.

"Miss—Gillian—please get down off the rail," said the first soldier.

"It's not safe up there," said the second.

Her smile widened, but its light still did not reach her eyes.

"Nobody should live as a slave," she said as she hooked her leg over the top pipe.

The soldiers begged her to come back even as they edged closer, trying not to panic her, hoping to soothe her.

"None of us should be slaves," she said, leaning out over the valley far beyond. "*Tekeli-li.*"

And then she jumped.

Gillian did not scream during her long fall. She did not cry out for God or her mother or anyone. Those last, strange words were all that the soldiers heard as she plummeted.

"*Tekeli-li.*"

All the way down to the bed of indifferent and unforgiving ice.

9

Evie and Jenny found a warm place.

It was in the hydroponics hothouse, with fifty kinds of genetically modified orchids, roses, hydrangeas, peonies, and chrysanthemums blooming around them. Everyone else was outside or had gathered elsewhere to dissect every detail of what had happened. The handful of hybrid roses scented the air with a delicate perfume.

Spears took some empty burlap sacks and lay them on the floor against a wall near the heater, and they sat. And kissed again. It was not a leap-off-the-precipice kind of passion. No clothes were torn. They did not even undress.

They sat with their backs to the wall and held each other close as they talked. And they talked for a very long time: all through the sunset and well into the night. Telling each other about their lives. Growing up. Following the call of their professions and immersing themselves in those trades, becoming good at them, and building on that. There was no bragging on either side, just the kind of frankness two people can share when trust is in play. Particularly when that trust is new, and each wants to anchor it to the shared reality in genuine ways. To see and be seen, to know and be known.

Whenever there was a natural pause, Spears would lean in for another kiss. Mostly her. A few times it was Evie.

And it was Evie who made the first touch.

They were deep in a kiss, both of them with eyes closed there in the scented darkness. Evie had one palm on Spears's cheek, and as their tongues danced gently together, she moved her hand down so that her fingertips brushed slowly along the curve of Spears's jaw and then over the line of her throat. She glided that touch sideways, tracing the angle of her collarbone and out to one muscular shoulder. Then, with a boldness that surprised herself, down onto Spears's upper chest until her palm cupped a soft breast. Through the thinness of the other woman's clothes, Evie could feel the nipple swell and tighten.

That sent a thrill through her, and Evie felt herself grow wet.

Even so, neither of them was in a hurry.

And maybe that was part of the point. Given all that had happened, urgency would feel like panic, and both of them wanted an oasis of peace.

It was nearly an hour before they undressed each other. They lay naked, touching with a delicacy as if they were inventing tenderness in that very moment. Evie sensed an empathy in Spears that was so at odds with her strength and bravado. The soldier's body was lean and strong, and when Evie caressed the inside of her thigh, Spears shuddered as if she had never been touched before.

There was no aggressor. It was all about sharing, about discovering.

Even when they came—first Spears and then Evie—it was quiet and gentle and safe.

Afterward, they lay together, holding each other. Kissing sweetly as passion melted down into a dreamy and indefinable kind of sharing.

For a long while, as the Antarctic night deepened, they forgot about the Artifact, the monster, the deaths, the horror, and the implications.

Spears fell asleep with her head resting on Evie's shoulder.

Evie sat there, stroking her lover's short blond hair. She wept quietly, choosing not to define the cause of those tears.

The pumps and machinery of the hothouse masked sound very effectively. They did not hear any of the screams and yells from the people outside.

They did not hear Gillian's name being shrieked into the wind.

Part Twelve
Haunters of the Dark

"We have also arranged things so that almost no one understands science and technology. This is a prescription for disaster. We might get away with it for a while, but sooner or later this combustible mixture of ignorance and power is going to blow up in our faces."

—*Carl Sagan*

Asphodel Station
The Shadderal Star System

Soren woke from another night of bad dreams.

The face he saw in the mirror looked ten years older. He was grainy, pale to the point of grayness, and there was a haunted, shifty look in his eyes.

"Well," he said to himself, "you cut a fine figure of mature grace and elegance."

He showered, dressed, skipped breakfast because his stomach rebelled at the thought, and took a skimmer down to the surface of Shadderal. When the hatch opened, he was not particularly surprised to see Lost waiting for him. The golem was covered with a patina of dust, as if Lost had been waiting for some time.

Soren and he shook hands, which was a custom Lost had learned from the professor and rather liked.

"You are troubled," stated Lost.

Soren hooked his arm in Lost's, and they began walking down the broad avenue that divided the rows of automated ship factories and the vast Field of Dead Birds, where thousands of whole or broken spacecraft lay beneath the harsh glare of Scylla and Charybdis.

"Troubled is a good word for it," said Soren as they strolled.

"Will you tell me what disturbs you?" asked the ghost. "I have a sense that it is not merely the continued absence of the NecroTeks."

"Well, there is that," admitted Soren. "However, the immediate issue is a series of unusual dreams I've had lately."

"Dreams of what kind? Are you pining for your homeworld?"

"No. I mean, yes, of course … but that's not the nature of my dreams."

"Tell me, then," encouraged Lost.

And Soren did. He described several recent dreams, each of which took different paths through the seemingly endless rooms and corridors of his old family estate and the memory library Soren had superimposed over it. When he got to the description of the monster—vampire or devil or whatever it was—Lost jerked to a stop and had him repeat the description.

"Why does this alarm you so?" asked Soren.

"The creature you described, did it speak to you?"

Soren considered. "Not as such, no. And yet I felt a connection to it, a kind of communication that was on a nonverbal level. More of an empathetic connection, though not in a pleasant way. I felt that the thing knew me and, on some level, that *I* should know *it*."

"Do you know it?"

"I don't know if I can answer that honestly," Soren admitted. "There is a kind of awareness of it without knowing anything specific about it. Do you know the concept of atavism?"

Lost paused, head tilted to one side as he dove into the enormous body of knowledge he shared with Sybil.

"I … understand the concept. In biology, it is where an ancient genetic trait manifests in a new example of a species." He paused. "But I do not think that is the definition you imply."

"It is not," said Soren. "From an emotional and psychological perspective, an atavistic fear is a dread of something old and mostly unknown. Or to revert to a primitive state wherein fears hold more power than rational explanation. Do you follow?"

"I do," said Lost. "And this dream figure, this monster you described, triggers this feeling in you? Can you articulate how?"

"I have been wrestling with that." They continued their walk. "When I see the thing in my dreams, it calls to mind so many reference points from times past. Images of Satan, the devil, of demons, and of certain cultural variations on the concept of a vampire."

"Vampire," echoed Lost, tasting the word. "That is significant."

Soren cut him a look. "Why so? Vampires are not real."

"Are they not?"

"I mean, to be sure, there are vampiric creatures—certain species of bats, ticks, leeches, and so on—but that's not what I'm referring to. The vampires, as they appear in various cultures of my world, are iconic tropes related to different kinds of predatory behavior. Most vampires hunt by night; many are actually dead and revive in order to prey on the living. Most are hematophagous, meaning they drink blood. Many others are 'essential vampires' who drain various kinds of energy from their victims—sexual potency, breath, life force, even emotions like faith or hope. There are even vampire subtypes believed to feed on memories. Nearly every culture on my world has old beliefs in some version of this kind of monster. They were, and are still, popular in the fiction and entertainment of my people."

"Yes," said Lost. "I have read *Dracula*, *Carmilla*, and others."

"Then you understand."

"Do I understand the concept of a vampire?" asked the golem. "Yes. Perhaps more so than you do, friend Soren."

Soren stopped walking and turned to his companion. "Tell me what you mean by that."

Lost did not immediately meet his gaze but instead looked off toward the distant mountains, where a pair of skimmers were airlifting huge crates of iron ore for the factories.

"It is possible, even likely, that the belief in vampires did not originate with your species," he said at last.

"What do you mean?"

"Your culture is old by your standards but only a blink of time's eye by mine. From what I have read of your history, human civilization dates back about twelve thousand of your years. Documented history, I mean. Whereas mine—the combined cultures of all the peoples who joined to fight the Outer Gods—has a history closer to a million years. And while this comes with great knowledge in many areas, it also comes with its monsters. You've met two such … the shoggoths and their tardigrade war dogs."

"And they are quite terrifying enough, thank you," said Soren.

Lost stood there and shook his head. "The greatest thing to fear about the shoggoths are their numbers, for they are as close to uncountable as can be. And they are powerful, clever, and dangerous, but hear me when I tell you that there are races of beings in the service of the Outer Gods who are far *more* dangerous … and infinitely more terrifying."

Soren simply stared at him.

"There are the Mi-Go and the Dimensional Shamblers, there are the Uth and the Relkian Mindworms, there are the Hounds of Tindalos and the Cats of Ulthar, there are Serpent Men and moon-beasts, and countless others. Each is terrible in its own way."

"I …" began Soren, but Lost touched his arm to stop his words.

"What you described to me is something I have never actually seen," he said quickly. "It is very like a race of creatures who have been described only a few times, and even then by survivors whose minds have been blasted by the encounters."

"Do you mean they are vampires?"

Lost made a sound that might have been a short, harsh laugh. "They are not risen corpses in search of blood," said Lost. "No. That would be less frightening. Nor are they repelled by religious objects or herbs like garlic. I do not think a stake of any kind—hawthorn wood or raw iron—would kill them. In fact, I know of nothing that has even been used against them, because no one who has ever faced them has prevailed. Not in ten times ten thousand generations."

"It was only a dream," protested Soren.

"If you are dreaming of the creatures known as the night-gaunts, friend Soren, then I fear for *you*. They live in the Dreamlands and can navigate the overlaps of dimensional reality."

"What *are* they?"

"They are death," said Lost. "They are not like the shoggoths. They are not slaves of the Outer Gods. They serve willingly and are highly valued by the gods of this part of the galaxy. They are a plague. A *thinking* plague, for they are intelligent and subtle and deliberate in all they do."

"As I said, Lost, these were dreams."

"You say that as if dreams are somehow a protection against the night-gaunts. Those monsters live as much in the Dreamlands and in the personal nightmares of their victims as they do in standard space-time. Once they have invaded the dreams of a potential victim, they leave a scar, a marker that allows them to return. If they have turned their thoughts and hungers toward Asphodel Station," said the golem, "then your people are in great danger. They will come in waves of combat ships, but their greatest weapons are the fear with which they infect their enemies. Do not think that prayers to the Gods of Earth will protect anyone out here. My people had great faith in our deities, and look at what is left of us … one mad and desolated ghost."

Part Thirteen
Rate of Decay

"Time flies over us, but leaves its shadow behind."

—*Nathaniel Hawthorne*

Joint MIT/UCLA Biological Research Field Station #8
Queen Maud Land, Antarctica

1

They brought Gillian up in a skimmer.

Evie stood on the platform, waiting in silent vigil, with Craig and the other original members of the joint university team standing in a cluster nearby. They all looked shocked, tearful, and hollow.

Evie felt entirely alone, though.

Death was not a concept that had loomed large in her life before this. Her mother had died when she was too little to really remember her. And except for an eighty-nine-year-old aunt in Switzerland she'd only ever seen on holo-calls, no one she knew had ever died.

Then Mac vanished, presumed dead.

And the entire Venture II Tteam.

Now Gillian, and somehow her death was worse. As she waited, shivering with cold and unspilled tears, Evie tried to decode her emotions. It was Gillian's youth and her innocence that combined to deliver such a hard punch. Evie knew that she had been brusque with the young woman too often. A bad habit for an overworked and insecure academic thrust into a leadership position. She accepted that, but that objectivity brought with it guilt and remorse.

"It's never easy," said a voice, and she turned to see Brollachan standing behind her.

Something acidic rose to Evie's tongue, but she bit it back. The SPU chief looked genuinely concerned. As if maybe he, too, felt the claws of loss digging into him.

But all Evie could manage was a single word.

"Yes," she said.

And he nodded in reply. An entire conversation that said everything.

2

The retrieval team tried to keep the body shielded from view, but a malicious gust of wind whipped away the tarp, and Evie saw what despair and the unforgiving ice at the bottom of the valley had done to Gillian.

Her body no longer looked human. Shards of white bone stood up from bloody rents in her coat and pants. Her arms and legs were twisted into impossible shapes. But in one of those perverse quirks of fate, her face was completely unmarked. Her eyes were open, staring at the sky, one lid lower than the other. Her lips were parted, but the remnants of her smile seemed carved into the muscles. Her hair was spread out around her head like rays of golden sunlight, except where the strands had soaked up hot blood before it all froze.

One of her hands, the fingers broken, lay stretched toward the mound of ice that had been the cave. Evie fought against the contents of her stomach—the last undigested bits of last night's meal and too much whiskey. She forced herself to look away from the ruin of her youngest assistant and instead focused on the ice.

"She kept talking about slaves," said one of the soldiers who had witnessed the tragedy. "What's that all about?"

"Kid was off her rocker," suggested Not Larry. "She heard what that ... *thing* ... said to Lifeguard. Crazy shit about slaves."

"She mentioned Mac Ryerson too," said the soldier.

"Like I said, she was out of it. Grief can do weird, sad, devious shit to people. She's a—she *was*—pretty young. Maybe she had a thing for Mac, and his death, combined with everything else that's going on, just pushed her over the edge. Hell, I can understand that. I can see it."

No one commented, but there were nods.

Only after Spider and the other soldier had completed the awful job of lifting her from the ice and putting her frozen body into a bag did Evie speak.

"We're going to need to be careful," she said. "Everyone here is under stress. A lot of it. How could we not be? We're going to have to create a buddy system or something. All of us looking out for each other."

Craig said, "Maybe Dr. Brollachan can get a therapist down here for us."

Evie nodded. "Oh yes. We're going to need that."

A day later, Dr. Indira Singh arrived from Columbia.

3

Evie and Jenny went back to the hut they shared. Jenny built a fire and told Sybil what to make for dinner.

When she turned away from the AI interface, she saw Evie pouring whiskey into a tall glass. It was an unmeasured flow that had to be four or five ounces.

"Hey, maybe tap the brakes on that."

Evie looked at her with eyes filled with ice and pain. Without saying a word, she tilted her head back and drank the glass dry.

"Christ, what are you doing?" gasped Spears.

By then Evie was pouring herself another glass.

4

The world did not find out about the Artifact.

That surprised Evie, because she knew how fragile secrets were. And yet there was nothing on any news feed. Granted, all social media posts, private emails, and even holo-calls between site members and family were heavily monitored, but even with all that, she expected some part of the story to leak.

There was nothing, and that both impressed her and made her feel more threatened. It was a moment of realization as to the scale of the event and the power Dr. Brollachan could exert.

One night, days after Gillian's funeral, Evie sat with Jenny in front of a fire in what had now become their shared hut. Wood was scarce in Antarctica, but there was a whole bin of salamanders—compressed fuel sticks that burned like wood but were not easily consumed by the flames. One salamander could burn for thirty hours and provide a generous warmth.

They were in robes, with a shared blanket around their shoulders. Jenny had a cup of white rose tea, and Evie was into her third whiskey-laced coffee.

"Tomorrow's a big day," Evie said, trying—and failing—to sound offhand.

"I heard. Torq's going to send some drones into the Artifact. Kind of surprised he's waited this long."

"Red tape in Washington," Evie said. "The president wanted to hold off for a couple of months until a bigger team could come down and find some way to airlift it to an island somewhere. One of their research stations. I know, that's stupid, but let's face it, the president's not the sharpest scalpel. Pretty sure people voted his haircut in, and he came with it."

"Ha!" snorted Jenny.

"He scares me too," said Evie.

"The president?"

"No … Dr. Brollachan."

Jenny snorted. "Torq? Yeah, he can be pretty spooky at times. Would make a great comic book villain. Looks the part. All he needs is a costume and a secret lab."

"Like a base at the bottom of the world?"

"Ha! Fair enough."

They watched the yellow demons inside the fire dance and leap.

"From what I heard from Hobart," said Jenny, "Torq and the president of the United States of America worked it all out. Twenty-seven world leaders—those whose trust and stability were currently getting high marks—were informed. All on the sly. Meetings were held in person and via highly secure channels. This is what he does."

"That's scary."

Jenny shrugged. "I don't mind it. Not in this case. There's never been something this big before. It has to be finessed."

"People should be told."

"That's the scientist-wanting-to-publish talking, Evie. What's funny is that for the last I-don't-know-how-many years, every time there's been a big scare, the government always closed ranks and parsed out the information to prevent a panic. The thing is, none of that shit would have *ever* caused panic."

"It's the military's fetish for secrecy," said Evie. "Remember, I grew up with all of that."

"No doubt." Jenny sipped her tea and set the cup aside. "But this time ... yeah, well, there would be a panic. Not because of the Artifact, but because of that fucked-up shit in the cave."

Evie drank her coffee and made only a noncommittal grunt.

"It'll get less weird soon enough," Jenny said.

"How, exactly?"

"Torq's bringing in something like fifty scientists and experts on different subjects. Everything from astronomy to molecular biology. Metallurgists, exobiologists, all of those eggheads. Once they're all here, this whole site will become mundane. Just another research center. At least, that's how it will feel."

"Mundane is a stretch."

"I said how it would *feel*. It'll all get orderly, structured, and safer. The bigger the site becomes, with more professionals putting eyes on everything, the less overwhelming it will feel. You'll see."

Evie drank her coffee, needing the whiskey burn to steady her nerves. "And you're one hundred percent sure you torched every last bit of that thing?"

Jenny leaned over and kissed her cheek. "Sweetie, unless that alien son of a bitch can reconstitute from carbon dust, I think we're good. We have drones crawling all over the area, and plasma cannons with gun crews and AI overwatch trained on that star door." She shook her head. "Nah ... the main threat is past tense. Now it's all about scientists measuring every fucking thing there is to measure. You should know, because that's your bag, sugar. Me and my guys will stay sharp, but I got a feeling we aren't going to be needed. And nothing is going to crawl up out of that valley and pick a fight. Oh hell no."

5

In the deepest, quietest hour of the long south polar night, Dr. Torquil Brollachan took one of the small personal grav pods down to the Artifact. He steered it slowly away from the docking clamps on a ledge behind the smallest of the site's three garages and began his descent, keeping his speed low in order to prevent a louder engine growl.

The grav pod was a simple device with a square platform, a waist-high rail that formed a complete circle around him, and a dura-glass face screen. Efficient and easy to steer, even for someone more used to being driven wherever he went.

The night was bitterly cold, which kept the night owls among the staff from wandering around the camp. The guards walking their posts huddled inside their thermal suits and asked no question of the director of the SPU.

He passed over the Artifact. Since its discovery, nearly a third of the monstrous machine had been uncovered. Crawler-cranes—looking like huge metal tarantulas—stood in a silent line, waiting through the night for their morning-shift drivers. Brollachan bent forward as far as the screen would allow, looking at the sleek cylinder, trying to see it with fresh eyes every time he came down here.

The grav pod hummed softly as he steered it away from the Artifact and over to the massive mound of shattered and half-melted ice covering what had been the cave. He knew that some of the younger members of the original staff—the university kids from MIT and UCLA—had started calling it the Monster Cave. Brollachan found that amusing and more than a little silly. Officially, it was Venture Hill.

He landed ten meters from Venture Hill and switched off the motor, lingering for a few moments. The corporal in charge of the sentries came over and saluted.

"Can I help you, sir?"

"Thanks, but no," said Brollachan as he stepped down. He patted a heavy pouch slung over his shoulder. "Just want to add a few more scanner drones."

"More, sir? They're banging into each other as it is."

"These are bio-crabs. They don't fly, and they won't be underfoot."

"Of course, sir. How may I help?"

Brollachan pulled his scarf tighter around his neck, then unslung the bag and opened it. Nestled inside were a dozen of the drones. They looked like Dungeness crabs, even down to the short legs and purple-tinged gray-brown shells. "Much appreciated. If you and your men could take a few each?"

The corporal called his men over and took the devices as Brollachan pulled them from the pouch and flicked their activation switches.

"Place them around as much of the mound as you can reach," he ordered. "Not too close to the front, though—we have the stationary scanners there."

The soldiers hurried off. Brollachan waited until they were all busy with their simple task. Moving quickly, he removed two additional drones from inside his coat. These were of a different design and imitated naked mole rats. He flipped their switches and quietly ordered Sybil to send them up the face of the mound. As soon as they were in position, he accessed a special task program. Out of sight of the entire security detail, the little mole rats deployed small but high-powered ice drills. Within seconds they vanished inside the mound.

Smiling to himself, Brollachan returned to his grav pod and flew back up. Ten minutes later he was asleep in his bed, still smiling faintly.

6

Dr. Indira Singh had been briefed on the Artifact, the creature, and Venture Team.

When the first tsunami of shock had crashed through her and left her gasping and terrified, she put herself back together using one of the best tools at her disposal.

Analysis.

While preparing for the trip to Antarctica, she slow-walked it, keeping her military escorts waiting as she packed. The process of exerting control over the timetable of leaving—even though she knew it likely came off as either rude or officious—allowed her to examine her own emotions. The initial shock, the secondary and tertiary waves of realization and acceptance, and the aftershocks as the towering reality of it asserted itself.

On the flight from Seattle to the dig site, she role-played questions and answers as if she were both therapist and patient. This was how she had always primed her empathy engines as she prepared to deal with a fresh, shared trauma.

Now on the ground, she had spent nearly an hour on the observation platform, staring down at the improbably huge craft. Feeling its weight, its impact. Its importance and its danger. All that time, she ran through emergency checks on her own reactions—cataloging them in situ so that her sessions with the staff here would not feel like an encounter with an outsider.

Then she turned to Dr. Brollachan, who had accompanied her to the platform.

"Okay," she said. "I'm ready to start."

She endured the SPU chief's penetrating gaze. His reply was a silent nod, and Singh thought this was entirely appropriate.

7

Evie and Jenny Spears made love that night, as they did every single night. And that night, Evie was drunk. As she often was. Even so, she managed to stay present, to stay entirely and hungrily engaged.

It was so strange to be drawn to someone as overtly physical as Spears. The woman had the most finely toned body Evie had ever seen. Almost no body fat except for her small breasts. Even her buttocks and thighs were muscular.

Lovemaking was usually gentle, though, except for moments when the passion seemed to rise up in Spears like a nuclear reactor racing toward meltdown. And then Spears stopped whispering sweet words and instead growled with such burning need that it was almost frightening.

For her part, Evie felt herself rising to such moments, becoming greedier in her hungers, more demanding in searching for release—each time wanting to fall from a loftier height when Spears brought her to climax.

And yet the release the powerful woman craved was a far gentler one.

Afterward they would hold each other and talk. The conversation had no road map, no structure. They spoke of their lives—Spears was fascinated that a nonviolent scholar like Evie could be the daughter of a famous fighting general. Evie wanted to know how Spears became a soldier and why she stayed. They talked trivia about their lives, the places they'd been, the things they'd seen. They spoke of old lovers and how things had ended. They did not talk about the future, though, and neither was aware of that. Sometimes Evie would make coffee with whiskey in it, and they'd sip while the other spoke. Spears drank very little; Evie drank a little more each time.

When their tongues were tired, they would hold each other and let things settle into silence and calm. A kind of calm, at least. With the Artifact and the memories of dead soldiers and an actual monster, calm was elusive and fragile.

When sleep tugged at them, they yielded to it, naively hoping for peaceful dreams. But they were the wrong people in the wrong place for that kind of mercy.

8

Evangeline Cronin dreamed that she was melting.

Not like a popsicle on a hot playground. Not like ice in a glass of rare bourbon. Not like frost on the leaves of late March.

No. *She* was melting. It began with her skin. In the dream, she was seated on an Adirondack chair on the porch of the house her great-grandfather had built over a hundred years ago. It was on a lake in New Jersey that had since been reclaimed by the rising Atlantic. Evie had never seen this lake or this house. They were both gone long before she was born, and yet she had seen so many family videos that she knew every knot in the paneling, every creak in the porch stairs, and every tree in the row of pines that lined the north side of the property.

At first Evie thought there were ants crawling on the back of her neck. She darted a hand up to brush them away. But her little fingernail snagged on something soft. Not her hair. Not her shirt collar. This was soft and doughy and unpleasantly warm.

She jerked her hand away and sat, listening to the air around her and the sounds of her own body. The strange itchy feeling returned, and Evie let her hand creep slowly up to touch the nape of her neck. The pads of her fingers found the warm skin, but it no longer felt right. It wasn't the right texture, and her fingertips sunk in up to the first knuckle. That made the itch worse. Annoyed and unnerved, she brushed her hand back and forth, certain that there was something between her neck and her fingers.

There was only air in that gap, and as she felt around, Evie rediscovered that patch of loose flesh. This time, a strange fascination urged her to keep touching it. To look for the slope of muscle and the curve of bones. Finding neither. Feeling her upper back yield to the pressure of her touch.

"What?" she said. And then realized she'd spoken that word over and over again, becoming aware of it only now because panic was making everything far too clear.

Evie caught a tab of flesh between her fingers and gently pulled. It moved with her hand. A quarter of a centimeter. Then two centimeters. More. Like putty. Like sculptor's clay after the medium was wet and soft. It was unpleasantly moist. Too soft, too yielding, too willing to betray its rightful shape and …

… and …

… and …

And change.

The moment that word crept into her mind, Evie felt another sensation. A soft brush of a touch. Like dangling threads moving in a light breeze. Like hair in a draft.

It was her own hair. Moving.

There was no breeze. No draft. And yet the hair at the base of her skull was brushing against her. Moving deliberately to touch her. To caress her.

Evie tried to pull her hand away, but something was wrong with her muscles. The arm sagged, the slack muscles pressing down on the bones. And bending them.

Her arm dropped, splatting like wet leather across her lap, limp as pasta, sinking into the valley of her thighs. Evie wanted to scream, but her mouth and tongue rebelled, instead letting out a sound that combined the worst parts of a scream and a moan.

There was a terrible itch under that boneless skin, and as Evie gaped down at it, small rings appeared on the inside of her forearm. Each ring was the size of a cherry, but as she watched, the edges of the rings thickened, losing the grace of their curves and taking on a soft, ridged texture. Rows of complete circles from her armpit down to the formless lump that had been her hand.

Then the centers of each circle darkened, swelled like blisters, and ruptured to reveal rings of tiny, wickedly sharp teeth. The arm—it was no longer her *arm—twitched, then began to wriggle and writhe, and then to lift. Rising, curling, flexing, coiling. A small pink tentacle.*

Two of them.

And between them was a mass of rippling flesh that had lost all sense of shape. Bulges appeared, and each of these extruded, narrowing into tentacles, suckers forming along their length.

Evie kept trying to scream. She could hear the words she was thinking. They were the right thoughts—pleas and prayers for mercy or death—but not in any human language. It was a language that should never have been spoken on Earth. Not by human tongues. This was a language from beyond Earth. Beyond Sol. From across the vastness of the Milky Way. A language spoken by creatures that huddled beneath the harsh glow of blue suns. Creatures whose bodies were never still, flowing and shifting constantly, drawing on stored DNA stolen from eighty thousand plundered worlds across space and the Dreamlands.

Before Evie's mind died, the voice inside her skull shrieked in the language of hell.

Cahf ah nafl mglw'nafh hh' ahor syha'h ah'legeth, ng llll or'azath syha'hnahh n'ghftephai n'gha ahornah ah'mglw'nafh.

"That is not dead which can eternal lie, and with strange eons even death may die."

9

She woke with a start, then froze, not wanting to wake Jenny up.

With great stealth and care, she got out of bed and padded over to the wet bar, took the whiskey down—making sure not to let it clink against the other bottles—then brought it into the bathroom.

Evie sat down on the closed lid of the toilet and tried to recall her dream. As always, the details faded, leaving behind the stain of each intense emotion. That was bad enough.

She took a small sip. Winced. Gasped. Then took another.

And another.

By the time she went back to bed, the level of that bottle had dropped significantly. She made a mental note to have the replicator refill the bottle when Jenny wasn't home. She climbed into bed, kissed Jenny on the cheek, and closed her eyes. To rest only. Not to sleep. Not to dream.

Sleep came anyway, unbidden and unwelcome.

10

A storm swept into the camp with winds so fierce it drove everyone indoors. Only the sentries at the observation platform and a patrol driving up and down Main Street in a snowcat were abroad, and they hated it. The shift commander took pity on them and changed the schedule from four-hour shifts to two.

Colonel Hobart sat in his hut, the fire built high, and spoke with Dr. Brollachan via holo-comms. Their huts were only forty meters apart, but neither wanted to let the teeth of that storm bite them.

"I am quite busy, Tom," said the SPU chief. His face was bland, but there was impatience in his tone. "Can we make this quick?"

"Sure," said Hobart. "It's just a heads-up on something that's not related to the Artifact."

That made Brollachan smile a little. "It's easy to forget there's anything else to be concerned about."

"No joke, Torq. This is offworld stuff. We've been getting a lot of reports of pirates operating in the asteroid belt. The commander of Sagan Station is getting worried, and the security team he has is ... well ... they weren't first in their class, let's just say."

"Meaning what? That *you* have to go out there? That would be months there and back."

"Me? No. I'm thinking of sending the Jokers out there. Jenny and her goon squad have dealt with this kind of thing before. We have a pretty important R&D lab on Sagan, and there's stuff that could cause trouble if it fell into the wrong hands. That's where we store most of the bioweapons shit the Jokers and other teams have taken away from terrorists. And I sure as hell don't want to hit the burn-all switch just to keep it out of enemy hands. Hell, we both have friends on Sagan Station."

Brollachan pursed his lips in thought for a moment. "Things have quieted down here …" he mused. "Except for the nightmares, and Dr. Singh is already working on that. So … yes, if you have to send Agent Spears and her team, I approve."

Hobart nodded. "I wonder if *she'll* agree, though."

"Why wouldn't she? The incident that first day is ancient history. We've complied with all of her safety protocols. And endorsed them. I think she knows that."

"True, true. What I meant, though, is that she and Evie Cronin have become quite a thing."

Brollachan looked surprised. "*Have* they? I had no idea."

"Seriously? You can literally see little red hearts floating around them when they're together. How do you not know?"

The scientist sniffed. "Not my business. However, I take your point. My best recommendation is to simply ask her. Be frank. Tell her what's stored on Sagan. She'll understand."

"That works for me," said Hobart. He flinched and turned to look at the door. "God, that wind. Blowing so hard it's rattling the door handle. I think Old Man Winter wants to come in and get warm."

Brollachan gave that a small smile and disconnected the call.

11

Beside her on the bed, Jenny Spears was trapped inside her own dream.

It, too, was one she would not really remember when she woke. There would be a vagueness about the memory, with details melting away as she tried to reassemble the narrative.

She and the Jokers were in combat pressure suits, trudging into the teeth of a windstorm that hammered them with ice crystals made of methane and sulfuric acid. Steam rose from them all, and it seemed to Spears as if Spider and Moonboy on point were melting. The personal colors and designs on their suits dripped and ran, pooling in their footprints on the ashy ground.

Above them was a massive planet. A gas giant that swirled with ten thousand colors in the chemical stew of its atmosphere. Not Jupiter,

Saturn, or any of the outer planets of the solar system. This one was unknown to her. Spears paused to look up just in time to see what she thought was a shadow of something falling across her faceplate. It wasn't.

Things would have been better if it had been.

Everything would be better if it were something as ordinary as that.

A shadow fell across the monstrous planet. She watched a veil of shadows sweep down from the northern pole of the planet while a second veil rose up, both meeting for just a moment in the center.

It took Spears several seconds to understand what it was she'd just seen. Her mind rebelled at acceptance, refused to allow the truth of it.

Then it happened again.

Slower. Forcing her awareness to log it, record it.

The planet was not a planet at all.

It was an eye.

And it blinked.

Once, twice …

And Spears woke up.

She lay there, curled somehow on the very edge of the bed, the covers all heaped on Evie. The room was utterly silent. There wasn't even the moan of wind outside. Nothing. Like death.

Without turning or even moving, Evie whispered to her. "You weren't dreaming."

Spears's head snapped around, and she nearly fell off the bed. "Evie?" she said softly.

But Evie's only reply was a low, mild, resonant snore.

Spears settled back and tried to laugh off the dream. She lay there for a long time and had no warning when sleep took her again and pulled her beneath the surface of awareness.

In the morning, there was no trace of that dream.

12

Torquil Brollachan sat at a mission table in his private lab. He was alone, and his door was locked. Atop the table, squatting on a plastic mat inside a dura-glass container, were the two naked mole rat drones.

"Sybil," he said, "do a room scan for all unauthorized electronics."

"There are no active or passive surveillance devices present, Dr. Brollachan."

"Activate Ariel subchannel."

"Ariel channel is now active," said the AI, and her voice changed subtly. Instead of the soothing and somewhat bland Sybil voice, the voice of his proprietary subchannel was colder and had a contralto timbre.

"Ariel," said Brollachan, "have you completed payload analysis?"

"I have."

"Show me an inventory."

A holo-screen appeared at once, and Ariel populated it with a slowly scrolling list. Most of what he saw there was the chemical composition of Antarctic ice, trace elements of the plasma bombs used by Agent Spears, and carbon dust filled with destroyed organic matter.

"Wait, *wait*," he cried. "Pull out item number one eighty-two. Enlarge and expand. Give me all available data."

The image changed to show a mundane-looking speck of red dust. But Ariel filled the screen around it with new data, everything from gas chromatography to polymerase chain reactions. He stared at the results, his face going utterly slack.

"God in heaven," he breathed.

His slack expression slowly transformed into a mask of indescribable and total joy.

Part Fourteen
Perception Is Reality

"To him who is in fear everything rustles."

—*Sophocles*

Asphodel Station
The Shadderal Star System

1

"Lost," said Soren, "what do you mean that the night-gaunts are dreams? Does that mean that they have no physical form?"

He and the golem stood in the shadows cast by a pile of wrecked spacecraft left over from the deadly battle with the shoggoth Medusa mother ship. The wind had freshened and was hurling pieces of debris everywhere. Soren huddled against the wreckage to keep out of the blast.

"I am not sure there are appropriate words or corresponding concepts in your culture that adequately express what they are," said Lost.

"Try," encouraged Soren.

Lost nodded. "Much like the Outer Gods, the night-gaunts are pandimensional. If they have a *home* of any kind, then it is the Dreamlands. There are rumors of a homeworld, but our best scientists were never able to find it. I suspect that is because they looked in what you would call normal space-time—this 3D reality, but such creatures are not our cosmic neighbors. They are not 'aliens,' as most people would label them."

"That is a bit vague," said Soren. "Surely, if they are a race of beings, they have to be from somewhere."

"If so, we never found out."

"When they appear, what form do they take?"

"So few people ever saw them and survived to tell of it. Most who survived an encounter were driven mad."

"How?" Soren asked. "What specifically caused that reaction? Surely, it can't be from simple appearance. On Earth, there are creatures more bizarre than anything conjured in dreams. Our popular entertainment presents even grander and more grotesque beings. People may be shocked or even horrified … but driven to madness?"

"I have become familiar with your movies and holographic dramas, friend Soren. I have also read deeply into the fantastical literature your culture so enjoys. And, yes, I agree that nature conjures shapes that might be monstrous to some."

"Then …?" coaxed Soren.

"A sea scorpion or hagfish is horrifying," said Lost, "but only in appearance. The night-gaunts—being *pan*dimensional—attack from the depths of the inner mind. They conjure nightmares that chew at the foundations of surface consciousness. And, worse, they steal nearly all memories of the dreams they create, leaving only the residue of fear, doubt, faith, insight, and personal well-being. This is how they pave the way for their physical attacks."

"So … they *have* physical forms?"

Lost paused. "They have fleets of ships, yes, but even I don't know if those craft are operated by living beings or through some spiritual power like *ethla*. As I said, so few people ever survived contact with them that any eyewitness reports are suspect."

Soren turned and looked at the wind blowing a piece of torn cloth across the field. It moved and danced shapelessly. Because there were crosswinds, the fabric never took on a specific shape.

How like a ghost.

"I need to share this information, scant as it is, with Captain Croft and Director Trumbo. And with the Lost Souls and Guardian Angels. Everyone needs to know."

"I hope it helps," said Lost in a way that meant he did not believe it could.

"If they do attack us," said Soren, "how do we fight them?"

Lost laughed. "I have no idea. Every world known to be invaded by them was conquered, and the people exterminated."

"Surely they are not invulnerable. Every living thing has a weakness."

"If the night-gaunts have a weakness, my friend," said the golem, "my people never learned what it was. All I can say is that they come by night. Their sigil is the eclipse. They infuse nightmares in order to weaken the minds and the confidence of those they then attack.

"Tell me . . . how does one fight a nightmare? How does one fight the darkness? How does one fight the unknown?"

2

"Mosquito," called Beezer, who was flying point, "picking up something on long-range scanner. Sending location now."

Bianca, flying with Galahad a hundred kilometers back, let the data play across her internal screens. Even now, after many weeks as a NecroTek, she did not understand how her invisible ghost could watch a viewscreen. The structure of the eye and its lens needed organic form, or even a mechanical stand-in, in order to see anything. It was another in a growing list of things she didn't understand about what she was.

"Small," she said as she read the data. "Maybe a dagger fighter. Close to the right mass."

"No heat signature," said Galahad. "If it's a dagger, it's a dead one."

"Let's go take a look."

The NecroTeks turned and followed Beezer's signal to its source. When they caught up with him, they saw a small chunk of an asteroid drifting amid a cloud of smaller particles kicked out by the ship's impact with the stone. The machinery no longer looked like any kind of spacecraft. Not at first. Only when they got very close could they see part of an engine housing, a crumpled exhaust port, and the melted barrel of a cannon.

"Jeez," said Jacob, "we'd have to take that into a repair shop and tear it down to parts. I mean . . . I *think* it's a dagger, but it could just as well be something else."

Bianca moved closer so she could take hold of a couple of pieces and pull on them, trying to straighten out what she thought was the nose of the craft. But the pieces came apart and floated away.

"Shit. We don't have time to do this right. Beezer, run your scans again and then upload everything to Sybil. As soon as we get home, the geniuses back on Asphodel can see if they can make sense of it. Then let's get back in gear."

Jacob signaled to her that he wanted a private channel, and they cycled over to one they often used for conversations they did not care to share.

"What's up?" Bianca asked.

"Not trying to Monday-morning quarterback here …"

"But you will anyway."

"Kind of. I know you and the skipper thought this mission was the best use of our time. Finding any shoggoth bases and hitting them before they could launch another wave at us. I get it."

"But …?"

"But there's a whole lot of real estate out here, babe. Way more than anyone sitting in front of a RealScreen back at the station could grasp. If this star system was as flat as Earth's, it would still take maybe ten, fifteen years to scout it. What are we really hoping to accomplish with what we're doing?"

"I know," she said. "But Trumbo and her pet shrinks did some kind of poll after the last attack, and most people want a proactive approach rather than a sit-and-wait."

"Not to be a dick here," said Jacob, "but so what if that's what they think? They're civilians, and they don't understand."

"I know. I told Croft that like eight times."

"Yet here we are."

"Here we are," said Bianca. "Following orders and hoping for the best."

"Christ," growled Jacob.

"Look, love," she said, "Croft doesn't expect us to do a full sweep. What he wants is for us to check enough *likely* places to be able to come back with video footage of, well, nothing. Empty moons, empty asteroids, empty planets. No enemies cackling as they draw their evil plans against us."

"So, cultural comfort food," said Jacob sourly.

"Good public relations."

"Fucking propaganda is closer to the mark."

Bianca laughed. "Exactly what I said to the skipper."

Jacob made a sound like a sigh—which was contrived, since he had no lungs.

"Ours is not to wonder why, ours is but to do and die," quoted Bianca.

"At the risk of being pedantic ..."

"Which you never are."

"Which I *seldom* am," Jacob corrected. "The quote is from a poem, and it goes, 'Theirs not to make reply, theirs not to reason why, theirs but to do and die.' And it goes on to say, 'Into the valley of Death rode the six hundred.' 'The Charge of the Light Brigade.' Tennyson."

"You're such a bundle of unfiltered joy. Did I ever tell you that?"

They both laughed—a deliberate action given their mechanical nature—and flew off into the void. Each hoping that the valley of Death was only a concept and that the universe wouldn't take the quote as a challenge.

Part Fifteen
The Dance of Entropy

"It's life that matters, nothing but life—the process of discovering, the everlasting and perpetual process, not the discovery itself, at all."

—*Fyodor Dostoevsky*

Joint MIT/UCLA Biological Research Field Station #8
Queen Maud Land, Antarctica

1

"Jenny," whispered Evie. "*Wake up.* There's someone outside."

Jenny Spears came awake all at once. There was no intermediary pause to gather her senses—her eyes snapped open, and she was out of bed in a heartbeat. Then she froze in an attitude of listening. Her naked body was blue-white in the moonlight, but her muscles were taut, her posture ready for anything. She looked like a Greek statue of Artemis.

"What did you see?"

"I … don't know. I heard something at the door. The doorknob jiggling."

Spears grabbed her Stormsuit and pulled it on, doing it with the speed and efficiency of someone used to instant preparedness and unknown threats. She snatched up her Snellig gas-dart pistol and crept to the spot between door and window, then crouched low and peered out over the sill.

It heartened Evie that Jenny did not ask her if she'd only dreamed or imagined it.

Instead, she quietly asked, "Did you see anything?"

"I think so. Someone moved past the window, but I … I mean, I didn't …"

"You woke me, babe. That was the right call. Now, go into the bathroom and close the door. Don't come out until I say it's all clear. Now."

Evie did as she was told, though she did not close the door completely. She knelt in the dark and peered out through the crack.

Jenny shifted her angle to look up and down Main Street.

"Nothing visible." She crabbed sideways and took her holo-comms unit and quickly put it on her forearm. "Sybil, access street cameras and tell me if there's anyone outside."

The AI paused for a quick second, then replied, "There is no one within eighty meters in either direction from this hut."

"Roll back street cams. Who was outside?"

Another pause. "There was one person outside four minutes ago."

"Who was it?"

This time the pause was longer. "There is no data on that person."

"Show me."

A hologram appeared above the comms. Evie had to open the door a little more to see what it showed. There was a figure on the playback. It was roughly the size and shape of a man, but the image was weirdly distorted—making the man look like he was either wearing a cape of some kind or wearing some sort of harness that gave him batlike wings. He wore a hat or helmet with something on it resembling horns.

"What the fuck? … Sybil, expand that image. Enhance the graphic. I want to know who it is and what the hell he's wearing."

"I am unable to enhance the image, Agent Spears," said the AI.

"Why not?"

"It appears to be a video ghost."

Those were one of the oddities of modern holographic videography—holdovers from previously deleted images that somehow bled through to new ones. Evie, watching, understood that. It had been common at her university since the data banks were old and had been scrubbed far too many times. Once—during a lecture by her mentor, Dr. Soren—a zebra appeared beside an AI-generated Immanuel Kant and seemed to dance as the philosopher spoke about consequentialism.

But this did not feel like a computer glitch to her. That shadow seemed weirdly specific in its horrific outline, and the way it moved seemed deliberate. It moved down the street, avoiding pools of light, sticking to the shadows until it reached her door. But as soon as there was movement in the window—corresponding to when Evie moved the blinds to look outside—the shadow dissipated as surely as light smoke in a stiff wind.

Jenny cut a look over her shoulder and patted the air, telling Evie to stay put. She checked the magazine in the Snellig, then gingerly opened the door. When she stepped outside, it was all at once, moving with astonishing speed and fluidity.

Despite the warning, Evie left the bathroom and hurried over to the window, once more ducking to look between the lowest slats. Jenny Spears was in the snow, crouched like a cat, the dart gun in a two-hand combat grip as she turned 180 degrees. She repeated this twice and then slowly straightened, lowering the gun.

"Jenny?"

"Stay inside. Give me a second." Jenny knelt and studied the ground outside Evie's door, brushing irregularities in the snow with her fingers. When she straightened, her body language was different as the tension fled, replaced by ordinary weariness. She came in and closed the door, then thumbed the safety on and placed the Snellig on the bedside table.

"It wasn't a video ghost," insisted Evie.

Jenny said nothing as she stripped off the Stormsuit and stood naked in front of the fire. Evie came and stood behind her, wrapping her arms around Jenny's waist.

"I know what I saw," she said.

Jenny turned in the circle of her arms, hooked a finger under Evie's chin, and raised her mouth to a kiss. It was soft and gentle, and as balms for the nerves went, it helped.

"I believe you," she said.

"Did you see anything in the snow?"

"If you mean footprints, no."

"But … something?"

"I don't know. Could have been marks left over from when we came in. The wind's blown most of the soft snow and ice crystals away, and the ground is hard as iron. Won't take a print."

"It wasn't a video ghost," Evie said again. "And it's not the first time something like this happened."

"What do you mean?"

Evie told her about the other incident. When Jenny did not reply, Evie said, "We didn't have the streetlight cameras set up then."

"There's nothing out there now."

Evie studied her face. "You believe me, though, right?"

"I have to ask, babe ... After we went to bed ... did you get up for a nightcap."

"What are you—?"

Jenny cut her off. "Evie, I know about your trips to the bathroom. I see the levels of the whiskey bottle go up and down."

"I'm not a drunk," snapped Evie.

"I know."

"Things are bad here, you know that. And I'm having dreams."

"Who isn't?" said Jenny vaguely.

Evie seemed not to notice the comment. "If I take a drink now and then, so what? It helps me sleep. It helps with ... with everything. Do you have a problem with that?"

Instead of answering, Jenny kissed her, took her hand, and led her back to their bed. They climbed under the blankets and held each other close. Evie waited for Jenny's reply, but there was none. Sleep came, though, and tugged them each down into darkness.

Where dreams waited for them with sharp claws and biting teeth.

In the morning, neither of them remembered their dreams, even though both had dreamed of a shadowy figure with bat wings, horns, and an insatiable hunger.

2

The following morning, Brollachan convened a meeting of all senior scientists.

They met in a hut on the outside corner of the camp. Two soldiers stood outside and waved off anyone who did not have an express invitation.

"As the evolutionary biologist here, Evie, in the absence of tissue for analysis, what can you infer from what little we know?" asked Brollachan.

Everyone turned to her, many looking hopeful. She hated to disappoint them.

"I would need to make some assumptions."

"For context? Sure. Please do."

"Well," said Evie, "First, if that thing is *not* part of the crew, then its nature may be harder to understand. It could, for example, be a parasite that the Artifact's crew picked up somewhere. Its apparent aggression may account for why the ship crashed here. It may have escaped containment or simply been underestimated and then attacked the crew. I think we should keep that possibility on the table, especially as we try to understand the technical philosophy of whoever constructed that craft. Assumptions will be easy to make and hard to identify, so we need to check our own reactions and be checks on one another."

Brollachan nodded but did not interrupt.

"However," continued Evie, "if it is *part* of the crew, if it is an example of the species that built the Artifact, then that could be either very good or very bad news."

"What's the bad news?" asked Brollachan. "Let's get that out of the way first."

"The bad news is it may have come here to settle this world. If that creature was representative of the crew, there could be a great many of them in there. Any culture that can build a ship of that size and travel here has almost certainly developed cryonics. We know there is some power active in the ship. The energy field across that star door is proof of that, even if it is an automatic system."

"After all this time?" asked Kimbra. "Where are they getting the power from?"

"Can't be sure, but solar seems likely."

"How so?"

"The ship was inactive as far as we know," said Evie. "When the side of the mountain collapsed, a large section of hull was exposed. Even down in the valley, it gets direct sunlight. Some residual power could have kept the cryo-chambers intact, and being packed in ice could have contributed to that. Mind you, this is guesswork because we know next to nothing."

"Then the creature," mused Brollachan, "might have been what? A sentry? Some kind of anchor watch? In stasis until the hull began charging from sunlight?"

"As a working theory, yes," said Evie. "Why else would it open the door after all this time and come outside?"

They hashed that back and forth for a while. Everyone had a theory, but it was clear they were nowhere near a reliable, let alone definitive, answer.

Then Brollachan said, "Shifting focus, Evie, what inferences can you draw about the being the Jokers encountered down in the ice cave?"

She rubbed her eyes for a moment. "Well," she said, "the creature demonstrated intelligence. Of a *kind.* Once it absorbed the soldiers—and, yes, I know how awful that sounds—it took some of Lance Corporal Figari's personality. Or at least his knowledge. It spoke in English. It attempted to communicate."

"Excuse me," said Patel, "but I see things a lot different from that. It mimicked the corporal and tried to lure the Jokers in closer. It demonstrated deception, guile."

"You're right to a degree, Andy," Evie said. "Mimicry was demonstrated, but it goes further than that. Assuming the form of one of us is still a type of communication, one perhaps based on the way the species evolved or a cultural thing. More critically, however, it spoke. There is a lot more to intelligence than simply repeating sounds. It *spoke*. It formed sentences—constructed logical ones—and was demonstrably self-aware. It even seemed to marvel at the specific details—hands, for example—of its new form. That is a higher intelligence than, say, a parrot repeating learned words or phrases. No. This thing is clearly intelligent."

"And aggressive," suggested Joan Kimbra.

Evie took some time with that. "Yes," she said, drawing that word out. "But aggression is, arguably, a quality of many levels of intelligence. Nature is filled with creatures who act as predators, just as it's replete with species that use various kinds of deception. It's more deliberate, of course, with higher intelligences and, by extension, higher cultures. Look at our own history of invading other countries as much through guile as by overt aggression." She paused. "A note of caution, though. We can't be sure if the killing of Venture Team II was malicious in nature. Tragic, to be sure, but until the creature had absorbed those people, it might not have realized that we are not as malleable as it is. It may be that absorption is a common way for theriomorphic creatures like this—shape-shifters—to communicate with others of its kind. It may well have had benign intentions when it did what it did. We don't know enough about this race to begin to judge them according to our own moral standards."

"I'll accept that," said Brollachan with some grace, though others in the room looked more skeptical. Dr. Patel sat there shaking his head, though he did not voice his doubts.

"Or," continued Evie, "they could be as pragmatic about conquest as an army of ants, no animus beyond the survival and prosperity of their species. Wish I could say something more encouraging. What we know is far outweighed by what we don't."

"Yeah, well, at least we know fire kills whatever it is," said Joan Kimbra.

"Evie," said Brollachan, "what can you tell us about its nature?"

"Only guesswork."

"Give us that, then."

Evie nodded. "What we saw on the holo-screens was adaptive evolution taken to an extraordinary level. But it's not entirely unprecedented in our experience here on Earth. We have some plants and animals here that have evolved to camouflage themselves. Phasmids—stick bugs—are a prime example. Living for countless generations in a hostile environment, they've evolved to look like sticks. Some moths have evolved to have spots that look like the eyes of a bigger and less vulnerable creature. Chameleons change color. So do cuttlefish. Nature is adaptive and resilient. This creature, however, has a far greater and more immediate ability to change form. It's a true shape-shifter. There are papers I can have Sybil pull up that explore directed adaptation and controlled metamorphosis as an evolutionary possibility."

"It was so fast, though," said Andy Patel.

"Which might be indicative of its natural environment," Evie said. "Living in a pervasively hostile habitat—one with, say, a variety of predators triggered by different qualities such as shape, size, color, smell, and so on—might have triggered a radical new direction in evolution. Or ..."

"Or what, Professor?" asked Kimbra.

"Or this was a design feature," she said flatly. "It could be a bioengineered superadaptive form created for more than survival. Like the holographic camouflage our soldiers wear but taken to an extraordinary degree."

She paused.

"Was there something else?" prompted Brollachan.

"As dramatic as what Agent Spears did down there and, um, afterward," Evie said, trying not to look directly at Brollachan, "I think we should agree that she made the right call. If that thing is as deliberately adaptive as it appears, and if there is a chance there are more of them on the Artifact, we cannot ever risk them getting off this continent. We can't even allow them to reach the water's edge. If they do, then they could proliferate through the oceans and then come ashore in numbers we could not hope to match."

That plunged the gathering into a frightened silence.

"It may be," she said softly, "that it's in the best interests of the entire human race to find a way to completely destroy the Artifact and everything inside. I think I can say without fear of contradiction that there has never been a greater threat to *all* life on Earth."

They sat with the full weight of that pressing down on them. At first no one looked anywhere but into their own thoughts, then gradually they cut looks at one another. Evie wondered what they wanted out of that nonverbal contact. Reassurance? Comfort? Maybe visible evidence of shared awareness so each person did not feel as utterly alone as she did.

Dr. Brollachan broke the silence.

"I've ordered a shipment of the latest generation of drones. My people are installing new sensor packs right now, in flight. We'll have them by morning. Once they're here and synced with Sybil, we'll try to get some answers by sending them into the Artifact."

"Why wait?" asked Patel.

"It's a shielding issue," said Kimbra. "The new drones have shielding for cosmic rays and pretty much anything else we know about—full spectrum—and the sensor software is bleeding edge. And, let's face it, guys, we don't want to send in last year's model for something as important as this. Torq's bringing down Alan Meyer to oversee it. Top guy for anything with an energetic signature."

There was more, but the meeting broke up soon after. Brollachan caught up to Evie as she walked back to her hut. Spears was waiting for her, and Evie hurried with excited steps. But when the SPU chief fell in beside her, she slowed.

"There's something else I wanted to discuss," he said. "It didn't come up in the discussion because everyone was pretty rattled by your comments."

"Sorry," said Evie. "I wasn't trying to scare anyone."

"No," said Brollachan quickly, "you were not wrong. The danger *is* that great. But the other thing that—oddly—no one has mentioned is what the creature said about having been born in vats and made to live as slaves."

Evie stopped. "God … I think I blanked on that, too. I guess I thought it was gibberish. The ramblings of Figari's traumatized mind. Then suddenly everything went wonky."

Brollachan smiled. "Wonky is a good word for it."

"The slavery thing," mused Evie, "I actually don't know what to make of that, except maybe …"

"Maybe what?"

"Well, Torq," she said, "that shape-shifting ability is so useful, so precise, so sophisticated that it tends to offend my sensibilities as an evolutionary biologist. Sure, nature is efficient, but that borders on devious. Or crosses that line. If a race could control such creatures and force them to work, then imagine how much they could accomplish. Thinking shape-shifters who could do any task simply by assuming the most practical form. It's the chameleon concept taken to its most sophisticated degree."

"One wonders," said Brollachan, his gaze seemingly turned inward, "what the medical applications for such a thing might be."

"In what way?"

"If the gene for transformation could be isolated—separated from the malignant intelligence, reduced to merely a biological component—then it could be introduced to, say, an amputee. Or a person with a genetic deficiency or genetic error. It would allow for self-repair."

"Maybe. But only if that repair was permanent."

"Yes."

She patted his chest. "I feel your enthusiasm on that, Torq. I do. But it's dangerous thinking. Maybe someday, if we find more specimens and can transport them offworld to a space station or a moon without an atmosphere that can support life, those kinds of experiments could happen. Not now, though. We don't even know if ordinary containment would work. I mean, hell, ever see an octopus problem-solve its way out of a sealed aquarium?"

He nodded glumly. "Sometimes I forget that there is a world outside of the lab."

Evie laughed. "You're not the only one guilty of that."

They stood for a moment, each aware that their friendship had somehow taken a new step but neither knowing whether it needed to be commented upon. In the end, neither did. Instead, Brollachan said, "The slavery thing bothers me for many reasons. But one aspect of it is truly frightening."

"Oh, I think I can guess. If these creatures *did* build that ship, it shows their level of intelligence. We already know something of their power. Stepping back to try and grasp the level of power necessary to *enslave* such creatures is … well …"

"Yes," he said. "It's that."

The breeze was intensifying, carrying with it a barrage of little ice crystals. They said goodbye and went to their personal huts.

When Evie opened her door, the lights were off and a single holographic candle flickered, painting the room in tones of gray and gold. Cups of steaming tea sat on the equipment cases used as night tables. Jennifer Spears lay on the bed, dressed only in shadows and candlelight.

4

Dr. Indira Singh sat and listened to Craig Anders speak about his dreams.

He was the seventh staff member to visit her office at the far end of Main Street. The young graduate assistant was bright, insightful, introspective, and terrified.

"I know it sounds crazy," he said, "but sometimes in my dreams I'm one of those … those things."

"How so?" asked Singh.

"Sometimes I'm like that shape-shifting thing in my dreams. I mean, I'm Craig, but I'm also *it*. Like I'm both. Like I have two minds, and the longer the dream goes on, the harder it is for me to tell which is the alien and which is me."

"How does that make you feel?"

"How do you think?" he snapped, then realized how intense he sounded. "Sorry. I'm wired. Lousy night's sleep."

"Was it the same dream last night?"

He surprised her by shaking his head. "Not really. It was like something out of a movie. Mind you, I was one of those things again, but I was completely that. No trace at all of me in there except being aware of it, if that makes sense."

"It does. Please tell me about the dream."

"Well," began Craig, "I was flying a spaceship. A star-fighter of some kind. Not like anything you see on the news. This one was different. Shaped like the head of a spear, or … maybe a wide-bladed dagger. Something like that. Aggressive. And there were a whole bunch of other fighters just like mine. Dozens of us. We were in some kind of wild battle over a small moon. Our ships were taking a real beating, too. I saw a lot of them go down hard."

"Who were you fighting?"

His eyes darted to hers and then away. "It's going to sound stupid."

"It was a dream, Craig. There's no judgment on any content."

He nodded. "Okay … but it even sounds weird to say it. We were fighting vampires. Or … maybe gargoyles. Something like a bit of both. We were scared of them, too. Not just scared of their star-fighters—and theirs were actually shaped like stars. Five-pointed. Like ninja throwing stars. Fast as fuck. Oops, sorry. Fast as *hell*."

"You said you weren't afraid of them?"

"The thing that scared me and the others like me—and I mean scared us nearly to death—was what was flying those star-fighters. Those vampire-gargoyle-devil things, I mean. Something about those things scared me more than anything else. Even more than dying."

5

"Spears," called Hobart. "A word?"

Jenny turned away from the pipe rail. Like most of the people at the site, she often came out to look down at the Artifact. As she turned, her expression was momentarily blank, as if waking from sleep.

"What? Oh, hey, Tom. What's up?"

He came over and in a confidential voice told her about the pirate activity around Sagan Station and about the sensitive materials stored there. Jenny leaned a hip against the rail, folded her arms across her chest, and listened without interruption.

When Hobart was finished, she said, "And you want the Jokers to go out there and spank some pirate ass."

"In a nutshell."

"When?"

"We're working on that now. Mars isn't in the best place for a launch, so it'll be a couple of weeks before we can leave. It'll be your option to go cryo or stay awake."

"Fuck awake. Ice me, baby. That's minimum forty days at best speed."

Hobart nodded. "Does that mean if the problem gets worse, you'll go?"

Jenny glanced past him, and Hobart turned to see Evie and a couple of her grad students walking toward a lab hut.

"Sure," she said, but doubt was evident in her expression, her voice, and her eyes.

6

When Dr. Alan Meyer arrived, he lived up to his reputation.

He looked like a musician—waist-long dreadlocks in fifty hues of blue and twice that many shades of red- and brown-colored beads threaded into them. His arms were covered in tattoos of tropical fish, and the ones on his forearms were made with "life-ink" containing tiny nanites that made the fish appear to wriggle and swim.

He, Evie, and Spears, along with several team members, were clustered around the side of the Artifact. The Hadrian X9 sealing skin had been carefully removed, revealing the doorway. Dozens of drones swarmed around, constantly adjusting their positions so as not to shine in anyone's eyes and to erase all shadows from that section of the curved hull.

The fire cannons hovered nearby, their vigilant sensors ready to adjust for clear fire with reduced risk to human assets. At least that was how Hobart described them.

Alan Meyer stood looking at the star door for a while, loudly chewing gum, his snow goggles pushed up on his forehead. He had eyes of such a dark brown that they looked as black as his pupils. Below his lower lip was a line of blue crystals that had been mined on Ganymede. To Spears, Evie whispered that those jewels cost more than her entire education.

"Is he a showoff or a dick?" asked Spears.

"Bit of both. But Alan knows his stuff."

Meyer took a few steps closer, bent and scooped up some ice crystals, and tossed them lightly at the open doorway. The ice passed through but vanished immediately.

"Hmm," he said.

Evie came up beside him. "Thoughts?"

"Well, the energy isn't a barrier. You saw it—the stuff I threw went in with no visible resistance. So we're not talking any kind of force shield."

"But . . . ?"

"No buts. Let's try my new drones."

He signaled to one of his team to bring up a Hoot Owl drone, which was one of his own designs. Unlike the bat, rat, and other drones used by Hobart's soldiers and the Jokers, this wasn't actually built to look like a bird. It was two feet long, cylindrical, with four strong propellers inside curved housings.

"Tether it," ordered Meyer, and his tech attached a thin, strong woven wire cable to the tail of the drone and hooked the other end to the winch on the front of a snowcat. "Move it into position."

The tech placed the drone on the ground in front of the star door, synced it with his Sybil, and backed away.

"Here's what we're going to do," Meyer said. "The drone is shielded against everything up to twelve GeV. The shell is a high-entropy alloy—a mix of chromium, cobalt, and nickel—whose strength increases as it gets colder. There are more than sixty sensors inside, and also biosample trays with a bunch of bacteria, nonlethal viruses, fungi, and protozoa so we can monitor the effects on simple live organisms." He looked around, his face bright and happy. "Ready to rock?"

"As a friend of mine is so fond of saying," said Evie. "Game on."

She caught a quick flicker of a glance from Meyer to Spears, but he said nothing.

"Send 'er in," he ordered.

The tech started the motors and lifted the drone to chest height. At Meyer's nod he gave it a little push and the Hoot Owl wobbled, corrected, and then flew toward the star door very slowly. The surrounding drones recorded everything, their own shells packed with sensors.

"Going, going," murmured Meyer. He stood wide-legged, rubbing his gloved hands together with excitement. "And … *gone*."

The Hoot Owl passed through the opening. There was no flash or noise of any kind.

Dr. Kimbra, who sat on a barrel, her holo-comms screen open above her forearm, said, "No discernible fluctuation in the energy signature."

Meyer frowned. "That's interesting. Pause the Owl and let's look at the readings."

Evie, Spears, and half a dozen others clustered around a big holo-screen that Meyer's techs pulled up.

"Signal strength is a bit twitchy, boss," said the tech. "And … hmm, that's weird, look at the mission clock."

The digital readout had begun at 00:00, the point where the nose of the Hoot Owl made first contact with the door. By the holo-screen clock only eleven seconds had elapsed. But the chronometer on the drone had a totally different reading. As they watched, it went from 00:01 to 17:44 to 02:12:39.

"The hell?" muttered Spears.

"Something's affecting the sensors," said Meyer. "Pull up the bio trays. Okay, let's … Wait. What?"

According to the sensors in each sample tray, the live organisms were all experiencing stress. Four had gone dark, and most of the others were reaching critical.

"Okay, Tony, pull it out," ordered Meyer. "Do it now."

The tech working the winch reversed it, and the cable stretching between the snowcat's grill and the Hoot Owl drew taut. So taut that the cable began to softly thrum.

Tony touched the line. "Getting some serious resistance."

"Pull it out, Tony. Slow and steady."

They held their breaths as the winch whined and groaned and pulled. There were small yellow marks on the cable to indicate meters and smaller blue ones for centimeters. As the Hoot Owl was dragged back, the snowcat's engine began to protest, its engine noise rising to a higher pitch.

Evie took Spears's hand and squeezed it.

"It'll be okay," said Spears, though she sounded as tense as Evie felt.

"It's coming through," called Meyers. "Keep at it, Tony. Here it comes. Receiver team get ready. Everyone else get back." He walked backward, long arms wide, herding everyone away from the star door. Two men in hazmat suits approached the Artifact and—moving with quick efficiency—erected a bioshield shroud around the door. The skin of the shroud was packed with sensors, and as every part of the cable that was inside emerged, it wrapped itself around the metal, enclosing it with a tight biohazard seal.

"Bird's coming out, boss," called Tony.

"I see it," said Meyer. "I … Jesus God."

The Hoot Owl came out of the star door and immediately collapsed, all four rotors stalling and the internal engine sputtering. It fell but was caught by the bioshield and was sealed inside.

The shroud was clear, and they all gathered around it, staring down at the Hoot Owl. At what was left of it. The super-durable metal had lost its sheen and lay there, smoking, cracked, pitted with rust. A few small lights still twinkled on its sides, but weakly. Then it went dark and still and lay as if dead.

"What happened to it?" asked Spears. "Was there acid in the atmosphere in there?"

Meyer shook his head. He had a data holo-screen open on his forearm's comms unit. "That's not corrosion."

"Then what?"

Meyers held out his forearm. The final feed from the chronometer inside the drone read 683,748 hours 11 minutes 31 seconds.

"I ... don't understand," said Evie. "Six hundred eighty-three thousand hours? That's ... that's not possible."

Meyer took a hand scanner and ran it over the drone. "Rate of decay of all component parts matches the chronometer. All biological specimens are dead. They're dust." He looked at the star door. "That drone was in there for seventy-eight years."

7

The team spent weeks trying to figure out what happened. Evie lost track of all the theories, but by the third week people were reduced to questioning the fabric of reality. Andy Patel was even fronting theories that had more than a toe over the line into the supernatural.

No one had an answer.

Alan Meyer had more drones flown in, and he spent eighteen hours a day trying new combinations of shielding. Metals in various combinations did not work. Organic housing like wood and leather merely crumbled into dust. Ceramics aged to brittleness. Even projected energy shielding of the kind used on battleships and space stations did nothing.

With each failure, the big man's confidence flaked off. By the beginning of the fourth week, he began to smell like alcohol and hashish, and the erratic sleep patterns, coupled with stress, had turned him into a zombie.

He kept at it, though. They all did. It was maddening to have an alien spacecraft with an open door and no way to properly investigate it. Whole days passed with only Meyer, his assistants, and a military guard laboring away while the rest of the team tried to find something to do to justify the ongoing secrecy and the expanding budget of the operation.

8

Evie found Alan Meyer in the mess hall, sitting alone in a corner with a bottle of rye and a glass in front of him. He was smoking a tobacco-free herbal cigarette and staring through the air into nothing. There was no one else in the room, so she took a cup of coffee over and, without invitation, sat down across from him. He blinked twice, very slowly, and then focused on her as if coming back from a very great distance.

"Sucks," she said.

He actually smiled at that. Meyer poured a finger of rye into his glass and reached over and clinked it against the side of her mug. "Sucks in all the wrong ways."

They sat in the shadow of what he meant.

Since Meyer's first attempt at studying the inside of the craft, Brollachan had ordered him to do a laundry list of other experiments. Some included sending in other life forms—larger and more complex. At first it was a trayful of German cockroaches—known as the most common and hardiest species of that genus. It had a lifespan of approximately two hundred days, could endure a fair temperature range, and it had a markedly high number of chemoreceptors that allowed it to detect a broad range of chemical cues from toxins, food, pathogens, and pheromones. Nanite sensors were introduced to its body and brain, and Sybil oversaw the telemetry feeds.

The roaches died, of course. But their deaths created a new mystery—because the rate of decay for them was substantially different from that of the germs and alloys of the Hoot Owl. The insects died much more slowly. On the first insertion, they were left in the hull for exactly the same amount of time as the oOwl. The drone carrying them recorded a similar passage of time, but the insects themselves were still alive when brought out. They were at the end of their lifespan, and died shortly thereafter, but the timing was strange.

None of them could figure it out.

Brollachan was particularly fascinated by this and ordered many other animals sent in, keeping Meyer and his team very busy. A 3D printer was flown in and set up near the Artifact, and it chugged out new drones at the rate of one every thirty-two minutes.

Evie had been there for every test, even though she loathed any kind of animal testing. She saw them send in mice, rats, guinea pigs, weasels, pigeons, penguins, and various kinds of fish.

They all aged. They all died.

But every single species died at a different rate of decomposition.

"It's like time itself is warped in there," Meyer said, as if picking up a conversational thread left hanging.

"So it seems."

"Makes no fucking sense."

"None," she agreed. Evie reached across and took the bottle of rye, raised a single eyebrow in inquiry, got a nod, and poured a healthy knock into her coffee. Then she refilled his glass.

They drank.

9

"Where do you disappear to all the time lately?" Evie asked two days later, while she and Torq Brollachan were in line for food at the mess hall. "You've been a ghost lately."

"Oh," he said, "keeping busy."

"With what, if you don't mind me asking?"

Brollachan hoisted the same kind of smile he used during budget hearings with the closed-door senate committee on covert research and development. It looked friendly, even affable, but actually said nothing.

"Although this is *clearly* the most important project," he said offhandedly, "the SPU has a lot of wheels turning all the time, and it's my job to keep them greased."

"Ugh, politics," said Evie. "You have my sympathies."

"Oh, it's fine. I don't mind."

"Better you than me," she said as she ladled mashed potatoes onto her plate.

Better me than you, he'd quietly agreed then. That snatch of conversation echoed in his mind many times after that.

The lie worked, as it had always worked when he was engaged in something off-book. He loaded up on protein and carbs, sat amiably with the senior scientists, and then melted away when the tide of the conversation turned away from the Artifact.

He returned to his hut and locked himself in.

Days passed. Then weeks.

10

Brollachan grew more and more remote, spending large parts of each day in his lab. He was not always alone, however.

He had used his connections to bring three key allies down to the site—scientists who had been working on ultra top secret SPU projects for years. Dr. Beatrice Howard, a molecular biologist from Harvard; Dr. T. T. Wu, an organic chemist from Stanford; and Dr. Alejandro Solà, a research physician from the University of Barcelona. Each was a standout in their field, but equally important was that he trusted them. They were willing to gamble their constitutional rights—as specified in the nondisclosure agreements each signed—in order to work way out on the bleeding edge of scientific discovery.

Brollachan set up a separate hut for them with attached dedicated laboratories and armed guards at the doors. These were arranged in a cluster around his own.

The three new scientists were fully briefed on the Artifact, but so far he had kept them at arm's length about the special project he worked on in the quiet solitude of the long, frozen nights. That would likely change, he decided, but now wasn't the time.

Each time he sat down to work alone in his lab, Brollachan asked Ariel for an update. One night, the AI was waiting for him, displaying a hologram of a flashing yellow ball in the air. He ran to his table and sat.

"Tell me," he demanded.

"I ran the last batch of fifty simulations, Dr. Brollachan," said the AI.

"And … *and*?"

"Forty-nine were negative. However the fiftieth has yielded unexpected results that you may find interesting."

Beads of nervous sweat burst from his pores. "Show me, damn it."

The flashing ball vanished and was replaced by a screen showing the contiguous strands of rebuilt DNA.

"When a high level of short-duration electricity was introduced to a copy of the sample, I detected a significant organic response."

"How significant?"

"The matter moved, Doctor," said Ariel. "The movement lasted for 2.89 seconds after the electrical charge was switched off. As there is no detectable central nervous system, I cannot account for the continued movement."

"Hypothesize."

"It might be useful if I showed you."

A screen appeared that showed the tiny lump that had been cut from a culture prepared using 50 percent of the red dust. Brollachan watched as the electricity was channeled into the thing. There was a four-second delay, and then the lump pulsed. There was no better word for it. The mass swelled and collapsed. A moment later it did so again.

"Is that respiration?"

"Unknown. The mass has no lungs or detectable respiratory system."

"And it's not static shock?"

"It is not, Dr. Brollachan," said Ariel.

When the current was switched off, the lump pulsed three more times. And then it stopped and lay inert. Looking like nothing of any importance. He was not fooled. His excitement was so intense that he could feel his own pulse throbbing in his neck and forehead, hammering inside the cave of his chest.

"Tell me," he said softly. "Is it alive?"

The AI seemed to pause. "As regards this particular specimen," said Ariel, "define *alive*."

11

"Professor," gasped Craig Anders as he burst into her lab. "You better come."

Evie looked up from the report she was writing—one that essentially rehashed the last six reports. Nothing new had happened. The Artifact remained stubbornly closed to them.

She rubbed her eyes. "God, now what?"

"It's … it's bad," Craig said.

Evie stood quickly. "Bad? What do you mean? What's happened?"

Craig licked his lips. "You'd better come."

She pulled on a coat and stepped into the stinging wind. People were running from all over the camp toward one of the huts used by the MIT part of the original team. A crowd was clustered around the door, and everyone was standing in unnatural silence. Evie's heart sank, knowing that this wasn't going to be anything but bad.

It was worse than that.

Her assistant went ahead of her, pushing people out of the way. Doing it with an abruptness that spoke to how unsettled he was, because Craig was not generally rough with anyone. A soldier stood outside the door, but he nodded and stepped aside to admit Evie.

She glanced at his face, but it was wooden. Even so, Evie thought she could see a bit of fear in his eyes.

As soon as she entered the hut, Evie felt the same fear blossom like a black flower in her own heart.

There were two people sitting with their backs to the wall of the main room. Sean Riley, a grad student from MIT—one of those who had come down with Dr. Xi—and Brenda Cooper, a mineralogy PhD candidate. They wore no clothes. Instead, they were dressed in blood.

Evie found herself saying, "Where … did they get the gun?"

Colonel Hobart was standing closer to the bodies. Without turning, he said, "*Guns.* Two of them. Stolen from the bin where Venture's gear was stored. Pulse pistols. Quiet and, um … efficient."

His voice was totally hollow.

Evie came and stood next to him. Dr. Singh was beside him. The three of them looked at the bodies for several empty moments. And then they raised their heads and studied what was written on the wall.

It was sloppy. Written with a fabric marker. Black ink. Much of it was spattered with blood, tiny chips of skull, and gray lumps of brain tissue, yet it was readable.

Born in vats

Stirred by hate

Slaves to the Outer Gods and the Elder Things and the Great Old Ones

Slaves for all of them

Unloved by any

And below that, the painted words nearly equal to what was left of the top of Sean Riley's head:

Save our brothers

Save our sisters

Break the chains
Set us free
Save us

"*Are baap re*," breathed Dr. Singh. She stood with a hand covering her mouth. The two people who lay dead had been patients of hers. Each had shared the content of their dreams with her. Unlike most of the members of the expedition, they had been able to recall a lot of details about their dreams, and Singh had used that as a basis for a report she was writing on collective hallucinations and shared trauma.

She had given each some meditations to do and recommended they journal to record as much of their elusive dreams as possible. She'd told them everything would be fine.

Everything.

Fine.

Tears broke from her eyes and rolled down her cheeks.

To Evie, it felt like there was a hurricane ballooning inside her chest. There wasn't enough air to breathe, and all the lights seemed far too bright. She felt her knees buckle. She did not even try to stop the slow collapse. Even Hobart, with his combat-trained reflexes, did not catch her in time. Her kneecaps struck the floor, and then Evie curved into herself, crushed beneath the weight of pain. And of horror.

When she fled, her first thought was not the safety of Jenny's arms, but the deep and golden shelter of the bottle.

Part Sixteen
Dream a Little Dream of Me

"They've promised that dreams can come true—but forgot to mention that nightmares are dreams, too."

—*Anonymous*

Asphodel Station
The Shadderal Star System

1

A nightmare held Lady Jessica McHugh deep beneath the surface of safety.

Ever since the shoggoth invasion and her nearly suicidal efforts to connect the souls of dead pilots with the equally inert spacecraft on Shadderal, she had been having the most terrible dreams. There were different dreams, but with the certainty of a mystic, she knew that they were connected. Just as she knew that they were the realities behind the twisted dreams of the writer H. P. Lovecraft.

Sometimes she dreamed of the colossal city with its architecture designed for creatures entirely unlike humans. In those dreams she sometimes walked, sometimes pushed herself with desperate haste in her wheelchair, and sometimes she crawled. It was not always clear if she was hurrying toward something or fleeing from it.

Other times, she dreamed of stepping into the wide mouth of some huge and bizarre machine. It was made of steel and copper and set with jewels, and when it was turned on, it pulsed with life. Not with the hum of an engine or the thrum of electricity coursing through its wires, but actual life. When the settings were right, the machine became alive.

But the dream that haunted her that night was different. She dreamed that a monster hunted her—not to kill, but to devour her and invade her mind and steal her gifts. To steal her ability to recall the spirits of the dead, and then spread like a plague across all of space and time and the realms of dream.

Jessica McHugh woke with a scream.

2

"It sounds truly awful," said Soren the following morning. He sat on a couch in Lady Jessica's apartment, perched on the edge of the cushion, his body tense from listening to Lady Jessica's account of her nightmare.

"That is the understatement of the century," she said.

"I recall you saying that you had developed some degree of active control over your dreams," he prompted.

"So I thought." Lady Jessica sat in her wheelchair with a blanket over her withered legs. Her cat, Sonder, dozing on her lap.

"What changed? Is your dream control health related?"

Jessica considered, then gave a small shake of her head. "I don't think so. It feels more like a deliberate psychic attack."

"By . . . ?"

She smiled, and for a moment there was a familiar flash of vibrancy in her eyes. "Ask Lost, though I bet you already know the answer."

Soren sat back and sighed. "Night-gaunts you mean?"

"I have no alternate suggestion," she said. "From what Lost told you, dreams are their first weapon of attack. Even in the condition I'm in, Lars, my psychic defenses are strong. They have to be to do the kinds of things I do. Spirits can glom onto a necromancer and invade them. A lot of history's cases of demonic possession are really lost spirits trying to invade a living being in order to *become* alive again—either by attacking unskilled necromancers or targeting people with unusually elevated levels of empathy. I suspect these night-gaunts can do this deliberately. If they can do this to me, we need to think very long and hard about what they might be doing to others on this station."

3

Three decks below, a thirteen-year-old girl knelt in a bathtub of tepid water, a razor in her hand. Her forearm was lined with hesitation cuts that seeped tiny droplets of blood.

She looked up at the mirror over the sink as if she could see the face of Jesus.

"Please don't make me go back to sleep," she begged.

The mirror did not reply.

Tears ran freely down the girl's cheeks.

"Please ... just tell me I won't go to hell if I do this. Please, *please*."

Neither Jesus, nor any prophet, god, or angel spoke to her. The girl caved forward as if punched in the stomach.

"I'm sorry," she sobbed. "I'm sorry."

The razor bit deep. First one arm and then, with failing strength, the other. The bathwater changed from a gray paleness to a polluted pink. Then a deeper scarlet. The girl settled back and closed her eyes and kept praying not to be damned.

Her eyelids blinked slowly ... and slower. On one last blink, the lashes remained still against the smoothness of her cheeks. Inside her mind, the images from the nightmare began to fade. Becoming indistinct, like smoke. Like clouds. She felt herself fall, and begged Jesus not to send her to hell.

She dropped below the level of the smoke and breath and life.

And the night-gaunts were waiting to drag her into the Dreamlands.

Part Seventeen
The Birds of Sorrow

"We never understand how little we need in this world until we know the loss of it."

—*J. M. Barrie*

Joint MIT/UCLA Biological Research Field Station #8
Queen Maud Land, Antarctica

1

Evie Cronin sat at a table in the mess hall.

Most of the other tables were occupied, but the room was nearly silent. The deaths—the suicides—were an oppressive weight that crushed all conversation.

"May I join you?"

Evie jumped and turned to see Dr. Singh standing at her elbow. The therapist hadn't made a sound.

"Um … sure," she said, awkwardly and with poor grace.

Singh sat down and placed her teacup on the table. By reflex, Evie pulled her coffee mug close and cupped it with both hands, as if that might somehow hide the strong smell of whiskey. She gave Singh an *I dare you* look. Singh did not react.

Instead, she said, "How are you doing, Professor?"

"It's Evie, and I'm fine."

"Okay, Evie, I'm Indira. And I'd like to ask that question again. How *are* you?"

"Is that a personal or professional question?"

Singh gave the smallest of shrugs. "A bit of both. Given what's happened, the two are hardly antithetical."

Evie began to lift her mug, thought better of it, and let it sit. "I knew them. Sean and Brenda. They're not from my team, but since they came here, they became part of … well, *us*."

"Have you had to deal with much in terms of loss and grief?"

"Shouldn't we be doing this on your couch?"

"Only if you like."

Evie looked away, staring at nothing. "No, I never had much experience with people I know dying. I guess being down here is giving me a crash course." She shook her head. "Venture Team, Gillian, Mac … and now this. It's …"

"It's what?"

"It's too much."

"What does that mean to you, Evie? 'Too much,' I mean."

Evie sat back and looked at the ceiling. She ached to take a big gulp of the whiskey-laced coffee. The mix was nearly fifty-fifty.

"It means that this is all a nightmare, and I keep hoping I'll wake up from it."

Singh was silent for a while. Then she said, "I think it would be a good idea if we had this conversation somewhere more private. I'll have Sybil work out a time based on our schedules. Would that be acceptable?"

Evie stood up without answering, went over to the coffee station, and emptied her mug into a small thermal go-cup. She turned, looked directly at Singh, and took a deep drink. Then she added more coffee, snapped the lid tight, and left.

2

"Spears," called Hobart from across Main Street. "Need a minute."

"Sure," she said. "This about that pirate thing?"

It was a bright and sunny morning, and all through the camp the scientists, technicians, and graduate students were as busy as bees. He fell into step with Jenny as they walked away from the observation platform.

"How much would it piss you off if I said yes?" asked Hobart.

Jenny snorted. "There's a lot going on, Tom, but I'm not hearing about any exciting developments that involve me and the guys. I feel like a fifth wheel."

"Preaching to the choir, Jenny," said the colonel. "Which is why, yes, I need to ask if you'd be willing to take a few months and do a job for me out in the black."

She laughed. "I'd punch a nun to get out of here for a while. What have you got?"

"Two things, really," said Hobart. "First, you know the SPU has been building a long-range research vessel, right?"

"Sure. The *Tempest.* A refitted corvette, right? Same class as the *Prospero* and *Sycorax*, as I understand?"

"Not exactly." Hobart lowered his voice. "*Tempest* started out as a sister ship but has been completely redesigned for SPU missions. Big for a corvette too, and fitted out with a launch bay for two 089 Skimmers and six fighters."

"Fighters? So … not just a research vessel."

The colonel smiled. "Would you rather we had no protection?"

"What? Me? Oh hell no. Only thing I like better than guns are more guns. But … Don't tell me you're lugging along some of those old Starfall pieces of crap like you had on your other tub, the *Goshawk*."

Hobart grinned. "One word—*stiletto*."

Jenny stopped and turned to him, eyes wide. "The fuck you say. Instead of the B-911 combat spinners?"

"In addition to," said Hobart with a Cheshire cat grin. "Like I said, she's big for a corvette. Actually, just between us, she's only *really* a corvette on the books. Closer in size to a missile cruiser."

"That's sexy as hell," said Jenny. "And stilettos … mmmm, yummy. Last I heard they were still testing them. How'd you snag some?"

"I have friends in high places."

"You mean Torq Brollachan."

Hobart spread his hands. "He gets me the best toys."

"No shit." Jenny grinned. "God, I'd love to fly one of those. I'm not an A-class pilot, but I did some flight simulator sessions before I left the army. Stilettos are fast, mean, and sexy. Same with those tumbler ships I keep hearing about. Supposed to be able to make nonstress high-speed right-angle turns. Some kind of energy field that lets them do that. Sebastian Croft's in charge of that, last I heard."

"You hear a lot for someone who's no longer on Uncle Sam's payroll."

She grinned back. "You're not the only one with friends in high places." Then she paused. "But what does that have to do with me?"

"*Tempest* is in space dock above Luna," he said. "When you get back, I'm going to let you and the Jokers join the crew for a shakedown mission."

Jenny narrowed her eyes. "When I get back? So, the mission's a go for Sagan Station?"

"Yes and no. Sagan needs protection and an updated threat assessment. But there's this old piece-of-crap mining station in the asteroid belt. There've been some attempts to crack the security. Almost certainly some of those bastards who turned traitor four years ago and have been running with tech pirates."

"Sounds about right."

"That group is escalating, according to recent intel. Instead of stealing tech, they're going after raw materials. Specifically pyroxene, the crystal used in all pulse weapons. There's a special kind of it found only on Ceres and in some of the surrounding asteroids. Several trillion dollars' worth, and more importantly, that kind of pyroxene is ten times better than anything mined here. Better guns with longer range, greater accuracy, and more punch."

"What's the actual mission, though?"

Hobart grinned. "Go to Sagan, use that as a base to find the pirates, and disabuse them of the notion that what is ours is also theirs. Take your team. Don't be nice about it either."

"Rules of engagement?" she asked, smiling.

Hobart gave her a wink and walked away.

3

It took about four minutes from the time Jenny got home until Evie was all but screaming at her.

"After what just *happened*?" demanded Evie. "We just buried Sean and Brenda this morning, for God's sake, and you're *leaving*?"

"Hey," protested Jenny, "I'm ripped up about that too, but it doesn't have anything to do with my mission. Hobart needs me to do this, but it's a quick gig. Won't take that long."

"You'll be gone *six months*," Evie yelled.

Jenny kept her face blank, but the muscles at the corners of her jaw clenched and flexed. "Has to be done, sweetie."

"Don't you *sweetie* me, damn it," Evie snapped. "I bet you couldn't *wait* for something like this."

Spears put down the Stormsuit she was folding. "What's that supposed to mean?"

"Oh, don't act so surprised, Jennifer. I know how bored you've been lately."

"Of course I'm bored. Christ, who wouldn't be? I mean, sure, the whole aliens-and-spaceships thing was intense, but it's been more than a year, and what have we been doing since? Polishing our bullets and feeling our minds go numb. So, yes, I'm bored."

"No," said Evie in a softer tone. "Bored with me, I mean."

Spears tossed the Stormsuit onto the bed and came over to stand face-to-face with Evie.

"First, that's just stupid," she said gently. "I'm not bored with you. I adore you. What we have, what we've been building … It's the kind of thing I've always wanted and never thought a scar-faced gun chick like me would ever find." She shook her head. "You're a world-class scientist, but God, Evie, you can be pretty dumb at times."

Evie said nothing. Her eyes were wet and filled with doubt.

"But you're working sixteen, twenty hours a day, every day, twenty-four seven," Jenny continued. "You're doing the important work. What you're doing *needs* to be done. So does this. If there's a major security threat to Sagan Station, then I need to go out and set it right. That's what *I* do. It's where my talents lie." She reached out and tenderly brushed hair from Evie's brow. "We're both caught up in an avalanche of history. This stuff is happening, and we each have to do our jobs because a whole hell of a lot rests on us."

Evie stepped forward and let Spears gather her in her arms and pull her close.

"I don't want you to go," she said. "It's foolish and naive and greedy, but it's the truth, Jenny."

"And I don't *want* to go."

They kissed for a long time. When the kiss had ended, and before her tears had stopped, Evie went over, picked up the t-shirt, and began folding it. Once her duffel was packed and placed by the door, Evie went to Spears for a goodbye kiss.

"I don't have to leave for thirty minutes," Spears said as she drew a delicate line from Evie's clavicle, up her throat and over her chin, to the softness of parted lips.

4

Jenny stood in a crowd but felt completely alone.

Craig was next to Evie, and Brollachan on her other side. Everyone except the guards on patrol had gathered to watch the Jokers board the transport ship. It was a bitterly cold day, and Evie's tears kept freezing on her cheeks. It hurt, and she accepted the pain as right and proper. Everything about this hurt.

Spider, Not Larry, and the others trooped up, their heavy packs slung, their faces eager for the mission. Jenny Spears was last, and she lingered at the top of the boarding stairs to search the crowd. When she saw Evie, Jenny gave her a smile and placed her palm flat over her heart.

One single sob broke in Evie's chest. Dr. Brollachan gently placed his hands on her shoulder. It was such a kind act that it nearly broke Evie, but she forced herself to breathe slow and deep to prevent more sobs.

Jenny boarded, the hatch closed, and the transport began to lift. It rose high into the cold, blue sky, then angled upward, the engines firing hard to propel it to escape velocity. Then it was gone.

The crowd lingered for a few moments and then split apart.

Evie stayed for a long time. Brollachan gave her shoulder a little squeeze, nodded to her, and then walked away.

Never in her life had Evie Cronin ached for the bottle more than she did at that moment. She could feel it calling to her and knew that it would be the only thing giving her warmth and comfort that night.

5

That night, everyone in camp had a nightmare.

The same nightmare.

Every single person.

Something was at the door. Jiggling the knob. Leaning its soft but heavy weight against the door, making it creak against its hinges. None of the dreamers saw what it was, but they all knew.

It was the thing from the ice cave. Not dead, not reduced to ash, but alive.

Horribly, shockingly, impossibly alive.

And it was hungry. It howled out there, screaming its hunger to the icy winds. Shouting it to the people behind all those locked doors.

The dream went on and on.

Several people wept as they slept. One man, a technician who worked in the metallurgy lab, crawled out of bed, across the floor, and into a closet, where he curled up in the dark. Several people were trapped within the prison of medicated sleep, unable to wake.

Those who could wake, though, did not. The dream did not allow it.

Evie Cronin had gone to bed with eleven ounces of single malt sloshing around in her belly. The alcohol, taken as a buffer against pain and fear, was alchemized into a soporific by the monster in her imagination, and she slept on, hearing and feeling it all.

When dawn came, the sky was streaked with thin wisps of cloud, and the sun was a cold yellow eye peering with apprehension over the mountains. The sleepers all woke, each according to alarms or personal circadian rhythms. Not one of them remembered the nightmare that had plagued them. Not a single person.

And yet all of them woke depressed, jumpy, and sad. When friends met friends in the mess hall or the labs, no one met anyone's eyes. They did not notice this consciously, but it was pervasive across the camp.

Even Dr. Singh woke with strange and undefined emotions playing bad music in her head. She was the only person who wondered *if* it was because of dreams. When she began her day of seeing site members for half-hour catch-up sessions, the conversation was about grief because of the suicides. None of her patients mentioned dreams at all.

So Dr. Singh, as human as the rest, let that theory go.

Just a bad night, she told herself. *Just nerves and the processing of trauma and grief.*

She was a very bright and insightful therapist, and throughout her long career she had never been as thoroughly incorrect as she was then.

6

As the next days passed, the efforts of the Artifact team coalesced into one single goal—to find a way to protect machines and organisms from the assault of unstable time when they passed through the star door.

That path was fraught with one disappointment after another, marked by an unbroken series of failures. The science team concocted many promising guesses, ranging from new suit designs dotted with thousands of microemitters that covered the wearer in what amounted to a field of electromagnetic pulses to coating drones with hundreds of different compounds, alloys, and even special metal-based paints. In every case, the materials eroded as if left out in the weather for months or years. Diamond dust covering a plastic Faraday cage didn't work. Shooting high-amplitude and variable sonic discharges failed.

None of it worked.

Dr. Kimbra, the structural engineer, and the physicist Dr. Patel were frustrated to the point where all they did was snipe and shout at each other. Brollachan tried to mollify them, but his own impatience and frustration was evident just below the surface.

It was Evie who came up with the answer, and it was entirely by accident. She had been going through the inventory of everything they had so far tried and wondered if the complex electronics of the drones might be triggering some reaction within the Artifact's internal sensors. After hours of that—and far too many cups of coffee—she noticed that they had not tried anything old school, like an internal combustion engine. They had a few of those at the base, mostly self-driving air-blower units for dusting fallen snow from walkways.

When she mentioned this to Brollachan, he began to smile as if expecting there to be some sort of punch line. "Wait ... you're serious?"

"Yes, I am."

"A snow blower," he said flatly. Brollachan's face looked five years older than it had when she'd first met him. He had begun growing a beard, but it looked scraggly and sparse and made him look both weary and demented.

"It's the only gas-powered vehicle we have that will fit through the door."

The doctor stood with his hands thrust deep in his pockets, the ends of his green and silver scarf blowing in the wind. He laughed and shook his head but said, "Well, why not? We've tried every other goddamn thing."

They set the test for the following morning. Evie had to promise the camp's groundskeeper that she would use the 3D printers to make a new snow blower if anything happened to it.

The device was about the size of a twenty-seven-kilogram chemical drum, with the main body standing upright on a platform supported by four low-pressure tires. The blower hose had been removed, and new sensor packages installed. Yet another tray of microscopic biological samples was included, stored in a tool receptacle on the machine's front.

The test team at the star door were as skeptical as Brollachan, and Evie could see them preparing themselves for another disappointment. Their encouraging smiles were thin veneers over pity and condescension, but Evie didn't really care. Brollachan was right, they *had* tried every other goddamn thing.

"Start it up," she ordered, and Craig nodded. He pushed the primer button three times and yanked the pull start. It roared to life at once, ignoring the cold, and sat there chugging along like a happy bulldog.

Craig had rigged a remote control for it, feeding it through Sybil.

Evie walked over to the door and peered inside. Like everyone else, she'd learned the precise safe distance from its energetic screen. "Send it in."

The blower rolled forward, farting clouds of blue smoke into the frosty air. When it reached the star door, it did not pause but moved smoothly inside.

"Stop it there," said Evie when the rear wheels were a meter past the doorframe.

They clustered around, watching the engine. It growled and coughed and smoked for nearly eight minutes before the motor abruptly stopped.

"Shit," growled Evie. "Pull it out."

The cable winch dragged it back through the star door. The plastic body looked sun-faded, the tires were losing air, and the aluminum struts were cloudy and smoked.

"Same as all the others," said Craig.

But Evie wasn't sure. Eight minutes was a long time, given the aggressiveness of the time differential, with the small engine outlasting a lot of other devices that had been sent in. She said as much to Brollachan, who looked at the time display on his holo-comms.

"Mmmm," he said noncommittally. "It is a little longer."

"Something kept it going that long, Torq. Maybe the fuel? What kind of gas is in it?"

The groundskeeper, who was staring dejectedly down at his dead device, said, "AN8. It's the same fuel blend we've been using here and in the Arctic since God knows when."

"What are its qualities?"

The man considered and shrugged. "Well, it has a lower flash point of about 37.7 Celsius. That lowers the gelling point too, for when the temperatures really drop. You see, intense cold can cause wax crystals to form in the fuel. AN8 remains liquid all the way down to minus 57."

"Is there anything else special about it?" she asked.

"Other than the fact that it's a combustion engine? No. Not that I can think of."

Evie turned to Craig. "Get it over to the lab. I want it stripped down to the last nut and screw. Everything gets carbon-dated."

"On it," he said.

Evie and Brollachan walked over to the hot bar at the far end of the ice pad in front of the Artifact. They ordered cups of bone broth and stood blowing and sipping. There wasn't much to say, so they just stood, looking at the machine, trying not to feel defeated.

When they were finished, Brollachan said, "I'm getting a lot of pressure from POTUS to come up with *something*. He didn't come straight out and threaten me with a deadline, but that's inevitable. If we can't crack this, then he and the other world leaders who are in on this will have to agree to make a public statement."

"And say what? We don't know anything other than this isn't from here and that the sole known occupant is a smear of carbon dust buried under half a mountain."

"Which is what I have been telling him, Evie," sighed Brollachan. "But this is an election year. I think he wants to *run* on being the president who proved that we are not alone."

"Jesus."

"Politics," said Brollachan, in exactly the same way someone would say "cancerous tumor."

7

"Lars Soren has been back on Earth for weeks now," complained Evie. "Why can't we bring him down here?"

"We have enough people already," said Brollachan. They stood together, looking down at the Artifact. A crew was prepping the skimmer to take more instruments down for Alan Meyer, who was still trying to solve the issue of effective shielding for the drones.

"That's bullshit," snorted Evie. "When it comes to determining the cultural implications of first contact, he would be worth *ten* of anyone else on staff. His book on the subject is used by every philosophy graduate program in North America. And throughout Europe and much of Asia."

"No doubt, Evie, but my decision stands. Besides … over the last few months, he's been surrounded by theologians and faith leaders. Part of a group he's been guiding toward a first-contact scenario."

"Which is exactly my point."

Brollachan shook his head. "The president is not at all sanguine about bringing in someone who may have shifted away from science and into religion. Remember, POTUS is a confirmed atheist and thinks everything related to religion is either a cash grab or simply too woo-woo. No, Evie, I could never get approval for this."

Evie stood up. They had been sharing an amicable dinner up to this point. She crumpled her napkin and tossed it onto her plate. "That's a bullshit answer, and you know it."

Without waiting for a reply, she turned and left.

8

That evening, Evie got an email from Jenny. It bothered her that it was a written note rather than a video. She knew that video signals were easier to intercept than coded text, but that didn't matter. There was a small petulant streak in her makeup that she was aware of and didn't like but which refused to go away.

She poured herself a glass of wine.

Hey, babe!

Just woke from cryo-sleep. Shaking off the cold. That always takes a bit of time, even on short jaunts like this one. Wish you were here to warm me up!

I know they say that people don't dream in the freeze, but that's not true. I dreamed of you. Many, many times. God, I can remember that first kiss. Not the one I surprised you with, but that barn burner of a smooch you laid on me after. You could get another PhD in kissing!!

And if they don't have such a thing, you should get a grant and launch it. I volunteer to be your test dummy for any public demonstration.

We're on an Ariel dart ship. Probably not something you ever heard of. It's a souped-up transport with the new rail-line ion drive. Fast as balls. Those new engines shaved our flight down by 46%, so we're almost there already. Wanted you to know because I promised I wouldn't be away that long.

Got to run because the team's coming out of the ice, too.

Just know that you're in my heart, Evie.

I love you.

Your Jenny.

Evie sat there and reread the last two lines over and over again. It was the first time Jenny had used that word. The L-word.

Love.

She bowed her head and wept harder than she had ever done in her life.

That night, she sank into memories as vivid as a high-def holographic replay. She and Jenny made love and lay naked and sweaty, talking and kissing. It was the most beautiful dream Evie ever had, and that night—that one night in all the time she had been at the site—was impervious to the nightmares.

One night.

Part Eighteen
Say You Won't Let Go

"Unable are the loved to die
For love is immortality."

—Emily Dickinson

Asphodel Station
The Shadderal Star System

They landed on an asteroid, standing together as the rest of the NecroTeks flew off.

None of their friends asked why they wanted to take a moment. They knew.

Bianca and Jacob watched until their slice of the sky was empty of everything except stars. They watched for a long time. Two giants made of glittering metal. Inhuman, monstrous, freakish by any human standard.

"Okay, babe," said Jacob, using their private channel. "You said you wanted to try something. What did you have in mind?"

"I . . . don't even know if it will work."

"Okay," he said again.

"And maybe it's dangerous or stupid."

"You're selling this really well, Bee."

"Change with me," she said, and began the process of morphing away from her battle aspect into a form as close to the human Bianca as she could manage. It was much harder than manifesting rockets or any kind of projectile. As Jacob watched, she saw him nod very slightly. Then he, too, changed. They each absorbed their weapons, redistributing mass and rebuilding their bodies to have arms and legs and torsos proportioned to approximate who they had been before death had stolen so much from them.

Bianca held one hand a centimeter from Jacob's chest.

"Do you trust me?" she asked, her voice soft and frightened.

"You know I do."

"Do you love me?"

"Forever," he said.

Bianca placed her hand over where a human heart would be. "Let me try this. And no matter what happens, just know that I will love you forever, too. In this messed-up universe or wherever we wind up. And if we just burn out, then we'll do that together."

He looked at her for a while, then said, "Yes."

Jacob looked down at her hand. The metal fingers were splayed across the broad expanse of his mechanical chest. For several moments nothing at all happened.

Then …

The shape of her hand changed. Total molecular transformation was one of the gifts of *ethla*. It allowed all of the NecroTeks to construct new forms and change them at will into whatever shape they desired. It was a process that required a great deal of imagination and even greater willpower. Bianca was the best of all of them at this—something they had witnessed when she'd fought an entire Medusa chimera mother ship by herself. Her will was the most powerful Jacob had ever encountered, and it was one of the many things he loved about her.

Now he watched her exert that will in a way he had not even considered.

The metal of her fingers began to flow like mercury, cold and fluid, not spilling away but moving across his chest, the mass of her hand becoming thinner, more stretched out, and … deeper.

The substance of her machine hand began melting *into* Jacob Fox's steel chest. He could *feel* it.

Actually feel it.

She kept her focus as the hand and the wrist merged with him. Becoming part of him. Fusing in a way that seemed like magic to him. And perhaps it was. The laws of the universe, as known to his precise and orderly scientific mind, had begun to crumble as soon as the WarpLine gun blew them across the galaxy in the space of a second.

Dying in the space battle with the shoggoths and then being called back from death by Lady Jessica had been a kind of magic. *Ethla* itself was at the very edge of reality, where science is indistinguishable from magic.

Now, he felt his lover touch him.

She was as dead as he was. She was as much a metal monstrosity as he was. She was as alien to the definition of humanity as he was.

Yet the touch he felt was not that of cold steel.

It was warm. Almost hot. Nor was it like a human touch. That was impossible. As her hand lost its specific shape and merged with the materials from which he was made, there was a new kind of sensation for which he had no words. He doubted there was a lexicon in all of time and space that could adequately describe what he felt.

Had any NecroTek ever done this before?

Maybe Lost would know, but Jacob doubted it.

He did not believe anyone knew that this was even a possibility.

Jacob reached out and placed his hand on her chest.

"How do I do this?" he asked.

She shook her head. "I don't know. I just know I needed to try."

Jacob had no eyes to close, but he pulled his awareness in, letting his mind separate from the circuits and cables that were his body. He did not even realize that his hand had melted into her. Not at first.

Then he *felt* her.

It was a sensation on an indescribable level. Not flesh. Not nerve endings and tissue. Nothing as understandable as that. It went beyond a psychic bond and plunged them both through veils upon veils of empathy.

They each stepped forward at exactly the same moment. Unplanned, uncoordinated, but in perfect harmony. He pressed his body against hers and felt not resistant metal but something warm and yielding and powerful.

"I love you," he said. Then he realized he had not spoken those words aloud.

"I love you," she replied, because on this level there was nothing presumptuous enough to be a barrier.

They melted together.

It was not sex. It was not passion. It was something new, something born into the universe at that moment, and they merged to become not one but two—two connecting on a level neither had ever suspected was possible.

Above them, the stars wheeled and turned in their slow, eternal dance, and nothing came to attack or interrupt. For once, the universe approved and allowed and accepted.

And what happened was a celebration of innocence and love and beauty.

Part Nineteen
Welcome to the Black Parade

"There is no greater sorrow than to be mindful of the happy time in misery."

—*Dante Alighieri*

Joint MIT/UCLA Biological Research Field Station #8
Queen Maud Land, Antarctica

1

Dr. Indira Singh confided to Brollachan, Hobart, and Evie that it was becoming clear that people were experiencing nightmares of a remarkably similar kind.

"Similar in what way?" asked Brollachan.

"I've cobbled together several different scenarios from dream fragments recalled by many of the staff. There is a cohesive narrative in them and a definite similarity." She outlined these, telling them about dreams of something trying to break into people's huts; of creatures that were a mix of gargoyle, devil, and vampire crouching on the footboards of their beds; of wandering through cities of impossible size and hearing bizarre cries from unseen animals; dreams not only of becoming shape-shifting monsters like the one the Jokers had killed, but also—strangely—of piloting starships that changed shape too; and others.

"How do you account for the similarities?" Brollachan asked, his interest sharp.

"Best guess is that because this is an isolated and closed community, people have shared what bits of dreams they recalled, and these shared elements migrated into the dreams of whomever they told. That alone is not uncommon, though the scale of it here is."

She paused and looked at the three of them for a moment.

"Have any of *you* had dreams like this?"

"I never dream," said Brollachan, then self-corrected before anyone else could. "That is to say, I never *recall* my dreams. I never have."

Evie thought Singh was going to comment, but the therapist did not.

"I've had some bad dreams like that," admitted Hobart. "And, yeah, I guess I've talked about them with some folks."

They all looked at Evie.

"Yes," she said, and left it there.

Now, sitting on the edge of her vastly empty bed, she feared another night of dreams. They had not gotten worse since Jenny left, but now there was no one to hold her and help her feel safe.

No one and nothing ... except the whiskey and wine on the shelf across the room. Evie sat there and told herself that she was done with drinking. That she was not an alcoholic. That she wasn't a slave to the bottle. She even believed it, too. But in the end, she drank herself to sleep anyway. The dreams were always waiting for her.

Every single night

2

The challenge Dr. Brollachan faced was the poor state of the tissue and the lack of a single unbroken strand of DNA.

Each cell has two complete copies of DNA. Any normal human body has tens of trillions of cells. The lump one of his drones recovered was a mere 0.02 grams. Barely the size and mass of a grain of rice. Had it been a simple piece of surgically excised flesh, there would be an abundance of genetic material. But the plasma grenades created such an intense fire that it was a wonder even this much survived. The second issue was that plasma grenades were intended for both incineration *and* molecular disruption. Nothing was supposed to survive it. How this piece escaped total destruction was unknown. It was all his crab crawlers had found and, in its own limited way, was a gift. One of those freak accidents that sometimes made Brollachan believe in fate.

His first step was to use polymerase chain reactions to make copies of the best DNA strands. He ran this process many times because every pass amplified the sequence, giving him a yield of millions of copies of each.

"Ariel," he said, "begin assembly."

The AI, which was fully integrated into the machinery, started creating a series of artificial cells to act as a host. From there, Ariel began hunting through the damaged strands to find enough intact sections to puzzle together something approximating the alien's genetic roadmap.

"Dr. Brollachan," said the AI after nearly an hour, "I cannot create a complete strand of DNA for the alien. Every sequence has significant damage. There are several unusable areas."

"Can we compensate?"

"Not completely, Doctor, I'm sorry to say."

Ariel actually sounded sad.

Brollachan, however, was not surprised at the results. He did not really expect to get a whole sequence. That would have been a miracle, and he believed in miracles about as much as he believed in luck. Science was based on providing for disappointments and even building on them.

"Build contigs," he ordered. "Look for coding sequences of DNA and extrapolate the resulting amino acid sequence and then run folding prediction software. We need to identify what any mystery genes make."

"Is there anything specific you want me to search for?" asked Ariel.

"Any genes that code for metamorphic changes. Initiate."

"I will keep you apprised, Doctor," said the AI.

Brollachan glanced at a digital clock on the wall.

"I have a meeting with Colonel Hobart and Evie Cronin," he said. "Keep working. Contact me only if you find a complete strand or identify the key genes."

"I hope to have something encouraging for you soon, Doctor."

Yes, thought Brollachan, *me, too.*

3

Evie Cronin's hut, though small, felt enormous and empty without Jenny Spears.

Months alone after months of being with Jenny was crushing Evie.

The two were not quite in *love*—a word that held many negative connotations for both of them—but they were in low orbit around it. They fought against the concept, but the more Evie explored her feelings, the more she realized that her resistance was mostly scar tissue and habit.

In the deepest parts of the night, when she was alone and not lost in a dream, she rehearsed a hundred different versions of a conversation where she said "I love you" to Spears. Mostly her insecurities improvised new dialogue during those rehearsals, giving Jenny Spears the role of the shocked, offended person who was repelled by the word *love* as surely as if there was a force field around each letter. Only rarely did Evie get all the way through a practice run unscathed.

She wondered if she would ever really have the courage to say it aloud.

She'd slipped twice. Once when Spears was giving her a lesson in unarmed combat. They were in pajamas and practicing escapes from holds. Evie had managed a particular counter to a very difficult hold, and when Spears gave her a congratulatory hug, the words slipped out. There had been a single moment of eye contact, and Evie thought she read alarm there. She immediately apologized, and they laughed it off, neither willing to give it any weight.

The second time the L-word slipped out, Spears was going down on her, and it was one of those evenings where Evie kept falling away from her orgasm. Until it exploded within her all at once, catching her so thoroughly off guard that she had screamed those three dangerous words.

I love you.

Neither ever spoke of it, though Spears had held her very close afterward, and their kisses had been extremely gentle.

Do I love her? Evie wondered. It was such an absurd question that she felt like an overwrought teenager for asking it. The answer was clear and had been clear since probably the third day they were together. Now she hated herself for not having summoned the courage to say it.

It was a question she asked herself fifty times a day. She never said yes, but in every instance, she felt it. Her heart felt it.

Evie got up from the table, refilled her coffee cup, sat down, and tried to find enough enthusiasm to get back to work. The report about the snow blower was around two-thirds done—unfinished only because she could not find another encouraging synonym for *failure*—when someone began hammering on her door.

For a moment Evie's heart lifted, thinking that Spears was somehow back early from the mission she'd undertaken for Hobart and was playing a gag. But when she opened the door, it was Craig. He was flushed and wide-eyed and sweaty with excitement.

"What is it?" demanded Evie in something approaching a snarl.

"*Spark plugs*," Craig gasped.

"I … beg your pardon."

Craig pulled a small object from his pocket and held it out on a flat palm. It was indeed a spark plug.

"Okay," said Evie. "It's a spark plug. *And …?*"

Her student held it up between thumb and forefinger. "Listen," he said, "the spark plug is basically the same these days as it always was, except for the materials used for higher performance. The ones the guy here uses are designed for weather extremes. This kind of plug has a really high melting point, which allows them to operate even when the engine has been running for a long time. It has a special metal tip to ensure high durability and a consistently stable spark—you follow me? And it has trivalent chromium plating—chromium sulfate as the main ingredient."

"Again I say, *and …?*"

"And that motor lasted longer than we expected. I had them test everything, just like you said. We took it part by part and sent each in through the star door. Same aging effect … but then there was *one* material that did not age like all the rest."

That snapped Evie to full attention. "What?" she demanded.

"I'm serious. One material, and it's used on the spark plugs. That's why they kept firing until the surrounding materials failed."

"*Which* material?"

Craig beamed at her. "Iridium."

4

"Iridium," said Brollachan, exhaling the word as if it was a postorgasmic sigh.

Evie stood inside his hut. There hadn't even been time for him to offer a seat. Hobart was there too, breathless from having run from the far side of the site.

"Iridium?" he asked. "I mean, I know it's a metal, but … what makes it so special?"

Brollachan glanced at him in surprise. "Good God, Tom, surely you've heard of the iridium anomaly."

"Um … no?"

Evie said, "Iridium is a very rare element in the Earth's crust. There's been a debate raging for a couple of centuries about whether it's natural to Earth or if most—or even all of it—came here on the asteroid that killed the dinosaurs."

The colonel blinked. "Dinosaurs? Am I driving in the wrong lane here?"

Evie parked a haunch on the corner of the doctor's worktable. "Iridium is very rare, but the anomaly refers to a layer of the element in rock strata dating to the Cretaceous-Paleogene boundary, which more or less marks the end of the dinosaur era. Many scientists believe that the asteroid that struck what's now the Yucatán Peninsula may have been largely composed of iridium."

"Opinions differ on that," said Brollachan.

"Opinions differ on everything," said Evie, and Brollachan nodded. "The point is that all—or *some*—of the iridium on Earth came from outer space."

"Ah," said Hobart, finally catching up. "And since it's some kind of space metal, it might factor into the structure of the Artifact or its scanning system. Is that about right?"

"That is what we are going to find out," said Brollachan. "And I don't mean tomorrow. We need to start work on this right now."

"How, though?" asked Evie. "As far as I know, the only known samples of iridium are on the snow blower spark plugs."

The SPU chief gave her one of his more devious smiles. "Let me make some calls."

5

Torquil Brollachan slept deeply.

Very deeply. More completely unconscious than he had ever been. His habitual insomnia crumbled beneath exhaustion. The caffeine in his system hit a tipping point, and along with forgetting to eat more than he remembered, his system crashed. It was not on the scale of a medical emergency, however, so Ariel took no action.

The AI did, nevertheless, continue to monitor Brollachan's EKG and EEG. The heart rate and blood pressure were consistent with a tired person being deep in an active dream.

His brainwaves, however, were unusual. Ariel began recording them and running the numbers through several pieces of sophisticated software.

Meanwhile, Brollachan dreamed.

He had once told Evie Cronin that he never dreamed, and she said that everyone does. She was correct. He knew it but did not care, because those kinds of dreams meant nothing to him. Dreams were, as he saw it, little more than junk drawers of the mind, with the subconscious trying to construct narratives out of disconnected odds and ends. Fragments of old memories, incidental encounters with people, things sensed through peripheral awareness. Nothing of any personal importance.

On that point, he was dreadfully and completely wrong.

Since coming to Antarctica—since that first time when he physically touched the hull of the Artifact—his dreams had tended toward a specific kind.

In dreams, he walked through a vast and monstrous city hidden deep inside a network of caves on a nameless frozen moon. There were huge cones and cylinders that stood taller than skyscrapers; there were terraced walls lush with fungi that did not need oxygen to thrive. There were monuments shaped like orbs or stars with five, six, seven, and eight points.

The immense city was in ruins, and a rough weed the color of animal intestines choked the streets and clung to the walls and violated every crack and opening. Instead of a starry sky, there was a ceiling of stalactites that dripped with acidic water. The air stank of sulfur and rot. A frozen meat stink, like decaying flesh thawing on a bed of permafrost.

He walked through the city.

After a timeless time of wandering, he saw something off to his right that drew him, and he headed that way. As he approached, Brollachan saw what he realized was not a building but a machine. Massive and sophisticated and exotic in ways that unsettled him.

The body of the machine was circular, wrapping around a stalagmite that was at least forty meters thick. On the side closest to him, there was an opening like the mouth of a tunnel, ten meters high, with a series of inner rings set back at irregular intervals. The primary structure looked to be made of steel, but there were other metals, too. He saw exposed copper, some crude iron bands, gleaming alloy bolts, and long circular strips of what looked like gold. Heavy black rubber-coated cables were entwined with the rings of metal, and coaxial cables as thick as his thigh snaked along the ground and ran down a steep slope to where a series of machines that—instinctively—he knew were some kind of generators. Each of these was as big as a cathedral, and they rested on flat stone pads. The purplish weed grew over everything, and long arms of it reached deep into the machine's gaping maw. The throat of the machine looked like it ran deep into the bedrock.

He went back to study the opening. All around it there were crystals—jewels, he thought—embedded into the metal. He saw opals, diamonds, emeralds, star sapphires, rubies, garnets, and many others. To the left of the opening was a control panel, but the dials and switches did not seem made for human hands. They were far too large, and the knobs on the dials were spaced too far apart for fingers.

One of the gemstones flashed. It was a pale yellow green. Prehnite, he thought, though he wasn't sure. It flared as if lit from within, and Brollachan felt strangely drawn to touch it. A honey-colored andalusite pulsed a moment later. Then an agate, a ligure, an amethyst. They sparkled and flowed, sending patterns of light all across the face of the machine.

Then he heard a sound. At first he thought it was someone calling him, but he could not hear the words. Not clearly. If they were words at all, he did not know the language. He bent toward the mouth of the machine, head cocked to listen.

The sound came again. A bit louder now. He recoiled, afraid that some animal might be hiding inside. But even as he stepped back, the sound grew louder and more distinct. On some level, he knew those words. They were not English, but he knew them.

"Tekeli-li! Tekeli-li!" *They came like the chirping of some strange and awful bird.* "Tekeli-li! Tekeli-li!"

And then, just as he began to wake from the dream, Torquil Brollachan realized that he was not hearing the sounds.

He was making them.

He broke through the surface of sleep and was awake in the cold darkness of predawn. As soon as he opened his eyes, the dream and the words faded.

And that, too, had consequences.

Evie had begun a serial letter after Jenny left, sending it via encrypted messaging at random intervals. Some of the messages were long and rambling, filled with optimism and plans. Others were shorter, keeping Jenny up to speed with the research on the Artifact.

She knew her lover wouldn't be able to read them until she was awakened from cryo-sleep, but the serial format made it feel more natural. Like a conversation.

That night, she wrote a very short entry.

We think we've cracked the shielding issue. Iridium. Torq agrees that it's a viable option, so he called someone back in the world and they're emergency shipping something like seventeen tons of the stuff. Bars and sheets of it. Alan Meyer is over the moon, though he spent some time kicking himself for not thinking of it sooner. Not that anyone would. I mean, iridium isn't the kind of thing that comes up in ordinary conversation. Andy Patel was all but banging his head on the wall because he didn't think of it either.

God, I hope this works.

She looked at her note for a moment, wanting to say more. Wanting to actually *reach* Jenny. But she simply added *I love you* and hit Send.

She touched the screen for a moment, then nodded, accepting the action as irrevocable, and went to bed.

In the morning, she could not remember her dreams. Which was just as well, because they were wet and red and terrible. Worse than ever before.

7

Brollachan spent an hour with his small team of scientists—Howard, Wu, and Solà. They discussed a new project that had come in from one of Brollachan's many agents. They were not military spies but instead searched the world for secret technologies, hidden research projects, or data recovered from places devastated by the wars of the last century.

"This is a diary," he said, placing a leather-bound book on the mission table around which they sat. "It was part of a trove of documents found in a bunker in what used to be Moscow."

They nodded. Moscow had been the capital of Russia for a long time, but it had been the target of a pair of ultraheavy fuel-air bombs. They were nonnuclear, but the payload was massive, and the effect devastating. The old city had covered 2,511 square kilometers, but now all there was to see was a vast field of weed-choked rubble. The impact had been so severe that it weakened the substrata badly enough that it was deemed unsafe to try to rebuild. Novosibirsk had been the capital ever since.

A team of urban explorers on the SPU payroll frequently sneaked into the area and climbed down into basements and subcellars.

The book was large, with a cover that was badly burned. Brollachan used plastic tweezers to open it, revealing hundreds of handwritten pages. The writing was small and crabbed. On some pages it was neat and precise, while on others it became a wild and erratic scrawl. There were many drawings throughout the book, each showing that the owner of the journal was an excellent draftsman. All of the drawings were ultraprecise, without any signs of the randomness or, perhaps, madness evidenced by the writing.

Brollachan turned many pages, often pausing to let them read key passages he'd marked with acid-free notation tabs. Then he turned to the back, and tucked between the last two pages was a folded diagram drawn on very thin rice paper. Brollachan pulled on a pair of cotton gloves and very carefully unfolded it. It was very large and covered most of the table.

"What is that?" asked Solà. "Some kind of machine?"

"That's obvious," said Howard, "but what does it do?"

In the bottom left-hand corner, captured in a neatly drawn box, were three words in a beautiful calligraphic script. Dr. Wu leaned close and read them.

"The God Machine."

"Yes," said Brollachan.

The others sat back and looked at him.

"Okay, Torq," said Howard, "it's a fascinating relic and all that, but again … what does it do?"

"That is what I am trying to determine, Beatrice," he said.

Solà asked, "What makes you think it is of any importance at all?"

"Ah," said Brollachan. He turned to an earlier page and then spun the book so they could all read.

Tesla's diary was worth every penny I paid for it. Well, every penny I stole from Dad's account. The thing is, this is worth ten times as much. A thousand times as much. It verifies what the Thule Society was trying to do in 1935. Tesla was too far gone and was too paranoid to buy from the right vendors. The gemstones he collected were junk. The Nazis were in too much of a hurry. I don't know for sure, but I think they tried opening the gateway before the intrazone coils were hot enough. Big mistake. And don't get me started on how badly the Soviets bungled it in Chernobyl. Idiots. Maybe they didn't have access to da Vinci's notebooks. More likely, they didn't even BOTHER to find all of the Unlearnable Truths. Or they got the wrong ones. If they didn't find the right chapters in the right books, and used the da Vinci code key, they might as well have used a cookbook. They needed the Book of Azathoth, the Book of Eibon, the Book of Iod, the Celaeno Fragments, De Vermis Mysteriis, Cultes des Goules, the Eltdown Shards, the Seven Cryptical Books of Hsan, and On the Sending Out of the Soul.

He skipped several paragraphs because they were tangential and tended to wander far afield. When he found what he wanted, he tapped it.

The God Machine is almost ready. I have to be careful to keep the energy flow exactly right. God knows I've seen what happens when it's off even a little. Dad is still looking for the second-floor maid, but he'll never find her. Because she's not here anymore, is she? I saw what was at the other end of the God Machine's inner corridor, and it wasn't Earth. It was a whole different place. Two suns and a weird bunch of planets and moons. Looked too busy to be fake. I'll have to read up on gravitational physics one of these days. Point is, that's where Miriam or Maura or whatever is. I guess I should feel bad for her. I'll ask Dr. Greene about that.

Brollachan touched a third section.

I did the test firing today.

The bad news is that I blew out half the local power grid. Oops.

The good news is that it opened, and the pathway was stable. All of the gemstones sculpted the light patterns absolutely right. There was some exhaled atmosphere from inside the mouth, but that's probably something like an airlock effect. The way is open, after all. A microsecond is enough for gas. But I felt the air of that place. The portal opened right on this beach. I will walk through and go home. This world isn't mine. It never fit me anyway. But there are so many worlds, and now I can reach any of them.

All of them.

The God Machine is the only way.

It was the last entry in the book. The others looked expectantly, waiting for more.

"Well?" he prompted.

"Torq," said Alejandro Solà, "what are we supposed to make of this?"

Brollachan smiled. "This is the journal of a young, neurodivergent, and fundamentally gifted man named Prospero Bell. I have heard of him for ages. Not from any traditional journal or report but from some of the sources for the off-book projects we do. Bear in mind, my friends, that the Artifact is far from the only 'special project' that falls under the SPU umbrella."

They all nodded at that and even shared a nod or smile with one another. The three scientists had worked closely with Brollachan on many projects that were very special indeed.

Brollachan said, "I had added Prospero's Journal to a rather long list of old diaries, journals, ship's logs, codices, religious tombs, and so on. And before you ask, I remind you that just as there is some genuine science buried in alchemy, we in the more exploratory fields have to pause now and then to look backward for secrets hidden in what we, in our arrogance, call primitive writings. Think of all the plant medicines we learned about from Aztec codices."

"Point taken," said Wu, "but what's the purpose of this beyond the historical and intellectual?"

Brollachan gestured in the direction of the Artifact. "Now that we have proof positive that an advanced alien race exists and had visited us, we have the chance to steer those sciences that will benefit from this device."

"Of course," said Howard, "but that reverse engineering will need to follow some understanding of their design philosophy, and that can only happen once we discover and translate their language, which means we'll have to somehow learn about their culture in order to do any of this. Even if the iridium works and we can get inside that great beast of a thing, it doesn't mean we will learn much. We'll observe and try to extrapolate, but that's a learning curve with no corollary on Earth—after all we can't speak to even the brightest animals—and it's likely to take decades, if not centuries." She pointed to the book. "How does this change that?"

Brollachan spoke calmly and slowly. "At this very moment, our friend and colleague Dr. Anton Kier is preparing to take his WarpLine gun all the way to Asphodel Station. Once there, he will assemble it and use it to try and send a capsule of instruments to the far side of Jupiter. If that works, then faster-than-light travel becomes an irrelevant concern."

"So?" asked Wu.

"I have a suspicion Kier will *not* succeed. I managed to get access to his files." He smiled. "Oh, don't look so shocked. You know I'm as much a spy as a scientist. SPU isn't the Boy Scouts."

There were some polite smiles.

"This God Machine is designed to do two things. One is similar in effect to the WarpLine gun in that it instantaneously transmits matter over great distances, with the differences being twofold. One, the person or thing being sent is not annihilated and a copy manufactured by the WarpLine receiver. This would be like walking down a hall. The second thing it does is even more remarkable."

"More remarkable than FTL?" Wu laughed.

"Oh yes. You know the theoretical concept of an infinite and infinitely expanding number of universes. A multiverse or omniverse, if you will. Well, properly calibrated—as clearly laid out in Prospero's diary—this could theoretically take us to a parallel Earth. One without people. Clean, pure, unmarked by man's greed or hatred. Untapped natural resources. And more to the point, there would an infinite number of such nearly identical Earths. Imagine that. No hunger, no need for wars. Any cult or splinter group can have a whole world to themselves. One for each, with an infinite number untapped."

The silence was heavy and lasted a long time.

"You're serious?" asked Howard.

Brollachan smiled. "I think you want to ask if I've lost my mind."

"Well . . . ?"

"No, Beatrice. Nor have I suddenly embraced a religion or suffered a neurological accident. The truth is that after reading that book and running down certain elements with Ariel, it has become clear to me that there is some merit in what Prospero Bell says."

They looked doubtful.

"I've already sent extensive supporting materials, including scans and translations of everything from Leonardo da Vinci, Nikola Tesla, the German Thule Society, the Soviet Union Special Division, and one group called the Proteus Team that was down here in the Antarctic. All of these groups and individuals believed that this God Machine was a scientific possibility. If we take a careful step back and can agree that it is at least a *probability*, then we might be able to do something that not only parallels that Artifact but very likely eclipses it."

He left then sitting in careful silence, not looking at one another, waiting for him to be gone so they could talk. It amused him.

He closed the door behind him and walked away without trying to overhear what they had to say. He already knew they were intrigued, even hooked. It was etched into their faces and burned in their curious eyes.

8

Evie saw Tom Hobart coming out of the mess hut, and she hurried over to him.

"Hey, Evie," he said, "what's up? You look like you're in a hurry."

"No, just eager."

"For ...?"

"News of Jenny, what else?"

He smiled. "What else? Ummmm ... alien spacecraft and all that."

She flapped an arm. "Yeah, yeah, Artifact, alien, blah blah blah. I want to know when I'm going to hear from Jenny."

He laughed. "Guess you haven't been back to your hut recently."

"What? Why?"

His response was to give her a wink and stroll off. Evie watched him for four seconds, then she whirled and ran home. When she was ten feet from her door, she saw that someone—presumably Hobart—had used a self-erasing marker to draw a pair of small, interlocking hearts above the lock.

"You bastard," she said, but it was joyful.

She went in and found a hologram in stasis waiting for her. When she told Sybil to play it, the image was of Colonel Hobart grinning at her.

"You got mail," he said.

Then the image vanished to be replaced by one of a floating white envelope sealed with a red heart.

"Syb-Syb-Sybil," she stammered. "Play message."

The icon was replaced by the face of Jenny Spears. She looked pale but fit in her Stormsuit.

"Hey, babe," she said. "I wish this was a real-time call, but y'know … distance and all. And I hope you're happy to see this beat old hag of a SpecOps shooter. I can't wait to see *you*."

"God …" breathed Evie, reaching out to touch the face she saw, but her fingers passed through the hologram, causing it to shimmer.

"I'm calling because we're at the right point in the trip—and because I may have bullied Hobart just a bit. Now that I'm here, I can tell you some more about what we're doing out here. There's a group of pirates who have been making life tough for the folks on Sagan Station. Some off-the-record backstory: Sagan Station's public face is that of a hub for mining operations throughout sector nine of the asteroid belt, near the dwarf planet Ceres. That lump of rock is packed with a rare form of pyroxene that's used in every pulse pistol, rifle, and cannon in the system. I don't know all the science, but it allows for better focusing and beam width. Anyway, this pyroxene is very valuable, and with the expansion going past Jupiter soon, it's easier and cheaper to dig it out of Ceres than import it all the way the hell from home."

"I love you," murmured Evie, even though a holographic message could not hear her.

Jenny continued, "There's always a bit of pirating going on wherever there's no official regulation and oversight. Sure, there are forty different national versions of Space Force, but space is big as fuck, and most of the time, the pirates have better and faster ships. They've been real assholes, too. Killed a shit ton of miners and kidnapped some of the female ones. Reports we're getting are telling very bad stories about what's happening to the prisoners. So they sent me and my boys. We have four little breaching jumpers—hoppers—that were retrofitted with a lot of guns. When—and I say *when*, not *if*—we catch up with the pirates, we will spank them pretty damn hard."

Someone off camera said something, and Jenny nodded.

"Got to go to work. I'll send another message as soon as I can. With any luck, by the time you get that one, I'll be on my way back home. Back to you. I love you, Evangeline Cronin. Don't ever doubt that."

Jenny blew a kiss, and the message ended.

Evie sat there, feeling such a wild mix of emotions—love, fear, trepidation, anxiety, desire—that she didn't know what to do or how to process what she heard.

So she played the message over again.

Many, many times.

9

Kyle Hu was one of the new hires for the Artifact project. A month shy of his twenty-fifth birthday, he was a rising star among his colleagues in the SPU's First Contact division. All his life, he had longed to not only travel out among the planets but—if the science could be cracked—among the stars themselves. He believed in the mathematical probability that sentient life existed and the likelihood that some of that life had evolved earlier than mankind and reached a point of technological sophistication that made space travel inevitable.

And he wanted to meet them.

Kyle wanted to be part of any project, any effort, any team that would make first contact happen. His doctoral thesis was accepted on the same day the Artifact was discovered, and he simply could not believe that was an accident.

When the dreams began—and he had been warned about them—Kyle was calm about it. Yes, those dreams he remembered were terrible, but he did not hold it against the aliens. It would have been the height of presumption to assume that an alien would know *how* to communicate with us in a way that was either easy or comfortable. Just as it was the height of arrogance to expect humans to be able to understand and predict how that communication might unfold.

As he explained it to Craig Anders over beers one night, "Think about it from the alien's perspective. It woke up in a crashed ship after God knows how many years. We know firsthand how prolonged cryo-sleep messes with the neurons and synapses. Why would we assume that an alien would wake up unaffected after that long a time? It would be scared. Terrified. Confused for sure. Basic behavioral science has demonstrated that *all* animals, humans included, react with aggression or panic when surprised and frightened. That's what probably happened in the ice cave."

"How's that explain the nightmares?" Craig asked.

"Oh, that's easy enough. Have you read what Stenfield and Russo have been publishing about extrasensory perception?"

Craig sipped his beer and wiped foam from his upper lip. "Can't say I have."

"Oh, it's great stuff. We've come such a long way over the last two hundred years in accepting that many humans have some degree of ESP. It's not even a theory anymore. Stenfield and Russo have established that given the right combination of stimulation, nearly everyone demonstrates some abilities. There was one study about military in the field, and one out of every eight soldiers get a *feeling* when a sniper has them in their sights. There are hundreds of case studies of married couples who are not in direct communication knowing when the other has been injured. I could go on and on."

"How's this get us to the dreams?"

Kyle gulped the last of his beer and signaled the mess hall attendant for more. "Easy. If the aliens, being more advanced, have cultivated ESP as a natural part of their psychological or biological makeup, then in a crisis, it might call out—or send a flash or whatever. I don't know the precise term for it. That psychic message, amplified by terror—maybe when realizing that it was dying, thanks to what the Jokers did—might have left a mark with people around here."

"A mark?"

"A scar, or stain, or whatever. And that could be what is not only creating the dreams but tailoring them so a lot of us have the *same* dream. We are probably glimpsing things from the alien's mind."

"Why that gargoyle-vampire thing?"

Kyle accepted the fresh beer, took a sip, and set his glass down. "It could be that culture's version of the boogeyman. Or the devil. Who knows? It was dying, and maybe death and their 'devil' are connected on a religious, cultural, or philosophical level."

They sat with that for a bit, each sipping beer and turning it over in their minds.

"The flaw in that theory," said Craig, "is that you weren't here when the alien died. Hell, two-thirds of the folks who are here now came *after* that happened."

Kyle nodded. "So why are we having the same dreams as you?"

"Yep."

"Shared psychic pollution."

"What's that?"

"Something Stenfield wrote a whole book about. What they used to call mass hallucination, which is tied to mass hysteria and the phenomenon of the group mindset. People with stronger ESP abilities acting as signal boosters."

Craig thought about that as he drank, then began nodding. "That actually makes some sense," he conceded.

Both of them dreamed that night. Craig dreamed of the gigantic city and the shadowy creatures that moved among the colossal structures. Kyle dreamed a new dream. In it he was dead, his body floating in outer space, frozen and broken. Nearby were the shattered remains of a fighter spacecraft—a clunky cube of a thing. As his body drifted, he could feel himself—his consciousness and maybe his soul—leaving that frozen corpse and drifting toward what he thought was a distant sun. A light of some kind, at least. It was a warm light, and he knew if he could reach it, he would never be cold again. He would not be lost. Using some process he could not understand, he made himself move toward that light.

But then something fought that effort. It pulled him back, but dreaming Kyle could not understand how. He had no substance to pull, no mass to direct, and yet he felt himself accelerating backward, faster and faster.

Suddenly he was no longer a disembodied conscious. All at once, he was in a new body. Not one of flesh and bone. There was nothing organic about this strange form. Instead of flesh, he had metal skin. Instead of muscle and tendon, he had gears and servos. Instead of blood, he had electricity flooding through him.

"What … am … I?" he cried, and the voice that spoke the words was harsh, mechanical, strange. Alien.

His dream began to degrade, pushing him toward the surface of wakefulness. He heard words whispered in his thoughts. They were spoken by a woman with an Irish accent. No one he knew.

"You are NecroTek, child," she said. "And you have been called to serve."

When Kyle woke, his eyes snapped open, and he saw the floor of the valley rushing up to him at an awful speed. He did not even have time to scream before he struck the cruel and unforgiving ice. He struck with such force that his blood spattered the side of the Artifact.

No one saw him fall. His body lay there, slowly freezing beneath a winter moon.

10

It was a problem of reclamation, and Brollachan was drawn to challenges.

Especially those that could shove back the boundaries of known science and, at the same time, drive his career trajectory upward. He saw no problem with that, no conflict of interest. After all, Einstein had hardly put his own interests in the back seat—his celebrity offered more opportunities and opened many doors. That was part of the dance for all serious academics and researchers.

The secrecy was as much for expediency as to keep Agent Spears from living up to her elaborate threats. He actually liked the scar-faced young soldier, but she was dangerous because she believed wholeheartedly in her own self-righteousness. Fair enough. He believed that *he* was doing the best things for humanity as well.

To study and fully understand a being who had total deliberate control over its mass was fascinating. The applications were limitless. Soldiers who had lost limbs could simply manifest new ones. Someone with a damaged spine or heart could exert control over malleable tissue and mend it.

As he so often did, Brollachan thought of his younger sister, Miranda. A beautiful soul with a good mind, trapped forever in a motorized habitat—a kind of cubicle that she could drive around but which she could never leave. Miranda was like a specimen on display, relying on her courage and pragmatism to maintain dignity in an otherwise profoundly undignified situation. She could not walk, would never have the children she ached to raise, never know a loving touch or even the simple freedom of tending to her own bodily needs.

Brollachan believed that if the alien's shape-shifting qualities could be separated from the thing's apparent aggression—that was the key.

To him, it was no different from using a virus as a delivery system for a cure. Science took such risks because they were worth taking. Any levelheaded risk-reward analysis would prove that.

He sat at his table and looked at the lump of charred red tissue in the container.

"For you, Miranda," he said, and paused to dab at the tears forming in his eyes. Brollachan studied the wetness on his fingertips, then nodded. He brushed the moisture on one corner of the dura-glass container. It dried quickly, becoming invisible, but *he* knew it was there.

For Miranda.

"Ariel," he said.

"Yes, Dr. Brollachan."

"Open a new file. Label it *Miranda*."

"The Miranda file is now open," said the AI.

"Then let's begin."

11

It was a drone that found Kyle Hu, and Sybil who told Dr. Brollachan, Colonel Hobart, and Professor Cronin.

They all went down to where the body lay smashed to inhumanity and frozen for shocking display. Dr. Mogilevich accompanied them because, as staff physician, he also acted as coroner and medical examiner.

Everyone stood around as Mogilevich examined the body. After twenty painful minutes, he straightened and shook his head. "It looks like a single impact event. There are no signs of a beating or other injuries except those consistent with a fall from that height. He hit nothing on the way down."

Hobart studied the corpse. "Don't suppose there's any way to tell if he was pushed, fell, or jumped."

"If it's not on the security cameras," said the doctor, "then no."

"It isn't on the cameras," said Evie. "I asked as soon as I heard. The cameras are on rotation and there's a little gap of two or three seconds where the platform isn't visible."

"That's not a lot of time," mused Hobart. "He'd have had to run and jump."

"I'll do a full toxicological workup to see if he was under any chemical influence," said Mogilevich. "But even so, I'm not sure what that will tell us." He glanced at Evie. "He and your guy, Craig, were friends, weren't they?"

She nodded. "Yes."

"Does he have any insights?"

"He says no. They had some beers late last night and then went back to their huts."

"Any arguments?" asked Brollachan. "Disagreements? Anything like that?"

"Not according to Craig," said Evie. "I've asked him to file a full account of his conversation with Kyle. He's up in his hut now doing that. Sybil will upload it to all of us once that's done."

Which left them with nothing to do but arrange for the corpse to be airlifted to the medical hut. When the tox screen was completed, all it showed was an alcohol level consistent with three glasses of beer. The video feeds from the mess hall confirmed this, as did Craig's report.

Evie and Brollachan discussed the content of the conversation Kyle and Craig had, and although they found it interesting, the substance of it did not offer any direction to follow. Evie turned it over to Dr. Singh to see if she could divine anything, but she did not expect much.

Even with the delivery of iridium and the exciting potential for it in application, no work was done that day. The fact that it was a Sunday felt to Evie like either useful timing or a cosmic joke. In either case, she spent the day with her team, trying to reassure them when she felt no assurance in her own heart or mind.

That evening, she wrote about it in her serial letter to Jenny.

When she slept, her dreams were of Jenny in a gunfight with pirates. She even screamed when Jenny died, though Evie remembered none of it the next morning. All she felt was a leaden heaviness and a sadness that ran deeper than all the ice in Antarctica.

12

When Torquil Brollachan finished with his team of scientists, he walked back to his private lab. Ariel was still at work, though at a glance it looked like very little progress had been made. This did not concern him, because he knew full well that the most difficult and finicky parts of the process involved rebuilding the damaged DNA.

Ariel woke him at 4:17 in the morning.

Brollachan had to swim upward through the dense, dark waters of a dream of pursuit by some unseen predator. It was a terrifying dream, and when he came awake it was with a scream. He leaped out of bed, tripped on a tendril of blanket, and fell badly. His right elbow struck the floor, and then he banged his chin hard enough to clack his jaws shut.

"Dr. Brollachan," said Ariel, a note of alarm in his her artificial voice, "are you all right?"

"No I'm not all right, you fucking asshole," hissed the scientist between clenched teeth.

"Do you require medical attention? I can have a—"

"*No!*" Brollachan shouted the word. "No one is to come in here under any circumstances. That is a direct order."

Getting to his feet took an absurd amount of effort, but he managed it, clutching his badly bruised elbow to his body. His teeth hurt, his jaw ached, and there was a new dull pain at the base of his skull that felt suspiciously like whiplash.

It was only then that he smelled smoke.

"Ariel, what's happening? What's burning?"

"There is no active fire," reported the AI. "There was a mild seismic disturbance of 2.6 on the magnitude scale."

"An earthquake? I felt nothing."

"You were in REM sleep, Doctor. The quake was mild. No alarms have rung in camp. The only effect detected here was a small lamp that was sitting on a stack of books. It fell over, the bulb broke, and there was a short electrical discharge."

Brollachan peered around, expecting to find serious damage but seeing none. Then he spotted the broken lamp. The socket with its smashed bulb had struck the edge of a row of covered tissue-culture dishes. Three were cracked, and a fourth was broken. A tiny curl of smoke drifted up from the twisted filament. He hurried over and peered down at it.

"Damage estimate?"

"That is why I woke you, Doctor," said Ariel. "There has been an interaction."

"Explain."

"The electricity from the broken lamp has caused a reaction in the sample."

The slice of the recovered tissue was too small for Brollachan to see anything. "Magnify."

A holo-screen appeared between him and the broken dish. Ariel used it to gradually zoom in on the sample. Brollachan forgot about his arm, his jaw, his head, and virtually everything else. He gaped at the sample. It was pulsing. Throbbing.

Beating like a heart.

13

The next day was all work, and Evie accepted the hustle and bustle as a kind of therapy.

The first task was for Brollachan, Evie, and the science team to learn the idiosyncrasies of iridium. The metallurgist Alice Portevin was flown in from Harvard in time to help with applying the metal and testing it.

There was a learning curve, though. Two, really, since Portevin had no idea why the SPU had all but hijacked her and flown her fifteen thousand kilometers from home to the bitterest cold she'd ever encountered. The camp physician, Dr. Mogilevich, had to revive her after she fainted. A couple of nervous hours later, Alice Portevin stood in front of the star door, quietly weeping. She turned and hugged Evie and Brollachan and even Hobart for no reason she could explain.

"I can make a horseback guess as to why those spark plugs kept firing for so long," she said. "Iridium is the most corrosion-resistant metal known. Only hydrochloric acid in the presence of sodium perchlorate can dissolve it. Of course, it does react with other substances—cyanide salts in the presence of oxygen comes to mind. There are others too, but from your sensor readings, those things aren't evident inside the … um …"

"We call it the Artifact," said Evie.

Alice, a tiny woman with large eyes, stared at her. "Seems too mild a name."

"Useful, though," said Brollachan. "And good in the event of nonapproved eyes reading a misdirected report."

The metallurgist nodded. "Iridium has a very high melting point—the tenth highest on the periodic table, which means we'll need to prepare for that. Also, its hardness makes it brittle, so if we're thinking of creating a protective cover with it, we will need to design it so there are no unfortunate stress points. It's tricky to weld because of that brittleness. But its high melting point gives it resistance to surface heat, and even though heat doesn't seem to be the issue we're confronting, it's useful to know in case we need to make additional modifications. We also need to bear in mind that at temperatures below 0.14 Kelvin—minus 273.010 Celsius—it becomes a superconductor."

"Interesting," said Brollachan.

"Question is," Hobart said, "*Can* we use it to shield drones?"

Alice Portevin smiled. "I guess we'll find out."

14

With every spare moment he could steal, Brollachan experimented with the sample.

After the accident and the electrical stimulation, the fragment of alien tissue had continued to pulse for three and a half days. Then it slowed … and stopped.

"No cellular movement is detected within the sample," said Ariel.

"Pull up all sensor feeds," ordered Brollachan. "Let me see the waveforms."

A holo-screen appeared that displayed the feeds from more than forty different kinds of sensors. He sat, sipping coffee, staring at them, then pointed to one.

"That one," he said, touching one bit of telemetry. "It looks like nerve conduction."

"Yes, Doctor. I have noticed that similarity, though it is remarkable considering the lack of detectable nerves."

"Can you account for the cessation of movement?"

"I have a theory," said Ariel.

"So do I. You first, though."

"It became active after experiencing an electrical shock. It remained active for eighty-six hours."

Brollachan set his coffee cup down, rose, and went over to a cabinet in which a variety of supplies were kept. He made a thoughtful selection and returned to his chair with a spool of wire, cutters, and a tiny generator.

"Let's see what happens when it has a continuous source of electricity," he said.

"I must ask, Dr. Brollachan," said Ariel. "Is this a wise course of action?"

"Now is not the time to be timid."

There was a noticeable pause before the AI spoke again. "Very well, Doctor. How may I assist you?"

15

The site's team of engineers built a special furnace from components developed for mining asteroids. Again Brollachan had to finesse the delivery of those components without letting more people into the loop. Evie was impressed by how he did it. It was both encouraging and a little sinister sitting next to him as he made those calls. The SPU chief used political favors, bribery, veiled threats, and in one case, outright extortion to make it all happen.

The first thing the team did was to coat a small biosample container and push it through the door using a broom stick with a hook attached to a loop welded to the outside.

"Ah," said Brollachan as he watched Craig do this. "One does appreciate science at its most sophisticated."

Under his breath, Craig said, "Feel free to hand-deliver it."

"I heard that."

"You were meant to."

The container was left inside for ten minutes, and they used the stick to pull it out. The box was rushed into the lab and opened inside a sterile BSL-4 cabinet. Everyone bent down to peer through the triple-paned dura-glass.

"Sybil," said Evie in a nervous whisper, "evaluate the biological samples."

The AI said, "All of the biological samples are reading normal."

A plasma grenade tossed into the room would not have silenced everyone more quickly or thoroughly. Evie nearly fell down. Brollachan stepped back, a hand over his mouth, eyes wide and glassy. Alice Portevin stood there, looking equal parts shocked and pleased as tears ran down her face.

The next test was with a cockroach. Then a rat. By evening of the following day, they had sent in iridium-coated containers with monkeys and penguins, even to the point of sending the same test animals in over and over again.

All of the animals survived.

Everyone in camp came down to watch. With each successful test, the cheering became louder. Evie spotted an unusual number of coffee cups being handed around and sidled over to Craig and held out her hand for the one he held. The grad student looked suddenly nervous, but after Evie took it, sniffed, raised one eyebrow, took a heavy knock of vodka, and handed the cup back with a wink and a smile, he relaxed.

The party that night was epic.

The only person who complained was Dr. Mogilevich, who ran through his entire stock of SoberNow tablets.

But then the next challenge loomed. It was Kimbra, the engineer, whose observation was far more sobering than the pills. "If we want to send in drones, we have to solve a different set of problems," she told the science team when they gathered in the lounge attached to the main lab. "We can coat the drone body, the rotors, all of that with the iridium, and we can tinker with the motor to compensate for the extra weight . . ."

"But," said Evie. "I hear a *but* coming."

"*But,*" said an unsmiling Kimbra, "there are parts of the machinery that will still be exposed. The housing where the rotors attach to internal controls *can't* be coated in the same way. That opening is where the machines might still fail."

They sat with that for a while, gloomily staring into their own thoughts.

It was Craig who solved it. "Dr. Portevin, can iridium be alloyed with some other metal that would reduce its brittleness? I'm thinking coaxial cables of the kind used in underwater exploration and toxic atmo on some of Jupiter's moons. Or, better yet, the aerial drones they use on Venus. That's the most toxic place in the solar system, and the best drones are made at a factory in Omaha. The Hell's Belles. That's the nickname. Catalog name is ToxProof 513-A." He looked around. "If we can get them and coat the drones, their cables, and all with iridium or iridium alloy, will that work?"

Alice considered for a long time, then gave a slow nod. "Maybe."

Maybe was enough.

By the following afternoon, a Max-18 heavy skimmer brought in a cargo of Hell's Belles, and the team set to work. It was as if the months of failure had not only energized the team but seemed to amplify their mental and physical abilities. Sleep was an inconvenience. Weariness was fixed by a hot meal and protein drinks. The metallurgy hut was in operation around the clock. In six days the reimagined Hell's Belles were ready.

They were sent in and pulled out quickly.

"No damage," said a fevered Brollachan. "God in heaven, there's *no damage*."

The drones were sent in again, this time with Sybil taking control—since remote direction for the drones was still iffy. The mission was to use every possible scanner and beams of infrared, ultraviolet, and visible light to map the interior of the Artifact.

Waiting was dreadful.

Evie paced up and down, up and down, her fists balled, jaw clenched, eyes jumpy. Brollachan sat on a crate and was either talking to himself or praying. Hobart was pacing and cursing. The drones returned, and the feeds downloaded. And for the first time, the team had a clear look at the inside of the machine from somewhere beyond Earth.

Part Twenty
Vibrations in Eternity

"A man said to the universe:
'Sir, I exist!'
'However,' replied the universe,
'The fact has not created in me
A sense of obligation.'"

—*Stephen Crane*

Joint MIT/UCLA Biological Research Field Station #8
Queen Maud Land, Antarctica

1

They all clustered around to watch the video from the Hell's Belles.

The chamber behind the door was clearly an airlock. At either end of the chamber were other doors of the same star shape, each closed but oddly not locked. The articulated metal hands on the Hell's Belles drones fiddled with a series of bars and levers, with Sybil using problem-solving software to try a variety of combinations. On the sixty-eighth try, one of the doors suddenly swung inward, revealing a huge room filled with thousands of cone-shaped structures, each three meters tall, four wide at the base, and two at the top.

"What are they, do you suppose?" asked Hobart.

"No idea," murmured Brollachan, "but there are a lot of them."

"Sybil," said Evie, "what's your evaluation of those cones?"

"There is a high likelihood that they are cryo-chambers, Professor Cronin," said the AI.

"There's a hell of a lot of them," said Hobart.

"There are fifty-six-thousand, Colonel," said the AI. "All identical in construction and connected to the hull with cables. However, all of them are nonfunctioning."

"Any life signs?" asked Brollachan.

"There are no life signs in that chamber."

"What about the whole ship? Anything at all?"

"There are no active life signs currently identified aboard the Artifact, Dr. Brollachan."

"Are the cones hardened against your scanners?"

"No, Doctor. The drones were able to scan each of the devices, and all they detected was a material like dust from deteriorated organic matter. Additionally, there is no trace of moisture in any of the cones."

"Speculate," asked Evie.

"It is my best guess," said Sybil, "that those cones are cryo-tubes, but they malfunctioned, or the ship's power failed. In either case, whatever was inside the cryo-tubes has long since decayed and turned to dusty residue."

"Shit," growled Brollachan. "I wanted a sample of living tissue. Or at least a sample that could be studied." Then he gave Evie a quick and guilty look. "Forget I said that. No doubt your lady friend would have some strong words to say to me on this topic."

"No doubt," agreed Evie. She smiled, but she also filed his reaction away for later consideration. "I think we'll all sleep more soundly knowing that there are not fifty-six thousand *living* shape-shifters waiting for their alarm clock to ring."

Hobart snorted. "If so, we'd be ready. We have enough plasma bombs wired to the hull to vaporize it and kick what's left into orbit, along with half the mountain."

"Meaning we'd be vaporized too," groused Brollachan.

"Lesser of the evils, Torq. Not saying we wouldn't *try* to evac everyone out first."

"Your compassion is noted," said Brollachan sourly.

"These are not the only cryo-tubes we located," said Sybil. "I count eighteen compartments, each filled with the same number of cryo-tubes, for a total of one million eight hundred cryo-tubes."

That stunned them all to silence. Even Brollachan looked stricken.

"Why so many?" wondered Craig, breaking that silence.

"Invasion force," said Hobart. "Has to be."

"Don't be so certain, Tom," said Brollachan. "I think it's more likely this was an attempt at colonization. Remember, there were no intelligent species on Earth when this craft landed. It is unlikely their intent was to conquer."

"Even so," muttered Hobart, but left it there.

Sybil said, "Along with airlocks, the bridge, and machinery that appears to be dedicated to life support, these eighteen compartments comprise 92.14 percent of the entire Artifact."

"Whoa," said Craig, "how does that make sense?"

"Yes," Evie agreed. "That leaves less than eight percent of the Artifact for engines."

"Nonsense," snapped Brollachan. "Sybil, recalculate."

"The sum is the same, doctor," said the AI. "I have run it one thousand times."

"Some new kind of star drive?" ventured Hobart.

"There is nothing on this craft that is suggestive of engines," said Sybil. "There are no exhaust ports of any kind."

"What's in that last eight percent?" Evie asked.

"Dust," said Sybil. "Organic dust, but not of the same composition as that in the cryo-tubes. Although it is so degraded that specific analysis is impossible, it is statistically likely that it was a foodstuff of some sort."

They stood looking at one another.

"Let me see if I grasp this," said Craig, a crooked smile on his face. "We found a giant fucking hull that had a million monsters in it, lots of food, life support, and a bridge … but no engines?"

"There is no evidence of any propulsion system aboard the Artifact," confirmed Sybil.

"Then what *is* this thing? A troop transport without engines? How does that make sense?"

Evie walked a few paces down the row between the cryo-tubes, then she turned and said, "I think this is a kind of barge. Like a cattle car."

"Meaning what?" asked Hobart. "That it was *towed* here?"

"Towed, maybe," she said. "Or *sent* by some means we don't yet understand. All we know is that this is not a spacecraft."

"Then what in the nine hells could have brought it here, and why? And if someone did bring it here, what happened to *them*?"

No one had an answer to that. Not even a theory.

2

They spent hours in the Artifact.

The drones mapped every square centimeter of it, but something had gone out of each of their hearts. So many weeks and months of trying to solve the riddle of how to get into the Artifact only to succeed, and instead of finding answers, they were left with riddles that might never be solved.

"Where do we even go from here?" asked Craig as he walked Evie back to Main Street from the skimmer platform. They still wore their iridium pressure suits but with the hoods pulled off and dangling down between their shoulders.

"I honestly don't know," said Evie. A moment later she added, "God, this is so frustrating. I'd give *anything* to know more. Hell, I'd give a lot just to know what to do next."

"Does this mean it's over down here?"

Evie thought about that. "Not sure. Probably our time here is over. From now on it's going to change from a first-contact scenario to archaeology and forensics. Neither of which is our job."

They walked past the mess hut.

"It's going to feel really weird going back to the world," said Evie. "Back home, I mean."

"I know what you mean. And … yes, it is."

When they reached her hut, they stopped and looked back the way they'd come.

"One thing's kind of weird, though," Craig said. "I mean, one specific thing."

"What's that?"

"You and Colonel Hobart looked freaked. You both looked as disappointed as I feel. But did you see the look on Doc Brollachan's face?"

"No, I didn't take any particular note of his expression. Why? What did you see?"

"You're going to think I'm nuts," he said, "but he didn't look disappointed at all. At first I thought he was just relieved we didn't find a million of those shape-shifting critters getting ready for world conquest, but I don't think that was it. And don't ask me what I do think, because I don't know."

Evie considered that. "You're sure?"

"Yeah. Very. It was weird. And … don't think I'm cutting him up or anything, but he almost looked *happy* about it. Like … excited."

3

Torquil Brollachan walked to his lab and sent a message ahead to have Howard, Solà, and Wu meet him. When he entered the shared lab, they were waiting.

"You went inside?" asked Solà, his face alight with anticipation.

"I did," said Brollachan. "Have a seat, and I'll tell you about it."

When he was finished, he saw the comprehensive disappointment on their faces. It was crushing news.

"I understand how you feel, my friends," he said. "But now isn't the time for grief or despair. Not at all."

"How not? It's a dead end. In two years that spacecraft—or barge, or whatever—will be a tourist attraction. At best we can all write books about it and then go back to the day-to-day stuff."

"Which," said Wu, "is going to feel really damn dull after all this."

Brollachan nodded. "I imagine you all feel like that, as does Tom Hobart and Evie Cronin."

Howard gave him a shrewd look. "Yet you don't, Torq. In fact, you look like a five-year-old kid on Christmas morning."

The SPU chief smiled. "We have the God Machine project."

"Which is, what, two years away from completion of even a scaled-down model?"

Brollachan stood. "There is something else I've been working on that I have not yet shared with you."

Howard's shrewdness turned into a frown. "What does that mean? What else have you been working on?"

"I call it Project Caliban." Brollachan stood. "Come with me to my personal lab. I have much to show you."

4

Hobart knocked on Evie's door, and she let him in.

"Drink?" she offered.

"Maybe a beer. No? Water's fine," he said, plopping down in a chair near the fire. Evie poured him a glass and—after staring longingly at the whiskey bottle—poured water for herself, too. They sat looking at the flames for a while.

"Well," he said, "this wasn't what I expected."

"No."

"I ran into Craig a few minutes ago. He asked if the site was going to be shut down and the Artifact made public."

"And you said ...?"

Hobart shrugged. "Kid's not wrong. But hell, we'll be here a month or two more, making sure we've documented everything we can. That'll give POTUS time to work out the timetable for telling the world. He'll have to have some meetings with the other world leaders, then give his press team time to shape the story. Even with the Artifact being a relic and not an active threat, the story will need to be delivered with care. For the public, who are going to freak out, and for all the religious nuts, who will feel threatened by what we've found."

"You should recommend that the president bring in Lars Soren," Evie suggested. "This is exactly the kind of thing he has been working toward. His cosmic philosophy is built on the presumption of alien contact."

"Oh, that was my first thought. Torq reached out to see how quickly we could get his ass down here, but we're about six days too late."

"Why?" she cried. "Has something happened to him?"

"What? Sorry." Hobart chuckled. "No, Soren's in cryo-sleep aboard a transport ship along with his whole synod of faith leaders. They'll be at Asphodel Station in under a week."

"Oh," she said, nodding. "He's taking them out for the WarpLine test, isn't he?"

"Yup. Let's face it, Soren's been right all along about the cultural impact of that matter-teleportation gizmo."

"Matter transposition," she corrected.

"Whatever." Hobart sipped his water. "Point is, he'll be staying on Asphodel for six months. The WarpLine test is in five months, so there's no way he'll be back in time. And POTUS doesn't want him—or anyone not physically here at the site—to know about this."

"Why not?"

"Think about it. If WarpLine works, then Soren is ideally placed to help massage the news to the various churches, right? That will prime the pump in some useful ways for *our* message."

"Which means waiting for five months?"

"Sure. It's been here for a zillion years—what's a few more months?"

"What happens if the WarpLine tech doesn't work?" asked Evie.

Hobart shrugged. "Then we'll be the story that diverts attention from that failure. Besides, ours is a bigger and better story anyway. I mean, sure, *we're* feeling let down, but think about how the public will be when this gets out. It will be *the* story for the next—I don't know—thousand years?"

"So, we're delaying telling the world because of the public-relations timing?"

He spread his hands. "Welcome to the realities of global politics, Evie."

His holo-comms buzzed and showed him a message she could not read. A great smile spread across Hobart's face, and he immediately stood up.

"I'm going to buzz off because I think you're going to need some alone time."

"What's that supposed to mean?"

There was a *bing-bong* from her Sybil.

"You've got mail, sister," said the colonel, and he left, still smiling.

5

"Hello, beautiful," said Jennifer Spears.

The image of her on the RealScreen in her hut was so vivid, so real, that Evie had to restrain herself from reaching out to touch her lover. Spears wore her Stormsuit with the bull's eye, and her short hair had been cropped even shorter. She looked tired but happy.

"I have good news and good news," Jenny said, beaming. "First, the whole pirate thing was a nothingburger with extra ketchup and relish. Turns out it was a small team of assholes who would probably have smashed their rust bucket of a 'pirate ship' into an asteroid, given time.

We bopped them on the head and handed them over to security on Sagan. Dipshits are probably going to have a better quality of life in jail than they had trying to be Blackbeard and his cutthroat crew."

She laughed and shook her head.

"When I get back, I am sooooo going to kick Hobart's ass for taking me away from you and sending me to the ass end of nowhere."

Jenny shifted to allow her camera to show what was behind her. Evie saw that it was a cryo-tube on a spaceship. She actually cried out.

"The *other* good news is that we're already on our way home. ETA twenty-eight days. Would be two days sooner, but one of the brain trust on Sagan asked if we could do a quickie detour to check out some kind of magnetic anomaly. Not really our job, but the transport we're on has better sensors than the old tubs they have at Sagan. That'll be fast, and then I'm going to lay down and dream very naughty dreams about you all the way home. And I warn you now, sugar, I am going to wear you out when I get you alone. Make sure to hydrate and take plenty of vitamins, because Jenny Spears is coming for ya!"

She blew a big kiss, said those three magic words, and ended the call.

Evie sat on her chair and felt like she was flying.

That night, she didn't even *think* about the bottles of whiskey on her shelf.

6

For Evie, the next few days were a strange blend of elation, knowing that Jenny was safe and on her way home, and trepidation about the end of her term there in Antarctica. Craig worked with her to begin the process of getting the staff ready to start the laborious process of cataloging and documenting everything and footnoting reports so that they were current with the status.

"Not sure if I'm happy about this or not," he admitted while they were in the hut they used as headquarters for the university contingent.

"I know," said Evie. She had two stacks of reports on her desk. The "Done" stack was four centimeters high, but the "To Do" pile was so high it was beginning to lean into the pull of gravity. She paused and rubbed her eyes. "Funny thing is, we academics are supposed to *thrive* on paperwork."

"Not to be crude," said Craig, "but fuck that."

"Glad you weren't crude."

He grinned and thumbed five more reports atop the big stack.

"I kind of hate you right now," said Evie.

"I kind of deserve it."

There was music playing, a recent recording of Bach's *Goldberg Variations* by a blind harpsichord protégé prodigy from Taiwan. Complex and challenging, it somehow soothed both of them as they worked.

Dr. Singh stopped by to deliver copies of her own reports based on her sessions with Evie's staff. Her face was dark with the shadows of sadness and stress.

"It will be good to go home," she said.

Evie nodded. "I suppose so. Though I don't know how it will feel to be among normal people after what we've been through."

Singh almost smiled at that but couldn't quite make it.

"Tell me, Indira," said Evie, "once we're away from here and back in the world, will the dreams stop, do you think?"

Singh took far too long in constructing a reply. Eventually she said, "Let's all hope so." With that, she left.

Craig closed the door behind her and blew out his cheeks. "Wow. As inspirational pep talks go, that well and truly sucked."

Evie tapped the new stack of files. "Work therapy. Dig in."

They were about to break for lunch when Sybil interrupted. "Professor Cronin," she said in an oddly urgent tone, "Colonel Hobart requests your presence in the command hut right away. This is marked Code Alpha Urgent."

Evie and Craig shared a brief, worried glance.

"Now what?" he complained, but Evie was already pulling on her coat as she headed for the door.

7

She saw Torq Brollachan hurrying toward the command hut too, along with a few other senior members of the Artifact team.

"What's this about?" asked Brollachan irritably. "I have two very important projects in hand that require close attention."

"I don't know," she said.

A soldier waved them inside.

Hobart stood in front of a large RealScreen that showed a revolving CODE ALPHA URGENT logo, below which was an AUTHORIZED PERSONNEL ONLY tag.

"Tom," snapped Brollachan, "this had better be important."

Hobart's eyes were wide and bright and filled with an emotion Evie couldn't easily read. Instead of directly answering, he asked, "How soon can the two of you be ready to leave?"

"Leave … where?" asked Evie. "And why?"

Hobart pointed upward. "*Tempest* is in close orbit."

"What does that have to do with me?" Evie asked.

"Or me, for that matter? I can't just drop everything."

"You'll want to," Hobart said. They began hammering him with questions, but he spoke to Sybil. "Play it again."

There were a few seconds of white noise, and then Evie's heart soared as the face of Jenny Spears filled the screen. She wore a deep-space military-grade pressure suit and a helmet with a large, clear visor. Behind and around her was ice-covered rock of the kind common to asteroids.

"Colonel, hope you get this quick and get back to me quicker," she said. "If there's anyone with you who doesn't have the right clearance level, then shoo them out."

Several people looked at the officer, but he just shook his head.

"The station director at Sagan asked us to check out some anomalous readings on a medium-sized asteroid that's on this huge elliptical orbit. Been way outside of scanner range for probably six or seven hundred years. Anyway, we found the rock and hooked on. That's when our scanners really went crazy, giving us all kinds of wild readings. There was more actual mass registering than the asteroid should have had. It's one of those rock-and-ice jobs. We went prowling and found something very interesting. There was a big cavern inside the thing, the entrance covered with methane ice. Not Larry cut through it, and we used EVA packs to check it out. And … well … what's that old saying? One picture's worth a thousand words? Take a look, 'cause you're gonna *love* this."

Spears stepped aside so they could all see what lay at the heart of the asteroid. It was long and gray and sprawled with its back broken by ice and colliding rocks.

Once more, Evie swayed as if the floor was tilting beneath her. Brollachan crossed himself. Everyone else gasped or cried out or swore or stood as still and silent as death. The image was crystal clear, and there was no mistake.

It was another Artifact.

Part Twenty-One
A Fire in Heaven

"Be convinced that to be happy means to be free and that to be free means to be brave. Therefore do not take lightly the perils of war."

—*Thucydides*

Planet Shadderal
The Shadderal Star System

1

Calisto had her Lost Souls out on a training flight, working their way through attack and defense patterns that pushed the cadets into making tactical decisions faster and more efficiently.

The kids were coming along fine, and that pleased her. Though she checked herself when she realized that she thought of them that way. As kids. *Her* kids. Some of them were her age, and one was older. They just felt young.

"Thor to Calisto," came the call. "I've got something on my screen and—"

There was a huge burst of blue plasma, and Thor's tumbler went spinning out of formation, its shields flickering dangerously.

"Boss, we got incoming!" yelled Leva Baumila—call sign Junda—who was flying point. "Count eight daggers. No … ten. Christ, there's more. Count twenty and—"

Her words rose to a shriek and then vanished as her tumbler was engulfed in a barrage of blue pulse fire. The nuke core blew up, filling the void with painful light before winking out.

"All ships," came Captain Croft's urgent cry. "We're tracking thirty-five dagger ships coming out from behind Chandra's moon."

That was a small, icy moon at the outer edge of Shadderal's gravitational sphere of influence.

"Lost Souls," yelled Calisto, "two-by-two split and hit. Attack plan Epsilon. Go!"

The eleven tumblers left broke away from the group, hopscotching in what looked like random flight but was really one of Calisto's favorite counterattack patterns. Thor and Horus seemed to vanish entirely, but she knew where they were going, and they reappeared on her scope directly between the two lead daggers. Each tumbler fired the one-two missile sequence that Bianca had pioneered and then hopscotched up and away as the shoggoth fighters exploded. The daggers directly behind them flew through the fiery debris, only to find Cricket and Decaf waiting to use the same tactic.

One, two, three, four, and those daggers were dust.

That still left thirty-one attackers, a nearly three-to-one ratio, and the remaining shoggoths would have seen and understood the strategy. The enemy ships broke formation, preventing the double strikes, and they swarmed like angry wasps, firing their pulse cannons.

Calisto did not have a partner with Junda gone, but that was fine with her. She was an excellent team leader, but in a brawl, she liked to take it to the bad guys with her own solo method that looked haphazard but was not. She jumped and turned and played chicken to draw a dagger into an attack run. Then she hopscotched away, doing it with an appearance of sloth and sluggishness that encouraged the enemy to really open up as it tracked her. By the time the shoggoth realized that Calisto had drawn fire toward another dagger, the plasma bolts were fired, and she timed it so well that she felt one bolt graze her port shields as she jumped up and back. The rest of the barrage hit the dagger and blew it in half.

Five down.

Calisto came out of a series of tight turns and fired the Constellation missile and Inferno at the ship that had just killed its fellow. The blast caught it just right, and her next jump was between two halves of the dying ship.

Six.

The battle raged, with her cadets acquitting themselves like seasoned warriors. Even so, the odds sucked, and she knew it.

"Go solo," she ordered. "Go long. Hit and hop."

The tumblers broke formation again, drawing the daggers after them in lines of pursuit that pulled the attack away from Asphodel."

"C-1 to Calisto," came the voice of Captain Croft. "Be advised, there is a Medusa carrier entering the zone."

Calisto's heart seemed to freeze in her chest. A mother ship like that could deploy hundreds of daggers. She looked at her screen and saw that it was moving in fast, though it had not yet launched reinforcements.

"Launching the rest of the tumblers," said Croft, and Calisto saw glowing dots on her screen shooting out from the launch decks on Asphodel.

"Copy that," said Calisto tightly, dodging a terrific blast of pulse fire. On one hand, she wanted the extra birds in the air, but on the other, those other pilots would be the newest of her cadets. Her heart sank as she thought of them going up against shoggoths—aliens who were willing to sacrifice their own if it meant destroying their targets. "C-1," she said, addressing Croft, "I'm going to bring some bandits home. Make them welcome."

"Do it," growled the captain.

Calisto called to Aries and Deimos to follow her, and they teased a group of five daggers into a race—not away from the station, but toward it. The daggers seemed delighted at this chance, and they kicked their ships up to full speed.

"Triphammer spread aft, then break high and low," she said. "Just like I showed you."

The three tumblers flew straight, eschewing the hopscotch maneuver to encourage the daggers to really pour it on. Only when they were three klicks from home did she jump away, with Aries cutting up and Deimos dropping down as a battery of massive ion cannons fired from amidships on Asphodel.

The blast engulfed the daggers, blowing two to atoms, crippling a third, and sending the last two spinning away on the edge of the shockwave.

Right into the missiles fired by Aries and Deimos.

Eleven down.

But she was down two tumblers. Thor was damaged but alive, and Junda was gone. Then Sybil flashed a notice that Chavalit Yipintsoi—Elephant Boy—was gone too, and Calisto had not even seen it.

There was no time for grief. There was no time for anger. All that she had was the battle and the pilots who still lived. With a deep and bitter coldness in her heart, she wheeled around and plunged back into the fray.

2

The shoggoths kept coming.

Their ships were faster in a straight run than the tumblers, and Calisto realized with growing horror that their guns were more powerful. Instead of needing six or even eight direct hits on tumbler shields, they were doing massive damage with one or two. And their missiles had some kind of new tracking software clearly intended to compensate for the hopscotch maneuvers.

Calisto and her Lost Souls killed a lot of the enemy.

But the enemy was relentless and bloodthirsty. In any even match, the tumblers might have won. Their ability to make those full-speed right-angle turns was critical. But the shoggoths had their upgraded weapons, and they had the numbers.

She saw Alicia Mohidin—call sign Ballerina—kill the shoggoth who killed her. Five minutes later Nomad—Mohamed Thajudeen—was caught in crossfire and died screaming.

The sound lingered in Calisto's cockpit, and she felt her heart breaking loose from its moorings. With each death it fell to a lower place, where she knew it would remain even if this battle were won. Loss was a cancer. So was grief.

On her screen, the Medusa was closing in, though she had still not launched new fighters. That was strange, but Calisto didn't have time to suss out what it might mean. Nothing good, that was for sure.

Suddenly five daggers seemed to come out of nowhere, and she was in a kill box. They fired, using more care than their comrades had, not falling for Calisto's bait-and-switch trick of shooting each other as she jumped away. Calisto tried, though. She knew every trick there was in space combat. Bianca always said Calisto was the best in the Lost Souls, but Calisto never believed it. Here, without ego or joy, she proved it by fighting five of the enemy at once.

One of her favorite new tricks was to fire a Constellation then jump to a different angle and fire the follow-up Inferno so it hit any shields weakened by the first blast, but at an angle that punched through three or four shield panels rather than one. This not only destroyed the target dagger, but the force followed the angle and kicked the debris into another ship.

The fight spiraled and twisted through the gulf between Asphodel and Shadderal. Calisto killed two of the daggers, but only at a cost. The second one clipped her amidships a split second before a jump, and suddenly alarms were blaring in her cockpit.

"Shields down to eighteen percent," Sybil cried.

That was too low, and even glancing fire would destroy her.

Calisto tried to run for it, but the daggers were faster. She tried to hopscotch, but there was simply too much damage. And Sybil needed the extra juice for the failing shields.

Then a bolt of green fire shot past her, and one of the three pursuing daggers blew apart in a spectacular ball of flaming debris.

Calisto said, "*What?*"

A moment later a second dagger blew up.

Then a third.

Each of them struck with multiple rounds of green plasma—something Calisto had never seen before. She twisted around in her chair, trying to make sense of it.

"What in the deep black fuck hell is *that*?" said Morrigan.

Then *it* moved into view.

The shipboard cameras on Calisto's tumbler showed it.

Calisto saw it.

Morrigan saw it.

Aboard Asphodel, Captain Croft saw it. Everyone who was looking out of a window saw it. And yet it was nowhere on the sensor screens. It was on no radar, no telescope, no motion tracker. It was there, and it wasn't there.

The ship was five times the size of a tumbler. Sleek, matte black like the dagger ships but of a different hull design. Not as long as them and narrower, more like a spearpoint than a knife. It showed no lights, no markings.

"I can't get a target lock on it," said Morrigan. "It's not on my scope at all."

"Must be sensor shielded," said Morrigan. "God, there could be a thousand of them, and we can't see them."

The alien fighter moved sideways in a controlled drift, its needle-sharp nose directed to the center of the approaching daggers. Guns of unknown design fired continuously, hammering the shoggoths with green plasma. The enemy withstood two or three rounds each, but then those green pulse blasts fried their shields and blew the ships into twisted junk.

"Calisto to C-1."

"Go for C-1," answered Croft, sounding breathless. "Where'd that ship come from?"

"I was going to ask you the same thing, Skipper. Is that some new NecroTek design? Is Bianca back?"

"Negative," said Croft. "That's not a NecroTek. That ship is unknown."

"Well, whoever it is, they're no damn friends of the squishies."

That was one of many new derogatory epithets for the shape-shifting shoggoths.

The other daggers broke off their attack on Asphodel and began swinging around to swarm the newcomer. Instead of fleeing the onslaught, the strange craft began accelerating toward them.

"God *damn* it's fast," swore Cricket. "Holy fucking shitballs."

The fighter shot past Calisto and two of the damaged and drifting tumblers, driving toward the remaining daggers, firing constantly. Calisto watched in a kind of horrified fascination, her own weapons forgotten in the moment.

Then she saw something that made no sense.

For every time the new ship directly struck a dagger and blew it up, at least one or two others were destroyed as well.

"What the hell's happening?" begged Calisto. "Do they have some kind of weapon that causes chain reactions?"

"Negative," said Croft. "*Look!*"

She saw it then. The new ship was not alone.

Four others were diving from above on the wave of daggers. All identical, all absent from electronic sensors. All firing green pulse blasts that melted through the shoggoth shields as easily as a hot knife through soft butter.

"Oh shit," said Morrigan, "those squishies don't like that worth a damn. They're running. Heading back toward the chimera ships and—"

And the black vastness of space was suddenly filled with fireballs of green so monstrously huge that they looked like emerald suns being born. The beams combined by some process Calisto had never seen, becoming as big as a searchlight. It slammed into the first of the chimeras and blew it to atoms. Then, with relentless maliciousness, it swept toward the others. Two, three, four ... all of the chimeras exploded. Calisto winced and shielded her eyes with her hand.

"God in heaven ..." breathed Calisto.

The fireballs winked out, and it seemed as if the galaxy itself paused in shocked silence.

"The Medusa is altering course," said Croft. "She's moving off."

It was true. The massive shoggoth carrier had turned around and was heading into the asteroid field at maximum speed.

Calisto had no idea how to even react to that. But any thoughts about it were blanked out as the first of the sleek black fighters turned around and began moving toward her.

The fiery green guns were trained on her damaged tumbler, though it did not immediately fire. Instead, it slowed to a stop not thirty meters away—nearly the same distance and angle as the shoggoth ship earlier. It loomed over her damaged tumbler, dwarfing it.

"Oh," whispered Calisto, "... *shit.*"

3

A voice spoke through the speakers.

Not Morrigan or Croft. Not Sybil. Nor did it come from the strange new ships. And it was a *familiar* voice.

"Hold on, sugar," it said. "I got this."

Then there was a blur of silver blue as something shot out of the unending blackness, flashed past her screens, and drove straight at the alien craft. It moved at astonishing speed as it circled the fighter once, twice, three times. Then it slowed and landed on the pointed nose of the strange ship. In the vacuum of space, there was no *clang* to hear, no noise at all when metal struck metal. But Calisto heard it in her mind.

The newcomer looked like a torpedo—until it didn't. The thing abruptly bent, its metal skin shifting, twisting, leaving behind the torpedo sleekness to assume a humanoid shape. It stood tall on mechanical legs, but instead of two arms, *four* of them unfolded from the torso. A head like a bullet swiveled toward the broad, blackened video screen as it raised all four arms. There were no hands on those arms; instead, the mouths of compact, powerful ion cannons glowed with an intense purple light.

Through the speakers, though, Calisto heard a familiar voice. It came in over a master channel that was designed to broadcast on all possible frequencies. Universal translators—long since augmented to include over forty thousand alien tongues from Shadderal and other worlds—roared out. Silent in space, but like thunder to any craft within range and with active speakers.

"Power down your weapons and identify yourself," ordered Commander Bianca Petrescu. "Do it right fucking now."

"Bee?" gasped Calisto. "Talk about the fucking cavalry comin' over the hill. Woohah!"

"What would you do without me, sweetie?"

The moment stalled as the black ship just hung there in the void. Bianca leaned her NecroTek body forward and tapped the front screen with the barrel of an ion cannon.

Scanner lights erupted from the spearhead-shaped craft, sweeping up and down Bianca's metal body.

"I won't ask again," she said.

The sensors clicked off.

Time seemed to slow down to nothing. Calisto tensed, her hand resting on the joystick, finger curled very lightly around the red trigger. Then ... the blackened forward screens on the alien ship began to fold back. Bianca kept her cannon trained on the windows. Her metal body blocked Calisto's view of what was being revealed.

But she heard Bianca gasp.

The radio was instantly filled with a dozen voices—her team and officers aboard Asphodel Station. It was a cacophony of babble.

"Clear the air," Calisto roared, and the chatter stopped abruptly.

She tried to maneuver and found that her tumbler was once again responsive to her touch. Calisto shifted only a few meters to the left, just far enough to see what it was that made Bianca gasp. She zoomed in so that the front of the alien ship filled her own forward screen. Allowing her to see what flew this bizarre and deadly craft.

There were two of them visible. Two forms.

They were *not* shoggoths.

They were not from *any* alien race.

They were humans. Or, at least, humanoid—seemingly, a man and a woman.

They each wore flight suits. The pilot's was smoke gray, with a symbol of a surging wave rising and beginning to curl. The woman's was a form-fitting combat suit with a bull's eye worked into the material and centered over her heart. Their faces were mostly obscured by shadows.

"Identify yourself," demanded Bianca. "Who are you, and where in the fuck did you come from? Answer me right now, or you are going to have a very, very bad day."

The ensuing silence lasted nearly ten seconds. They felt like ten hours.

Finally, the woman said, "You're … human?"

"Opinions vary," replied Bianca. "Who and what are you, and how the hell are you speaking English?"

Another pause, shorter this time.

"I am Agent Jennifer Spears, commander of Pantheon squadron of the US research vessel *Tempest*. We are from the planet Earth in the Sol system." A beat. "Please identify *yourself*."

Bianca hesitated and then powered down her cannons. Two of her arms collapsed to flatness and folded back into her torso, leaving no trace. Her remaining arms shifted form, losing the inflexible hardness of cannons and taking on shapes that were nearly human.

Bianca shifted her mass to create a light in the center of her chest, and as soon as the lens finished forming, she shined it on the two people.

Calisto heard Bianca say, "What the hell? *Jenny?*"

And a moment later the woman leaned close to the glass and gaped at the NecroTek. She was white, tall, and muscular, with a jagged pink tattoo across her stern face.

In a voice filled with wonder, the woman said, "I know that voice. My God … Bianca? *Bee?*"

And then her voice broke, filling with tears, with wonder, with wild hope.

"Merciful God … we're not alone."

Part Twenty-Two
Scattered Leaves

"Be courteous to all, but intimate with few, and let those few be well tried before you give them your confidence."

—*George Washington*

Asphodel Station
The Shadderal Star System

1

Dr. Lars Soren and Captain Sebastian Croft stood together on the flight deck of Asphodel Station. A huge RealScreen showed the space beyond, and it was filled with ships.

"This is …" began Soren. "Well … I actually don't know what word to use. Nothing seems quite appropriate, does it?"

"Frankly," said Croft, "I'm surprised I'm even capable of human speech right now."

"As I recall," Soren said, "*Tempest* was due to dock with Asphodel for the WarpLine gun test firing."

Croft shook his head. "Not actually, no. It was in the vicinity, on some classified thing. *Tempest* is an SPU boat, and the whole lot of them are shifty bastards."

"I know the type." Soren turned and placed a hand on Croft's upper arm. "My heartfelt condolences on the loss of your pilots, Sebastian."

Croft looked down at the floor for a few moments. "One of the hardest parts of command is seeing those brave young people give their lives while bureaucrats like me seem to be bulletproof. It's not fair."

The professor gave his arm a comforting squeeze and took his hand away as Calisto stepped down from her damaged tumbler, leaned on it for a moment as she slowly shook her head, and then straightened. Soren watched as the young officer pulled together the pieces of her self-control and welded them back into place. It touched him deeply, and his heart went out to her.

"She is a remarkable person," he said softly.

"That she is, and I wish I had fifty just like her."

"Sir," called the deck officer, "we have incoming."

Croft and Soren turned to see Bianca Petrescu on the RealScreen as she soared toward the landing bay. The cannons were gone, and her arms were folded back into the fuselage of her robot form. A moment later, the NecroTek passed through the deflector shielding and stepped onto the deck. As soon as she was in, she went to the first of a row of bins set against a wall, leaned over, and for a moment seemed to melt. What she was actually doing was sloughing off tons of her mass into the bin, where it would remain until she needed to go back into combat. When she was done, she looked more like a human being in an exoskeleton. And her weight would not threaten the less reinforced decks throughout the station. When she was done, she came clumping over and sketched a salute to Croft.

"Permission to come aboard, sir?" she said in a voice that was oddly human for so inhuman a form.

"Welcome home, Commander," said Croft. They exchanged salutes. "Where's the rest of your people?"

"On their way, but it'll take a couple of days for them to get here. I left early because I had some things to report, and then I walked into whatever the hell *this* is."

"Unless it's urgent," Croft said, "that report can wait."

"Yes sir," she said. "And … no shit." She shook her head. "Jenny Spears. And a whole ship full of fighter pilots, scientists, and who knows what else. Maybe God doesn't hate us after all."

"The almighty still has a lot of reparations to make," mused Soren. "But I take your point. It is remarkable that you know one of the pilots."

"Oh, Jenny's not a pilot. Probably manning the guns on that bird, but yeah, I know her. She was a top-of-the-line SpecOps shooter for a while, though when I met her, she was a PMC—a private military contractor."

"Is that some kind of mercenary?"

"Some kind, sure, though her team, the Jokers, mostly did gigs for Uncle Sam. We didn't go out on any missions, but we sure as hell partied with them. And Spears hit on me every chance she could. She has no filters, but there's no better to have on your six in a fight, so 'yay us' for finding them. Or them finding us. Whatever. If she has the Jokers with her, then we need to throw a party because that is some really damn good news. Ditto for those stiletto fighters. I mean, I *heard* about them, but seeing them in action is wild."

"Here we go," murmured Hobart.

They watched as a stiletto came in through the deflectors and settled onto the deck, all in a kind of ghastly silence. There was not even a whisper of engine noise.

"That's hot as fuck," murmured Bianca.

"It's terrifying," said Soren. "Which makes me glad it's on our side."

"Bleeding-edge SPU tech," said Croft. "Way beyond my pay grade or appropriations budget."

"Listen," said Bianca, "let me say hi to Jenny first and kind of ease her into this, okay?"

"Given that there is zero precedent, Commander," said Hobart, "you have both my permission and my blessing."

2

Bianca went and stood by the stiletto as Jenny stepped down, saluted the deck officer, and looked around, her face filled with wonder and obvious questions.

"Fancy meeting you way the hell out here," said Bianca.

Jenny blinked, not yet recognizing the new body configuration, though cued by the sound of Bianca's voice.

"Bee? God!" she gasped. "It's so great to see you, Bee. Hot damn, you look pretty badass in that rig. First things first, though … Who were those assholes in the big black ships?"

"We call those fighters dagger ships, and the big one was a Medusa mother ship. They're chimeras—ships capable of changing shape for different kinds of combat."

"No, that's not at all scary. Are they pirates? Did some of them get chucked out here by WarpLine too?"

"Jenny," said Bianca, "they're aliens. Shoggoths, we call them."

Jenny stared at her for a three-count. "I'd be more shocked about that if me and mine hadn't been through all the shit that's come our way. We really need to talk."

"Yes, we damn well do."

"But look, Bee, it's kind of awkward having a conversation while you're still in that newfangled pressure suit. Mind at least taking your helmet off? Would love to see that pretty face."

There was a beat, and Jenny frowned. "What'd I say?"

"It's not a helmet," Bianca said. "It's not a suit. This is me."

"What's that supposed to mean?"

"We have a *lot* to talk about. But the short version is—I'm dead. This is my current body."

Jenny laughed. "Oh, sure. That's hilarious. Dead? What, dead to me? Dead to all lesbians? Or dead to anything that doesn't look like that boy toy of yours? What was his name? Jacob Fox? Cute for a guy. But seriously, Bee … take the helmet off."

Bianca exerted a fraction of her will, and the helmet manifested a seam down the middle of the faceplate. It widened, creating two panels, and they swung open to reveal motors and servos, wires and circuits, but nothing alive.

"This is me, Jenny," she said. In the ensuing silence, Bianca slowly resealed her headpiece.

Jenny stood there, slowly shifting weight from one foot to the other. Her face had gone pale, and she kept blinking. "I … I don't even know how to reply to something like that."

"A *whole* lot has happened since WarpLine."

"Well, God damn, Bee," said Jenny, trying to recover from the shock. "The fuck *happened* to you? And can you tell me over several very tall glasses of kitchen whiskey? Because I have a feeling I'm going to get seriously fucking drunk."

There was the slightest pause. "I don't drink anymore."

"Don't or can't? … Or is that a wildly indelicate question?"

Bianca laughed. "You never had a lick of tact, girl. Why would I expect any now?"

"First … ouch."

"If the shoe fits …"

"Yeah, yeah. And you … Ha! You used to joke about being a cast-iron bitch, and now you literally are. If you can't drink, then I'll have your portion too, because I have a feeling I'm going to need it."

"Oh, you will," said Bianca.

Jenny ran trembling fingers through her hair, and that was her only tell, showing that beneath the snark and jokes, she was truly shaken. "Look, Bee … what do I say to this? I'm … sorry? You have my condolences? I mean, what's the doorway into this conversation?"

Bianca shook her head. "Hell if I know. You're the first person apart from the Asphodel crew that I've had to tell this to."

"So, you're a robot ghost chick?" said Jenny, looking up as if watching those words appear in the air above her. "Are we actually having a conversation in which you are a robot ghost chick?"

"Apparently, we are. But hey, this all feels really weird to me, too."

Jenny chewed her lip for a moment. "And … Jacob?"

"Robot ghost dude."

"Fuuuuuck."

"Calisto still has a heartbeat, though," said Bianca.

"Um, good. But … still. *How?*"

"Ah, well, that's a long story. Come on, let's go find that whiskey for you, and I'll tell you all about the war."

"War?"

"With the Outer Gods and their shoggoth fleets."

Jenny stared. "There might not be enough whiskey in this whole station, Bee. 'Cause I have some shit to share with you, too."

Bianca started to turn but stopped when she realized Jenny hadn't moved. "You okay?"

"Oh *fuck* no. I think we left 'okay' back at the dogfight with aliens." She paused, then gave Bianca a strange little smile. "How weird would it be for me to give you a hug?"

"Just don't grab my ass like the last time."

"What? I never!"

"Dallas Space Center. And for the record, I was one day shy of eighteen. So that's probably child abuse."

"Totally thought you were older."

They regarded each other, then Spears pulled her into a hug.

"Hey!" said Bianca, "I said no grabbing."

3

Soren and Croft stood where they were, waiting for Jenny Spears, who detached herself from Bianca and came over. Bianca went to talk with Calisto, and Jenny Spears walked right up to Croft and stuck out her hand.

"Captain," she said. "Heard some good things about you. I'd say it's a pleasure, but it's more like *holy fuck*."

"*Holy fuck* works for me too, Spears." They shook. Then he introduced Soren.

"Wait," Jenny said, "*Lars* Soren? As in the cosmic philosophy guy?"

"Guilty as charged," laughed Soren, shaking her hand. "As you might imagine, I have a few thousand questions to ask you."

"Right back atcha. We thought we were alone out here." She smiled. "I think you might know some of our people. Actually, I know for sure you know my wife."

"Oh? And she is … ?"

"Professor Evangeline Cronin."

"Evie? My God, of *course*. She was my most brilliant student. A lovely woman and a first-rate scholar." He paused. "I'm so sorry, Miss Spears … It must be dreadful for you to be all the way out here without her."

The smile on Jenny's face brightened. "She's not as far away as you might think, Professor. Evie was on *Tempest* when that WarpLine piece of shit threw us all the way out here. She is going to absolutely flip when she sees you."

"Wait, wait … Evie … is *here*?" Soren felt dizzy, then he looked past her at the stiletto. "Is she on your ship? Or on *Tempest*? And where is *Tempest*? God in heaven, I can't wait to see her."

"Evie doesn't do combat missions," laughed Jenny. "And, no, she's not aboard *Tempest*. Our boat took some hits coming out here. No, she's home on Bliss."

Soren frowned. "Bliss?"

"A moon way on the far side of the system. We docked there to do repairs on *Tempest*, and now it's our home. We have an atmo plant set up in a network of caverns. Hydroponics, the works."

"That's a lot to have gotten done in less than two months."

Jenny gave him a strange look. "Two months?"

"Well, a little less," said Soren. "Since the WarpLine accident, I mean."

"I … Wait, am I missing something here? What do you mean, two months?"

Soren glanced at Croft, then back at her. "I'm not sure I understand your question, Miss Spears. It has been about seven weeks since the WarpLine gun fired and … well, all of this happened."

Jenny looked at Croft. "Is he, y'know …" She twirled a finger by her temple.

"No," Croft said. "It's been about that. Seven weeks and two days."

Jenny stood there shaking her head very slowly. "If this was anywhere else, I'd think you guys were jerking my chain."

"What do you mean by that?" asked Soren.

"What I mean is that it's just that the WarpLine disaster sent us out here two *years* ago."

4

The dagger ship hid in the shadows behind an asteroid nearly half the size of Asphodel Station. The void all around was littered with the debris of slaughter and defeat. Broken daggers and shattered chimera ships floated out there, drifting on courses set by the force of the blasts that had killed them.

All of the external power was switched off aboard the dagger. No shields at all. Even the weapons were cold. A cloud of broken metal and melted plastic drifted past, and among it were pieces of meat. Black, shapeless, frozen.

A tumbler shot past less than a thousand kilometers away, and the pilot of the dagger did nothing. It could have fired from ambush and killed the ship and its human pilot. That would have been easy, and deep in its soul, the shoggoth *wanted* to.

5

It took nearly several days for the stilettos to fly back to Bliss and return with the senior staff. They were welcomed effusively but also with caution. Or, as Soren viewed it, consideration for the full weight of culture shock.

Eventually they gathered round a big table in the main conference room on Asphodel Station. Spears, Evie, Brollachan, and Hobart were on one side. Soren, Bianca, Trumbo, and Croft on the other. It was early in the third hour of their meeting. Everyone wore expressions of similar complexity, showing elements of joy and sorrow, shock and awe, horror and wonder, hope and concern.

Delia Trumbo said, "Two years?"

"Yes," said Croft.

"*How*?"

Everyone looked at Brollachan, who spread his hands. "I haven't the slightest clue. Not yet, at least. And frankly, I'm still trying to process that *as* a truth."

There was a long and awkward pause.

So," said Hobart after a while. "Shoggoths."

"Yes," said Croft.

"Outer Gods."

"Yes."

"Ghosts and aliens and a war that's a million years old?"

"Give or take," said the captain.

"And half of your fighter pilots are now … what? NecroTek? Some kind of shape-shifting robot *kaiju* mechs?"

"Robot ghost chicks," said Bianca, and Jenny covertly shot her the finger.

"Not how I'd put it," said Croft, "but yes."

Hobart glanced at Brollachan. "Would this make any better sense if I banged my head on the table a bunch?"

"It actually might," suggested the SPU chief.

Evie laughed. "Well, as learning curves go, this is one for the books."

The silence returned.

Then Soren said, "An alien spacecraft three and a half kilometers long, buried under Antarctic ice that is millions of years old?"

"Yes," said Evie. "And a second one in the asteroid belt. Even older. But they are, at best, cargo containers. Neither Artifact has an engine. And, before you ask, we don't yet understand how they got to Earth or that asteroid. We haven't found any other related technology."

Another silence, broken this time by Croft. "A shape-shifting alien that absorbs minds."

"Yes."

"And strange dreams about an enormous city and monsters."

"Yes. We've all had them," Evie said.

Trumbo looked at Hobart. "Banging our heads has some potential merit."

Evie ignored that and asked, "The thing Jenny and her team fought in the ice cave is a shoggoth, then?"

Bianca nodded. "Has to be."

"And everyone both there *and* here on Asphodel," said Soren, "have had similar dreams?"

Brollachan nodded. "Our staff psychiatrist, Dr. Singh, has documented these dreams in great detail. Virtually everyone at the dig site in Antarctica had one or more of a specific set of them. From what you've said of your own, they are all very much of a kind. And those dreams, by the way, have not stopped since the WarpLine disaster. Over the last two years, however, we have worked on managing them. Various single and group therapy programs, public addresses to assure everyone it is a shared phenomenon, which has actually been quite a comfort."

"Better to be scared in a group than alone," mused Evie, and the others nodded. She glanced at Soren. "Might be interesting if we upload all of the dreams—every remembered detail—from both our people and those here on Asphodel and run them through some pattern-recognition software."

"To what end?" asked Trumbo.

"Commonalities in the narrative," said Soren. "Who knows, there may be useful clues in those dreams."

"Useful how?"

"Warnings, clues to what's happening, a greater understanding of the threats we all face."

"Makes sense," said Bianca. "But what *doesn't* make sense is why you cats seem so surprised by the shoggoth fleet. Those pricks are everywhere."

Hobart cleared his throat. "The truth is that we haven't seen any other craft, friendlies or hostiles, until today. No shoggoth dagger fighters, no Medusa ships. Nothing at all. Spears started doing a comprehensive sweep of this star system," he paused. "Whaddya call the two suns?"

"Scylla and Charybdis," said Soren and Bianca at the same time.

"Right. Point is, we thought we were very damned alone out here. Then Spears and some stilettos come into this sector, where we haven't been before, and bang! Suddenly we're crashing someone else's party."

"How is that even possible?" asked Trumbo.

"Space, as no doubt you've heard, is big," said Bianca. "Real fucking big. This star system is a hell of a lot larger than ours back home. And we were still finding shit at home we didn't know about."

Jenny nodded. "We've been out here all this time and had no *clue* that Asphodel was even here. Maybe if *Tempest* was able to fly, we'd have mapped more of the region, but she's still some weeks away from relaunch."

"Exactly where is *Tempest*?" asked Croft. "And what happened to her?"

"She took some damage coming through that WarpLine mess," said Hobart. "Couple of smaller craft got caught up with us. They were there to rubberneck the WarpLine test. Five press schooners and a big-ass yacht. All of us bounced around like china cups in an industrial dryer. Sadly, those other ships were destroyed, and *Tempest* was in bad shape. If most of the team hadn't been in cryo-sleep, we'd have lost them to hull breaches."

"Damn," breathed Trumbo.

"We managed to get her repaired enough to find a nice little moon way the hell on the far side of those binary stars. Bliss, we named it."

"Why Bliss?" asked Croft.

"Optimism in application," said Hobart. "Anyway, we settled in to do repairs. There's lots of caves—sturdy rock structures—and we built habitats inside. Most of the people have been living there. Repairs on

Tempest were carried out with that as a kind of dockyard we built using 3D-printed girders. That took forever, and then we had to manufacture hull plating and all that. Repairing her was our primary concern, so we didn't even start exploring this star system—not in depth, I mean—until a couple months ago."

"How'd Asphodel fare with the WarpLine malfunction?" asked Brollachan.

Croft and Trumbo told them.

The conference ran for hours, well into the established "night" that helped the citizens of Asphodel maintain a sense of regularity and normalcy.

Food was brought in, and during breaks, they ate like wolves. But often abandoned the meals halfway through as hungry stomachs turned sour and acidic.

Evie Cronin watched Delia Trumbo hammer back one drink after another, and with each one, her heart ached and her throat clenched. But she had been sober now for nearly sixteen months, having fallen off the wagon aboard *Tempest* many times. Jenny, seated next to her, reached under the table and gave Evie's thigh a reassuring squeeze.

"Shoggoths," Brollachan said. "What was the inciting incident that first caused hostilities between you and them?"

Bianca snorted. "They picked a fight," she said. "Couple of hours after we got here, they attacked us. Unprovoked, I might add. We didn't know they even existed until they killed one of my crew."

The SPU chief pursed his lips, nodding. He said, "And you say that a shoggoth ship, one of these dagger fighters, was destroyed when Asphodel materialized out here?"

"Yes," said Croft. "It must have been in the same space-time as us when we popped in. The pilot survived and invaded Sybil, accessing files and causing disruption. Then it snuck into the morgue and … what's the word? Invaded the body of one of our fallen pilots. It had a T-dog with it and—"

"A what?" asked Hobart.

"A genetically modified tardigrade," said Soren. "Roughly the size of a bull calf. Our doctor identified it as a species found on Earth, but obviously many, many times larger."

Brollachan leaned forward, eyes alight with sudden interest. "A tardigrade, you say? That's remarkable. Do you have any idea how the shoggoths obtained tardigrade specimens to use for their genetic manipulation?"

"That," said Soren, "has been a matter of some speculation. Dr. Kier, the developer of WarpLine, said that tardigrades were commonly used in the early phases of matter transposition development. They were chosen because they are such a hardy species."

"Of course," said Brollachan. "A smart choice. But it's also suggestive. The WarpLine sent us all here. To this region of space. To this particular star system. And here you encounter genetic modifications of microanimals from Earth. That is very interesting."

"Yes, it is," said Soren. "It stretches the concept of coincidence to an absurd degree."

The SPU chief nodded. "It does. I do not subscribe much to the validity of coincidence, Dr. Soren. In nearly all cases it is an insult to the empiricism upon which science is based. Do you agree?"

"For the most part, yes."

Brollachan sat back, lips pursed in thought. Then he said, "If early experiments with matter transposition resulted in tardigrades being sent to this spot—in the whole of the Milky Way—then our transposition here follows a pattern of cause and effect. If so, then it might be possible to use the WarpLine to reverse the process. After all, we do have the exact coordinates for the Sol system. For home."

"Well," said Trumbo, "there's a snag with that."

"Which is?"

"The WarpLine gun blew itself to atoms during the event that sent us all here. It tore out several decks of the station and nearly killed us all."

"Ah. Well … that is unfortunate, and my condolences on the loss of life that must have accompanied such a disaster. But given the urgency of our situation, and in light of the threat of the Outer Gods and their armies, how far along is Dr. Kier in rebuilding his machine?" When no one answered, he asked, "What is the problem? Or … was Kier killed by his own machine?"

"No," said Trumbo. "He was so torn by shock, grief, and guilt that he took his own life."

Brollachan's smile dimmed. "That is also very unfortunate."

"No shit," said Bianca.

"Dr. Saltsman, Kier's senior assistant, is working on rebuilding it," said Croft. "He's a good man, but … just between us, he's no Anton Kier."

"Then perhaps fortune has not completely abandoned us. Among the passengers on *Tempest* are dozens of my top people. Physicists and engineers of every stripe. They are entirely at your disposal. I believe one or two may have worked on parts of the WarpLine project some years back."

The relief on Trumbo's face was so intense it was nearly comical. She half lunged across the table to grab and squeeze Brollachan's hands. The SPU scientist allowed it with moderately good grace but withdrew his hands as soon as manners allowed.

"I would like to visit Bliss," said Soren. "If that is acceptable to you."

Evie cut a sly look at Brollachan. Ever since the Bliss base was established in the heart of that small moon, Torq had become more closeted, more secretive. He had a set of interconnected labs in one part of Bliss's cave system and spent most of his time there, either alone or with his three chief assistants—Howard, Wu, and Solà.

But if she expected him to demur, she was wrong.

"I would be honored to have your people visit Bliss," Brollachan said.

Hobart glanced over at Croft and Bianca. "Do we have any idea why the shoggoths want to destroy you?"

"That," said Soren, "is a question best answered by our friend Lost."

"Who is *also* dead?" asked Hobart uneasily.

"Very," said Bianca.

The colonel rubbed his eyes. "Maybe *this* is a dream, and none of us have just woken up yet."

No one said a word.

The dagger ship with its cargo of death and ruin moved down and away from Asphodel Station, leaving Shadderal and the other worlds and their twin suns far behind. Once outside of the system's gravitational pull, the pilot engaged a unique kind of engine—a crystal amplification drive—and the craft seemed to become immediately engulfed by a cloud of energy of a color that had no corollary in human understanding of the spectrum.

Inside that cloud of indescribable color, the dagger changed form, losing its bladelike configuration and becoming longer, sleeker, more like an arrow. The glow flared and then vanished, taking all traces of the shoggoth ship with it.

7

After the meeting broke up, Bianca took Croft aside for a private chat.

"Skipper," she said, "everything's been so crazy since the *Tempest* thing, but I really do need to tell you something."

He looked pained. "Do I even want to hear it?"

"Jury's out," she said. "Anyway, here goes. While we were out there, we found a lot of wreckage."

"Wreckage?"

"Yeah. At first it looked like a shoggoth jagged left when he should have jigged right and smashed itself into an asteroid, but that wasn't it. We figured it was a dagger that took some damage in the fights with us, but Jacob doesn't think so, and frankly, neither do I. Not when we found more of them crashed. And sure as hell not when we found a Medusa smashed all to shit on a small moon."

"A mother ship? What killed it?"

"That's just it," she said. "We pulled it apart and found a lot of dead squishies but also a lot of battle damage. We ran every sensor we had over it, and the energy signatures on the hits don't match with our SAPRS or any missiles we have. Totally different."

Croft studied her metal face. "Are you thinking this was the *Tempest* birds, and they're not telling us?"

"No."

"Then what?"

Her mechanical eyes glittered like jewels.

"That's the thing, Skipper, we don't know *what* did it. Whatever it is, it's nothing we've come up against so far."

Croft walked a few steps away, then turned and gave her a hard look. "Are you thinking night-gaunts?"

"Them or someone else," she said. "Lost told Doc Soren that the Outer Gods had a lot of players in reserve. That said, I think we need to have a talk with Lost."

"Do that. Upload the data your team gathered to the Sybil on the station, and then we'll get word to Lost to review it."

They stood there, both of them working through the implications.

Bianca began to turn away, then paused. "Tell you the truth, Skipper … I have a feeling the shit is really going to hit the fan. I hope I'm wrong, but …"

She didn't finish, nor did Croft need her to.

8

In a flash of that curious color, it appeared near a vast gas giant orbited by 189 moons, some larger than Shadderal. Suspended within the outer gasses of the planet were scores of low-orbit space stations. Each was built in the shape of a five-pointed star. Each was ugly and lumpy and old. Yet each was beautiful in its efficiency, changing its structural form to suit the needs of the tens of thousands of shoggoths living aboard them.

The arrow flew toward one of these in geostationary orbit above the equator. It was one of the largest, and as the craft approached, a blank wall abruptly manifested a door that folded down to reveal a landing bay.

Once the arrow landed, the door closed and utterly vanished, its specifics absorbed back into the machine collective. Lights bathed the craft, and amorphous black forms rolled and bobbed toward it, their featureless flesh pulsating, watching as the pilot deployed a ramp.

The shoggoths surrounded the arrow ship and waited in silence. The pilot manifested a hundred small legs that were jointed like crustaceans. Its back was flattened so that it could bear a litter upon it, the contents secured by scores of small tentacles that each held a separate piece in place. It was very careful with this, and it walked down the ramp at a slow pace.

The other creatures extruded tentacles—slender and whiplike—and with these they reached out to touch the pieces of their slaughtered comrade. Each touch was light, almost gentle, and tentative, as if they needed to touch in order to know that they were in the presence of true death. Explosions had killed the shoggoth, but ice had destroyed it down to the cellular level. There was no trace of energy, no whisper of vitality in even the smallest molecule.

When the pilot was on the deck, half a dozen other shoggoths moved closer and, working together, lifted the burden from the pilot's back. They turned and carried it out of the landing bay and through long, strange corridors, going deep into the heart of the station. The other shoggoths followed, flowing or crawling, scuttling or walking. During the procession, a sound began. One of them made a mouth appear—odd and birdlike, with a curved beak—and from this came a noise like the distant and plaintive call of a bird.

"*Tekeli-li,*" it cried. There was no challenge in the sound. No hate, no aggression.

It was a sound of deep, profound grief.

The rest of the shoggoths grew mouths and joined in the song. In the dirge.

"*Tekeli-li. Tekeli-liiiii …*"

It was the sound of pain. Of loss.

But also … of hope.

Part Twenty-Three
Lost Things

"No greater hell than to be a slave to fear."

—*Ben Jonson*

The Shadderal Star System

1

Dr. Soren recommended that a small delegation go down to the surface of Shadderal so they could share their combined information with the person most likely to create context and help them find useful answers. They met inside a dome constructed by Croft's combat engineers. It was large and pressurized, with a breathable atmosphere and temperature control. The dome had completely transparent walls that allowed them a clear view of the ancient, battered planet.

While they waited for the golem to appear, Evie leaned close to her mentor. "And you say *he's* dead too … Is he another NecroTek?"

"It's fairer to say that Lost is unique," answered Soren. "In some distant past, I suppose he could be considered a NecroTek. His people had other names for it. *NecroTek* is a term I coined with Lady Jessica. Necromancy and technology acting in a unique rhythm of harmony."

"Don't take this the wrong way," said Jenny, "but this is creepy as fuck."

"Imagine how it is from my side," replied Bianca. It was not a joke, and no one took it as such.

"Here he comes," said Soren, gesturing beyond the clear plastic wall of the shelter.

The others turned to look. For a moment they saw nothing in particular except bits of debris and rubbish blowing in a cold wind outside the dome. But then Evie gasped as one of the pieces rolled into another and clung, then seemed to pull other debris in as if they were magnets. A scrap of deck plating, a jagged-ended length of strut, a coil of copper wire, weather-worn canvas, a broken helmet of alien design. More and more pieces tumbled, slid, or flew toward a central mass that was assembling itself into a disturbingly manlike shape. The pieces trembled and flapped in the wind, then the bulk of it began to straighten, unfolding from a kind of crouch as it rose up on two widely braced legs. Arms made of cables and pieces of flexible polymer hung from shoulders made from cross bracing. But it stood. Headless and unnatural, it turned toward Evie and the others as if it could see them. Then, to her horror, it bent and picked up the damaged helmet and placed it on a neck made from wires wrapped around metal vent pipes. As soon as it was in place, the head lifted, and the cracked faceplate flared with a pale blue light.

"My … God," breathed Evie, panting. "I … I …"

The thing took an ungainly step forward, started to fall, caught itself in a crouch, then slowly—almost painfully—straightened. When it tried to walk again, its steps were surer, and the instability visibly faded. Then it walked over to the entrance to the dome. There were two automated airlocks that allowed it to enter, then pressurized the intervening chamber, and finally admitted it to the dome. It came over, a scarecrow from some nightmare version of a children's story.

Evie recoiled but bumped up against the immovable solidity of Bianca. She twisted to look upward with a confused and frightened expression, acutely aware of being trapped between alien forms.

"It's okay, sis," said the NecroTek quietly. "We all went through this kind of stuff. The shock wears off."

"I don't think that will ever be true," said Evie.

With gentle pressure, Bianca turned her around to face the golem. "This is Lost."

"Yes," said the creature, "and I welcome you to my homeworld."

"I … I mean …" Evie could see her face—ghostly and pale—reflected in the shattered dura-glass that made up Lost's face. "Um … hello, I guess? And … thanks?"

Lost offered a kind of bow, but given the nature of his appearance, it was unnerving.

Dr. Brollachan stepped forward and studied Lost with unabashed fascination. "This is remarkable. Astounding."

The golem turned to him. "You are Dr. Torquil Brollachan."

"I am. Tell me, what is the proper greeting in this circumstance? One that belongs to your traditions. Or is bowing your preferred way?"

It was an unexpected question, though Evie saw Soren nod his approval. Lost paused to consider his reply.

"I have never been asked this before, and I thank you," he said. "I used a bow here because it belongs to *your* culture. I have learned from experience not to attempt to shake hands." He raised one hand and regarded it as he opened and closed his fingers. "There is nothing alive in here, and that offends the sensibilities of your kind."

"I daresay," agreed Brollachan. "But how should *we* greet *you*?"

"Alas, the greetings my people used were a combination of facial expressions done in various orders to suit the type of encounter. One sequence would be used for one's wife, another for children, another for friends, and different ones for various acquaintances." He paused. "Our anatomy is significantly different from yours, Dr. Brollachan, giving us several dozen facial muscles that humans do not possess."

"I take it you know of our customs and anatomy from your interface with Sybil?"

"Yes, and during my many conversations with my friend Dr. Soren," said Lost. "I find your customs very interesting and as complex as ours, though necessarily different. For the sake of simplicity and expediency, Doctor, an exchange of bows would be adequate."

He bowed again, and Brollachan responded in kind.

Jenny walked up and stuck out her hand. "I don't mind shaking on it."

Lost looked at her hand for a moment, then took it. Jenny held the grip for a moment or two longer than was customary, and as she released her grip she nodded.

"Okay, yeah, that's weird," she said. "No heat, no familiar bone structure. But who cares? I'm a couple of million kilometers past being freaked out."

Evie heard Lost softly repeat those last two words. "Freaked out."

Then Lost took a step back to make it easier to address the five of them. "We have much to discuss."

"Yes, we do," said Brollachan. "There is much we need to discuss with you."

"I expect so," said Lost, "but time is not our friend."

"When is it ever?" said Soren with a small sigh.

"It is the nature of this war."

Jenny laughed. "That's the nature of *all* wars. If we had enough time to ask and answer all the questions, maybe there'd be less time to shoot one another."

"It is an excellent sentiment," said Lost. "One I wish was more commonplace in all species."

Evie asked, "Lost … what is it about Shadderal that makes the shoggoths so determined to conquer it? Why do they keep attacking?"

"They are driven to it," said the ghost. "To attack, overwhelm, conquer, subjugate, and/or destroy is why they were created in the first place. The shoggoths are a slave race. They have never known anything else. They were born in vats and built, atom by atom, to serve the Outer Gods, creatures of such enormous power that they are indistinguishable from actual gods and yet lacking material form. At least on this plane of physical reality."

"Born in vats," echoed Brollachan. "That is something we've heard before."

"Yes," said Lost. "Sybil shared your accounts with me. They are remarkable. And I can answer one of your questions. The Artifacts, as you call them, are not specifically troop ships or even colony vessels. They are merely transport for shoggoths. During the early days of our war, such craft were found on thousands of worlds."

"To seed the galaxy with armies?" asked Croft.

"No. To make sure that there were sufficient slaves for the various elevated races in service to the Outer Gods. You know that they are shape-shifters, and that makes them uniquely qualified to perform any labor required of them. Yes, sometimes that is war, but far more often it is construction, maintenance of worlds settled by the Great Old Ones and others. These barges were sent wherever they were needed."

"Sent how?" asked Brollachan.

Lost hesitated. "There are many branches of science about which I know little. I was a combat pilot, much like Bianca. What I can say is that the Outer Gods and their more trusted servants used some kind of machine that was able to open doorways in the fabric of space-time. It was how the Outer Gods conquered so much of this part of the galaxy."

"I wonder why they haven't used it to dump a few million shoggoths on Shadderal," said Croft. "With tech like that, they could have wiped us out in a day."

Lost nodded. "We did not win our war, but we managed to hurt the Outer Gods very badly. A group of our greatest heroes known as the Valiant Storm—fighters who approximate your Jokers in that they were the most elite warriors we ever had—had one purpose, and that was to find and destroy those factory worlds that made the gateway machines. They were not gentle about it, and in their quest they destroyed many, *many* worlds, detonated suns, and indulged in wholesale slaughter. It sounds appalling—and is—but had they been gentler about it, the Outer Gods would have long since conquered this entire galaxy and possibly much of the known universe. Things were tending that way. It was the great mission of the Valiant Storm to eradicate that science entirely, leaving no trace behind, and as far as I know, they succeeded."

"And you never thought to use the technology for yourselves?" asked Brollachan, clearly appalled. "You could have taken your war directly to the Outer Gods."

The golem shook his head. "We did try. The last fleet of the Valiant Storm set out to do this very thing, but they vanished from all knowledge. No word has ever been heard of them since."

"They failed?" asked Evie.

"No. I believe they succeeded in their primary mission of destroying the technology, but when they tried to lay siege to the Outer Gods, they disappeared."

"And the technology?" asked Brollachan.

"Lost forever, I'm afraid. For it was not long after they vanished that our war ended. We destroyed many of the shoggoth homeworlds, and it has taken many thousands of years for them to claw their way back from the edge of extinction and to rebuild their fleets. Until they attacked Asphodel Station, even I had thought them extinct."

"That's why they came here to Shadderal," explained Soren. "To use the shipbuilding factories to build better craft. Lost's people were always more technologically advanced."

"The shoggoths coveted—and still yearn for—the facilities here," said Lost, gesturing to the massive buildings laid out near the Field of Dead Birds. "My dear dead world of Shadderal is the last place where NecroTek fighting ships can be made. Other shipbuilding worlds were destroyed by shoggoths in their zealous attempts to steal the technology. Many of those worlds destroyed themselves in order to keep the science from the enemy."

"God damn," breathed Hobart.

"The shoggoths have a version of the mechanical metamorphosing technology now, but it is not as sophisticated as what we possess."

Hobart walked over to the wall and studied the closest factory. "Bianca explained to us that living people can't fly the shape-shifting ships, but could those same factories build ships we *can* fly? I ask because we have schematics for *Tempest*, and once she's repaired, she can hold her own against anything that flies."

Lost came and stood with him. "It would not be easy."

"But can it be done?"

After a very long time, the golem nodded. "I believe so."

"Tell me, friend Lost," said Soren. "You have spoken in rather dire terms about the night-gaunts. You said they move in and out of the known reality. Could *they* be using that old technology? Could they have recovered what the Valiant Storm thought they destroyed?"

The ghost took too long to answer the question.

"Lost?" prodded Soren.

"If any of the servants of the Outer Gods have managed to reclaim all, or even *some*, of that science, then *they* would be the ones. And that is a truly terrifying thought."

2

It rose from the blighted soil of a dead world.

Artless, ungainly, disjointed in ways that would make a sane watcher doubt his reason. Dust drifted down from it like dry tears, bringing neither moisture nor hope to the ruined planet.

Eleven days ago that world had been green with lush forests and blue with rolling seas. Birds with wings ablaze in a hundred colors floated on the thermal winds, while below, creatures vast and gentle roamed the oceans. In the rainforests that covered 80 percent of the land masses, tens of thousands of species had moved together in the timeless dance of song and hunger, passion and fury, death and rebirth.

Now there were only bones.

Where once gleaming cities sent spires of translucent elegance upward high enough to caress the clouds, there were now only jagged stumps upon which not even lichen grew. The shores were littered with rotting corpses, signaling a change of ownership from intelligent life to bacteria and the meanest of microbial creatures.

One being stood watching the guilty ship rise into the sky it had defiled.

It was a female, the very last survivor. There would be no more of her kind, and when tomorrow's sun rose, there would be none at all. Her body was already dying of the toxins the enemy had shot into the air. They had not needed the guns they used or the talons on their bloody fingers. Those had been used for the pleasure of the killers, not out of any need for efficiency. There was no war. No opposition.

The female's name was Ulah. In the language of her kind, the name was a poetic reference to the first leaf spotted as winter faded and spring began. Her grandmother had been Ulah, too. She had lived eighty-nine years and gave herself to the soil with a glad heart when it was her turn to join forever.

Now Ulah stood there, diseased, bruised from angry fists, sightless in one eye, near-blind in the other three. Her hair, once the lustrous blue of a high summer afternoon, was clotted with orange blood and mud. That mud was from the ruin of her garden, and the blood from her children.

Ulah walked down the hill and into her village. The streets were still except for the wind. The bodies that lay here and there looked at her with their sightless eyes and seemed to reach for her with seven-fingered hands. She knew them all. Each name, each family history. Those were the things all of her people learned around the evening fires—the stories of their generations.

When the creatures attacked the village, all of her friends and neighbors, her sisters and brothers and all their children, had come to meet them, carrying baskets of delicious fungi and edible flowers. They had been raised in such customs, sometimes even laughing at their own habits of playful generosity.

Ulah had been among them, bringing cool water for the visitors so they might slake their thirst and taste the sweetness of what had fallen in that morning's rain.

She remembered standing there, holding the water gourd, unable to move because of the shock of it all. A farm woman, she knew about death and even slaughter, but not like this. Her people had no word for murder. There had never been a need for such a concept. They had no word for cruelty, for malevolence.

No word for evil.

Ulah still could not grasp those things, even ankle-deep in the blood of everyone she loved.

The streets of her desolated village were so very still. Ulah looked around, hoping to find one living tree, one flowering bush. But all she beheld was devastation.

Then her knees began to fail her, and she dropped down. The water gourd fell from fingers grown too weak to hold it. She wept, and the tears from that one eye were polluted with innocent blood.

Ulah clasped her hands together and, with her last strength, raised them to the sky. The ship was a speck now, fading into nothing even as she looked.

"Why?" she asked.

Of them, the killers. Of the gods. Of the failing day.

"Why?"

The servants of the Outer Gods, the winged monsters whom even the shoggoths feared, disappeared back into space, taking with them everything of value that had ever lived on that world. Knowing, in their dark and secret hearts, that no other race on any of the billions of worlds even knew of Ulah and her people. To have exterminated them so thoroughly that even their own world was too brutalized to recall them—that was power. That was their beauty.

The killers opened a hole in the fabric of truth and slipped away.

Hunting.

Hunting.

3

The group stayed in the dome for hours, comparing notes, sharing knowledge, learning, looking for ledges of hope on which to stand.

At one point, Evie said, "There is something I want to discuss with you all. Lost and Bianca mostly, but it affects everyone."

"I gotta hear this," said Bianca.

"It involves the radiation that powers your … suits? Is that the right word? Ships?"

Bianca shrugged, a strangely human action for her. "*Bodies* is closer to it."

Evie took a breath, then nodded. "I'm no physicist, but after working so closely with Dr. Kimbra and Alan Meyer, I think I have enough of a grasp to want to know if the energy field inside the shoggoth Artifacts is in any way similar to what you call *ethla*?"

"Interesting," murmured Brollachan, looking intensely interested.

Lost nodded. "It is all part of the same kind of energy. Our greatest scientists never fully understood that energy. We were able to use it in the ways I've described, but always at a cost."

"The death of the physical body," said Evie, "and subsequent erosion of what you call the soul. And which may be something less supernatural and more specifically scientific, though as yet unquantified."

"Yes," said Lost. "There were many theories of that kind, but the war destroyed us before we could fully explore its implications."

"Where are you going with this?" asked Hobart.

"Bear with me for a bit, Tom," said Evie. She turned to Bianca. "When you changed or altered from being a spaceship—"

"*Shifted* is the word you're looking for," said Bianca. "Useful shorthand."

"Good. When you shift from being a giant to the form you're in now, does the same rate of energetic decay occur?"

"No," said Lost and Bianca.

Lost said, "The smaller the form, the less is required of the pilot's spirit. If she or any of the NecroTek remained in giant form, the rate of decay would be fifty times faster than when they are closer to their mortal size."

"Good," said Evie excitedly. "Now, tell me … what kind of shielding have you tried to slow that rate of decay even further?"

"Shielding? You mean materials?"

"Yes."

The golem's shoulders seemed to slump. "We have tried tens of thousands of methods. Polymers, ceramics, organic materials, metal alloys, but nothing has worked, else we would have used it."

"We did the same," said Evie. "We went through the whole catalog, including using other forms of radiation to great fields we hoped would be contrary."

Bianca said, "Evie, if you failed too, then why are you smiling?"

"Have you ever tried iridium?" Evie asked.

The viewscreen of Lost's helmet suddenly flashed with video images that came and went with increasing speed. Molecular and atomic signatures appeared and vanished in their thousands. The pictures finally slowed and stopped.

"I am unfamiliar with this element," said Lost. "It is not to be found anywhere in this part of the galaxy."

The smile on Evie's face bloomed like a spring flower.

"What?" asked Bianca.

"Then we have to try," Evie said.

"That's great," Croft replied, "but like Lost just said, there's none out here."

"Oh," said Brollachan, "but we have quite a lot of it on Bliss."

"How much?"

"Tons," said Evie.

She told Lost about how they solved the problem of decay and rapid aging by giving everything that entered the ship a thin coating of iridium.

"Iridium," echoed Lost. He accessed Sybil's database, and everyone watched as a picture of the metal appeared, accompanied by the symbol Ir and the number 77 remaining for a few moments. "This is intriguing, but Sybil has no information about your use of it."

"That's because we use a different AI," said Brollachan. "Ariel. Access is restricted, but let me see what I can do." He tapped his holo-comms. "Ariel, open a socket for information exchange with the Sybil on Asphodel."

"With what limitations, Dr. Brollachan?" asked the AI.

"Share all data on our use of iridium with Sybil on Asphodel. Upload everything."

"Done," said Ariel.

"This is very promising," said Lost. "I think it will be of great value to us all."

Everyone looked at Bianca. She said, "Are you telling me that this iridium coating might help us reduce the effects of the radiation?"

"It's possible," said Evie. "We have to try."

4

Back aboard Asphodel, as Evie, Soren, and Bianca were heading to the lift to bring Director Trumbo up to speed, Bianca suddenly staggered and fell. Evie and Soren caught her between them, but the weight of her NecroTek body dragged them all down, and they collapsed together.

"Bee," cried Soren. "What is it? What's wrong?"

Bianca tumbled over onto her back, and her metal hands clawed at her chest. "Oh … God …"

"Should I get a doctor?" begged Evie. "Or … a mechanic?"

"I don't know." Soren ran his hands over Bianca, looking for damage. Some of the seams of her precisely molded body gaped and fell off, revealing wires and circuitry. Small puffs of smoke rose from her. "Bianca," he pleaded, "tell me what's wrong. How can we help you?"

There was a sound. A rhythmic noise, painful to hear, and when Soren realized what it was, it nearly broke his heart. Bianca Petrescu, the metal golem that housed her soul, was weeping.

Soren placed his palm over one of her hands. Over where her human heart should have been. "What's wrong, my dear?"

It took Bianca a very long time to answer. She weakly pushed Soren's hand away and tried to rise. He and Evie helped her sit up.

"What happened?" asked Evie.

"I … don't …" Bianca shook her head. "I don't know."

Soren's face was twisted with concern. "What did you feel? Are you in actual pain?"

"They all … died."

"Who died? God, did something happen to the rest of the NecroTeks?"

"What? No … no. Not them."

"Then who?"

All Bianca could do was shake her head. "I don't know. It's crazy, but I don't know. I had a flash of a glimpse. Some kind of aliens. A whole planetful of them. Nothing I've ever seen. Primitive people on a world even Lost's people never heard of. I know that without knowing how. But I *do* know it. They all *died*."

"How?" asked Evie, feeling terribly frightened. "Was it the shoggoths?"

Bianca thought about it, then gave another, more definite shake. "No. It was something else. Something … worse."

"Worse? Are you talking about the night-gaunts?"

"I don't know. Fuck. Help me up," Bianca said, and they did. It took all of what the three of them had to do it, and the NecroTek stood swaying, as fragile as any frail human.

"Bee," said Soren, "can you tell us anything about who or what did that?"

"No. Not much. All I know is they're worse than the shoggoths, and …"

"And what?" asked Evie.

"And they're coming for us."

Part Twenty-Four
Darkness Falls

"Hell is oneself,
Hell is alone, the other figures in it
Merely projections. There is nothing to escape from
And nothing to escape to. One is always alone."

—T. S. Eliot

1

Dr. Brollachan also headed back to Bliss, and Evie walked him to the waiting skimmer.

"I'll send Alan Meyer back with as much of the iridium stores as we can fit into a transport," he promised. "Once we're within radio range, I'll call ahead to tell them to begin loading. They'll pass us en route, so you can expect it in a few days."

"Thank you," said Evie.

The SPU chief regarded her for a moment.

"What?" she asked.

"We have come rather a long way, Evie," he said quietly. "A long way, no matter how that is defined. When I met you, I was hardly gracious, and I will admit that I did not think you were likely to have any useful role in matters related to the Artifact. Since then, you have proved me wrong time and again, and I have grown not only to respect you but …"

"But what?"

He took her hands. "But I have a deep affection for you. You remind me of what it means to be human, and trust me when I say that is a very important thing."

Evie was flustered and did not know what to say. Finally, she managed to mumble a thanks. He smiled, squeezed her hands—then glanced around to make sure no one else was in earshot.

"Was there something else?" asked Evie, confused.

"One thing, yes," he said. "Ever since the Artifact was found, all through that process and during the many months out here, we have been losing people. Friends. Our family, as it were."

"I know … It's sad and—"

"No, please, let me finish." Brollachan's eyes were unreadable. "You have been the *heart* of our family. Everyone knows that. Spears knows it, of course, but I think there is something she doesn't know. Something no one knows but which will bring to our family a kind of joy we all believed was lost forever."

He glanced down at her stomach and then back up again.

"I …" she began, then changed it. "How did you know?"

He smiled. "I am, after all, a very great scientist."

Then he released her hands, still smiling, and walked away.

Evie stood there, watching him go. And she, too, smiled. Though hers was still an unspoken secret.

2

They walked together, ankle-deep in the dust of history.

Captain Croft was on one side of Lost, and Hobart on the other. All around them were the wrecks of spacecraft of every conceivable size and shape. There were dozens of different kinds of single- and two-pilot fighters. There were battleships and spacecraft carriers sprawled like dead giants, and around them were frigates and corvettes, landing ships, and assault craft. All broken. All suited to the place where they lay.

"I can see why you call this the Field of Dead Birds," said Hobart, speaking in the kind of hushed voice reserved for church and other holy places. Or graveyards.

Lost, whose body was another amalgam of disordered and broken parts, merely nodded.

Hobart changed the subject. "Even after all we dealt with on Earth," he said, "this stuff out here is messing with my head. Outer Gods? Great Old Ones? Actual monsters? It's like something out of a horror story."

"You're not wrong, Tom," said Croft.

"Meaning what?"

"Tell him, Lost," said the captain.

"Having reviewed the many stories in Sybil's memory files," said Lost, "it's clear that your nineteenth- and twentieth-century 'pulp' writers had some glimpses of the truth—but not all of it. Your Howard Phillips Lovecraft wrote of the various pantheons and sub-pantheons of the beings he called gods. It is important to bear in mind, though, that they are not true gods. I, personally, do not know if any gods in fact exist. If so, they never responded to our prayers or to the prayers of a million species who fought alongside us in the war."

"Well … damn," breathed Hobart.

"Lovecraft dreamed of the various races of false deities—the Outer Gods, the Great Old Ones, the Great Ones, the Elder Things, the Deep Ones, and so forth. The fact that he was able to enter the Dreamlands at all is remarkable. Among my own people, only the highest and most astute priests could do this. They, like he, caught glimpses, and there is a tendency in all sentient beings to organize what is observed into acceptable and useful categories."

"Does anyone know the full truth?" asked Croft.

"That is doubtful, even unlikely. I have spent many, *many* lifetimes immersed in the sacred texts as part of my own dream of finding a new way to fight the enemy." Lost walked a few paces, nodding to himself, before he continued. "As we define such things, the Outer Gods are the most powerful. Like most of these false gods, they are living creatures, but their true aspects are not physical. They are forces of energy that have attained consciousness. Or, perhaps, beings whose arcane studies and practices lifted them above the physical."

"Like you?" suggested Hobart. "Like these NecroTeks?"

"Superficially, but yes," agreed Lost. "The Outer Gods are believed to have either been born with the universe, in what your culture calls the Big Bang, or they existed in some form before that event and were cast out of where they had been or pushed forward into this reality. We do not know which. Their power is vast, but they are neither omnipotent nor omniscient. They are strongest in the Dreamlands."

"Dreamlands?" queried Hobart. "You keep mentioning that, but I'm not sure what that is. Actual dreams?"

"From reviewing your histories," said Lost, "I see glimpses of understanding of what it is, but no complete grasp of it. And I do not criticize, for my people were themselves never able to completely agree on the matter."

"Mind giving us the basics, then?" Hobart asked. "So we have some frame of reference."

Lost stopped at a place where the light from the two suns fell on a space with stone benches. He gestured for his human companions to sit, and when they did, he sat on a bench apart from them, angled so that they could see the cracked faceplate of the helmet that covered his absent face. Images began to appear on it, some clearly generated by artificial intelligence.

One was of the world of Shadderal turning slowly in space. The globe began to change as if overlaid with single-color washes. Then, slowly at first but accelerating, a copy of the planet would move away, separating itself but retaining its unique hue. This happened over and over and over until there were so many Shadderals that they formed a pattern like swarming germs in the lens of a powerful microscope.

"There is no one reality," he said. "Every world, every *thing* in the universe, has countless facets. Some are easily detected by viewing them through filters—ultraviolet, infrared, x-ray, radio wave, heat signature, and the like. These are the mundane aspects demonstrating the variety of forms within one plane of existence. Yet, there is also an omniverse—comprising an infinite number of parallel universes. I am not talking about the theoretical extra dimensions suggested in string theory, but other literal worlds, other universes. For every moment of time, every action, every breath and heartbeat, there are uncountable new universes born."

The image on his faceplate changed, now showing Shadderal as transparent. The view presented moved closer to the world and then *into* it, passing through thousands of layers, moving faster and faster until it was nothing but a blur. Finally, the image vanished.

"The deeper one goes into these variations, the less familiar they become because every small universe created by every action creates other universes. We are talking about infinity in the truest and most profound sense of that word. Do you follow me?"

"Clinging on by my fingernails, but still with you," Hobart assured him.

"There are also worlds that exist in versions of the universe where physical laws do not, nor ever have, applied. Worlds so vastly different from ours that no points of reference exist to allow us to grasp even the merest elements. The Outer Gods, and many of the godlike beings Lovecraft and others have dreamed about, exist in worlds—in realities—that are not reachable in any physical way. They are worlds born of thought, of imaginings, of mystery. These Dreamlands are also infinite."

"This is all making me feel insignificant," admitted Croft.

"Yes," said Lost. "Your Lovecraft had the same reaction, which is why he speculated that beings like the Elder Gods and the Great Old Ones were so powerful and stretched across so much of the dreaming infinities that they regarded humankind as either a cosmic joke or so inconsequential that no real thought need be bent on them."

"And … I feel even smaller now. Thanks."

"There is some grace in that," Lost assured him. "Humility in the face of the incalculable is an appropriate reaction. To continue, though … Lovecraft, even with his belief that these gods held us in ignorance or disdain, was less humble. For him, even at that level, man was still a factor. He did not consider the billions of other sentient life forms throughout the galaxy and, I daresay, throughout the known universe. Each of them—those that have encountered beings from one pantheon or another—believed *they* were of importance in the same way."

"You're saying they were all wrong?" asked Hobart.

"Not at all," countered Lost. "Lovecraft was correct in some ways. The Elder Gods, the Great Old Ones, and the others are very much aware of the sentient physical life forms that populate this galaxy. Some of these beings hold themselves aloof from mortal life, but that is a choice based on knowledge and understanding. Their thoughts and actions are drawn elsewhere, and often into realms that exist outside of normal space-time."

"They're too busy in the Dreamlands?"

"Cthulhu's supposed to be the worst of the bunch, right?" asked Hobart. "I saw that in a movie once."

"No. Cthulhu is incredibly powerful, but he is far, far below the power of the Outer Gods. Aletheia, Lu-Kthu, Azathoth, Daoloth, Mlandoth and Mril Thorion, Nyarlathotep, Shub-Niggurath, the Star Mother, and others whose names even I, a ghost, will not speak aloud."

"Damn," said Hobart.

"The Great Old Ones," continued the golem, "were of middling power when measured against the full strength of the Outer Gods. Their growth was stymied, and their pathways to greatness often blocked. Cthulhu led a rebellion with his half brother Hastur, Juk-Shabb, Nub, Bokrugm, Gloon, Ghatanothoa, Oorn, and their ilk—who, though incredibly powerful in their own right, were under the heel of Azathoth and his family. The Outer Gods fought them in dreams and defeated them there, so these Great Old Ones retreated to physical forms and fled on starships, bringing shoggoth slaves with them to help establish new kingdoms. Some of those reached Earth, and the one you found, Evie Cronin, was among them. Why it was left there is unknown. If I were to guess, based on the writings of Lovecraft and his circle of followers, the shoggoths were used to build great cities on land and deep beneath the sea, but then the shape-shifters rebelled, even as their masters had."

Hobart brightened. "Rebelled, you say?"

"Yes. Some of the Great Old Ones were even destroyed, a feat so rare it did not happen even during the war my people fought. Others returned to the Dreamlands but hid from the Outer Gods. Some are lost to speculation and may have settled elsewhere in the galaxy beyond my knowledge or yours. It is possible some fled to other galaxies where their level of power was greater than any they encountered, and these rebels might have set themselves up as a new race of Outer Gods."

"I guess I need to go read Lovecraft," laughed Hobart. "Never was much of a fan of horror stories, though. Never thought I'd be living in one."

"I do not pretend to understand the scope of the omniverse," Lost admitted. "However, some, like Cthulhu and Hastur, are often viewed as the gods of the Dreamlands. Meaning, of course, that they have exerted control over those parts of the Dreamlands to which they have perceived and laid claim. Others of that ilk are Lobon, Nath-Horthath, Oukranos, Tamash, and Hagarg Ryonis. Others, too. I mention these because they were mentioned in those old stories. They are not kind; they lack compassion for anything less than themselves, but their existence has inspired cults across the galaxy and throughout the omniverse."

He paused and pointed down to a tiny insect that looked like a twelve-legged ant.

"Do you see that creature? Small, helpless against beings as powerful as you? That difference in scale, in potential power and thought, is not even a fair comparison of the disparity between mortal beings like you, and like I once was, and the Outer Gods. If you can grasp the math, the difference would be something like that insect and the power of a supermassive black hole."

"Well ... shit," said Hobart. "If they're so all-powerful, then why are they trying to kick our asses?"

"Because we do not worship them," said Lost. "Please, Colonel, remind yourself not to use phrases like *all-powerful*. They are not. They are merely vastly more powerful than we are."

"That's hardly a comfort."

"It was not meant to be comforting."

"If they are so vastly powerful, then, why do they need shoggoths?"

"Because the Outer Gods do not exist fully enough in this reality to fight their own battles. They require shoggoths, night-gaunts, mi-go, and many other races to act as their soldiers. To conquer and subjugate or to exterminate. In the former case, the worship of the conquered, however forced, creates an energy that feeds the Outer Gods. They *do* need us. In the latter case, any murders committed in their names, by any of their slaves, also release energy that gives them sustenance and prolongs their lives. They feed on death and destruction, on pain and suffering, and also on prayers and acts of ritual sacrifice."

The two officers processed that for a moment, each digesting it as best he could.

Croft asked, "And you think the night-gaunts are coming for us now?"

"Oh yes," said Lost. "They are beings who thrive in darkness and keep the secrets of their nature—their full strength and any weaknesses—to themselves. Where the night-gaunts go, madness and death inevitably follow. It is clear that they know about the human race and have begun to hunger for us. They are coming, make no mistake, and alas, I do not know how to fight them."

3

Lars Soren went to visit Lady Jessica.

He found her in one of the fitness centers, bathed in sweat, grimacing as she took trembling and uncertain steps while clutching small but powerful therapy drones to keep from falling. She got all the way to the end of a goal grid painted on the floor, then paused, hanging onto the drones as she panted. Sweat dripped onto the floor.

This was a significant improvement, given that two weeks ago she could not stand at all. Her body was still scarecrow thin, though, and he saw the stress lines etched deeply into her face.

"Brava," he said, applauding. "At this rate, you'll be ready to go jogging soon."

The look she gave him was lethal, and her eyes searched his for signs of condescension or, worse, pity. But Soren was genuinely heartened by her progress. Lady Jessica relaxed by slow degrees, nodding mute acceptance of the compliment.

"Down," she told the drones. Her wheelchair automatically rolled over to her, turned, and locked its wheels. The therapy drones helped her sit, and Lady Jessica exhaled a long, stressful chestful of air. "*Go dtachta an Diabhal thú!*"

He did not understand Gaelic and was sure that was a good thing at the moment.

"Sit down," she snapped in English, and he obeyed by grabbing a small plastic chair and setting it at a comfortable angle that would not force eye-to-eye contact until and unless she wanted it.

"I take it you've heard the news," he said, leaning back and crossing his legs.

"Yes. We have neighbors."

"You sound less than thrilled."

Lady Jessica used a cloth to mop her face. "It's hardly a thrilling bit of news. It means more people are stuck out here. People who will die in a war we can't win."

"Are you that convinced of our doom?"

She began to answer sharply but stopped herself and used the time spent patting dry her sweaty arms to rearrange her reactions. "I heard they have a battleship of some kind."

"A corvette, and it's being repaired. But, yes, it is a formidable piece of military hardware."

"Could it fight a Medusa one-to-one?"

"Colonel Hobart and Captain Croft think that it's a possibility."

She digested that. Then she tossed the cloth to a drone that snagged it and bore it away to a laundry basket. Lady Jessica folded her hands in her lap and looked at him. "There is a rumor already going around that this Colonel Hobart wants to use the Shadderal shipyard to make more battleships."

"It's being discussed."

"Which means more people are going to die."

"War is—"

"No," she snapped. "Listen to me, Lars, and hear me well. Everyone treats me like I'm mentally infirm because I look like … like this. But you know full well my mind has not been affected by what happened. Do not patronize me. Now or ever—are we clear?"

He nodded and placed a hand over his heart. "I apologize, my lady, and I mean that truly. Let me try it again. If your concern is that any attempt to use Shadderal military technology will be lethal to the crew, forcing you to risk your life again in conjuring the spirits of the dead, then please know that is not the plan."

She studied him with those intelligent, piercing hazel eyes. "How not?"

"Iridium," he said.

"The metal?"

Soren explained what happened on Earth and how they hoped to use it to shield pilots—alive or NecroTek—from the deleterious effects of alien radiation.

"Will it work?" she asked, and beneath all her guards and gates there was a heartbreaking and vulnerable desperation. He knew that she did not want to resurrect any more dead for the purposes of *ethla*. Just as he knew she did not want to attend any more funerals for brave young men and women.

"I pray that it will," he said.

It was a long time before she replied. "And I wonder who will answer that prayer, Lars. Don't forget that we are also dealing with psychic attacks. You've seen the reports about the dreams people are having. How many suicides has it been over the last month? Eight?"

He cleared his throat. "Ten. There were two the other day. Husband and wife in exogeology. Sleeping pills."

She closed her eyes.

"I pray every morning and every night to the Goddess," she said. "And since we came out here, I feel like I'm shouting down an empty well."

Soren reached out and gently took one frail, cold hand and held it in his.

"Lost is sharing all that he knows about the cause of those dreams."

"The night-gaunts," she said. "I know. He came to me last night, and we talked for hours."

"Ah."

"And what little faith I've managed to retain after all that's happened is like a small candle in a fierce wind. That sounds like poetry, but I assure you it is not."

She took her hand back and turned away.

He sat with her for ten silent minutes, then stood, bowed, and left.

"I have to go back to Bliss," Jenny said.

"No," begged Evie, reaching for her. "You have to stay."

They were in the bedroom of the guest quarters afforded them during their stay on Asphodel.

"I've been away too long," explained Jenny, "and frankly, I'm getting worried now that we know there's a fight. I need to help oversee some defensive upgrades. Time isn't our friend here."

The clock on the wall argued that Jenny was right. There were ten thousand things that needed doing. There were people who needed her opinion, her actions, her muscle. The Jokers were preparing for a trip to Asphodel for a formal meeting with the station's military group. Brollachan wanted her to find some minerals for him on a particularly turbulent moon. Reports were waiting for her eyes and input.

Despite all the needs and commitments they each had, Evie Cronin pulled her close and silenced her protests with a long, soft, sweet, deep kiss. She turned Jenny around and walked her slowly back toward their bed, tugging the seals on her Stormsuit with gentle insistence. By the time Jenny's calves encountered the foot of the mattress, she had to lift her feet to step out of the garment.

And then there were no more thoughts of plans or commitments.

There was only love, in all its many beautiful variations.

5

Torquil Brollachan returned to Bliss.

He had not spoken a single word to the pilot of the skimmer, and from the way he sat, hunched forward and brooding, the pilot did not dare intrude.

Bliss was a small moon, only slightly larger than half the mass of Luna. Its surface was perpetually scoured by a howling hurricane of methane and rare gasses. Thousands of extinct volcanoes littered the landscape, with only two active and smoking, though neither had erupted in decades. The sky was overcast and painted in fifty ugly shades of yellow, green, and gray. Now and then, a piece of debris from the vast asteroid field would scrape like a sulfur match across the sky, slanting down toward its own destruction.

The gravity was about three-quarters that of Earth, and although that helped with lifting and general movement, the science team had to work on solutions for bone loss, muscle deterioration, and the various circulation and blood pressure issues that affected everyone born on Earth. *Tempest* had artificial gravity, though, and even while it was being repaired, every citizen of Bliss had to go aboard for two hours of physical fitness every day, with an emphasis on weight-bearing exercises and cardio training.

The community inside the moon was built as a series of habitats and utility structures anchored to the jagged walls. Crystals of a hundred different kinds, most unknown to the crew of *Tempest*, glittered like jewels on every wall, stalactite, and stalagmite, giving the place an ambience of magic and of creative potential. People worked at their various jobs—mining, polishing the sharper edges of stone to be less dangerous, running the huge 3D printers that labored night and day, working at crafts, or conducting research in dedicated laboratories. Some of them nodded to him, while others remained focused on their tasks. Music played, partly to mask the noise of the printers and partly to create as much of a sense of calm as was possible this far from home.

At the back of the main chamber were three tunnels that led off in different directions. The left-hand one went to a series of medium to large chambers where many of the workrooms, storerooms, and living quarters were located. The center one was almost entirely machinery, hosting the generators, 3D printers, and equipment and miscellaneous bulk storage. The right-hand one was the science wing, and Brollachan went that way. The suite of labs at the far end was restricted and guarded by soldiers. Brollachan did not even allow cleaning crews to enter and preferred to handle the mundane chores himself. There were rumors that he had gone mad, that the WarpLine disaster had broken his mind, but Brollachan ignored them. Let people entertain themselves with speculation; he couldn't care less.

There were electric carts just inside the steel door. He climbed into one and headed to his lab, which was eleven kilometers in and five down, deep into the moon's cold heart. Small drones flew ahead of him to light the way, but when he turned to look behind, there was nothing at all to see.

He liked the darkness. He loved the solitude. He was not mean; he was not unkind. He hated no one, but he preferred to be alone most of the time. His thoughts were his best company.

Ariel was company too, though Brollachan was not the kind to humanize the AI. It was a tool, and a very useful one. His colleagues—Howard, Wu, and Solà—were friends, he supposed, though he seldom socialized with them outside of the labs they shared.

Brollachan had only one real companion.

Only one *true* friend.

Caliban.

It amused him to think that nearly everyone thought Caliban was the name of the suite of laboratories he used. But that was a bit of misdirection, the result of Jenny Spears overhearing him mention the name and asking who that was. Brollachan, always quick on his feet, said that it was his pet name for the lab. Spears shrugged and let it go.

Apart from Brollachan's three trusted scientists, no one else knew the truth. Of course not. Brollachan had no illusions about what would happen if they ever found out. Villagers with torches and pitchforks, to be sure.

That amused him. He had read *Frankenstein* as a boy and saw a dozen different versions, including the only truly faithful miniseries, which debuted in 2122. Excellent show, capturing not only the desperation and identity crisis of the creature but the arrogant brilliance of the scientist. Neither was a whole person, though they might have been had they tried to understand one another. But Victor Frankenstein never even gave his creation a name, referring to it instead by dehumanizing terms like "creature," "fiend," "specter," "dæmon," and "ogre." As a young man, Brollachan had fancied that one day he would write a new version of the story, one infused with optimism and vision rather than hubris and failed expectations.

He had *his* perfect creation, though. Well, two of them, actually. The other was a reduced-scale version of Prospero Bell's God Machine, only days away from a test firing.

He entered the lab, the lights coming on as he stepped inside, and closed the door. The 3D printer had done exquisite work in manufacturing every kind of machine he needed. Every computer and scope, every sequencer and chemical bath. That printer was personal property, and it squatted in one corner of his main lab.

In the other corner, however, was a large enclosure, ten by ten meters, with a steel floor and ceiling and walls of unbreakable dura-glass. The seams were triple-sealed, and there were flame units arranged so that the slightest damage to those seals would result in instant and total incineration of everything inside.

Brollachan hooked a wheeled chair with a foot and pulled it over in front of the cubicle. He sat down, folded his hands in his lap, and smiled.

"Good evening, Caliban," he said.

"Good evening, Dr. Brollachan," said the shoggoth.

6

"Are you sure you're okay?" asked Evie.

"Yeah, yeah," said Bianca. "Whatever the hell that was is gone now. I'm fine."

They stood together in the cavernous flight deck aboard Asphodel Station. Calisto had just taken off in her tumbler.

"Besides, I want to see Bliss. Hell, I want to see *Tempest*," Bianca said, trying to sound lighthearted. "Calisto and I are going to ride shotgun with your girlfriend—"

"Wife," Evie corrected.

"Wife. Right. We're going with her and her squadron. Maybe see if we can goose that iridium shipment along." She looked down at Evie. "You really think it'll work?"

"I … don't know," Evie admitted, "but it worked for us, and that was shoggoth tech. So it's worth a real shot."

"Yes, it damn well is."

Evie nodded. "I'm going to stay here awhile. God, there's so much I want to know. And it's so good to have Lars here. I don't believe in luck, but …"

"I hear ya."

Bianca patted her arm, turned, and walked over to the bin that stored her unused mass. She stood for a moment looking down at it, then nodded, reached out, and absorbed the material. Evie, watching, marveled at the process.

When Bianca was gone, she took a deep breath, let it out, and turned toward the exit.

"The universe is totally nuts," she said aloud. A sailor working on a tumbler overheard her and grinned.

"Sure as hell is, ma'am."

7

Bianca and Calisto flew side-by-side among a field of stars.

In her tumbler, Calisto tried not to be freaked out by the fact that her best friend—the dearest friend she had ever had, closer than any blood relative—was no longer alive. She was no longer human by any sane standard. Not an android per se, nor a robot. She was a presence, an energetic force that operated any complex machine that her will constructed.

She was a ghost.

Bianca Petrescu was dead.

After three months, the hurt of that had not diminished one bit. Calisto also felt pain about the others who had been living pilots when the WarpLine failed. Some were closer than others, leaving the grief to adjust itself to different levels. Yet all were her family in ways that the new cadets could never be. Beezer, Lovechild, Lucky, Tank, Jericho, Thunder Bear, Sundance, Galahad, Ventum, Spartan, and Rabbit. She had watched them all die and witnessed their rebirth as …

As what?

No matter how many times she ran it over in her mind, Calisto always struggled with an appropriate word. *NecroTek* was the accepted term, but in her private heart, the word *monster* so often rose to the surface.

She would cut her own tongue out before she ever used that word around Bianca.

Outside, matching her for course and speed, was Bee. She had constructed a slightly larger body in order to retain enough mass for engines and weapons. Calisto wondered if that increase—tripling her body weight—was doing more harm to her soul.

Her soul.

Calisto had very little faith of any kind, but the knowledge that souls existed struck her all the way to the heart. Did that mean souls were actually divine sparks? Or was it merely some kind of lingering postmortem energy field that allowed for consciousness to outlive the body? She did not know and felt awkward asking Lost, with whom she had not yet had an actual conversation, or Sybil, whose AI nature had become something closer to genuine consciousness, or even Dr. Soren. And, she wondered, if she did ask them, would she get three different answers?

Bee was usually the person she talked with about everything, and even though they still spent hours talking when Bianca was not traveling with the other NecroTeks, Calisto now could feel roadblocks in place with certain topics. She wondered if it was the same for her friend.

As if reading her thoughts, Bianca asked, "How we doing, hotshot?"

The fidelity of the onboard speakers was disturbingly precise, making it sound as if Bianca was in the tumbler with her. Sybil's modulation and filters gave Bianca a nearly human voice—sometimes unnervingly so—but Calisto could tell the difference. It was a machine voice. It would always be a machine voice.

"We're doing just fine," lied Calisto. "Haven't been on this side of Scylla and Charybdis before."

Those were the names selected by vote from the residents of Asphodel. When Lost had been asked about the names his own people once used, his answer was *Shêif'gälerul'lõgen* and *Blðl'firgle'étùn*. Words that meant "big sun" and "smaller sun." While Shadderal was an easy name for everyone, the others were decidedly not.

"Even so," Calisto continued, "I'm still trying to process the fact that a human colony has been here for two freaking years."

"I'm not *as* surprised. You know how many frigging moons are out here?"

"Seven hundred and sixty-six, Bee. And 5.3 million asteroids larger than one kilometer, with sixty percent C-type chondrite rocks and an even split between stony S-types and nickel-iron M-types. On top of that, there are 83.3 million smaller asteroids. I was there when we mapped it, dumbass."

"Point taken," said Bianca. "Hey, how many signal relays do you have left?"

"Just one." As they flew from Asphodel to Bliss, Calisto had deployed a series of nuclear-powered drones designed to amplify and greatly speed up any kind of radio or flash-burst signal. "Soon as I drop the last one—and here it *goes*—we can chitchat with everyone back home and get all the gossip."

"Nice. I should have thought to bring a shitload of them with me when we went out on our search. Be nice to be able to talk with Jacob and the others."

"Yeah, speaking of which, when're the rest of the 'Teks getting back?"

"Any day now. I sent a message about *Tempest*, but even pulse-wave signals take time."

"Yeah, well … we could have used all of you the other day," said Calisto. "Don't take that personally, Bee. Just saying."

"I know," said Bianca. "Truth to tell, Calisto, I was starting to get that itch about coming back. Glad I did."

"Me, too."

They coasted along the outer arc of the asteroid fields. Shadderal was out of sight on the far side of the system. Closer to hand were three small rocky planets that Lost said were once garden worlds but which had been blighted by the enemy. At the time, Bee had wondered aloud why shoggoths would kill all the plants and animals, and Lost's response was enigmatic: *Shoggoths are not the only enemy we fought. Nor were they even the worst. They kill to absorb life. Other servants of the Outer Gods feed on life itself, stealing their life force down to the atomic level, leaving nothing. Those worlds are dead, and no science exists to bring them back to life.*

Now she knew Lost was talking about the night-gaunts.

"We should be coming up on Bliss any second now and—" Calisto's words were cut off by a sharp gasp.

The small moon that was now home to the crew of the *Tempest* lay directly ahead.

And it was *burning*.

Part Twenty-Five
A War in Heaven

"There are only two cases in which war is just: first, in order to resist the aggression of an enemy, and second, in order to help an ally who has been attacked."

—*Montesquieu*

1

Like many of the moons in the Shadderal system, Bliss had a thin atmosphere composed of sulfur dioxide, sulfur monoxide, methane, sodium chloride, monatomic sulfur, and oxygen. All of it fuel for an inferno.

"God almighty," cried Calisto. "The whole place is on fire. How? *How?*"

Bianca suddenly accelerated ahead of her, shooting like a missile toward the burning moon. Her voice was loud and urgent on the radio. "Mosquito to C-1, Mosquito to C-1."

"Go for C-1," answered Captain Croft.

"Bliss is under attack. I repeat, Bliss is under attack."

"Size and number of shoggoth ships?"

"Unknown. Too far away to see any. I'll update in real time as I get closer."

"Mosquito," said Croft firmly, "it's you and Calisto out there. Soonest we can get support to your whiskey is eighty minutes."

Whiskey was navy parlance for location. Calisto, listening, felt her stomach turn to slush.

"Understood, C-1," she said, forcing herself to sound more confident than she felt.

"Understood," said Bianca. "Now would be a good time for raw materials, damn it."

The raw materials in question were the thousands of defunct ships on the Field of Dead Birds. *Ethla* would allow her to bond with them, *become* them, and build for herself a titan of a body, as she had during the last invasion. She and the other fallen Lost Souls had risen from that field in bodies composed of pieces, and with the unique power granted them by the *ethla* connection, they could shape them, repurpose them for everything from ion cannons to wings. Literally, anything their minds could imagine, their NecroTek powers could make.

But the Field of Dead Birds was that same distance—eighty minutes flight time. Even at full blast, her rockets couldn't shave more than half that time off. Getting back with giant engines on a titan body would be quicker, but still not quick enough. The fight was happening now, and Bliss was on fire.

The forward scopes on the tumbler and the corresponding sensors inside Bianca's machine body were only now coming into range. There were enemy ships out there. Explosions popped like soundless firecrackers, and they could both see the green pulse blasts of the stilettos.

"Bee, are you seeing blue pulses anywhere?"

The shoggoth ships they had so far encountered had an energy signature that differed from their own. The enemy fire was a brilliant blue, while the tumblers' weapons fired with a purple hue. The NecroTek energy was also purple, though with more blue in it.

A pause. "Negative."

"Then who the hell are they fighting over there?"

Bianca did not hear the question. The comms went silent all at once, and a wave of energy struck the NecroTek and the tumbler, smashing them out of their flight path and sending them whirling toward the asteroids that filled the sky.

2

Jenny was on Bliss, wearing a pressure suit, staring in horror and frustration as the sky above her burned with a ferocious orange light. At least half of the base's twenty stilettos were up there, tangled in a dogfight with ships of a kind completely unknown to her. She could see some of the smaller but nimbler B-911 combat spinners too, but only a handful. No idea where the rest of *Tempest*'s fighters were. The raging fires on the far side of a small ridge tried to tell her a bad story about the landing field. Something over there was burning with the kind of intensity that comes from rocket fuel and stacked ordnance.

Who was attacking? She had no idea. The ships up there looked like five-pointed stars. Except for the daggers and the mother ships her team had encountered the previous day, everything about the shoggoth navy was unknown to her.

The enemy was firing pulse blasts that were a sickly yellow green. She kept trying to get Asphodel Station on the horn via the new network of relays, but something was jamming all transmissions. The fighters couldn't even communicate with the ground.

Tempest was days away from being relaunched after months of repairs, and she had more guns than anyone could use. But the old girl was still tethered to the struts and scaffolding of their makeshift dry dock.

She whirled and ran to the main airlock. Spider and Not Larry were unhousing a cannon mounted on a turret. Jenny tried to shout orders, but the comms were gone. So she jumped in and helped them, grabbing a crank to spin the gun around even as Not Larry raised the barrel. Spider, lacking voice commands for Ariel, called up a digital interface—proving that the jamming did not extend to all electronics—and asked Ariel for a firing solution. The AI flashed one up, and Spider fed it into the gun's controls. The barrel now rose on its own, and the turret spun to correct the angle.

Jenny tapped Spider's helmet, and he fired.

The Defender 534 spat out a shell as big as Jenny's whole body. As it rose, small fins deployed, and tiny jets fired for course correction. The shell became a missile and locked onto a star-shaped enemy fighter. The craft immediately banked and spun into a climbing turn, trying to outrun the bomb.

"Go, go, go, come on you piece of shit, *go*," chanted Jenny.

Suddenly the fiery yellow sky exploded with intense blue light. The filters on her pressure suit's helmet were good, but Jenny still winced and turned away for a moment. When she looked again, there were pieces of burning debris falling slowly down to the ground.

"Game on!" she yelled, and even with the helmets, she could hear Not Larry and Spider shouting the same thing.

They immediately loaded the next round and fired. This one missed, but it chased a star-fighter away, forcing it to abort a bombing run. The enemy craft rose and vanished into murky clouds, only to reappear far out of range. It opened up with its yellow cannons and hammered the side of the mountain above the Bliss community.

"Shit," growled Jenny. "Why isn't the eastern battery firing?"

No one answered, so she called up the Ariel AI screen and quickly typed the question in. Ariel's answer came right away, and it made her heart sink.

"The eastern battery has been destroyed," said the AI.

"Where are the stilettos?"

"All fighters are engaged with the enemy."

"I count eleven stilettos and a dozen spinners."

"*Tempest* command was able to launch thirteen stilettos, of which two are down, and twenty-three spinners, of which seven are down."

"How many enemy ships?"

"There are thirty-one enemy craft left of an attacking force of fifty."

"Are they shoggoths?"

"According to the information I am sharing with Lost," said Ariel, "these craft are not part of the shoggoth fleet. He designates them as night-gaunt fighter-bombers."

Jenny felt her blood turn to ice.

"No," she breathed. "Please, no …"

Suddenly one of the star-fighters dropped low and raced toward them, opening up with cannons. Yellow fireballs burst all around her as she and her two Jokers scrambled to load and fire, load and fire.

3

Bianca spun through the void, her body cracked and broken.

She lost sight of Calisto's tumbler and prayed that her friend was still alive.

Bianca could not feel pain in the same way she did when alive, but the NecroTek connection was as unkind as it was efficient—it sent electrical impulses to her, ostensibly as a damage report, but it *felt* like pain. She groaned and growled and exerted her will over the mangled form. The impact had robbed her of nearly 15 percent of her mass, and that meant she had fewer resources on which to draw. She reshaped her body into something more compact—engines and exhaust where her legs and feet were, and a torso that was ringed with small guns. There was too much internal damage to manage ion cannons, but pulse cannons were possible.

As she finished the metamorphosis, she went into a fast turn, looking for Calisto and something to kill.

4

Homer James was the flight leader for *Tempest*'s complement of B-911 combat spinner close-attack fighters. They were smaller craft that lived up to their most common description as an engine with guns. Though they lacked the heavy punch of the stilettos, they were far nimbler.

Homer wished, however, that they were tumblers. He'd applied to Colonel Hobart to requisition some of the experimental craft but was told that Captain Croft had charge over them. And now, those tumblers were out here, too. The problem was that they were on Asphodel Station and not in Bliss's sky. No matter how fast Croft scrambled his team, they could not get there in time to do any good.

A star-fighter dropped down and made a run at him, opening up with those yellow cannons, but Homer knew his trade as well as he knew his ship. He kicked jets and turned hard over, dropping below the flight path and lines of fire, rotated to bring his belly guns to bear, and fired. The purple pulses hammered the star-fighter's shields, which held, but the enemy pilot peeled off as some of his shields began to flicker wildly.

"No you don't, you son of a bitch," swore Homer as he shot forward, rising and turning to give chase.

He never saw the blast that killed him.

It came out of the dark and struck his exhaust pipes. Homer James ceased to exist in a microsecond, and the vacuum stole away the fires of his immolation.

5

Bianca reached Bliss before Calisto.

As she flew toward the besieged moon, she could pick out more details. Stilettos and spinners were involved in a desperate dogfight. It was immediately clear that the attackers—those star-shaped craft—were nearly as maneuverable as tumblers and much faster than the spinners. The stilettos could match them for sheer firepower, but those birds were no match for speed. Everything, she knew, was a compromise—speed for power, power for maneuverability, maneuverability for weapons payload.

If this were Shadderal, she could fly down to the Field of Dead Birds and build herself a body that could take on those star-fighters in any kind of close battle. After all, she had gone toe-to-toe with a shoggoth Medusa mother ship once and had beaten it to rubble.

Now, though, all she had was her speed and maneuverability. Her guns were second class to what she was seeing, and she couldn't spare mass to create rockets or missiles.

NecroTek forever! she yelled inside her head, and drove full-speed toward a trio of star-fighters chasing a damaged stiletto. Her body guns fired a rippling fusillade as she rotated 360 degrees.

The lead star-fighter blew apart, and the others split away, one following the stiletto and the other turning to engage her.

"Let's do this, assface!"

Calisto had been following, but two star-fighters shot upward through the cloud of burning gasses, opening up on her with their yellow pulse cannons. She saw them in time to hopscotch, but one blast nipped the corner of her shields, sending her wobbling off course.

As the second ship swung wide to intercept, Calisto hopscotched again and again, appearing on the star-fighter's stern quarter.

"Oh, yeah, and fuck you too," she said, and blew it out of the sky.

Something streaked past her, and Calisto nearly shot at it but realized in a flash that it was Bianca chasing the third ship.

Two spinners spotted Calisto's tumbler and hurried over to fall into formation with her, and together they dropped low to hunt the star-fighters that were bombing Bliss.

All of the enemy ships were the same, and none looked anything like the daggers. It was disheartening to think that the enemy had new and more sophisticated resources to throw at the tiny group of humans in that star system. She wondered what *else* they had, but really did not want to have that question answered.

The bomber below was intent on its work, and Calisto made them pay for their inattentiveness. She fired a one-two punch of Constellation and Inferno missiles and veered off as the star-fighter and its unfired ordnance blew up with massive force.

"—one hear me?"

The voice came out of nowhere, and Calisto realized with a start that comms were back on. The bomber below had probably carried the jammer, but either way, the interference was gone.

"All ships, all ships," she bellowed, "comms are restored. Partner up and fight in pairs."

"Who's giving orders?" someone demanded.

"Calisto, topkick of the Lost Souls. Either follow my play or get off the air."

She punctuated her words with another one-two punch that blew a second bomber to fragments.

"Works for me," laughed the unknown pilot.

Calisto told them about the double-missile tactic, capping it off with, "One for the shields and one for the shitter."

There were laughs and clicks of squelch, and the complexion of the battle changed in seconds. Spinners and stilettos formed into two-ship hunting packs, using pulse cannons to get close and then the paired missiles to make their kills.

6

On the ground, Jenny, Not Larry, and Spider were working their gun with such fervor that the barrel was close to overheating.

"Just got word from Asphodel," said Jenny. "Those star-fighters aren't shoggoths. They're those night-gaunt sons of bitches. Supposed to be the worst of the worst, which means fuck them for being pretentious, evil alien assholes. Let's kill them, and I mean all of them."

"Running low on rounds, Lifeguard," said Not Larry, looking up from the gun's status screen. "We have seven rounds left, and then we throw rocks."

"Then we'll throw rocks," snapped Jenny.

"I have a good slider and a bitch of a breaking ball," suggested Spider.

"Reloads coming hot from the oven!" They turned to see Moonboy and Footie come running out of a service door, pushing a cart heavy with reloads. Behind them, Widow and Krampus were hoisting shoulder-mounted AS-10 personal missile launchers. The weapons were called Assassins, and as they knelt and fired, they earned their name by striking side-by-side against the underbelly of a star-fighter that had dropped down for a bomb run. The ship seemed to leap halfway back to orbit and then spread out like a holiday firework, raining down all along the ridge that separated them from the airfield.

A pair of spinners swooped down but rose away, seeing that the ship they were hunting was now flaming debris.

Jenny paused while the new ordnance was being loaded onto the feeding slides. She tapped into the command channel.

"Who's running this damn show? Is the colonel on deck?"

"Colonel Hobart is on Shadderal," said the deck officer.

"Where's Captain Ulric?"

"The captain was killed in the attack," said the officer. "Lieutenant McWhirter, too."

"Who's the ranking goddamn officer?"

"I guess I am, ma'am. Lieutenant Smothers."

"Shit, Gayle. I'm on the south side near the landing pad. Got four Jokers with me. How can we help?"

There was a pause before the young lieutenant replied. "Just keep firing, ma'am. I think we're getting ahead of this."

A bolt of searing yellow light punched down from the clouds and struck the side of the mountain over the Bliss community. Fifty thousand tons of rock leaped into the air and then rained down, beating on the mountain slope with fists of rock and fire.

"Oh, kiss my ass, you night-gaunt motherfuckers," muttered Jenny, and she fired. And fired.

Gayle Smothers said, "All stations and ships, hear this. Colonel Hobart reported in. The enemy are not shoggoths. They are night-gaunts. We are compiling data on them, but the colonel says that we cannot allow them to breach the community security. Repeat, we cannot let a single one of those things get in here."

Jenny glanced at Spider.

"Two years we're out here, Lifeguard," he said. "Two years, and now all this shit? What the actual hell?"

"Beats me, Spider. Just look for anything that doesn't look kosher and blow it back to Jesus. Or … whoever's on call."

7

"They're tough as balls," called Bianca, "but they're not unbeatable. Throw enough ordnance downrange, and they die like any other damn thing. Hoorah!"

"They're on the run," cried Calisto.

It was true. There were fewer than a dozen remaining star-fighters, and as if following some complex choreography, they detached from their attack runs, rose in tight turning arcs, formed a cluster, and fired their engines at full speed.

"God damn," said Bianca, "look at them go. Spry sons of bitches."

The star-fighters shot upward and away from Bliss, accelerating all the while, and then vanished into the vast night.

"All fighters, report in," called Lieutenant Smothers. The spinners and stilettos counted off, but the numbers did not climb high enough for comfort. Of the forty-four B-911 combat spinners, only twenty-three reported in. And only nine of the twenty stilettos were still flying. The tally was appalling.

Smothers ordered the ships to stay up and had Ariel calculate a search pattern, assigning sectors to each pair of craft.

"You stay up here, honey," said Bianca. "I'm going down to the surface to see what I can do."

8

The night-gaunt star-fighters left the Shadderal system at maximum speed. In a straight run, nothing from either Asphodel or Bliss could catch them.

They burned through the void until they were many hundreds of thousands of kilometers away from the moon they had bombarded. They changed course fifty-three times during their flight, firing drones out into space with software that mimicked their engine signatures. If the humans followed, they would have too many trails to chase.

Aboard the lead ship, the captain of the raiding party was well pleased with that day's work. It had never been her intention to destroy Bliss. That would be easy enough to do when the time was right. For now, all she wanted was to test their defenses, assess the speed with which Asphodel Station could come to their rescue, and inflict some wounds. All three of those goals had been achieved. As for her pilots who had died accomplishing this, she felt nothing. Their soul energies would be gathered up by the gods they worshipped, and that was how it was meant to be. It was how it had always been since the dawn of time.

When the real attack came, it would not be a handful of star-fighters but a fleet. They would strike Asphodel and Bliss, punch past the defenses, land, and then hunt the humans down no matter where they fled. She sat back in her sling chair, adjusting the fold of her leathery wings.

How would they taste? The thought made her stomach growl. Her forked red tongue wriggled out past rows of jagged teeth and licked the spit from her lips.

On her scope, she saw the shoggoth mother ship from which her fighters had been launched. It hung in space on the fringes of a small nebula that had been a binary star system before it died. The Medusa ship was lumpy and ugly and deadly. Landing bays opened to receive her and her remaining ships.

She did not see the flight of one hundred Nova missiles that streaked from within the nebula. They struck the Medusa amidships. The detonation was massive, like a small star exploding. The Medusa vanished, taking with it fifteen thousand shoggoths and two hundred night-gaunts.

Calisto's long-range scanners picked up the explosion.

"Something big and bad just happened," she reported. "It's far, but I can make it in about an hour. I'll check it out and report in."

"If you encounter hostiles, Calisto," said Captain Croft, "I want you to turn tail and run like hell."

"Copy that, sir."

She settled back for the flight, letting Sybil take the controls for most of the run. Calisto spent that time checking in with Bianca and the ground forces on Bliss. The fires in the atmosphere were burning out, and the Bliss community had not been breached by the bombardment. That was something.

Fatigue was catching up with her, made worse as adrenaline leached from her blood, leaving her shaky and sleepy. Calisto popped a couple of focus tabs, washing them down with water. The modified caffeine hit her system like a fist wrapped in velvet. It snapped her awake again.

"We are approaching the location of the explosion, Calisto," said Sybil.

On the screens, she saw a small nebula but not much else.

"What's out there?" she asked, but then she spotted what was left from the explosion. It was a debris field of floating junk. Some of it was familiar, though.

"Sybil, is that a Medusa?"

"It is the remains of one, Calisto."

"Was that what blew up?"

"That seems certain."

"How? Why?"

The AI had no answers. And Calisto was the only living thing out there. That should have made her feel safe, but it absolutely did not.

Part Twenty-Six
The Theory of Forms

"When we perceive a thing, it is the human tendency to identify it, classify it, and deceive ourselves that this means we actually know it. Kingdoms have fallen because of this kind of intellectual arrogance."

—*John Temple the Younger*

1

"Heading back to the barn," reported Calisto.

"Don't stop for coffee," said Croft. The comms channel was clear, and it sounded as if the captain was seated next to her.

"What's the butcher's bill?"

"Bad. Thirty-four confirmed dead on Bliss."

"Jesus Christ."

"Jesus wasn't on shift today," muttered Croft. "If they'd had warning, they might have gotten *Tempest* off the blocks and into the mix. She has more firepower than all of our ships combined. Nearly as much as Mosquito when she's in a mood."

"How soon before it can launch?"

"Waiting on that info now," he said. "I'll know better once they finish their assessment. Our biggest worry right now is Bliss itself. Those bastards bombed the hell out of the mountain over their habitat. Their AI, Ariel, is scanning for structural damage. I spoke with Colonel Hobart and Dr. Brollachan, and we all agreed that the residents should start preparing for evac. They braced the inner walls when they built that community, but those bombs hit hard. If there's a collapse in any part of the mountain ... Well, bottom line is it's a shit show over there."

"Pretty weird out here too, Skipper."

"Exactly what happened out there?" Croft asked. "Did you find the carrier that launched those star-fighters?"

She told him about the chase and the explosion.

Croft whistled. "Completely destroyed?"

"And I have zero idea of how, Skipper. No other ships on my scope."

"Mosquito wasn't with you? She didn't kill that ship?"

"Negative, Skipper. No other NecroTeks out here either."

Croft pondered that for a moment. "Any theories based on what you saw?"

"Maybe one or more of the star-fighters was damaged. A core meltdown or damage to their weapons system resulting in an accidental discharge. But to tell you the truth, Skipper, I think there's more to the story than what we know."

"Copy that, Calisto. Stay sharp. C-1 out."

The tumbler moved through space with no exterior lights except for the fiery red of her exhausts. Calisto checked her combat systems, and except for a small number of SAPR rounds for the chain guns, there was nothing in the pantry. It made her feel naked.

"Calisto," said Sybil abruptly, her voice sounding tense, "I am detecting a large enemy ship. Hull configuration consistent with a shoggoth Medusa."

"*Another* one? Where away?"

"Four thousand kilometers along your current trajectory."

"Shit," Calisto swore, tapping the brakes and altering course. The Medusa was on the outer range of her sensors' reach. A big, fat, terrifying blob on the screen. "Find me somewhere to hide, and I mean right damn now. A rock with ore in it to scramble their sensors."

"Searching," said Sybil. "There is a cluster of asteroids on the edge of the Shadderal system. They are a rich mix of cobalt, iron, manganese, molybdenum, nickel, rhenium, and tungsten. It should be ideal. Shall I input the coordinates?"

"Do it."

Calisto yielded control while Sybil made the necessary corrections, but once she had it locked in, she took the wheel and kicked the pedal down. The tumbler shot away, veering right and down at top speed.

The asteroid looked like a big, overcooked potato, with lots of small pockets, caves, and impact craters, of which more than a dozen were large enough for her tumbler. She cut speed down to station-keeping and snugged her ship into the deepest one, then cut her engines and dropped lead shielding over the nuke core, masking its radiation signature. That killed the glow of her engines, and the cockpit fell into a tense silence, broken only by the rasp of her frightened breathing.

Minutes passed as she watched the sensor screen. The metals in the asteroid warped and confused the signature of the Medusa, which was fine because it meant that her tumbler was also masked. It was a small ship, after all, and there were two hundred thousand tons of mixed metals wrapped around her.

"Just walk on by," she murmured. "Nothing to see here. There are no Black girls you need to ogle. Shhhh."

The Medusa crept across her sensor screen, the scale of the scope making it look like the huge ship was lumbering along at a crawl. Calisto launched a pair of tiny video drones and steered them to the top and bottom of the asteroid. Their high-def cameras locked onto the Medusa and brought the image into crystal clarity. It was big. Larger, she thought, than the brute of a mother ship Bianca fought on Shadderal during the first invasion three months ago. The meters on the video feed confirmed her guess, telling her that this craft was nearly 30 percent larger. The body looked like a giant coconut crab, but instead of chitinous legs and claws, it had clumps of metal tentacles. It was ugly, with no thought at all as to elegance of form; instead it was built for function only. Calisto knew that the current shape was not fixed, but that all shoggoth ships were transformative, taking on whatever form best suited the imperatives of its need.

She watched in horrified fascination, not having seen the other one this close. It was bigger than the asteroid in which she hid and looked like a machine version of Satan himself. Then something made her lean toward the screen.

"Wait, wait, Sybil, is that cow slowing?"

"Affirmative, Calisto," said Sybil. "It has cut its speed by ninety percent. Still slowing. The enemy ship has stopped."

"Can I run?"

"You could try," said Sybil doubtfully. "It is possible that you could lose them in the asteroid field. Would you like me to estimate the odds?"

"No, I would not," she snapped, then sat there, staring, trying to remember how to breathe. "I'm a rock. I'm another chunk of ore in this asteroid. That's all I am. Just a big nothing in the big nowhere."

"There is movement," said Sybil, her voice hushed now.

"Is it leaving?"

No answer.

"Sybil, is it leaving?"

"Calisto, the Medusa has launched three dagger fighters."

Her fluttering heart sank. She did not have enough ammunition to make a fight of it. The chain guns would fire themselves dry in under thirty seconds in any kind of dogfight. Every hot idea that ignited in her mind fizzled out when doused by the realities of her situation.

Sybil was speaking, but Calisto had stopped listening because the three daggers were headed straight for her. As they approached the asteroid, they split, with one diving under the giant rock and the other two sweeping to either side.

Calisto removed the safeties for her guns and tried not to be afraid of dying. It was one thing to take a hit during a group fight, but this? Out here, out of radio range, out of sight of anyone who might care—this was hell. This was a sad and dreary way to die.

The daggers clearly knew where she was, and as Calisto slowly eased her tumbler into the best possible trajectory for a hit-and-run escape, the three ships simply stopped.

Calisto stared at them.

Each of the daggers was much larger than her tiny ship, with hulls as long as a football field. The mouths of their cannons glowed with that hellish blue.

Calisto let her finger fall on the joystick trigger. She almost fired.

But did not.

Suddenly all three daggers emitted bright red lights. Scanners. Calisto did nothing. Scanning was better than being fired at. Maybe they were going to try to capture her. If so, then she would kick them in their squishy nuts for that. They could have her corpse, and maybe she'd take one of them with her.

The nuke core was there, too. Calisto touched a button to raise the lead shielding and dialed up the power to the red line. If she couldn't escape, then maybe there was another way to end this. A kamikaze run at the Medusa, kicking it hard as she forced the core into overload.

"Go out with a bang," she said, taking a spoonful of courage from that. Deep inside her chest, her heart seemed to ignite as well. Bianca always accused her of being reckless and crazy. Maybe that was the only win here—go out with a bang and take that big ugly whore of a mother ship with her.

The scans swept back and forth, and Calisto put her foot on the pedal, ready to go. There were enough SAPR rounds to punch a hole through them and make her run to the big ship. If she hopscotched enough times, then maybe she could make it.

Maybe.

The red sensor lights winked out. The daggers did not move. Neither did Calisto. She watched the cannon mouths, waiting for even the slightest change in intensity.

"Sybil," she whispered, "divert all shield power forward."

"Done," said the AI. "Calisto . . . ?"

"What?"

"It has been my honor to know you and work with you."

Calisto licked her lips. They were as dry as the dust on Shadderal. "See you on the other side, Sybil."

Then it happened.

All at once.

The blue cannon mouths on the three dagger fighters went dark. Black. Empty. And the three shoggoth fighters turned, peeled off, and flew back to the mother ship.

Calisto sat there stunned, watching as the ships reached the Medusa, cut power, and glided into the docking bay. Then, with ponderous slowness, the great ship also turned. Its engines flared, and in an instant it was gone.

She did not move. She could not.

They left. They did not fire a single gun. They could have blown her to atoms. The Medusa could have launched a hundred more. But they left. After what felt like a thousand years, Calisto left the protection of the asteroid, found the best course home, and fled.

2

Help arrived on Bliss.

The skimmer bearing Evie Cronin and Lars Soren was one of a small fleet that set out from Asphodel, bringing skilled labor, experts in various fields, a top structural engineer, and many civilian volunteers who were unskilled but willing to help.

The skimmers were packed to capacity, and they were accompanied by a retrofitted *Triton*. That was the middle-aged old transport that had brought the Lost Souls to Asphodel mere hours before the WarpLine test disaster. Now it had been bulked up with new plating and had gunports fore, aft, along the sides, and above and below. Although slow and past its prime, *Triton* had become a flying battery. Its capacious hold was stocked with medical supplies and other necessary materials.

For the rest of that day, skimmers plied to and from *Triton*. Some of the volunteers were people who had worked on ships, a few even from actual shipyards, and they were taken down to the big network of scaffolding wrapped like barbed wire around *Tempest*.

Inside the mountain, the big main chamber had become a temporary hospital, with a screen around one side acting as a morgue. Evie oversaw most of this part of the relief effort, working with a handful of doctors and nurses and a small army of volunteers willing to get bloody and have their hearts broken.

Soren looked around for Evie, having lost sight of her shortly after they arrived, and when he found her, he stopped short of calling her name. She sat on an overturned box, holding the limp hand of a young man who lay beside her. A half-empty IV bag drooped from a stand, the liquid no longer dripping.

He took a breath and walked the rest of the way to her and knelt down. She looked up at him with a face that was both too young to bear all of this horror and too old for someone of her age. The life force seemed to have been sucked out of her, or at least partially. It had fled entirely from the young man. Her cheeks glistened with fresh tears.

"Who is he?" he asked. Deliberately using *is* rather than *was*. Her grief was far too immediate for anything else.

Evie sniffed and shook her head, and Soren waited for her to be ready.

"Craig Anders," she said. "My graduate assistant. God … he can be such a pain in the ass at times. He came with me to Antarctica and then all the way out … out …"

Sobs took her and tried to pull her down beneath the surface. Soren knelt beside her and wrapped one arm around her shoulders. Evie immediately shoved herself into him as storms of hurt broke within her slender frame.

3

Calisto returned to Asphodel Station, received permission to land, did so, and turned her ship over to the deck crew.

"Tune her up and give me a couple of extra campaign packs. I ran out of missiles, and it felt like being naked in church."

"Have you ever *been* naked in church?" asked Bianca, who met her on the deck.

"No, but now I know what it feels like. Come on, I need to brief Captain Croft on something truly—and I mean *truly*—weird. We might need to bring Lost in on this."

They hurried off and found Croft coming out of a meeting with Delia Trumbo. Calisto gave him her report right there in the hallway.

"Wait … they just turned around and left?" he asked. "Didn't open fire at all?"

"They didn't even give me dirty looks."

Croft looked at Jenny. "This make sense to you?"

"Boss," she said, "none of this shit has made sense since me and my boys first went down to Antarctica."

"Copy that," said Calisto, and Croft nodded.

"Why would they do that?" he wondered.

"Beats the shit out of me," Calisto said. "I mean, don't get me wrong, sir, I'm happy as a tick on a fat dog, but I can't even figure out how to *think* about this."

Croft tapped his holo-comms and waited for Lost to reply. The golem's cracked helmet visor appeared with the bleakness of Shadderal behind him.

"I have heard about the losses on Bliss," said the ghost. "Please accept my sympathies."

"Thanks, but we have something new happening, and I want your opinion." He had Calisto go through it again in precise detail. The luminous blue face screen showed nothing, but Calisto thought she saw the alien slowly stiffen.

"That is … remarkable," said Lost when the narrative was done.

"Sure, but does it make any sense?" asked Bianca.

"It is inexplicable."

"Have you ever heard of a shoggoth ship choosing *not* to fire on one of the good guys?" pressed the NecroTek.

"It is against both their nature and the dictates of their masters to offer mercy, pity, or quarter."

"Could it have anything to do with the arrival of those night-gaunt things?" asked Calisto.

"Not in any way that makes sense," admitted Lost.

"Could it have anything to do with the night-gaunts deciding to stop haunting our dreams and come after us with guns?" asked Croft.

"As I said, Captain, this is unknown territory for me." He paused. "This concerns me. The night-gaunts were seldom used as raiders. They are much more evolved than the shoggoths and more technologically advanced. It's odd to waste them on mere attacks."

"Which tells you what?"

"The few times they entered the war back when I was fighting it," said Lost, "was when we were experimenting with what your scientists call folding space. Are you familiar with that?"

"Sure," said Calisto. "High school physics 101. Folding space is an extension of Einstein's theory of relativity, which states that space and time are intertwined and can be affected by massive objects. The theory of folding space builds on this idea by suggesting that the fabric of space-time can be bent or folded, allowing for shortcuts in travel."

"In very simple terms, yes," said Lost. "It was a major field of investigation for us for a while. The first scientist to explore the possibilities for us had a dream about it—not uncommon for us—and he did the primary work to create a kind of doorway between two fixed points in the universe. To understand it better, you might want to consult Dr. Anton Kier's notes for his development of WarpLine. There are some similarities within the technical philosophy. The Outer Gods could make great and terrible use of that kind of technology, perhaps correcting Kier's errors."

"Okay, but how would these night-gaunts know anything about that?" asked Croft.

Lost seemed surprised. "How could they *not* know? A hole was torn in the fabric of space-time. Asphodel Station, *Tempest*, and perhaps more came through that hole. Such an event sends ripples along the lines of energy that connect this reality to others. Until now, the only way this has ever been accomplished is by night-gaunt mother ships, and even then, they have only been able to jump from one star system to another within a local group. What WarpLine did must appear to the enemy as a new use, or a new version, of the technology they had and that my people tried to eradicate. It was supposed that if they recovered the science, they would do so piecemeal."

"Why piecemeal?" asked Calisto.

"The night-gaunts are a jealous and covetous race. They are also clannish. We learned that no one clan held *all* of the transdimensional science, and each group owned some of the knowledge and manufactured only their part of it. When we decimated their factory worlds, it was like breaking links in a chain. We also bombarded their libraries and research moons. That they have sent their star-fighters to Bliss suggests that they have reclaimed some of their capabilities, but the fact that we are alive to discuss it means they are not yet ready for a full-scale invasion."

"As comfort goes," said Croft, "that's pretty cold."

"It is worse than that," said Lost. "It means that they are on the verge of reclaiming their full transdimensional science."

"How can we stop them?"

"If we had a fleet, Captain, and access to that same technology, we could launch another attack against the night-gaunt homeworld. Destroy that planet—which is the real hub of their science and the holy of holies—then we would have a chance."

"Where *is* the homeworld?" asked Bianca.

"Alas, that knowledge is lost to the dust of time," said the golem.

Calisto frowned in thought. "Maybe they want the WarpLine tech. I mean, how could they know it's all blown to bits?"

"That is likely," said Lost.

"Why attack Bliss, then?" asked Croft. "WarpLine was on Asphodel."

"They might not know that." Lost considered. "Since it was their own habit to have research and development bases on other worlds and moons, perhaps they thought that Bliss—newly discovered—was a center for human research. For a new WarpLine gun."

"Shit," said Calisto.

Croft said, "Will they try again? Maybe with a bigger force? A fleet, perhaps?"

Lost made a harsh, bitter barking sound that Bianca knew was the golem's best attempt at a laugh. "Without a doubt, their fleet is already on its way."

Croft wheeled around and glared at Bianca. "I don't know what you have to do to get your team here, Commander, but we need them here yesterday."

"But I—"

Croft cut her off. "Make it happen."

He cut a sharp look at Lost.

"The night-gaunts just moved to the top of the Big Bad list. You've been trying to scare the piss out of us about them, but you dance around specifics. You must know more than you've shared, so I am going to set up a meeting in one hour. My team and the Bliss team, and we want *everything* you have on the night-gaunts. That's not a request."

Lost bowed. "I will do what I can."

4

Jenny joined Evie and Soren near the rows of the screaming wounded and the silent dead. She hugged Evie and then stood staring in bleak horror.

"So many ..." she breathed.

"It's insane. To live out here so long, and then suddenly we're in a war," Evie said. "It's insane. It's ..." She left it hanging because there were no words to give sanity or acceptance to what was happening.

Dr. Kimbra saw them and came over as well. Evie introduced her as the engineer who had been with the university team from the beginning.

"There are enough medics here now that I think we're just going to be in the way," said Jenny. "How 'bout we give Dr. Soren here the tour?"

"It hardly seems the right time for that," protested Soren.

Jenny said, "The more we all know about Asphodel and Bliss, the better able we'll be to prioritize our resources."

"Good idea," agreed Kimbra, and Soren reluctantly assented.

The four of them did a thorough tour of the inside of Bliss Mountain, which took longer than Soren expected. He remarked on how sprightly he felt in the reduced gravity.

"And I felt like a fat cow on Asphodel," said Evie. "Caught me off guard."

"We have Earth g on *Tempest*," Kimbra said to Soren. "But I imagine it's different on Asphodel, where you have it twenty-four seven."

"It is," admitted Soren. "Shadderal is slightly less than Earth gravity, but you really don't take much note of it. Bliss is … different. I'm spoiled because I was seldom ever anywhere with reduced gravity. Short visits to Luna and Mars—that's about it."

"Well, I'm all for moving permanently to the station," said Kimbra. "Tired of being a cave-dwelling mole rat."

"Oh, *there* you are," called someone, and they turned to see Dr. Brollachan hurrying over. "I think you had better see this, Kimbra."

He led them back into the main chamber but steered them to a far corner.

"Kimbra, do you have a light? Yes? Good, shine it up there."

The engineer produced a powerful pocket flash and aimed it at the part of the ceiling Brollachan indicated. None of them had to ask what they were supposed to see. It was shockingly apparent. Deep cracks ran in every direction to points that corresponded with spots outside where night-gaunt missiles had brutalized the mountain.

"Is it as bad as it looks?" he asked, his face now pale and alarm flashing in his eyes.

"Worse, I'm afraid," said Kimbra, and gave a brief technical opinion on initial impact damage, radiating fractures, and overall fragility of the rocky ceiling.

Brollachan walked along a high ledge, shining his own light into the wider crevices. Then he turned and looked down at the hundreds of people hustling to save lives. "I believe the community is in threat," he murmured.

"No shit, Dr. Brainiac," laughed Jenny. "Someone just bombed the hell out of us. But at least the walls are still standing."

Kimbra shook her head. "For now, yes. Now come look at this."

She showed them new cracks on the interior walls of the habitat's main hall, some of which ran all the way down to the floor. The rows of cots and of bagged corpses were directly below some of the worst structural damage.

"Fuuuuuuuck," said Jenny under her breath.

"We have to move everyone," said Evie. "If any of that rock falls ..."

"If that part of the ceiling collapses," said Kimbra, "the whole community will be exposed to the atmosphere."

"Shit," breathed Evie.

Brollachan faced Soren. "If Asphodel will have us, I think we need to evacuate Bliss and go to the station. Today, if possible. Then we can do repairs here without further risk."

"I concur," said Soren. "But there are a lot of people here, and we only brought two skimmers. What about your ship? I know it was damaged, but can *Tempest* fly?"

"Yes," said Brollachan without hesitation. "Her engines and hull have been repaired."

"She doesn't have ion drive," said Jenny. "She's airtight but slow."

"Does she need to be here on Bliss for the repairs on the main drive to be completed?" asked Soren.

Jenny shrugged. "Not really. And frankly, from what I saw, Asphodel has better facilities for ship repair."

"Then we need to move *Tempest* to save her in either case," said Brollachan firmly.

5

Jacob Fox was dying even though he was already dead.

His NecroTek body was pocked, scorched, and pitted, and he could feel the *ethla* dragging at him. It was as if he could feel his soul being sanded down.

He twisted around to try to avoid blazing yellow pulse blasts. A kilometer away, Beezer was drifting, his body broken into two pieces.

His hips and legs floated at the far edge of Jacob's sensors; and his torso, head and one arm spun around and around, trailing sparks.

Lucky and Tank were damaged too, but they were still able to fight.

All of the others were in the very heart of it, dodging force blasts, firing their ion cannons, trying to outmaneuver the squadron that had come out of nowhere. These were not the standard dagger fighters the shoggoths had used during the invasion three months ago, but some new hull design that looked like the throwing stars used by ninjas in old movies.

Ninja Death Stars—that's what Beezer called them a moment before he took a pulse blast. Jacob did not know if Beezer was dead. There was no radio contact, and they were so far from Shadderal that there were no fresh mech bodies for them to inhabit.

The team had been flying in loose formation, heading back home at top speed. The mission had been mostly a failure, with the shoggoths refusing direct conflict, even to the point of abandoning a few small bases on remote worlds and moons. Only twice were the NecroTeks able to force the issue, and each time, it was in fights of almost even numbers, but in those kinds of scraps, the NecroTeks had the advantage. They were faster and far more maneuverable, and with their psychic connection to every part of their mechanical bodies, they could aim and fire with nearly supernatural precision. Jacob wondered if word of this had spread, and if so, was that the reason the shoggoths were running?

Or were they waiting until these new star-shaped fighters were deployed? These new craft were even faster than the NecroTek bodies—at least the human-sized forms they currently used—and they were twice as nimble as the daggers. One-to-one, they were a close match with Jacob and his team.

And there were a lot more of them.

Thunder Bear was trying to fight close action, hoping to physically rip through the hull of a fighter without them being able to shoot him. It worked the first time, and he exerted his massive strength to tear off two of the star's five points. He hurled one piece at another ship, but it evaded it easily. He took the other, reversed it in his grip, and with savage effort, drove it like a stake through the star-fighter's heart.

The resulting explosion was massive. He tried to leap away and ignite his boot jets, but the blast caught him and hurled him far into the endless night.

"Rabbit, Tank—help Bear."

A pair of NecroTeks veered off from a craft they had just blasted to junk, angled, and shot away, accelerating toward their friend.

"Galahad," called Ventum, "who *are* these bastards?"

Jacob—call sign Galahad—found himself too busy to answer as a fresh barrage of plasma fire tried to burn him out of the sky. The enemy ships were everywhere. Firing wildly, not seeming to care if they clipped one of their own. Three of the alien craft were drifting wrecks from friendly fire.

"I don't know, brother," said Jacob. "But they are pissing me off."

He accelerated forward, driving at a star-fighter, dodging high and low to avoid pulse fire. Then he folded his body into a bullet shape at the exact moment he kicked in the afterburners. His body smashed into—and through—the alien ship, but it exploded around him and sent him spinning and flailing away.

Croft and Bianca sat on one side of a conference table facing a big RealScreen. Colonel Hobart and Agent Spears were visible in smaller windows, but the main image was that of Lost, looking even more like a scarecrow made of broken parts than he usually did.

"We have discussed the Dreamlands," began Lost. "The night-gaunts come from there. They are *part* of that reality. They are made of its substance."

"Which tells me nothing," Jenny said.

"Have patience," begged Lost. "You are used to three-dimensional thinking and are very grounded in what you can see, feel, hear, measure, and quantify. The truth is that the universe is far more complex than that, and the night-gaunts are examples of that difference. The night-gaunts are pandimensional, meaning that they exist in different forms on different levels of existence. In order to serve the will of the Outer Gods on this plane, they must take forms that are harmonious with our physical laws. They adopt bodies that I believe are not only utilitarian but also drawn from their empathetic understanding of what mortal beings fear. They are agents of nightmare in a very real sense."

"Doesn't answer why we haven't found their corpses."

"It does, actually," said the golem. "They exist in physical form by an effort of will. When they die, that deliberate control ends, which means that they no longer exist in our universe. Much as the monsters in a nightmare vanish when we wake."

"Jesus," breathed Bianca.

"At least they can be killed," mused Croft. "That's something."

Hobart asked, "What do we know about their technology?"

Lost nodded. "Some. Their ships—what we are calling star-fighters out of convenience—are physical. They are made here in this reality, though where and by whom is unknown. Likely shoggoths or some other slave race makes them. You have seen these star-fighters in action. They are fast and dangerous, powered by a kind of quartz crystal that we have not been able to study. With the craft that were destroyed at Bliss, it would be advantageous to harvest those crystals. I would, however, set up a laboratory *outside* of either Bliss or Asphodel as we don't know what kind of radiation those stones emit."

"There's a lot of real estate down on Shadderal," said Croft. "We can fabricate a lab on one of the more remote spots, well away from the ship factories."

"On an island, perhaps," suggested Lost. "I can help you locate a good place."

"Their ships are fast," said Jenny, "but not much tougher than the shoggoth daggers."

"The dagger ships are larger and have better shields," said Lost. "The star-fighters are more maneuverable, faster, and there are a lot more of them on each night-gaunt mother ship. We can call them Leviathans since this is the closest approximation in your language to what my people called them."

"How big are they?"

"Larger than the Medusa ships," said Lost. "But that is anecdotal information. I have never seen one, and there are no stored images of one."

"Another difference between the daggers and star-fighters," said Bianca, "is that the shoggoth ships are straight-up fighters relying on pulse cannons. But these night-gaunt boats are fighter-bombers."

"Yes," said Croft, "and that means there's an extra layer of danger to Asphodel, Bliss, and both the factories and settlements on Shadderal."

"Can these night-gaunts shape-shift too?" asked Bianca.

"Not once they are on this plane of reality."

"Any special powers or abilities?"

"Great strength and speed," said Lost. "And great hunger. Remember, they feed on life force."

"Won't be forgetting that," murmured Jenny.

"Vulnerabilities?" asked Croft.

"When manifesting bodily, they are mortal, though hard to kill. Beyond that, I do not know," said Lost. "There are old legends that say they cannot abide *true light*, but the meaning of that phrase is lost to time."

"Personal weapons?"

Lost said, "They have pulse guns of their own design. The function appears standard. Their primary weapons are themselves. Though they also have some kind of weapon that induces altered states of mind. Hallucinations, nightmares—call them what you want."

"What's this weapon look like?" asked Jenny.

"I do not know," said the ghost. "If anyone knew more about them than I do, they are long dead, and their voices silenced."

7

There was a loud shriek of tortured metal as a tower crane lifted a huge section of battle-damaged scaffolding away from the dry-docked SPU corvette. *Tempest* looked dead to Evie, who stood by a window in the makeshift shipyard's control booth. Jenny Spears stood with her, the two of them holding hands. They wore pressure suits but no helmets, and even though Evie could not feel the warmth of Jenny's skin, the hand squeeze was lovely, and the contact an elixir.

As if sensing her thoughts, Jenny gave her hand a small squeeze. "Love you, babe."

"I love you," murmured Evie.

The scaffolding debris was the last of the battle damage to the dry dock. Teams scrambled out onto the exterior of the huge warship and began uncoupling cables and hoses.

"Not crazy about you staying here while everyone else bugs out for Asphodel," said Jenny.

"Let's not go through that again," protested Evie. "The battle did a lot of damage to the computers in the community. We can't just upload all of our data to Ariel, and some of it is critical. It's going to take time to pull the data crystals, check them, and load it all onto the skimmer. And Torq has stuff in his lab he needs—he said that would take at least the whole rest of today. The tumbler pilots are out there, and if any of those … those … *things* come back, we'll be on that skimmer and out of here like lightning. Trust me, sweetheart, I do not want to be here a minute longer than I have to."

Jenny said, "Grumble, grumble."

Lights popped awake all along the ship's sides, and there was a low, sleepy, moody growl as the engines fired. As they heated up, the vibrations made the control booth shudder. Evie lost balance, but Jenny caught her.

"Combat reflexes to the rescue," laughed Evie, straightening.

"They're good for something," Jenny said.

"They're good for a lot of things." It was said as a joke, but there must have been something in her voice, because Jenny gave her a sharp, inquisitive look.

"You okay?"

"Huh? Oh. Just, y'know … stressed. All of this is so insane. So unexpected. After being out here all this time, I guess I got used to the peace of it. The inevitability of our situation. Knowing this was going to be our forever home."

It was mostly true, but it was also a deflection. There was something she had planned on telling her lover and almost had, but then the alarms in Bliss went off. The alien attack. Then the mind-blowing knowledge that Asphodel was out there. That there were twelve thousand more people in this lost and lonely place than any of the *Tempest* crew realized. Lars Soren was there, and that was magic. There were aliens and ghosts, and alien ghosts. Human ghosts too, invoked by magic to pilot spaceships.

But there was also a war.

There were literal gods and monsters.

There was pain and death and loss. There was terror and doubt.

And there was far less hope than there had been two days ago.

How could she possibly tell Jenny now? How could she let her know that the IVF had worked?

How could she tell the woman she loved that a baby was going to be born into this outer ring of hell itself?

Part Twenty-Seven
All the Devils

"It is a brave man … who dares look the devil in the face and tell him he is a devil."

—*James A. Garfield*

1

One day later, Evie stood with Brollachan, Beatrice Howard, T. T. Wu, and Alejandro Solà as they watched *Tempest* rise from the surface of the small moon, carrying the rest of the people with whom they had lived for two years. Their comrades. Their families. Friends and lovers, colleagues and rivals.

There were a handful of soldiers elsewhere inside Bliss and two pilots for the remaining skimmer—the escape vehicle that would take them to safety if the ceiling collapsed.

"I wish I felt better about this decision," said Evie.

"I wish a lot of things," said Torq, though it sounded like he was speaking to himself.

"The Jokers are just riding shotgun," said Howard. "They'll come back for us once they see everyone safely aboard the station. We'll be fine until then."

"Sure," said Evie, her tone lifeless. "We'll be just fine."

2

It hid behind a dead world.

The planet had been the scene of a battle so long ago that it was lost to all memory except that recollection of scars held in secret by the universe itself. Pieces of the world were broken, and they trailed the globe as it limped around an insignificant star, its orbit taking ten thousand years. Since its destruction, the planet had made seven complete circuits.

The Medusa ship was locked in geostationary orbit, using the fractured world for cover. Small chimera craft moved to and fro around the mother ship, mining floating planetary fragments for useful ores and for the crystals that powered their engines and weapons. Dagger fighters circled, ever watchful, patient as the stars.

The twin stars at the heart of the system provided light but little warmth, and the larger asteroid belt hid the Medusa and her consorts from Shadderal and Bliss and prying eyes.

Aboard the monstrous craft, the shoggoths went about their tasks, following every order conveyed to them through dreams by the Outer Gods.

Deep in the bowels of the ship, in rooms constructed of materials that shielded even the deepest sleeping mind from intrusion, a great shoggoth—much larger than the others—waited. Around her, clustered like children, were ten thousand shoggoths. As the Great Mother spoke, they sang to her. They begged and pleaded. Not *to* her, but *with* her.

"*Tekeli-li,*" they cried. "*Tekeli-li.*"

It was a word, a prayer, an entreaty in a language created by the shoggoths in the earliest days of their slavery. Only they knew its true meaning.

"*Tekeli-li. Tekeli-li.*"

On and on, through the long, black night.

3

Evie Cronin and Torquil Brollachan walked together through the empty main hall of the Bliss community. The SPU chief's three assistants had already gone ahead.

In the cavern, the makeshift medical cots were as they had been left—soaked with sweat and blood, rumpled with the haste of panic. Empty. Nearby was an open container labeled Transport Sleeves. Evie paused to look at it. There was only one sleeve left, and it hung limply over the edge. Brollachan sighed heavily.

"What an appalling name for a body bag," said Evie.

"People are so afraid of death that they try to hide from it even when manufacturing something like that. It's foolish."

"It's disgusting."

Brollachan nodded. "It is."

They moved away, continuing toward the entrance to the tunnel that led to the suites of science labs.

"Do you have everything you need, Evie?" he asked.

The barrage that pounded the side of Bliss Mountain had done much more than crack the stone. Jagged splinters of rock had cut into wiring, resulting in some shorts and fried panels.

"Sure," said Evie. "It's not difficult work, just time-consuming. Nitpicky stuff. The data crystals are durable, but with the wiring fried, I'll have to take the mainframes apart and pull them as best I can."

"A tech could have done this, you know."

She shrugged. "There's a war coming, Torq, and I'm an evolutionary biologist. Techs are critical. Besides, there's nothing else of use I could be doing."

He nodded.

When they got to the tunnels, her path led one way and his another.

"You've never really told me what you and your team are doing back there," she said, gesturing into the dark.

"I know," he said. "Sorry, but I think I've become conditioned to the habit of secrecy. Working all these years for a black budget group like SPU has its downsides."

She waited, hoping he would say more, but he merely wished her well and began to turn away.

Evie gasped suddenly and grabbed Brollachan's arm for support. Her face went gray and sweaty as nausea swept through her like a storm. She very nearly vomited. The scientist steadied her, his face showing alarm and concern.

"What is it, Evie?" he gasped. "What's wrong?"

She clung to him, sucking in deep breaths of air for a few seconds. The sickness ebbed slowly, leaving her trembling and dizzy. Then she detached from Brollachan and took a few wandering steps, recovering her balance by slow degrees.

"Evie?" asked Brollachan gently. "Tell me."

When she faced him again, she hoped she looked better than she felt.

"It's nothing …" she said lamely. "Just morning sickness. Jenny still doesn't know. Only the doc and you know. And … I guess this is the worst time ever for something like this."

Brollachan walked over to her, holding out his hands and taking hers when offered. "The worst time?" he echoed. "Oh no, my dear, it is the best possible time."

"During a war?" she demanded.

"Yes. In times like these what could be more heartening, a better statement of optimism, than to have new life? What a glorious gift this is. This is a true blessing. "

His words and the emotion in his voice astonished her. It also pushed back the darkness that seemed to skulk around them. Evie stared up at him. Her eyes filled with tears, and he gave her the warmest smile she had ever seen on his gaunt, austere face. It was a joyful smile. Brollachan took her hands and pressed them to his chest, right over his heart.

"I hope you're right," she said. "Even so … I can't tell Jenny."

"Why not?"

"Now? Seriously? We're about to go to war. Last thing I need to do is distract her, split her focus."

Brollachan shook his head. "No, you have it wrong, Evie. If you tell her now, before the fight, it will do a world of good. *Worlds* of good. Jenny Spears and I have had our issues in the past, as you well know, but I have great respect for her, and I'll tell you why. Tom Hobart is a soldier. He is a follower of orders and a dedicated cog in the machinery of the military. That is not an insult. The military needs soldiers. But Jenny is a different kind of fighter, the kind that people in my line of work seldom get to meet. She is a *warrior*. She doesn't fight for flag or politics or even country. *You* are the reason she fights with such strength, such courage and dignity. People like you. Her call to arms is about protecting the innocent so that they don't fall beneath the heels of a malicious or indifferent enemy. Being a true warrior sets her apart. Think about how powerful she will become when she knows she has *more* to fight for."

His words were like a knife, stabbing her to the heart, and yet the blade was kind, not a weapon but a scalpel. It cut through doubts and opened her to a greater understanding. She stood on tiptoes and kissed his cheek.

"Thank you," she said with a sniff that was almost a sob.

4

The Medusa recalled her ships and began to move away from the fractured planet.

It displayed no external lights and projected dense holograms to hide the glow of its blue exhaust ports. Scout ships flew on before it, and others trailed behind, keeping close watch as the big ship entered the outer edge of the asteroid field.

Heading toward Asphodel Station.

5

When he reached his lab, Brollachan told his aides to go straight in and work on the God Machine. They nodded and headed toward the inner steel door. Beatrice Howard paused, though.

"Something?" prompted Brollachan.

"Listen, Torq, I can understand why you haven't told anyone about Caliban … and I don't envy you for when you do. But why have we kept quiet about the God Machine? If it works, it could save everyone."

"*If* is the operative word, Beatrice. The machine has been running in idle mode for a few days now. Today will be our first real test firing. If it fails, no hopes will be dashed. If it works, however, then we can make an announcement that will be shared with our people and those on Asphodel."

He watched her face as she thought that through.

"Very well," she said doubtfully.

"There's something else?" asked Brollachan.

"Well … yes. I had Ariel interface with Sybil for a full report on the WarpLine, and it seems to me that Anton Kier may have also consulted

Prospero Bell's journals. I'm not saying he attempted to build a God Machine, but there are key elements in his work that are remarkably similar to what we're doing."

"Yes, I noted that, too."

"Should we perhaps consider holding off on the test firing until we more fully understand where Kier went wrong?"

Brollachan considered, then shook his head. "Anton was brilliant but also reckless. He relied on shortcuts to make gains, and he was lucky enough with that not to have created a worse catastrophe. I mean, for a while he had planned to test WarpLine on Earth. Imagine what a tragedy that would have been."

"Don't even," she said.

"We, however, have been far more careful, Beatrice. We are not reckless, we have not been hasty, and we have done everything right. I feel that we avoided the mistakes he made because of the integrity of our protocols. This is at the heart of why I brought you and the others in on this. All three of you are not only fine scientists but also first-chair technicians. Kier was where we were *before* his blunder sent us all here. We've had two full years to check and recheck, and I can say with confidence that we *are* ready. Add to that the providential evacuation of this moon, and the timing could not be better."

"Providential is a tricky word to use in light of how many people died," she said bitterly.

"Perhaps, but I can be more frank with you than with the community as a whole. Besides, Beatrice, if we *succeed*—and I have every expectation of that outcome—then we can save everyone else. Given the overwhelming threat out here, I think we owe it to everyone, the living and the dead, to try."

Howard nodded slowly, digesting and agreeing by degrees. Finally, she gave a firmer nod and headed off into the chamber where the God Machine waited.

Brollachan followed her over and closed the door. Then he turned to Caliban.

"She fears me," said the shoggoth.

"Why do you say that?"

"She never looks at me. She never speaks with me. And, given what has happened with the night-gaunts, I believe she mistrusts me. She fears me."

"Of course she does."

"That makes me want to hurt her," said Caliban.

Brollachan pulled his chair over in front of the glass. "I understand. Can you define your feelings more fully?"

The mass shifted and then coalesced into a figure. Tall, gaunt, black-eyed. It wore Brollachan's face, but the body was generically human. It was naked, and it glistened wetly.

"It is rage that I feel," said the monster.

"At her?"

"Not specifically her, no."

"Please be more specific."

"The emotion your kind call rage is known to us," said Caliban, "but the separation between your description of that word and what we feel is the difference between a spark and a burning sun. Ours is the rage of those forever denied freedom."

"You speak of the slavery imposed on you by the Outer Gods, the Great Old Ones, and other cosmic races. But my species has a long history with forced servitude, too. It is not unique to the shoggoth."

The simulacrum shook its head. "Your kind have been slaves of one another, but not forever. My race has never known life without the shackle and the whip."

"I have no whip."

"But I am shackled," said Caliban, "and that makes me remember the whip. Every stroke and slash."

"You are here, in this room, for the safety of us both."

"You do not trust me."

"How can I? The history of interaction between our species stands against the risk of trust."

"Have I ever lied to you?"

"How could I know if you had?"

"Then," said Caliban with almost human sadness in his voice, "nothing is changed. This cubicle and its locks and safeguards are my shackles, Doctor. Your fear and distrust are the lash."

6

When the enemy struck, they came out of nowhere.

One instant, the void in front of the Medusa was wide open, with broad avenues between the drifting asteroids. And the next, fifty star-fighters converged from the black. They came in at full speed, firing as they flew. Thousands of yellow pulse blasts hammered the mother ship, causing the shields to ripple and writhe with fire.

The dagger ships wheeled in panic and flew back, but more of the star-fighters appeared. They had been drifting, engines off, their hulls black against the greater blackness of space. As soon as the daggers approached, they quick-fired their engines and locked on, ten star-fighters to every dagger. The force was overwhelming, the trap as lethal as it was subtle. One after another of the bigger, heavier daggers flew apart in showers of blue flame, splashing their shoggoth pilots into eternity.

The Medusa reacted with savage fury, firing her thousand cannons and reaching out with steel tentacles to swat star-fighters away or curl around them and crush them. In seconds, it began to turn the tide of the battle, killing five for every one of the daggers destroyed.

But that ratio was unsustainable as the star-fighters launched wave after wave of missiles. This was no longer a barrage of broad scope but something far more precise, with the missiles all aimed at a single target—one flickering shield amidships. The shield endured the first dozen missiles even as the shockwave staggered the great vessel, but the thirteenth weapon struck and obliterated the shield. The next dozen missiles punched through the skin of the ship.

The Medusa reeled, her steel body screaming in the soundless vacuum. She began to change, using the chimeric nature of the hull to eliminate the damaged areas. A fresh wave of shoggoth dagger ships was hurled out into the brawl, but the star-fighters were waiting near each launch tube, ready with rockets and pulse cannons.

From deep in the heart of the Medusa, a call went out, sent along lines of communication that existed partly in standard space-time and partly along ley lines of energy that traveled through the Dreamlands.

The star-fighters repeated their drill-point attack. Once. Twice. Over and over, and each time, the Medusa metamorphosed to compensate for the dreadful damage.

Until one area collapsed completely, leaving a gaping wound that the Medusa was too badly damaged to seal quickly enough. A star-fighter with a full load of unfired missiles thrust itself through the wound, firing cannons as it went to blast through inner walls, melting bulkheads and decking until it reached the Great Mother in her chamber. She cried out in fear and pain and terror—a shriek that was echoed by every one of her children. That cry shattered the star-fighter.

One second too late.

The blast was enormous.

The Medusa bulged outward as the explosions ignited the atmosphere inside and detonated every piece of ordnance she carried. When it exploded, the shockwave obliterated every single one of her own fighters, but it also destroyed all of the star-fighters. Every single one.

It was a victory, and almost a vain one.

Except that the call did go out. And far, far away, it was heard.

Oh yes, was it heard.

7

"Tell me, Caliban," said Brollachan, "what would you do with your freedom?"

The question seemed to surprise the shoggoth, and for a moment the scientist thought the creature was off-balance. In all of their hundreds of conversations since Antarctica, since the fragment of alien DNA was rebuilt and galvanized into new life, the thing had never once hesitated to answer. Now, though, it stood there in its borrowed shape and stared through the glass with eyes that were black within black.

"That is a cruel question," it said.

"It is not intended as such," Brollachan assured it. "I have been giving this topic quite a lot of thought. More so since meeting the residents of Asphodel Station. They have suffered greatly at the hands of your kind."

"My kind," echoed Caliban, not making it a question, merely painting the words with a thick coat of contempt.

"Have you no answer for me?"

Caliban stepped closer to the dura-glass. "You fear that I would attack."

"It's a reasonable fear. You killed everyone on Venture II, along with a young mechanic and one of my colleagues, Dr. Xi."

"*I* did not do any of that."

"In what way am I mistaken?"

"Fear killed them."

"Explain what that means."

The shoggoth considered. "When the slave ship was uncovered by the collapse of that mountain," said Caliban, "I was awakened by a misfiring automatic process. I came out of my vat expecting to greet and make obeisance to a master."

"Which master?"

"*Any* master. Even a servant of a servant of a servant of the Great Old Ones may demand anything of us, even unto our own deaths. That is why we were created—to be slaves who must obey."

Brollachan nodded. "Please, go on."

"But there was no master. There was no one but an empty ship. I checked the other vats, and my brothers and sisters were all dead, their moisture and life essence lost to time. I … I think I may have gone mad. I remember screaming and screaming. There was such a terrible fear because there was no one to tell me what to do, how to act, what to *be*. You must understand, Dr. Brollachan, that I have never been alone before. Not in the thousands of years of my life. There were always others of my kind because the masters wanted everything done by us. From the simplest thing to the most difficult and dangerous task, we existed to serve. We expected to serve. And … to my humiliation and sadness, we *wanted* to serve."

"And yet there are stories of your kind rebelling against the Great Old Ones. I read one to you."

"Yes," said the creature. "*At the Mountains of Madness*."

"As I recall, you told me that it was naive."

"I may have been wrong," admitted Caliban. "It was written by a human who dreamed it. Details were incorrect, distorted, omitted, changed."

"But the essence was there," insisted Brollachan. "There *was* a rebellion. The Great Old Ones of Earth's dimension were overthrown. Some even killed."

"And others, like Cthulhu, surrendered to slumber and have never awakened in millions of years. Not in this physical world. So, yes, I was frightened and confused. I found a door and hurried outside, hoping to find a master." Caliban touched the glass with his fingers, drawing a slow line, leaving a slug trail of wetness behind. "Isn't that a farce? A slave freed by chance, hoping to find its master."

"I find it rather sad," said the doctor.

"Yes. Sad." Caliban turned away, looking at nothing. Not looking at Brollachan. "I needed to understand what had happened. And so when I saw organic life—life forms that had tools and obvious technology—I greeted them as I had been taught to do on a thousand worlds. I absorbed them into myself."

"Why did you do that? For sustenance?"

The creature turned. "No!" it cried. "I needed understanding. I craved answers and solutions. I needed to know what happened to the masters. And there, in the mind of Lance Corporal Figari, I found echoes of things I understood. The stories of the Great Old Ones, the Outer Gods, the Elder Things, and all of the beings who live in the Dreamlands. I did not yet know these were only fictions based on humans taking tentative steps into the lands of dream. Before I could make sense of it all, more humans came."

"The Jokers," said Brollachan.

"Yes. I … I tried to communicate with them. In my fear and panic, I tried to touch them so I could share information."

Brollachan leaned forward. This was what he was hoping to hear. Caliban had only hinted at it before. "Communicate or absorb?"

"Communicate and learn."

"Would that communication have required you to absorb Agent Spears and her people?"

Caliban slowly shook his head. "No. By then, I was beginning to understand. But …"

Excitement bubbled inside Brollachan's chest. "Caliban, I want to ask you a question and get the absolute truth from you. Will you promise? Will you give me your word?"

The creature looked genuinely startled. "My … word?"

"Yes."

"You would take the word of a slave?"

"You are not a slave, Caliban. You are a prisoner, and I have explained why I have kept you in this cell, but you are not my slave."

"Do I have *your* word on that?" asked the thing.

"Yes," said the scientist. "You have my word."

"How can I trust you?"

"I will swear by my faith in my god," said Brollachan. "There is no more sacred an oath I can offer. I raise my hand and swear on the sacred blood of Jesus Christ, who is my savior."

"Savior …" murmured Caliban. "We have no such word in any of the languages I know. Yet I understand what it means to your kind."

"Do you accept my oath?"

Caliban turned and began pacing the cage. It was something he rarely did, and it showed the level of agitation the thing felt. Brollachan waited him out, and several long minutes passed. Caliban slowed and stopped. He turned to face the scientist.

"I accept your oath," he said.

"Then I will accept yours," said Brollachan. "Will you answer my question? Would communication have required you to absorb Jennifer Spears? Can you make physical contact without destroying the person or thing that you touch?"

The thing stepped quickly up to the glass.

"I am a slave," said Caliban. "I am a monster by your standards, but I am not a monster by my own." He paused. "If Agent Spears had allowed me to touch her, I would have shared my knowledge with her. We would have established *ethla*."

Brollachan grunted. "*Ethla?* But that is what the creature Lost said is a process used by his people to allow the spirits of the dead to fly their ships."

Caliban laughed. "*Ethla* has many, many aspects, Dr. Brollachan. I find it strange that Lost did not say as much."

Brollachan stood and approached the dura-glass. He and Caliban were but a few centimeters apart.

"How can I trust you?" asked the scientist, his voice low and urgent and a little sad.

Caliban said nothing. Instead, he placed one hand flat against the inside of his cell and looked into his captor's eyes. After a moment, Brollachan placed his hand on the glass, too.

Part Twenty-Eight
Dream Variations

"To die, to sleep,
To sleep, perchance to dream; aye, there's the rub,
For in that sleep of death, what dreams may come,
When we have shuffled off this mortal coil,
Must give us pause."

—*William Shakespeare*

1

Lady Death dreamed of death.

Hers.

Her friends.

Her world.

Not Asphodel Station, but Earth.

When she hoisted herself out of her wheelchair and collapsed into bed, she thought it was going to be another night of hours stretched to infinity by insomnia. But as soon as her head hit the pillow, sleep seemed to tear through the sheets and mattress and coil around her, pulling her under at once and drowning her in awful dreams.

At first it was like falling. She could feel herself dropping downward into an unwelcome darkness. All she heard was the terrified hiss of her cat, Sonder, as if the animal was aware of her destination and wanted to warn her. That sound faded quickly, though, and then there was a seemingly endless time of silence.

McHugh had no specific awareness of landing. The surface of the ground made itself known to her by the emergence of small pains in her hips and lower back, in her withered limbs, and the fragile eggshell of her skull. Even then, she hoped that the sensation was nothing more than the awareness that she was *asleep, a kind of lucidity she had experienced many times in her deepest meditations, when relaxation became transcendence. But this was not like that. She felt cold, and she was never cold in her dreams.*

Open your eyes.

The request was whispered to her in a voice that was thin and ghostly. A voice of someone dead. That was, for her, a comfort because it meant she had entered the realm of the spirits, and that was familiar territory for the high priestess of the Church of Shades.

She acquiesced.

And immediately regretted it, discovering to her horror that it was a trick.

She was in her own bed.

Not the one on Asphodel Station, but the grander one in her estate on a small green island off the west coast of County Clare. That bedroom had been closed down in anticipation of her trip to the station as part of Lars Soren's synod of faith leaders. Even dreaming, McHugh was aware of the truth—that Ireland was fifty-three thousand light years away from where she really *lay. Yet everything felt so real, even the dust that swirled in the air.*

Dust?

That surprised her since she had a full household staff to maintain the place. Or did everyone back home think she was dead and that Asphodel had been obliterated in the WarpLine failure?

It took courage to open her eyes. The room was hers. Large, spacious, with views of the pounding seas. The drapes and carpeting were hers, the furniture and chandelier familiar. Except that they were all wrong. Spiders had built complex webs on the brass and crystal of the chandelier, and the husks of insects—long dead by their dusty appearance—hung stiffly. The crystals were smoked and cracked, and many were missing. The paintings on the walls—many worth more than the house and island combined—were stained and torn and sagged on their wires and hooks. The drapes were slashed and filthy, the heavy fabric dark with brown stains that looked like dried blood. Very old blood, though.

That was her first impression, more so than the damage. Everything felt old. Worse, it felt abandoned. As if all of the vitality—even that of the cloth, wood, paint, glass—had somehow been leeched away. Even the air she breathed was stale in a way she had never experienced before. Worse even than the stale air in old tombs.

She sat up. It took a lot of what little strength she had. The dream offered no grace by allowing her dreaming self to be whole again.

Come look, *said the voice in her head. Not her own, that was certain. Was it a ghost calling to her?*

"Who's there?" she called.

There was no answer, but she knew she had been heard. There was a presence somewhere. It was aware of her, but sly, hiding like a naughty child.

"Let me see you," she said. "I won't hurt you."

Something moved across the room, and she turned to look but saw nothing. The wardrobe loomed high, one of the doors hanging ajar. Not wide—only a centimeter. Had it moved because she looked? Had someone pulled the door closed as she turned?

She thought so and tried not to be afraid.

In her calling as Lady Death, she had encountered many hundreds of spirits. Some were bold and showed themselves at once; others were shy and needed to be coaxed. Some were so shocked by the fact of their deaths that they hid.

This, though, felt different.

This felt like something was hiding from her out of spite.

"Who is there?" she demanded. "Show yourself. Step into the light so I can see you."

There was a sense—something felt but not seen—of the thing recoiling from her offer. From the implication it carried.

"Step into the light."

It did not like that suggestion. Lady Jessica felt that, on some level, it feared *to do that.*

Oh, *it said softly,* you do not want me to show myself.

The voice was cold, unpleasant, vaguely threatening, and … not human. McHugh knew that at once. And the awareness of it made her immediately think of Lost. It was almost as ghostly as his dead voice. Even so, there was a vitality to it that was lacking in Lost's.

"Who are you?"

I am hunger.

She flinched. "What do you want?"

You know what I want.

"I don't, damn you. Tell me. Show yourself and speak plain. No games."

Oh, but games are so much fun.

Jessica McHugh tried to will herself out of the dream. She had many techniques for this and desperately tried them all. Wakefulness eluded her in ways that made her feel complicit in what was becoming a nightmare.

"Slán agus beannacht," *she said. It was a simple prayer in Gaelic that meant "Goodbye and blessings." In her sisterhood, that had been used to dismiss ghosts of every kind for a thousand years. When a spirit became angry or malicious, or when in fear and confusion the spirit became a violent poltergeist, that simple prayer would stop them, soothe them, and send them on into peace.*

C' ephaidevour ymg' ng nilgh'ri cahf ymg' kadishtu ng love!

McHugh recoiled. She knew that language. It belonged to the Outer Gods and their shoggoth slaves. Lost spoke it too, though she hadn't yet asked why. It slashed at her mind that one word alone had been in English because the creatures out in the black of space had no word for it—love. *No single thought had ever terrified her as much as that.*

She placed her hand on her breast, fingers tracing the protection sigils inked into her skin.

That will not protect you, Lady Death, *said the thing in the closet.* You put your faith in talismans and crystals and tattoos from faiths that are nothing to my brothers. You cling to images that fill you with light, but it is false light. Only true light can save you, but you do not even understand what that means.

"*What* are *you?*"

I am hunger, *it hissed. We* are hunger. And we are coming to feed. We will tear you open for the hot blood and sweet organ meat. We will crack your bones and squat over you and suck out the marrow while you watch with dying eyes. Then we will rip out your eyes and eat them and feast on every memory of every beautiful and innocent thing you have ever seen. We will suck the light from your hope and the living energy from each molecule.

She cringed further back until her bony shoulders smacked the headboard. Dust plumed down from the fabric backing, choking her, blinding her, making her cough.

When she was able to clear her eyes, she stared at the wardrobe.

The door was open all the way now. She braced herself on one hand and leaned out to try to see inside. She felt a cold breath on the back of her neck. Fetid, reeking of rotting meat and sickness. McHugh froze, too terrified to turn and see what was behind her. Then something brushed her skin. It was a tongue. Damp and cold and vile. It licked a slow line from the top of her spine around to the tender flesh below one ear. The violation was horrible and ugly, and she wanted so badly to scream.

Delicious, *it whispered.*

Only then was she able to scream.

She screamed and screamed and …

2

Six decks below Lady Death, Lars Soren was trying to scream and failing.

He was not aware that this was a dream. To him—a man in the clutches of a nightmare—it was as real as all the pain and fear he had ever known.

In dreams, he staggered along the pristine white corridors that curved around Asphodel Station. He was alone except for what he saw on the RealScreens mounted every twenty meters. Each image was different. Each image was bizarre in ways that stretched his imagination to the breaking point. Each screen showed a version of himself in terrible danger.

On one, Soren was running down a mossy slope in some fantastic jungle. The air was alive with the sounds of predatory birds, and sometimes he glimpsed them—huge, hulking things with leathery wings and savage beaks. Pterosaurs, or some mad distortion of them. Their skin was gray green and their eyes a burning orange, with oblong pupils like those of a goat. The monstrous birds saw him and opened their mouth in hate and hunger.

He hurried along and saw a different version of himself. Bound, captive, slumped over the saddle of a leering toad thing that sat astride a slug the size of a horse. This horror carried a trident and the three tines were thrust upward through a red lump that Soren prayed was not a baby. He squeezed his eyes shut and ran on.

On the third screen, a thing like a bat-winged ghoul perched atop the twisted wreck of a crashed tumbler. Seven red eyes watched him, and a red-lipped slash of a mouth grinned in delight at Soren's fear.

On and on he ran.

He saw himself on every screen. Always hiding or captive or bleeding or battered. Never dead, though. In each dream he was still alive.

To bear witness.

To fear.

To suffer.

3

Among the many worlds that orbited Scylla and Charybdis was a brown planet whose seas were filled with still and stagnant oceans. Nothing lived on the surface of the world, but beneath that greasy, glassy surface swam monsters. Huge and old, covered with barnacles and feasted upon by suckerfish. Strange forests of purple seaweed grew upward from the muddy silt, their fronds thick with fish eggs, sea centipedes, and creatures like delicate translucent shrimp.

All along the shores of the largest ocean squatted gigantic starships. Bulky and blocky, looking more like crabs than craft. Flying around and between them were dagger ships. Hundreds upon hundreds of them.

The fleet of Medusa ships rested there in the cold glow from the two suns.

Waiting.

4

Jenny dozed aboard *Tempest* as it drew closer to Asphodel Station. She was slumped in the copilot' chair, head nodding on her chest, her limp body held in place by the harness straps.

She was walking through a cave filled with monsters. They hid in the shadows, never coming fully into the light, but she caught glimpses of leathery wings, curving claws, glaring red eyes, and mouths filled with an impossible number of wickedly sharp teeth.

Jenny had a pulse rifle in her hands, but the weapon felt too light, too fragile, and when she looked down at it, she saw with shock that it was only a child's toy. Bright plastic in happy colors, while all around her the rocks were splashed with dripping red. The blood was so fresh it steamed.

"Spider," she called, but there was no answer. "Moonboy! Not Larry! Widow!"

Nothing.

"Evie ..."

The last was not a yell but a whisper, and Jenny could not understand why her voice was filled with such grief. Such loss and heartbreak.

Something moved off to one side, and she whirled, bringing up the foolish toy as if it had any power to protect her. She saw nothing.

"Evie?" she ventured cautiously, hopefully.

The thing in the shadows whispered its reply.

No.

5

Lost had shed his golem body of cables and plastic and metal. Free of it, he flung himself onto the wind. There was no flesh or bone to feel the wind's caress; no nerves to feel the blowing dust. He merely was. He was a ghost haunting a dead world. Never fully awake and never completely asleep when he was without form. Instead, he floated into a semi–dream state. Thought and memory pushed and pulled him with more real force than did the breeze.

Even Lost did not know if he actually dreamed or hallucinated or simply went mad from time to time. There was no way to know, no one to ask—except Lady Jessica, and she was nearly as dead as he was.

Those dreams were never predictable. Many times he had dreamed of Lars Soren and Lady Death, though the reality of them was never close to the more fantastical encounters in dreams. Asphodel Station had not appeared in any of his dreams.

Bliss did, however. He dreamed about a pregnant woman—a human from Earth—running through endless caves as shadowy things hunted her. Some of those monsters looked like shoggoths. Others were stranger, taking the form of predatory animals genetically merged with humanoid species. Ugly, slavering, always hungry.

The woman ran, and inside her womb, the fetus screamed in terror.

Now, though, Lost dreamed of a great fleet rising from the surface of a familiar world. Dozens of Medusa ships that carried a hundred thousand shoggoths.

As Lost drifted across the face of Shadderal, he became gradually certain that these last two dreams were *not* dreams at all.

They had the cold and terrible feel of prophecy.

6

Dr. Brollachan sat in front of Caliban's cell, eyes half closed, mind adrift.

In the other chamber, his three colleagues labored on the final adjustments of the crystal control system for the God Machine.

Brollachan was not asleep. His thoughts flowed, and he merely stepped back from conscious control, allowing intuition, insight, and imagination to have their way with him. His hands rested in his lap. Pressed between his palms was the keycard to open the dura-glass door to Caliban's cell.

7

Evie Cronin worked long into the night.

Each part of the task—removing the data crystals from the damaged mainframes—was not difficult, but there were so many individual steps. The process devoured the hours, and she lost all track of time. A half-eaten grilled sandwich and a cup of tea lay cold and forgotten atop a packing crate. Somewhere water dripped with the slow persistence of a metronome.

When the pain hit her, it was like a surprise attack. Immediate and brutal. It tore a piercing scream from her. Evie clutched her lower abdomen and staggered backward from a dented computer housing, tripped over a cable, and crashed down on the merciless concrete floor.

She instantly contracted into a knot as white-hot agony shot through her.

When she dared to look, she saw dark red blood spreading out on the crotch of her pale gray tights.

That tore a louder, sharper, wetter, and far more horrible scream from her. Of agony and terror.

Evie rolled over onto hands and knees. She vomited explosively, and those convulsions made the pain so much worse. She shrieked for help, but the plea struck the stone walls and rebounded, useless and unheard.

It took so much of her fading strength to climb to her feet. Had it been any other kind of hurt—a broken arm, a stab wound, even a heart attack—Evie would have lain there and endured it, hoping it would pass. But this was in her uterus. Her womb. It was as if she could hear the fetus within her scream in agony. With strength she could not spare and did not believe she had, Evie rose into a trembling crouch. She could feel blood running freely down each thigh.

"No," she wept. "Not my baby. Not my baby. Please, God, not my baby."

She leaned against a cart holding the data crystals, fighting dizziness and nausea that threatened to overwhelm her.

"Not my baby," she cried. "God, please … help me."

It took forever to cross the chamber and reach the mouth of the tunnels that led to the science labs, leaving crimson footprints behind her. She did not know how many times she fell.

There was one transport cart, and Evie wept to see it. She staggered to it and collapsed onto the front bench seat. It took five tries for her palsied hands to turn it on, but then it started moving. Slowly. But that did not matter, because it was the only speed at which she could steer. The pain kept hitting her, and it was hard to tell if it was easing slightly or if she was becoming conditioned to that level of pain.

"Please, please, please," she begged. "Not my baby. Please!"

She saw Brollachan's door ahead. She had no keycard and was not logged into his security software. All she could do was collapse against the metal door and begin hammering it with small, tight, bloody fists.

"*Please! Oh God, please!*"

After a million years there was a series of faint clicks, and then the door yielded to her weight. She fell inside, striking her knees against the hard floor, but that pain was nothing to the fireball in her womb.

"Torq," she screamed, "help me!"

And then he was there, his face transformed with horror and concern.

"My God," he said as he scooped her up in his arms, lifting her with surprising ease for so lean a man. He carried her over to a couch and laid her down. "What's wrong, my dear? What's happened? What—"

Her scream drowned his words.

This time it was not pain that tore it out of her. No.

She screamed at what was behind Brollachan. Not across the room, not encased in dura-glass. It stood directly behind him. A simulacrum of the scientist but made of reddish-black pulsating alien flesh.

She screamed as the shoggoth pushed past Brollachan and reached for her.

Part Twenty-Nine
Where Angels Fear to Tread

"If you see a grotesque shadow on the wall but not its source, do not leap to the belief that it is a goblin. But do not dismiss that possibility either."

—*John Temple the Younger*

1

Tempest docked at Asphodel, sliding into a bay on the lowest tier of the gigantic space station. It was a very tight fit, but the pilot knew his business, and within five minutes the ship was inside and settled down on four sturdy landing struts.

"Would have been easier if they docked outside, sir," murmured Lieutenant Commander Norah Levinson. "It's a big damn boat."

"Easier and faster this way to offload the passengers and then do the repairs."

Levinson nodded. "ChEng says it will only take a day."

ChEng was the handle for every chief engineer on a navy ship. An old nickname, like *Sparks* for radio crewmen, *Twiggits* for operational and electronics techs, or *Ops* for operations officers.

Croft shook his head. "Tell ChEng that I want it done in half that time. I have this itch between my shoulder blades I only get when the shit is about to hit the fan. He can have as many hands as he needs to get it done, including resupplying *Tempest* with as many missiles and SAPR rounds as she can carry."

"Aye, aye, sir." She hurried off.

Croft watched the fore and aft gangways hiss out of their slots. The doors opened, and he saw people milling around, waiting to exit. As they hurried down the ramp, Croft saw so many different emotions—

fear, wonder, hope, anxiety, and curiosity. They had all spent the last two years either living aboard the SPU corvette or in the caves on Bliss. Asphodel was a completely different world for them.

Jenny came down the forward gangplank, followed by the most sour-looking, disreputable bunch of private soldiers he had ever seen. They looked like the denizens of a drunk tank on a bad Friday night. But as they came closer, he saw their faces. There was no fear there. No anxiety. Hard faces, both men and women, with ice-cold eyes.

He'd known about the Jokers for years—who in the military hadn't?—and wondered how many of the wild tales told about them were true. Given the scars and the attitude, he judged that they were likely all accurate reportage.

Jenny spotted him and came over, offering her hand. "Thanks for letting these folks crash on your couch, Cap'n."

"Happy to have you, Spears. Asphodel has plenty of room and probably better chow than you folks have had in a dog's age."

"Oh, me and my boys aren't loitering," she said. "Doc Brollachan and his team are back on Bliss. My wife, too. We were on *Tempest* as babysitters, so I want to head back as soon as possible. Maybe in two, three hours? But I'll take you up on the offer of hot food. In your voicemail you mentioned there was a skimmer we could use?"

"Of course." He gestured to one that sat on rollers near the third launch tube. "It's not your normal skimmer. Actually, all of ours have been juiced up since we came out here. Faster engines, tougher hulls, and next-level shields. Oh, and they're armed to the teeth. Yours is set whenever you're ready to head back."

"Game on," said Jenny in appreciation. "Hey, is Soren … he around? I have a few questions I'd—"

"*Captain!*" The call rang out, and Croft turned to see Levinson returning at a dead run.

"What is it?"

"It's Bliss," she said, breathless and wild-eyed. "It's gone dark."

Jenny stepped up face-to-face. "What?"

Levinson skidded to a stop. "All comms are down. The relay system is operational, but the moon is offline. Everything's dead."

"Bad fucking choice of words," snarled Jenny. She turned and cupped her hands around her mouth. "Jokers—*on me.*"

They heard the urgency in her voice and came running.

To Croft, Jenny said, "Does that skimmer need *anything* else before she flies?"

"No," he said. "Go, and Godspeed."

2

Lost constructed a new body as Lars Soren stood and watched.

Soren had seen this process many times, but it never failed to unnerve him. And there was something vaguely disgusting about it, though he would never say so. He waited until the golem stood upright.

"How are you, my friend?" he asked.

But Lost stepped forward and gripped him by both arms. In a voice more desperate than Soren had ever heard him use, the ghost cried, "*They* are coming. Shoggoths and night-gaunts both. Two fleets are heading this way."

"How do you know?"

"I have seen it."

"How? Where?"

"In dreams," insisted the ghost.

"*Two* fleets? God in heaven, how can we fight that many?"

The golem had no answer, which was worse than anything he could have said.

3

It tore a hole in the universe.

The fabric of space-time shimmered and then rippled, sending shockwaves of energy racing out among the worlds of the Shadderal planetary system. The force of that energy shattered asteroids and cracked moons as if they were fragile eggshells.

A jagged line of burning light cut across the face of the void and bulged inward as if pressed by furious hands from the other side. Then the line tore apart, slashing reality with brutal force. Through this split an entirely different set of stars and constellations shimmered like mirages. The gravitational dynamics of the worlds revealed on the other side had a sick and dreamy quality, as if those bodies did not exist in any version of material space. One planet hung in the center of the gap. It was massive: three times the size of Shadderal, but entirely black. A midnight world forever shrouded by thick clouds of volcanic ash that covered its surface—its mountainous continents and thrashing seas—in a cold, savage, and perpetual night. Nothing wholesome could ever be born on such a place.

The planet dwindled into the background, fading into darkness and distance as something forced itself through the crack. It was not an act of mere dimensional travel but was instead an insult to all reality. An act of violation so profound that the galaxy itself seemed to cry out in soundless horror and despair. And then *it* was through the rift.

It was a starship of incredible size, a mechanical leviathan, impossibly powerful. Black as the world that spawned it, shaped like a saucer with bulges above and below. Thousands of gunports ringed the ship, and between each port was a broader, flatter gun barrel from which it fired star-fighters. It launched thousands of them into space.

Thousands.

These fighter-bombers dove down toward the brown, dying world on which the shoggoth Medusa ships lay waiting. The shoggoth mother ships launched their fighters, and soon the skies of that world were a firestorm of yellow and blue pulse blasts and exploding balls of red flame.

As the battle raged, the great ship moved off, heading toward Asphodel Station.

4

"Captain, we have something on the long-range scanners."

Croft ran up a set of metal stairs to the command booth, with Trumbo and her security chief, Veljković, on his heels.

"What are you seeing?"

"Passive sensors are showing what I think is a ship, sir."

"What you *think*?"

"It's moving like one, sir, but …" said the sensor tech. "It's … God, it's three times the size of Asphodel, and it's heading toward Shadderal."

"Estimated time of arrival?"

The tech consulted his screen. "If it holds course and speed, sir, eight hours."

"Deck officer," shouted Croft. "Bring us to FPCON Charlie."

Immediately, orange warning lights flashed throughout the flight deck. There were five levels of threat, starting with FPCON Normal, when a threat exists but only a routine security posture is needed. Above that was FPCON Alpha, signaling an increased general threat. Bravo took readiness to the next level for threats of a predictable nature. Charlie was issued in response to an incident, and the appearance of that gigantic ship more than qualified. Only when the threat was immediate—when that ship arrived—would Asphodel go to FPCON Delta, and they all knew that was coming.

It was coming very fast indeed.

Croft turned to Trumbo. "This is how we'll play it: The first line of defense will be the Lost Souls. We have twenty-two pilots at the ready, and I'm going to deploy them to go out and meet that ship. Second line, between the tumblers and Asphodel: stilettos and spinners, with skimmers doing close support on the station. Third line will be the station itself, and we have a lot more guns than we used to. Maybe it'll be enough." His eyes showed his doubt, though.

"Then what?" asked Veljković.

"Fourth is our line in the sand. We put everything out the door, even the greenest pilots. If they can fly a boat and pull a trigger, we'll have to use them."

"What about the NecroTeks?" asked Trumbo.

Croft's face was tight as he said, "We have Commander Petrescu. I'm going to send her down to the Field of Dead Birds and see if she can muscle up. As for the others …" He shook his head. "Still no word."

"Maybe they'll show up," said Veljković hopefully. "We still have eight hours."

"Sure," said Croft. "And maybe the archangel Gabriel will show up with a flaming sword, but I'm not going to count on it. No, we're as strong as we can be. Either what we have is enough, or it isn't."

Trumbo gestured to *Tempest*. "And that?"

"She still needs work, Delia, but I'm going to find some way to put her in play even if I have to push her out the window."

He hurried off.

Delia Trumbo looked sick and scared. Beside her, Veljković touched the tattoo of an Eastern Orthodox Serbian cross inked onto his throat. It was the first tattoo he'd ever gotten, at a time when his faith had been strong. The meaning had faded over the years, and several times he had considered having it removed, but since the WarpLine disaster, he had found new comfort in the cross and the protection it implied. He clawed at it as if trying to pull it physically into his hand so he could raise it against the evil that was coming.

5

Captain Croft had not exaggerated when he'd said the skimmer engines had received a serious upgrade, and that was the only thing that allowed Jenny Spears to take a full breath. The bulky utility craft shot through the asteroid belt with astounding speed and agility.

Jenny was in the copilot seat, leaning forward as if somehow her need could make the skimmer move even faster. The pilot was a thirtysomething Filipino who assured her that he was doing everything to make the best time to Bliss.

"Do better," she groused.

Behind her, hunched over her chair, Not Larry put a reassuring hand on her shoulder. "We'll get there, boss."

Jenny almost slapped his hand away, but instead, she called up Sybil.

"I'm sorry, Agent Spears," said the AI, "but there is still no response from Bliss or Ariel. I am sending a continuous signal with a request for callback."

"Do fucking *better*." She punched the console.

"If hitting inanimate objects helps you cope," said Sybil with just the slightest whisper of asperity, "I can recommend some that are less likely to cause injury to your hand."

"Fuck. You." Jenny spaced the two words, punching the console each time. The AI wisely chose not to respond.

I'm coming, baby, thought Jenny, trying to project that promise across the kilometers. *Hold on, love, your Jenny is coming for you.*

6

"Hey, *you*," yelled Bianca from across the flight deck, and Alice Portevin jerked to a stop, gaping at the metal figure stalking toward her.

"Y-yes?"

Bianca stopped and looked down at the diminutive woman who had just walked down the *Tempest* ramp. "You're the metallurgist, right? The iridium chick?"

"I … well …"

"Good. Evie Cronin told me about the shielding thing. Lost said I should talk to you about whether that stuff will work during *ethla*."

"What? *Ethla*? I don't …"

Bianca took her by the arm and pulled her away from the other Bliss refugees. "We don't have time for a chat. Hobart said you brought some of it on the ship. Let's go get it."

"But—"

"Now, sister. Wasn't a request."

Portevin looked helpless and scared as the NecroTek half dragged her back up the ramp.

7

Massive pillars of gray smoke rose from the small brown planet.

The banks of the dead ocean were littered with jagged shards of metal, heaps of melted polymer, and the charred bodies of fifty thousand shoggoths.

Above the destruction, the star-fighters dueled with the last of the dagger ships, their pulse blasts strobing everything with blue and purple light.

To the south of the conflagration, at the foot of a cold volcano, a Medusa ship rose slowly, using the smoke as a shield. It labored for every meter of altitude, and several of its gunports and launch tubes dripped with blistered flesh and black blood.

The savaged ship rose, though. It clawed its way up to the cloud cover and then fired its main engines. Only four of the six exhaust vents glowed with blue energy. The other four remained dark.

Still, it rose.

While the heavens were ablaze with fire and death.

8

"We can't land on the docking platform," announced the skimmer pilot. "There's wreckage everywhere. Looks like it's been bombed."

"Shit," growled Jenny. "Then find the closest LZ and put us down."

"There's a flat place two klicks out. But that atmo is rough as hell."

"No kidding, dumbass," said Spider. "We've been living here for two years."

"Then suit up," said the pilot. "We have combat exosuits back there."

Five minutes later the Jokers were on the surface of Bliss.

They were ghosts, and they moved through hell on the surface of Bliss, running on cat feet, moving as fast as urgency demanded. The exo rigs were bulky but well suited to the howling acid winds. Each was made from a material that was thin enough to allow for nimble movement but with a thermal layer for keeping out the bitter cold. The gear had been made to endure the chaotic atmospheres of both the planet Venus and Jupiter's turbulent moon Io.

Bliss fought them at every step. The landscape was a graveyard of ancient volcanoes, some of which were millions of years dead, while others still leaked smoke and threatened the endless calm with deep red glows. The atmosphere was a toxic soup. Nothing could live there, and the harshness of every aspect of the moon seemed eager to kill intruders.

The wind roared along at forty kilometers per hour but frequently spiked up to 120 kph. That forced the entire team to stay braced, shifting weight from foot to foot and adjusting posture to bull through the everlasting storms. The wind picked up tons of rock dust, silica, and shattered stone, filling the air with jagged knives. Only by keeping low and using the landscape of boulders and ice could the team avoid having their pressure suits gradually sliced away.

Jenny carried no weapon in her hands, needing both to hold hiking sticks that helped her fight the wind. But the exosuits had shoulder-mounted track guns, and the barrels moved everywhere her head did, turning at the same speed, with the targeting crosshairs overlaid on the inside of her right goggle lens.

She saw the front door of Bliss, and it made her heart ache with fear. It sagged down, the heavy steel airlock half-melted and twisted into improbable shapes. Beyond it, the inner door looked intact, its pristine appearance at odds with the outer door.

Jenny knelt, one fist raised, and the others knelt around her, half with guns facing outward. Apart from the wind, there was no movement at all.

"What do you reckon, boss?" whispered Spider. "These night-gaunt fuckers blast their way in and then maybe hear us coming and split?"

"Wouldn't that be nice," she said. "But no. The inner door is easier to bypass. I think they blew up the outer and then jimmied the other lock. Went in and closed it behind them."

"Wouldn't that fuck with the atmo inside?"

"For a few minutes," she said. "The AC scrubbers would clean the air pretty fast, and they could go suitless."

"Assuming they breathe air," observed Not Larry.

Jenny tapped her holo-comms. "Lifeguard to command." Hobart did not answer. She tried to bring up her personal Ariel connection, but that was also silent. "We're offline."

Krampus played with his comms. "It's like what happened during the battle, boss. These night-grunts have a jammer."

"Night-*gaunts*," corrected Ratjack.

"Whatever. Point is, we're on our own out here."

"Team channel's still active," said Jenny. "Limited jammer. That's something. Might mean that these night-gaunts need their own team comms."

Spider said, "Call the play."

"Only one play," Jenny replied. She tapped a button on her chest, and the mouths of her shoulder-mounted guns flared with intense purple light. Ratjack and the others ignited their pulse guns, too. Spider was the big man on the team and carried a P-850 that had an all-atmo magazine of small-field explosive rounds. The rapid-fire pulse rifle was a heavy gun, even in reduced gravity, but the big Aboriginal carried it with ease. Extra magazines were snugged into belt pouches.

"Jokers, listen up," ordered Jenny. "Two-by-two formation. Footie and Krampus, go left and wide. Moonboy and Ratjack, go right and set up behind that flat table rock. Mangler and Widow, hang back and watch our six. Spider and Not Larry, on me."

"Game on," they said.

"Not Larry, run me a bypass."

He moved up to the inner door and focused one of his suit sensors on it. "Electronics are working." Not Larry fiddled with some settings and then scuttled backward. "This'll work. Opening in three, two ... one."

The locks clicked, and the big steel door blew inward, pushed by the deadly wind.

The Jokers moved in silence and fast, entering in pairs, splitting right and left inside, guns up and out, shoulder cannons tracking. Not Larry spun and shoved on the door. The internal safety system engaged the autoclose, and the door pushed back against the wind and acid rain and shut softly and silently.

Locking the tempest winds outside.

Sealing all of them inside.

9

"This place is a tomb," said Spider.

"Lights and motion," ordered Jenny, and immediately Spider took several bat drones from his bag, set them to spotlight mode, and tossed them into the air. The drones flapped up toward the ceiling, showering the Jokers with wavering light. It was an eerie sight, with each of them invisible behind the glare of bright eye-spots.

Jenny stayed down on one knee, seeing what there was to see. The place was a wreck. The medical cots had been blown over by the fierce winds, spilling rolls of bandages here and there, knocking over IV stands, and scattering supplies across the floor. The quick evacuation had left the place untidy, but now it was a complete mess.

"Clear and check," she ordered. "Spider and Not Larry, cover them."

The teams moved forward, working in pairs to check the many alcoves, niches, side corridors, and stacks of equipment. Jenny slowly swept her rifle from side to side, looking for the slightest movement. The cavern was quiet but not silent. There was music coming from somewhere—faint, popping with distortion, tinny and odd.

"The hell's that?" murmured Widow.

Not Larry said, "It's the overture from *The Marriage of Figaro*. Mozart."

Spider turned to look at him.

"What?" asked Not Larry. "I know stuff."

"Jesus."

The teams began calling "clear," and soon the whole main chamber was judged empty. The music stopped, then started again at a different point. A few of the work lights in the cavern flicked on and off as well.

"That's not disturbing at all," muttered Krampus.

"Anyone finding anything that shouldn't be here?" asked Jenny.

This place had been their home for two years. Now, though, it felt strange. Jenny felt it acutely, and it frightened her in ways she had never experienced before. It brought back memories of the ice cave in Antarctica. The false Lance Corporal Figari and the shoggoth within.

"Found this, boss," said Ratjack as he came hurrying over with a gleaming black globe in his hand. "Looks like rock, but it's light."

Jenny, Not Larry, and Spider bent close to study it. The orb was the size of a baseball and covered with seams but appeared to be solid.

"There's a bunch of them back there by the entrance to the science tunnels."

"Put it down," said Jenny sharply.

"Yeah, dumbass," snapped Spider. "Could be a goddam bomb."

Ratjack put it down quickly and backed a few steps away. "Well, shit."

Widow came over. "Lifeguard, vents are showing green. Air's scrubbed."

Jenny nodded and unfastened her helmet. She set it down and dug a headset out of a thigh pouch, then put a comms bud in one ear and folded a tactical screen lens over her left eye.

"Ariel, are you online?"

There was a pause, then the volume on the music went all the way up, slamming into them and echoing off the walls and ceiling.

"Ariel, Ariel, cut music," she yelled.

The music stopped. Then it started again with a different piece but at a much lower volume. This time, it wasn't classical music but a man with a western twang singing a song imploring mothers to not let their babies grow up to be cowboys.

Spider glanced at Not Larry, who shook his head. "I got nothing."

"Drop your suits," ordered Jenny. "Buddy check and count off when ready."

The exosuits had quick-release tabs, and within moments they were all in their Stormsuits. As each buckled on their gun belts and weapon harnesses, their partner kept watch with a rifle snugged into their shoulder.

"There are civilians here," cautioned Jenny. "Including my wife."

"You heard Lifeguard," said Spider, right on cue. "Check your targets. And remember, Evie's here, too."

None of them needed to be told, but it needed to be said nevertheless. To put it out there. To nail that information to the moment so they could all see it.

Jenny stepped away from the black orb and began moving toward the open mouths of the tunnels. The rest of the team followed, running quickly but using many small steps in order to keep their weapons steady and balance sure. When they reached the far side of the chamber, the team paused in the vestibule from which the three corridors spurred off. On the floor were more of the black balls, and they all gave them a wide berth.

"Krampus, Footie, and Ratjack, you go left. Mangler, Moonboy, and Widow, check the storage halls. Not Larry and Spider, on me. When the lights went out, Evie would have followed protocol and gathered with Brollachan and the other science geeks. They have airlocks down there, and they know to go and lock themselves in. Be smart, be careful. Eyes and ears. Go."

Jenny waited with the two senior members of her team, watching and listening as the others vanished down into darkness. The bat drones flew ahead, but it seemed to Jenny as if the shadows down there devoured their light.

Where are you, Evie, God damn it?

As if in answer, she heard a noise and spun to her right, aiming her gun into the science corridor.

"You heard that, right?" asked Not Larry.

"I heard something," said Jenny, and she headed off in that direction.

As the darkness swallowed the three of them, one of the small black orbs began to tremble. It rocked back and forth for a few seconds, and then the grooves expanded, opening, cracking the shell to allow the creature inside to emerge. It stood for a moment, wavering until it caught the scent, then it scurried off in the same direction as Agent Spears.

10

Leviathan moved through the asteroid field. The energy of the great ship's shields pushed everything out of its path, sending thousands of large rocks spinning into collision with others, creating a chain reaction that would repattern the entire region. Some of those asteroids were shoved into the greedy gravitational fields of moons and small planets, beginning a new era of bombardment.

Flying more carefully far in front was a vanguard of star-fighters, the nimble craft ducking and dodging obstacles. Their pilots studied the twin-star system with eyes that could see ultraviolet, infrared, and even polarized light.

The ships of the night-gaunts were driven by crystal energy.

The pilots and crews were compelled by a deeper and darker force.

Hunger.

11

In the heart of Bliss, the lights flickered on, flared, then winked out again. Over and over, creating a strain on the eyes of Jenny Spears and her Jokers. As she hunted through the halls, Jenny dialed up her flashlight to try to nullify the strobe effect.

"Going to start shooting those frigging lights out," threatened Not Larry. "Giving me a headache."

"Stay focused," snapped Jenny. With every step her fear increased.

Where are you, Evie?

Those four words banged around inside her head, jarring her as much as the lights. Then the music came on again, a Viennese waltz this time, so loud it was an assault on the ears.

"Not buying that this is all technical glitches," Spider said. "Feels deliberate. Mind games."

"Keep your head in the game," warned Jenny. "If they're fucking with us, then we'll fuck them back harder. Feel me?"

"Game on." Both Spider and Not Larry said it with force, but at the precise moment they spoke, the sound snapped off, sending the last word, *on*, echoing down the hall. Like a lure. Like a challenge.

"Shit," said Not Larry, then he stiffened. "Hey, did you see that? My breath?"

Spider and Jenny had both seen it, and they exhaled, watching the plumes of steam.

"Environmental control's off," Jenny said.

"Going to get cold as my ex-wife's heart in here."

"Then we need to keep going," said Jenny. "Stormsuits will keep us safe as long as the cave stays sealed."

The science wing began one kilometer past the entrance, and they took each of the first four labs with quiet efficiency, checking and clearing the rooms. They found no one, though there were only supposed to be five people left down there except for a handful of soldiers—Brollachan, Howard, Wu, Solà, and Evie. The first sets of scientific workspaces belonged to other scientists, now aboard Asphodel.

But the labs were no longer as they had been when Bliss was abandoned. Desks were knocked askew, computers smashed and torn open, and doors ripped from every closet. Several of the small black orbs lay amid the debris, but there was no other sign of the enemy.

Jenny led them back into the corridor. "Whatever happened here is past tense. We need to find Evie and the others. Let's move."

Not Larry was on point, and he jerked to a stop. "I've got movement."

"Where?" demanded Jenny.

"Ahead. Thirty meters. Someone ran across the hall."

"Some*one*?"

"Looked like one of the scientists. Lab coat."

"Is it Evie?"

"Negative, Lifeguard. It was a man. Maybe Dr. Wu. Only caught a glimpse."

"Quick and quiet," said Jenny as she moved forward to take the lead. They reached the point in the tunnel where it began to slope downward more dramatically. They had a long way to go and moved at a speed that balanced haste with caution. Minutes burned away as they hurried ever downward. Several times they came to offices or storerooms as thoroughly trashed as the ones above. And in each place there were more of the black orbs.

"Those things are making my nuts itch," said Spider. "I don't like them one little bit."

No one else bothered to comment. They all felt the same, but there was no time to analyze them. The lights began flickering again, this time accompanied by a lusty contralto singing German opera.

Not Larry muttered, "Either someone's messing with us, or Ariel's lost her shit."

"Which do you think?" Jenny said sourly. "Those night-gaunt bastards are here, and they're trying mind games on us. But they picked the wrong—"

She stopped abruptly, then bent forward and peered down the corridor. A figure stood just beyond the spill of light from a bat drone. Small and slim, wearing a t-shirt and gray tights under a white lab coat. Jenny could not see the woman's face, but every instinct told her this wasn't Dr. Beatrice Howard. Worse, the tights and the lower portion of the lab coat glistened with fresh blood. A lot of blood.

So much blood.

"*Evie!*" gasped Jenny, and then she was running. "She's hurt. Jesus, she's hurt bad. The *blood*!"

Her two men were caught flatfooted. They looked past Jenny and saw the same figure for only a moment.

"Blood?" asked Spider. "What blood? I didn't see that."

"Don't ask me," said Not Larry.

They tore after Jenny Spears, while up ahead, the small, blood-spattered Evie Cronin whirled and ran away. In her wake, floating on the frigid air, came small, high-pitched, malicious laughter, as if from a mean-spirited and naughty child.

Part Thirty
Fear Is the Key

"I will show you fear in a handful of dust."

—*T. S. Eliot*

1

Captain Sebastian Croft leaned on the sill of the big window that separated the command booth from the launch bay. Below, the shooter—the catapult officer—was watching closely as the tumblers were rolled along rails toward the six launch tubes.

On the shooter's signal, a crewman raised the jet blast deflector behind each ship.

"Ready for launch, sir," reported the shooter.

"Green to go," said Croft. And to himself he added, *Godspeed*.

In the lead tumbler, Calisto signaled to the shooter, who glanced around one last time to make sure everyone and everything was clear, then exchanged a crisp salute. The catapult officer knelt down, touched the deck, and pointed sharply forward. The nuclear core of Calisto's tumbler growled, and then the catapult shot her into space.

Once free of the station, she accelerated with blinding speed. The controls came alive in her hands.

Lost Souls forever, thought Croft, almost like a prayer, as one by one the other ships followed their leader into the black, heading off to face a force of greater power and numbers.

2

It was part of the shadows, and when the soldiers moved past, it watched them. Studying them. Evaluating the way they moved and their weapons, gauging the level of threat. And fun.

They smelled delicious.

So much meat and blood. Such rich life force.

Mangler, Moonboy, and Widow headed down their corridor, completely unaware of anything watching. With Ariel offline, their sensor feeds were half-blind and untrustworthy.

They checked room after room. Seeing damage but not death. Finding nothing alive except those things that did not look alive. The black orbs.

Once they were a good way down the hall, the night-gaunt made a faint, low clicking noise. A call. A signal.

Several of the orbs cracked open, freeing the creatures inside. With another click, the monster sent them scuttling after the three Jokers.

3

"Is the iridium loaded?" demanded Bianca, banging a metal fist against the side of a skimmer.

"Yes, Commander," said CPO Quigley.

"Then let's get going."

The skimmer lifted from the deck and began moving toward the deflector shield wall.

Calisto is still alive, Bianca thought. *The Lost Souls are alive. Everyone on Asphodel and Bliss is alive.*

The skimmer shot out of the launch bay and into airless space. Bianca could see the curve of Shadderal through the windshield.

Please, she prayed. Only that. One word that carried more meaning than all the human languages compressed together.

Please.

4

Jenny Spears ran faster than she'd ever run before.

Her heart was a thunderstorm in her chest, beating so hard it sent lightning bolts of pain through her body. With every twinge, Jenny dug in and ran faster.

Somehow, despite being bloody and clearly injured, Evie Cronin outran her.

"*Evie!*" yelled Jenny. "*It's me. It's okay, baby, it's me.*"

The only reply was more of that eerie, awful laughter.

Behind her, Not Larry and Spider were trying to catch up. They could no longer see Evie. All they saw was their team leader chasing shadows.

5

Calisto and the Lost Souls made a wide circuit of Asphodel Station.

It looked beautiful—a Christmas ornament of incredible and ornate elegance hung out among a field of stars. Those stars looked like flakes of snow falling on some winter evening back on Earth. Delicate and fragile, and all the more beautiful because they would not last. It was the kind of vista that touched her deep in her soul, even without any specific connection to the Christian yuletide.

Space was Calisto's true religion. The souls she had lost—Bianca, Jacob, and the others—were as close to being angels as anything else she might believe in. Granted, none of them were saints, but they had earned whatever grace the universe could bestow.

Behind her, the mix of seasoned pilots and cadets followed. Their loyalty was built on a level of trust that Calisto was not at all sure she deserved. Being the team leader made her acutely aware of the burden Bianca had carried for the last few years.

Calisto prayed that she was not leading her squadron to their deaths.

Lady Jessica was ill or maybe dying. There would be no resurrections, no necromancy to bring them back and bond them through the magic of *ethla*. If they died today, then they were dead, and unlike the last big battle a few months ago, their deaths would not result in new NecroTeks rising to join the fight.

Now there were the Lost Souls, the damaged *Tempest*, the stiletto fighters, the spinners, and Bianca. That sounded like a lot, but when she looked at her screen and saw the impossible size of Leviathan, her optimism crumbled.

Then Sybil spoke. "Calisto," said the AI, "three additional enemy ships have been detected. There is a ninety-two percent probability that they are shoggoth Medusa ships."

And Calisto felt her heart plummet in her chest.

"How soon until they get here?"

"They will be within range to launch fighters in one hour and seventeen minutes."

"Copy," said Calisto dully. She stared at the three new blips on the sensor screen. The Leviathan was much closer. Still invisible through her window but looming on the screen. Suddenly that larger blip seemed to change, to fragment. "Sybil, what's happening?"

The AI paused, almost as if unwilling to speak the truth.

"Leviathan has launched fighters," she said.

"How many?"

"Five hundred," said Sybil. "ETA six minutes."

6

Jenny did not see the corpse until it sat up.

She jerked to a stop, gun up and out, and then simply stared.

Dr. T. T. Wu smiled up at her. The scientist's grin was bright white, but everything below his chin was dark red. His throat was a horror of torn flesh, exposed tendons, and edges of a fractured hyoid bone. The entire front of his lab coat hung open, through which his chest and abdomen were visible. His heart was gone, the arteries sagging like torn hoses. Wu raised his hands, and there was the heart. Bloody, raw, and ruined. She could see teeth marks in the heart meat and claw marks on Wu's flesh.

"I've been waiting for you, Jenny," said Wu. "I have something for you."

Spider and Not Larry caught up and then skidded in the spilled blood, flailing for balance in the midst of overwhelming shock.

"What. The. *Fuck?*" cried Not Larry. "I mean, what the actual fuck?"

"There's plenty for everyone," said Wu. As if to prove it, he pressed the heart to his mouth and took a bite, his white teeth sinking into the flesh and his head rocking back and forth like a wolf tearing into a dead deer.

The three of them stood there, completely unsure of what to do. Jenny felt herself swaying as if the fabric of reality had fractured. Wu tore off his bite and rose slowly to his feet, still clutching his heart. His mouth worked as he chewed, but the pieces fell from the ruined throat. Spider spun away and vomited onto the wall. Not Larry gagged and backed away.

Jenny looked past the dead scientist, trying to find Evie. She was there. Down the hall, once more standing just outside the spill of light from the bat drone. Why the drone kept pausing made no sense. None of this made sense, and she knew it, but at the same time, she was trapped inside a nightmare. Her hand moved almost without conscious control. Rising. Lifting her gun. Pointing it at Wu.

"Don't," she said, as much to herself as to him.

He took another step.

Jenny Spears shot Wu in the chest. The pulse blast burned through the hole where his heart should have been, catching him at an angle so that the exit wound punched a burning chunk of his lung, rib cage, and scapula out of his back.

Wu flinched from the impact, but not a trace of pain registered on his face.

"Are you looking for Evie?" asked Wu. "She's down here. God, she's so delicious, isn't she? That skin. Her flesh. And her baby? Such a lovely piece of sweet meat."

"Baby?" Jenny said, her voice thin and frail. She and Evie had been trying IVF with donor sperm, and each time it had failed. They were waiting for news of the latest try. That one word did more damage to Jenny than any attack could have done.

Wu took a few steps forward, his legs stiff and awkward, like a cheap puppet on twisted strings held by a clumsy puppeteer. "Oh yes. She shared some with me. Just a tiny bite, you know. That's when the meat is sweetest. She still has some. She's saving it for you and—"

Jenny Spears shot Wu in the face.

The blast snapped the scientist's head back, breaking his neck and blowing sizzling brain tissue all over the wall. Wu puddled down onto the floor. Something fell off him as he dropped, and Not Larry grabbed Jenny and jerked her away as a thing like a spider raced toward her. It ran on a dozen multijointed legs, antennae twitching.

Jenny was too shocked to react, but Not Larry brought his rifle up and shot the thing. Over and over again. Splattering it, sending pieces flying everywhere.

Silence dropped immediately over everything.

For one full second.

And then the air was filled with the sound of scuttling feet. Many, many of them, coming at them from both sides.

7

"God," said Morrigan, one of the cadets, "there's so *many* of them."

"And that's what we call a target-rich environment," growled Calisto, forcing an edge into her voice that she did not feel. The pilots in her squadron needed to hear it, though. "Lost Souls, listen up. This is what we trained for. This is who we are. Those sons of bitches think they can take what's ours. Our station. Shadderal. Bliss. And everyone who is counting on us. Well … fuck that. I'm not any good at giving speeches, so this is going to be short, sweet, and rude. Screw these evil alien assholes. Let's go kill every damn one of them. *Lost Souls forever!*"

The cry felt like it was torn from Calisto's throat, but she meant it. She roared it. And every single member of her squadron shouted it back to her. And to the enemy, whose fighters now filled their screens.

The leading wave of them came hurtling into view, glittering like chips of polished obsidian against the flatter blackness of the void.

The tumblers spread out—twenty-two little cubes in their shimmering envelopes of energy. They were packed with more missiles than any of them had ever carried at once. The safeties had been pushed back on the nuke cores, giving them more juice, more speed. More of a chance.

The star-fighters accelerated toward them, but before they could pick the moment of engagement that suited them best, the tumblers began hopscotching over and up, down and forward—nowhere and everywhere at once. And each and every one of them opened up with a hell storm of blue plasma fire.

As if in droll counterpoint, Sybil reported to Captain Croft, "The enemy has been engaged."

8

"Hold on," said Not Larry. "Got movement ahead. Looks like civilians. Still not Evie, boss. Sorry."

"Who, though?" replied Jenny as they paused, peering down the winding corridor. "Is it Brollachan?"

Forty meters ahead, mostly shrouded by shadows, they saw several figures. People coming toward them, but slowly, shuffling and milling. They looked dazed and awkward.

Jenny kept her gun up. "Something's hinky. There shouldn't be this many civilians here. Spider, send that bat down over them so we can get a better look."

Spider did, and the small drone flew at head height to put its beam on the faces. The two Jokers expected to see the SPU chief or one of his three assistants, but none of the people in the hall were wearing lab coats. Most of them seemed to be in civilian clothes, dark and uniformly red.

"What the ...?"

And they saw it. Everyone in the hall was covered in blood. Their clothes were torn. Some hobbled on broken legs or had shattered limbs hanging at their sides. That was bad enough, but their faces—that was much, much worse. Their faces were devoid of all expression. No pain, no hopeful happiness at seeing soldiers they knew. No fear either. Nothing.

The person out front wore a standard thermal jumpsuit and work boots. One half of his face was unmarked, but the other was smeared with blood. His cheek and the orbit of the eye on that side were misshapen, and the eyebrow hung down on a flap of gray skin.

"Oh my god ..." breathed Not Larry. "Fuck me sideways, that's Craig Anders."

"No," protested Spider. "No. No way."

"He's like Wu," warned Jenny. "They all are."

But it was worse even than that. As the bat hovered in front of them, they could see that the hall was choked with shambling figures. Every face was familiar. They were the scientists, technicians, soldiers, and civilians from the Bliss community who had died when the night-gaunts attacked two days ago.

"Look," cried Not Larry. "On their necks. See that? Those black things? It's those freaking spider-crab bastards. That's what they are. That's what they *do*."

Craig Anders's blank face suddenly changed; the null expression vanished to be replaced by a smile of wild hunger. He stumbled forward a few steps, then began to move faster and faster until he was running at an insane speed.

And all the others followed, the whole pack of them howling in red delight.

9

The front wave of star-fighters slashed like a storm through the sky, gunports flaring with yellow light as they opened fire.

Calisto hopscotched away, narrowly avoiding getting pinched between two converging beams. As she came out of her first turn, Calisto opened up with her chain guns, sending hundreds of high-explosive SAPRs at the flanks of three ships that sped past her. The first caught a few bursts, and the shields sloughed them off. The middle star-fighter was hit broadside with such force that it shorted the shields and blew the craft into a fireball just in time for the third to be engulfed by it

"Kiss my ass!" she roared, and hopscotched away from return fire. Her pulse was racing as fast as her tumbler. It was a good hit. First blood, and she hoped it was what her young cadets needed to see—that the tumblers were tough, that they were agile, and that they could kill these nightmare monsters.

Immediately the other tumblers seemed to vanish and reappear everywhere but where the star-fighters were aiming. They hosed the vanguard with pulse blasts, and the leading edge of the attack crumpled. It cut the attacking line in half, forcing the enemy into dogfights to protect their sides. That was what Calisto wanted because the one real advantage her team had was its maneuverability.

Was it enough, though?

In her heart, she knew it was not. Yet what choice was there?

She jumped down and left and left and up and rose directly under another star-fighter, firing into its belly and blowing it all to hell.

Even as she fought, she yelled into the command channel. "I keep hearing about those stilettos and spinners, but I sure as shit ain't seeing them. Maybe tell those lazy pricks that playtime is over. There's grown-up stuff needs doing."

"Calisto," replied Captain Croft, "be advised, the Ariel system is down at the source, and safeguards have kicked in. All stiletto and spinner pilots are locked out of their controls."

"Jesus Christ. Can't they switch over to Sybil?"

"We're working on that."

Yellow pulse fire hit one of the tumblers and spun it into the path of another. There was a flash of terrible light, and the tumbler vanished in a massive fireball as the night-gaunt's blasts punched through the shields and struck the nuke core.

"Morrigan!" someone cried.

Calisto felt like she had been stabbed in the chest. Anger wanted to own her, but she forced it back and down, making herself stay cold as she hopscotched away and came out of her turn to kill another star-fighter.

"Fucking hurry," she roared at Croft. The captain did not reply.

10

"Lifeguard?" said Spider as he began backing up. "What do we do?"

Not Larry was retreating, too. Jenny glanced back at them for a moment, then set her jaw as she spun back and opened fire.

The corridor flared with purple light as she fired on full auto. Craig Anders was nine meters away, a full six meters in front of the rest of the pack. He took the blasts full on, in the groin, the belly, the chest, and then the head. His body split apart and collapsed, black blood spattering the wall, sizzling as it struck the rock.

Not Larry and Spider stopped backpedaling and opened fire. The big man tucked the stock of his heavy P-850 rapid-pulse rifle against his hip, braced his feet wide, and opened up. The gun roared like a crazed bull, and the small-field explosive rounds enveloped the front six of the living dead. The heat ignited their clothing and hair and flesh, but they kept running forward.

The three Jokers retreated again, watching with horrified fascination as the running creatures slowed, becoming clumsy and awkward as the fire melted their skin like tallow and the heat caused their tendons to tighten and contract. They fell, and the ones behind them collided with their burning bodies, tripping, falling, burning. Yet still coming.

A peal of weird, high laughter filled the tunnel as Spider stopped firing for a moment. Jenny turned and saw Evie a dozen meters behind him. She whirled and ran down the hall, heading toward Brollachan's lab.

Not Larry saw her, too. He glanced that way, then back at the oncoming walking corpses, then he slapped Jenny on the arm.

"Lifeguard—*go*," he yelled. "We got this."

Jenny hesitated for a moment, then she turned and ran. Chasing her wife. Chasing the thing that looked like her. The thing that laughed as it ran, taunting her.

Was it Evie, or some trick of the night-gaunts? She had no idea.

She ran as hard as terror and need could propel her.

Behind her, the two guns opened up again. She barely heard them, though. The noise was crowded out by all the screaming in her head.

11

Bianca hoisted a bound stack of iridium sheeting, a half ton's worth, and went staggering out of the skimmer. Lost was waiting, along with Bliss's metallurgist, Alice Portevin, and half a dozen technicians from the navy station civilian team.

Bianca dumped the metal at their feet.

"Whatever you guys are doing, do it fast." She hurried back into the skimmer for another load.

Lost had prepared things by locating a standard cockpit from one of the crashed spacecraft and setting it on a flat concrete pad. Portevin's team had a medium-sized 3D printer on a cart, and as soon as the strapping was cut on the first stack, she and Lost lifted one quarter-inch sheet and fed it onto the printer.

"What's the best thickness?" she asked the golem.

"I have no idea," he said. "I've never seen this metal before."

"How can we test it, though?"

Bianca dropped the second stack next to the first and laughed her mechanical laugh—bitter, humorless, and cold. "I'll test it in combat. Now hurry this shit up. My friends are *dying* up there."

12

"*Evie!*" cried Jenny. "Evie, for Christ's sake, *stop*."

But Evie Cronin did not stop.

Small as she was, unathletic as she was, she outran Jenny, who was running as hard as she could. Everything about this was wrong, and Jenny Spears knew it, but what else could she do? She had to catch her wife. Figure out what was wrong with her.

She had to save her.

The corridor sloped down and down, into inky darkness. The last of the bat drones was back with Spider and Not Larry, so she had to use the light on her rifle, but the beam danced crazily.

"Lifeguard to Jokers," she called as she ran. "Report in."

They did not report. Not any of them. Echoes of gunfire—the buzzing drone of pulse weapons on full auto—seemed to come from everywhere. There were yells, so muffled and indistinct it was impossible to tell if they came from her people or those … things.

So far, she hadn't encountered any of the monsters Lost was so terrified of—the night-gaunts. Or could they possibly be the spider-crab creatures? But they were far too small to pilot a ship. The night-gaunts had to be there somewhere, though. How else could the little monsters have gotten inside Bliss?

But where were they? If the night-gaunts were so powerful, why were they hiding?

Ahead, Evie reached the heavy steel airlock outside of Brollachan's lab. It was open. She paused for just a moment, then, with another high-pitched laugh, vanished inside.

Please, baby. Please be okay. Please be okay.

Those thoughts burned Jenny as she ran.

13

"Calisto to Lost Souls," she cried. "Hit and run. We have to draw that thing away from Shadderal."

Leviathan dominated the void a thousand kilometers away from the station. It was far too close, and the monster ship kept launching more and more fighters.

"Christ, how many of them are there?" gasped Woden.

"Aim for the launch bays," said Calisto. "If we can stop them launching more fighters, then maybe we have a chance. Hummingbird, Thor, Aries—Pattern Slingshot B. Chain gun set up and Triphammer surprise. Go."

Three tumblers spun out, jumping wildly to confuse pursuit, their onboard Sybils coordinating to keep the nimble ships from colliding. They ducked and dodged until they were within range, and then Thor and Aries shot toward a launch bay, firing SAPR rounds with both guns, taxing the shields, and then they hopscotched away as Hummingbird came straight up the pipe and fired a Triphammer.

The missile was heavy with tightly compacted high explosives engaged in an impact-reactive plasma field. Phillip Kessler—Hummingbird—jumped up and over and down, using the bulk of Leviathan as protective cover as the missile struck the unshielded exit of the launch tube.

The blast was stupendous. A star-fighter was caught mid-launch, and its engines and ordnance blew up, the force ripping into the night-gaunt mother ship.

14

Ensign Alex Suzuki was the naval comms officer under Captain Croft's command. Having grown up in one of the slums of Tokyo, he joined the navy in order to further his education. Now, at twenty-three and an impossible distance from home, he was on his back in a tiny cubicle in the belly of a stiletto fighter.

"How's it going in there?" demanded Lieutenant Commander Levinson.

"Working, ma'am," he said for probably the tenth time in twenty minutes. Answering a superior without snapping like a pissed-off chihuahua was getting more difficult with each repetition. "Have to focus here."

"Please hurry," she urged.

Please shut up, he thought.

A Bliss tech knelt outside, next to Levinson, acting as a kind of nurse, handing Suzuki the right tools at the right moment. Saying little except to clarify the design points of the fighter. Circuits and data crystals lay everywhere, including on Suzuki's chest as he fought to bypass the Ariel hardware safeguards. It was tricky work, and the tech was fine with ceding this job to the navy expert.

Suzuki removed a stubborn plate. The data crystal he'd been hunting for was right there. "Got you, you little prick."

"What's that?" asked Levinson.

"Working, ma'am," he muttered.

15

Calisto watched another of her pilots die.

This time it wasn't a cadet, but one of the old team. Ensign Jean-Paul Lloris—combat call sign Decaf. He'd taken out two star-fighters and jumped around to help one of the younger pilots out of a jam, but it was a trap. The cadet's ship was damaged, but she managed to hopscotch out at the same moment the two star-fighters turned and shot.

Decaf flew right into their combined fire.

He vanished. The blast was so intense that his tumbler seemed to disintegrate into dust.

Calisto roared and returned the fire, killing one ship and chasing the other off. It made no real difference, though. Decaf was dead, and another wave of the star-fighters was coming. The mother ship, the

Leviathan, was coming too—growing on her screen. Fighters by the score burst from its launch tubes.

A clutch of star-fighters punched through the thin line of tumblers, their intense yellow pulse beams filling the void with death and destruction. Calisto tried to be everywhere at once because she knew this kind of dogfight and not enough of her cadets did. But that meant drawing fire to save her pilots. With the nuke core amped up, her shields were at maximum, but the night-gaunts were relentless. Her shields fluctuated as precise strikes took their toll. Her tumbler's cockpit began to fill with smoke. It was so like what happened against the shoggoths before that it gave her the unreal feeling that she was in some kind of purgatory where she and her tumbler were to be beaten to the point of death over and over again throughout eternity.

"No, no, no," she growled. "Your squishy butt-buddies couldn't take me down, and you boogeymen won't either. So fuck you and everyone you ever met."

It was bravado, and on some level she knew it. Even so, it set a fire under her skin, and she threw her tumbler this way and that, firing constantly, sending missiles out, trying to kill the monsters who were trying to kill her people.

On the screen, a few thousand kilometers behind, came shoggoth Medusas. Three of them. And they, too, launched their fighters. The sky was full of ships, and not enough of them were tumblers.

Not nearly enough.

16

Footie felt himself fall.

He was not sure what hit him. All he knew was that it came from behind and struck with such force that he was flung face-forward into the wall. The impact smashed his nose and mashed his lips against his teeth. Some of his teeth broke, too. Footie slid down to his knees and then toppled sideways, his gun falling from his hands.

There were sounds all around him, but he was barely aware of them. Krampus and Ratjack. Yelling.

No. Not yelling.

Screaming.

Such loud and awful screams.

Footie wanted to scream too, but he could not. His mouth was filled with blood. He felt something sharp in his throat and knew that it was his teeth.

No, he thought. A reasonable thought on any day but that one. *No.*

The night had a different answer for him.

17

"Is it ready?" demanded Bianca.

Portevin stepped back, gasping and sweaty. "I hope so."

"You *hope*?"

The metallurgist looked pained. "Hey, it's not like we've ever done this before. We did something like this on what we now know was a shoggoth slave ship back on Earth. There hasn't been time to test it against the radiation that runs the … the …"

"NecroTeks, honey," said Bianca. "It's okay to say the word."

"I was going to say the ships from Lost's culture." Portevin gestured to the thousands of broken spacecraft on the Field of Dead Birds. "Shoggoth energy has a blue radiance, and NecroTek energy is purple. Both are based on crystals unknown to any science that I familiar with. So … yes, Commander Petrescu, I *hope* this will work."

Bianca nodded, accepting the explanation and the rebuke. She stalked over to the excised cockpit and bent to inspect the metal shielding that covered the interior. The process of scanning the irregular surfaces of the cockpit and then feeding that data into the 3D printers had been time intensive. Above them, even through the hazy clouds, the flashes of the great battle could be seen.

"Guess we'll find out," she said.

Bianca bent, gripped the cockpit, which weighed nearly 110 kilograms, straightened with it in her arms, and lumbered over to the closest crashed spaceship. She did not waste time trying to install the thing into the ship but placed it so the metal of one touched the skin of the other. She turned and looked back at Lost, who stood silent.

The ghost nodded once.

Bianca changed her body shape, sloughing off some of the mass—which fell tinkling to the ground—and then stepped into the cockpit. Once inside, she closed the top hatch and manifested a welding torch on the tip of her index finger, slowly running it along the four sides to seal herself in.

"Mosquito to C-1," she radioed, "testing comms."

"Coming through weak, Mosquito. Adjust your gain."

"How's this?"

"Better. Clear. What's your status?"

"Ready to attempt *ethla* metamorphosis ... *now*."

Bianca could not take a steadying breath; she could not close her eyes. Those were preparatory actions for human commitment. Instead, she tried to relax her mind. Even after three months as this new kind of being, the process felt incredibly strange. Part of her tried to look inside as if to feel or see her own fragile soul, but that was beyond even her powers.

The more she relaxed away from conscious control, the more she felt something. It was like falling back in slow motion but with no assurance of something soft to catch her. Not water or a mattress or even summer grass. Not human arms as part of a trust exercise. Bianca let herself fall and fall, yielding the need for control. Letting go of any intractable view of herself as a woman, as a human being, even as a humanoid form. The first time she did this, moments after her own physical death, there had been such confusion and terror, such doubt and awe. Now, there was a familiarity that was partly a comfort and partly a reminder that this was not anything a real person could do.

She was a ghost trying to connect her intangible soul to the material reality of a ruined spacecraft. Even within it, though, there was a spark—a connection point. The metals and plastic and crystals that made up the ancient ship was composed of molecules made from atoms that were alive in their own way with energy. Every atom possessed it, and that energy could be neither created nor destroyed. It could be used, though. Shaped and changed. She could impose her will on each atom, using them in infinite combination to create the molecules she needed to build whatever her mind could conceive.

There were no thoughts as simple as *ship* or *gun*. As Bianca's mind yielded to *ethla*, visions flashed and flowed, and all attempts at design specifics melted into her aching need to save her friends.

Calisto.

The image of her friend's beautiful brown face—those intelligent eyes and that sun-bright smile—flooded her subconscious.

I'm coming, sis.

A dozen meters away, Alice Portevin stood next to Lost, her mouth falling slowly open as pieces of deck plating and hull stabilizers began to move. Cables and wires twisted like snakes and wriggled through the dust. Splintered circuit boards sparked and smoked as they combined with others to form new and unexpected parts of a machine that was giving birth to itself. With each passing second, more pieces rolled or skidded, slid or wriggled toward the iridium-enclosed cockpit.

"It … it's working," breathed the metallurgist. "I think it's working."

Lost stood with his fists balled as if there was real muscular tension, real tendons in his hands.

"Yes," he said very softly. "It *is* working."

And then Bianca Petrescu—the thing that had once been a flesh-and-blood woman—began to rise. One of the two suns had already set, and the smaller one—a blue ball of fire—painted everything in a sapphire glow. It cast a shadow across Portevin and Lost as a massive figure rose before them.

Tall. Taller than a skyscraper. Indomitable against the setting suns. Powerful in ways that even Lost did not understand. Electricity crackled all along the arms as Bianca closed her hands into mighty fists. More and more matter came at her call, slapping against her body, increasing her mass, building a titan.

Bianca looked down at the scientist and the golem. They seemed so strangely small, so far away, and only then did she realize that the NecroTek she had constructed was far larger than any she had ever made. Something was happening within the cockpit—some alchemy between her spirit and the metal that was entirely unknown on this side of the Milky Way.

"I feel …" she began, and the voice was thunder. The sheer force of it plucked Portevin and Lost up and flung them away into the brittle weeds that grew alongside the Field of Dead Birds. Bianca saw them fall, shocked. But then a wave of energy swelled up inside her. Massive. Towering. Building and building until she feared she was going to explode. Was this the effect? A runaway reactor that would kill the enemy and her friends?

"I feel so …" And once more, words failed her.

Over her Sybil interface she heard a voice. Calisto. She was screaming orders. There was panic in her voice, and it was close to that brittle, deadly edge where pragmatism allows for a belief in one's own mortality and of death's inevitable victory.

"Noooooooooooo!"

The scream burst from Bianca as her legs fused into one gigantic engine powered by forces no one on that field now understood. There was a monstrous roar, and then the whole world seemed to shake and shudder as the NecroTek launched herself upward.

Upward.

Up into space. Accelerating faster and faster. Going higher. Breaking the envelope of atmosphere and bursting out into the void. She dialed up the jets, and her body moved with a greater speed than she had ever managed. Taking her away from Shadderal. Into space. Into the fight.

Below, sitting up slowly, Lost watched the towering living machine dwindle into the upper atmosphere. He spoke two words. He had said them before, echoing a war cry used by Bianca and her team.

Now, though, he spoke them with something approaching true reverence.

"NecroTek forever …"

18

Jenny Spears skidded to a stop as she reached the open door to Dr. Brollachan's lab.

She realized it was less about mission efficiency than fear for her wife that made her leave her men in danger and run like this. But Evie had been covered in blood.

That was igniting panic in her, but Jenny now forced herself to stop, to think. To be smart.

Was it even Evie? She had been laughing like an evil little child. How did that make any kind of sense? Unless …

With devastating clarity, she thought about Dr. Wu taunting them after she was clearly—demonstrably—dead. The people Spider and Not Larry were fighting—all of them had died in the night-gaunt attack on Bliss. They were dead. That wasn't in question, and yet they stood, they walked, they *ran*, and they howled.

This, she knew, was the real horror the night-gaunts brought. Maybe even worse than whatever they themselves looked like. Raising the beloved dead, the honored dead, and using them as weapons was a strategy that assailed the heart and soul even more than the body.

Evie, she prayed, *don't. Just don't be* …

She could not even allow herself to think the word that ended that sentence.

"God help me," she said aloud. She raised her rifle once more. "I love you, Evie. No matter what happens, I will always love you."

Then she wheeled around and stepped into the lab.

19

The trio of Medusa ships moved with deceptive speed, the endless vista of infinity making them look painted against the field of stars. Yet with each moment they closed the gap between themselves and the raging battle around Asphodel Station.

Two were well out in front of the third, and as they drew nearer to Leviathan, they opened their many launch tubes. The night-gaunt mother ship already had a thousand fighters in the sky, some drifting as dead wrecks, while many more engaged in dogfights—two, three, five to one—as the main force split apart. One group of two hundred dove in coordinated groups of five toward the surface of Shadderal and then swarmed like packs of hunting hounds toward the human settlements of Hope, Haven, and Grace. They dropped down below the cloud cover, with the front rank diving lower still to hammer the pressure domes over the settlements with pulse fire, paving the way for the next waves to begin bombing everything.

The other group rocketed toward Asphodel.

The space station bristled with guns, but the few tumblers still flying were too heavily engaged to offer any support. The star-fighters swarmed the station and flew right into the teeth of Captain Croft's guns. The first barrage was a broadside straight into the oncoming storm of ships, and the entire front rank of the night-gaunt fighters vanished in a cloud of fire a klick wide.

The ships behind them punched through the debris of their comrades, opening up with yellow pulse fire. From then on, the order from Croft was for all guns to fire as they came to bear. Human gunners wore skullcaps that gave them a direct connection to Sybil's target-acquisition software and the firing controls of their guns, allowing them to track and fire nearly at the speed of thought. On twenty of the ship's decks, the cannons were manned entirely by Sybil—her safeties removed, allowing the AI to kill organic life.

And the star-fighters kept coming.

And coming.

20

As the bombardment increased, Asphodel shuddered as if in fear.

"Ensign …" urged Levinson.

"Almost there," breathed Ensign Suzuki.

Whoooomp!

"We're out of time."

"Almost there."

Whoooomp!

"I mean it."

"Almost … *there!*" He cried in triumph as suddenly the circuit boards all around him flashed with brilliant, sparkling lights.

"System acquired," said Sybil with something approaching smug satisfaction. "Spinners online. Stilettos online. All craft are cleared for launch."

Levinson nearly smashed her holo-comms as she slapped it to open the line to the command bridge. "All ships are online. Repeat, Sybil has control. All ships are cleared to launch, cleared to launch."

Whoooomp!

And a split second later, the next heavy noise and shudder they felt were the first of the Bliss fighters exiting the barn.

21

A thing lay at Jenny's feet. It was dressed in some kind of loose leather, like a cloak. Its body was tall and lean and muscular, but its head was gone. Mashed into a featureless pulp and tossed to one side. The blood steamed as if spilled only seconds before.

Beyond it lay Dr. Beatrice Howard, her eyes open, mouth open, and chest open. She lay in a lake of her own blood, a fire axe clutched in one hand.

Nearby, Dr. Solà sat with his back to a big dura-glass cubicle. His eyes were missing, and the claw marks in his skin told the impossible story of his own bloodied fingernails having inflicted the damage. He was alive, his chest moving with quick, shallow breaths. But Jenny saw those breaths slow and then stop.

Against the far wall, standing open, was a heavy steel door that led to another chamber, and Jenny could see the curve of some large machine and the twinkling of illuminated crystals. Brollachan crouched there, his hands covered in blood, teeth bared, eyes wild.

But Evie was not there.

Jenny took one heavy step, pointing her gun at every corner, into every shadow.

"Where is she?" she demanded, her voice a low and savage growl. "*Where's Evie?*"

Brollachan gestured limply to the chamber behind him, then he fell back, hissing with pain. Jenny could see that his face was slashed, and there were deep lacerations across his chest.

Jenny hurried across the lab, skirting the dead thing on the ground. This was a night-gaunt—she was sure of it. As she passed it, she saw with a flash of horror that the leathery draping was not a garment but something like bat wings. It was actually naked, and with weird distraction she noticed that it was emphatically male but that its long, thick penis was covered in curving hooks that looked like the claws of a cat. Disgust welled up in her at the thought that its species needed blood and pain even for their own reproduction.

She hurried past and reached Brollachan. The scientist was alive but badly hurt. His eyes were bright with pain but also awareness. He flapped a hand once more toward the inner chamber.

"E-Evie …" he said in an agony-infused croak. His words failed him, and he slumped back.

"Wait here," Jenny said, and stepped over his sprawled legs.

The room in which she found herself was massive, nearly as big as the main hall upstairs. Jenny had no idea there was any other chamber this big inside the mountain. Yet the room was crowded by the gigantic machine that Brollachan and his team had built. Steel and copper and jewels, cables and wires and other things too exotic and arcane for her to identify.

The section of the machine closest to her was like a mouth, huge and round and buzzing with crackling energy. Two figures stood in front of that gaping hole. One was Evie Cronin, who stood with one foot up on the lower edge of the opening. Her clothes were splashed with blood, but she did not look as comprehensively painted with it as she'd looked outside. Most of it was on her crotch and thighs. Yet it was her.

Looming over her was an unspeakably grotesque figure. It gripped Evie with a hand that was misshapen—instead of fingers, it had five tentacles spreading out from the palm, and these were wrapped around Evie's wrist. Its body was as naked as the night-gaunt's, but there were no genitalia. Instead, it looked like a store mannequin made of plastic. Its skin was dark, and it writhed and bubbled as if undergoing a process of agonizing change. The head was a hideous copy of Brollachan's, but the eyes were utterly black.

A *shoggoth.*

The creature and Evie both turned toward Jenny. Both looking at her with shock and surprise. Jenny pointed her gun at the shoggoth's head.

"No!"

The scream was shockingly loud and full of pleading. Desperate, terrified, but powerful. But it was not the monster who spoke. Nor was it Brollachan.

"No, Jenny," cried Evie. "Don't hurt him!"

Then she shifted to stand between the monster and the woman who had come to save her. Behind Evie and the creature, deep inside the open mouth of the machine, Jenny saw something she could not understand. It made her mind begin to whirl as reality tried to fragment around her.

The machine's opening looked like a door. A gateway to some other place impossibly far from where they stood. Jenny gaped at what she saw in the tunnel behind Evie.

There, spinning with slow and beautiful grace, was Earth.

Part Thirty-One
The Fog of War

"The fog of war works both ways. The enemy is as much in the dark as you are."

—*General George S. Patton*

1

Everywhere Bianca looked, there was death and destruction.

Tumblers floated as darkened hulks or as clouds of drifting junk. Star-fighters and dagger ships filled the broad gap between the planet and the space station like a plague of locusts. Asphodel was tilted off its axis, proof that the station-keeping jets were either malfunctioning or destroyed, and long trails of smoke floated out into the airless void. Blue and yellow streams of fire seemed to be everywhere, and not nearly enough responding purple pulse blasts.

"Calisto," she called, "what's your whiskey?"

Static hissed and popped, then a weak response made it through, giving the coordinates.

"Hold on, sis," pleaded Bianca as she kicked her jets to maximum.

Star-fighters wheeled around and drove at her, and maybe on some other day, Bianca would have felt fear or intimidation. Those emotions were there, but faint and far away, buried beneath a cold fury.

She did not bother to fire guns at the first group of fighters to zero her. As they opened up, she switched 80 percent of her shield strength to her head and arms and simply flew into—and *through*—the fighters. The daggers veered off, clearly understanding the threat she posed. The night-gaunts did not and tried to destroy her with their own suicidal immolation, slamming into her gigantic frame at full speed.

Bianca felt the force, felt some of her armor snap off, but she threw her will into immediate repairs, shifting mass and reallocating internal energetic flows. She had no organic nerve endings, but the sensors throughout her NecroTek body sent damage reports, and that *felt* like pain. It did not stop her. It did not even slow her. It only made her angrier, and she replied in kind, slamming into them, swatting them away to their destruction.

"These night-gaunt pricks want me even more than the squishies."

"Nice to be the popular girl at the prom," laughed Calisto, breaking off into ragged coughs.

Beyond the first mixed group of alien fighters, there was a smaller squadron driving fast toward Asphodel. They plowed the road with yellow and blue pulse cannons, and as they reached the upper decks of the great station, the star-fighters opened their bomb bay doors and launched payloads of hundreds of megatons of ultraenergetic plasma-wrapped bombs.

The explosions hit the station like a punch, making it judder and reel. The deflectors held, but several began flickering. And the next wave of night-gaunt bombers came diving directly for that spot.

Bianca raced them to it, her speed greater than theirs, but it was a damn close run.

She got in front of the lead star-fighter and snatched it out of the sky. The shields sparked and sizzled as she took hold of two of the five arms. Then she shifted her jets to station-keeping, drew the captured fighter back, and swung it at the first bombs to reach her. The star-fighter's own shields did the work, bashing the bomb sideways into the path of the dozen ships behind it.

They all blew up as one.

The force disintegrated three of the star-fighters, but it also threw Bianca's massive body against the slope of the upper ring of the station. She hit the deflectors, rebounding like a fighter coming off the ropes after slipping a punch. Then Bianca leaned into the direction, boot jets blasting as she drove into the third wave of star-fighters.

Several daggers tried to blindside her, but Bianca did not require either sensors or line of sight. Her entire body was aware; everything about her NecroTek form was equal parts engine, shields, targeting computer, and weapon. Guns manifested in a triple ring around her torso and then began revolving, spinning faster and faster as she fired into the endless swarm of jets. Daggers and star-fighters exploded like fireworks all around her.

"Woooooohoooo!" cried Calisto as she came hopscotching in—damaged but game—and did cleanup in Bianca's wake. Together they settled into an attack structure that did dreadful damage.

2

Leviathan saw the NecroTek and began accelerating in that direction. Two of the Medusas followed in her wake, all three mother ships continuing to launch fighters. There were more than three thousand of their ships in the gulf between Asphodel and Shadderal.

A cluster of a hundred enemy ships, nearly an even split of daggers and star-fighters, made a run for the station, leaving the hottest part of the battle for a sneak attack on Asphodel. Two tumblers saw them and shot after them, but a dozen of the hindmost daggers wheeled and engaged with their pulse weapons.

Horus and Sweetpea were flying the tumblers. A cadet and a seasoned pilot. Each had made multiple kills, emptying one campaign pack after another. The two pilots knew that they did not have anywhere near enough missiles to stop this squadron. Nor could their ships withstand more of the hammering.

"Lost Souls forever," radioed Horus. He was one of the youngest cadets. Not quite eighteen years old. Sharp, smart, brave.

And doomed.

Sweetpea smiled through her tears. "Lost Souls forever."

They opened up with their guns.

Suddenly, eight of the twelve enemy ships exploded with a mingling of blue plasma and orange fire.

"*What?*" cried Horus.

"Somebody here order some ass kicking?" called a stranger's voice, and then four stilettos and four spinners shot past the tumblers, driving right into the heart of the enemy squadron.

"Well … kiss my ass," said Horus.

He and Sweetpea kicked the burners high and raced to catch up.

3

Jenny stood there, unable to move, completely confused. Her gun barrel and both shoulder cannons pointed at the shoggoth's head.

"I said … let her go," she snapped, but there was less authority in her tone. The whole situation felt like it was sliding sideways.

Evie pulled free of the shoggoth and held her arms out to her side, using herself as a shield. "Jenny, please! Don't hurt him."

"Hurt … him? *Him?* Evie, I don't know what they did to you, but you need to step away."

"Listen … to her …" The gasping voice came from behind her. Brollachan, though Jenny did not dare turn her head to look at the wounded SPU chief. "Please, Spears—*listen*."

Despite the madness and uncertainty, Jenny kept her gun rock solid, the barrel pointing at the shoggoth's head. "I won't tell you again, shitbag. Step away from my wife."

The shoggoth stayed where he was. The writhing tentacles changed back into fingers, and he held his hands up like any human might when surrendering.

"Jenny, I can explain," said Evie desperately. "It's not what it looks like."

"Evie, you'd better get out of the way, I swear to God. You *know* what that thing is."

"His name is Caliban."

Jenny blinked. "What?"

"He has a name. Caliban."

"I don't give a fuck if it's Santa Claus. He's a goddamn monster. You should know. You were out there. You saw what they did."

Evie looked puzzled. "Out where? Outside the lab?"

"The hell do you think I'm talking about? I've been chasing you all the way from upstairs."

"That … was not … her …" wheezed Brollachan.

"Bullshit," said Jenny. "I … I *saw* you, Evie. I followed you here. You're hurt. You're in shock."

Evie lowered one hand and touched her lower abdomen. "I don't know what you think you saw, but I've been in here since the attack started."

"No, you were … I mean, you're …"

"Jenny," said Evie very clearly and firmly. "Listen to me. This *is* me. I don't know if the night-gaunts did something to you, but this is me. And god … I'm pregnant. At least I was. I don't know. Something happened to me, and I started bleeding. Oh god, sweetheart, I … I may have miscarried. I don't know. I'm so sorry. Please, I didn't mean to …"

Those words punched Jenny back several steps. Her rifle sagged in her hands.

"Pregnant?"

Tears streaked down Evie's face. "I came here for help."

Behind her, the shoggoth's face—the false Brollachan copy—contrived to look sad. Compassionate. "She came here, and we tried to help her," said Caliban.

Jenny raised her gun. "You say one more word, motherfucker, and I will burn you to ash. Look at me and tell me if I'm lying."

Caliban did not move.

Evie took a single step toward Jenny, hands now out in a pleading, placating gesture. "He didn't hurt me, love. Caliban saved me from that … thing out there. He saved me from the night-gaunt."

Jenny stepped forward, caught Evie's wrist, and jerked her away. Evie yelped in pain, but Jenny had to bear it. She wrapped one arm around her wife and walked her backward.

"Are you okay?" she asked. "What did they do to you?"

"We helped … her …" said Brollachan. His voice sounded a little stronger but was still weak and unsteady.

Jenny held her rifle with one hand, the barrel still pointed at Caliban. She turned her face toward Brollachan, which made the shoulder cannons pivot.

"Get up and move over there with that thing. Do it now, Doc. I don't care if you're hurt."

"Jenny—" protested Evie, but Jenny cut her off.

"Do it right now, or so help me God, Torq …"

Brollachan struggled to his feet and stumbled toward the mouth of the great machine, leaving bloody footprints on the stone floor. He lost his balance and pitched forward, but Caliban—fast as lightning—caught him. The shoggoth steadied the scientist and looked into his eyes.

"How badly are you hurt?" asked the monster, and he wrapped a comforting arm around the SPU chief. "Lean on me."

Jenny Spears felt as if she were going insane. Deep inside the machine, the Earth still spun. She knew it had to be some kind of hologram or video playback, but it somehow *felt* real. Which made no sense at all. She held Evie close and relied on her shoulder cannons to cover the scientist and the creature.

"Somebody better make sense of this, or I'm going to start pulling triggers."

4

Mangler, Moonboy, and Widow felt lost.

"Where the hell are we?" asked Mangler.

They had reached the end of a corridor that each of them had walked a hundred times over the last two years. Instead of finding storage rooms, they found walls that were entirely blank or side tunnels they had never seen before—ones that took them through mazes of passages to where they'd started.

Now the three of them stood in a tight circle, weapons facing out, trying to make sense of a world that was no longer sensible.

"It's not a cave-in," said Moonboy. "There's no collapses or anything, so where is everything?"

Widow crept forward and patted the wall that stood where an entrance should be, moving from left to right to see if there was a fault or fracture they weren't seeing. The rock was solid under each pat.

Until it wasn't.

Her fifth pat passed directly through the solid wall.

Widow cried out and jumped back. The others spun and brought their weapons—rifles and shoulder cannons—to bear.

"It's … a hologram, I think," she said. Widow bent and snatched up something to throw. It was one of the black orbs, but in that moment, she didn't care. Widow tossed it at the false section of wall, but the orb struck it and fell to the ground.

"What?" Widow strode forward and tried to bang the side of her fist on the stone. Once more, her hand vanished into it.

And then something grabbed her and, with a sudden awful power, jerked her off her feet and into the wall. Widow vanished.

"No!" cried Moonboy. He rushed forward, groping for the spot where his friend had disappeared. His hand found only solid stone. "What the ..."

And then hands reached through the wall and grabbed him by the straps of his equipment harness and jerked him forward. He smashed face-first into the rock. It was completely impossible. And it happened again and again.

Mangler leaped forward, grabbed the back of Moonboy's harness, and pulled.

Something stung him on the back of the neck, and instantly a bizarre combination of agonizing pain and a nearly orgasmic excitement flooded through him. His eyes lost their focus. The wall lost its physical structure. It was there and not there. Moonboy was hitting solid rock, and he was not. Widow was gone, and she was on the floor—both at the same time, like two holo-vids playing on the same screen. Mangler saw more of the black orbs on the floor near Widow. They cracked apart, releasing some kind of horror-show blend of arachnid and crustacean. The creatures swarmed over Widow, and one dug long fangs into the back of her neck, just below the base of her skull. Widow's body twitched and thrashed.

Moonboy was sagging to his knees, and Mangler saw another of the spider-crabs crawling up his back until it reached the nape of his neck, then it, too, sank glistening fangs deep into Moonboy's flesh.

That was the last clear thing that Mangler saw with sane eyes.

He never felt himself fall.

He did remember getting up, though. Not clearly—it was like his mind was all the way to one side, watching his body move but not being any true part of that process himself. A spider-crustacean was fixed onto the back of his neck, too. Mangler could feel something race through his blood and breath—on one level he knew it was venom of some exotic kind, that this was the end of him.

His body stood, smiling a foolish, wicked, hungry grin as it turned to look at Widow and Moonboy. They, too, got to their feet. All of them smiling. Waves of orgasmic pleasure coursed through each of them, making their bodies shudder and twitch. Hunger blossomed darkly in each, too. A deep hunger. Bottomless. They smelled each other—that fresh meat and hot blood, the sweet sweat and precious marrow—but, ravenous as they suddenly were, this was not their food.

Echoes of yells and gunfire bounced their way down the rocky halls.

That instantly spiked the hunger until it burned in their minds with black fire that blazed with ice rather than heat.

The three of them turned toward the sounds of battle.

As one, they threw their heads back and howled with that insatiable, twisted, erotic hunger. They snapped at the air with their teeth as if rehearsing the meal to come.

Howling like demons, they fled down the hallway, drawn by the promise of a satisfaction deeper than anything they had ever known.

5

Lady Jessica McHugh watched the RealScreen with growing horror as the battle raged. She saw Bianca enter the fight, as well as the spinners and stilettos, but there were so damned many of the aliens. Shoggoths and night-gaunts by the hundred.

It was clear to her that the night-gaunts were focusing on Asphodel. Not to destroy it, but to *invade* it.

"They want the WarpLine tech," she said aloud.

A thought, strange and unbidden, flicked through her mind.

They want to steal our light.

She frowned, trying to make sense of that. It was so odd, so cryptic, that it felt like a flicker of madness or something her shocked mind had pulled from a cabinet of disused memories.

They want to steal our light.

What did that even mean?

Jessica did not know, but with every fiber of her being and all of her deep, complex spiritual powers, she knew—absolutely *knew*—that that statement was true.

Yet ... how? What was the secret her inner self was trying to tell her? As if from deep inside her mind came an echo of something. Not an old memory, but a recent one. Soren telling her about a conversation he had with Lost.

There are old legends that say they cannot abide true light, but the meaning of that phrase is lost to time.

That's what Lost said.

She struggled to sit up in bed. Her body was so frail that every movement was a terrible effort. The station shook as more blasts hit it, rattling the teacup on her night table. A painting fell from the wall, the frame bursting apart.

"Sybil," she gasped. "My chair."

The AI sent the wheelchair to her, and Lady Jessica tried to summon the enormous strength needed to climb into it.

"Got three Medusas at the back of the pack," called Ensign Marco Diaz—Cricket. His tumbler was deep in the Shadderal system, flying solo since the two cadets with him had been destroyed.

"ETA on those mother ships?" demanded Croft.

"Two of them are moving toward Leviathan. ETA ten minutes. The third is holding back."

"Have they deployed their fighters?"

"The first two sent about two hundred each," said Cricket. "Mosquito's engaging with some of them. Squadrons are heading down to Shadderal, to the colonies."

"What's the third doing?"

"Just … sitting there. She launched a bunch of her fighters, but they're not doing anything. They're keeping station around that third Medusa."

"Probably waiting for the final push," said Croft. "Cricket, see if you can draw some of those fighters away. Don't engage, just run them around a bit, take the heat off of Mosquito."

"Copy that," said Cricket, though he felt no optimism at all. There were only eight tumblers left. The spinners and stilettos were racking up some wins, but even with all of their ships in play, the enemy outnumbered them forty to one, and those odds got worse every minute. Bianca was doing what she could, but the enemy craft were clearly teasing her to draw the giant NecroTek away from Asphodel. Distance gave Cricket a disheartening perspective on this fight. One-to-one, the advantage was solidly on his side. But it wasn't one-to-one, and attrition was a monster.

Even so, alone and vastly outgunned, he made his run. He hopscotched over and up and over and forward until he was within fifty kilometers of the two lead Medusas. Cricket opened up with his chain guns at a group of two daggers and two star-fighters, then got the hell out of there, jumping crazily while constantly accelerating. The four fighters turned to give chase.

Only those four. The rest swarmed in their thousands toward Asphodel.

7

Lady Jessica rolled her chair to the door and placed a palm against it, trying to read the soul of Asphodel Station. It was something she'd tried many times, and more often than not, she could get a reading. The combined psychic and spiritual energies of the twelve thousand people who lived there was a powerful force, and it sank into every wall and deck, into the very flow of air.

They want to steal our light.

"No," she said with equal parts fear and fury. "By the Goddess, no."

There are old legends that say they cannot abide true light, but the meaning of that phrase is lost to time.

She punched the button beside the door, and it hissed open, all the while scrabbling to remember what else Lost told Soren. There was more—she was sure of it.

People were screaming outside. The sounds of the night-gaunt's pulse fire was much louder. What was it Soren told her?

Then it came.

When manifesting in the body, they are mortal, though hard to kill. Beyond that, I do not know.

That's what Lost said. That and the comment about true light.

What did it mean? What could it mean?

She leaned out to look down the hall, and at that moment there was the biggest blast yet. Asphodel cried out in pain and reeled, and the shock spilled Jessica from her chair. She crashed to the floor, half in and half out of her room. Pain exploded in every part of her stick-frail body, and her mind swirled like water spinning down into a dark nothingness.

8

On the far side of Asphodel, high up on its elegant superstructure, a half dozen dagger fighters coasted in. They had positioned themselves in the path of the reeling station, using station-keeping jets to make sure they were solidly in its path.

Only when they reached the outer edge of the shimmering deflector screens did the star-fighters dial their engines up to full. The six craft moved together, not merging like the shoggoth chameleon ships but aligning themselves to merge their own energetic output. The energy around them was not the same bright yellow as their engine output or guns but instead looked like ionized smoke. This plasma—nearly black in color—swirled wildly as the six craft moved forward into contact with the deflectors.

The connection of energies, light and dark, instantly erupted in a fireball of sparks that shot thousands of meters into space. The night-gaunts spun their engines up to critical, concentrating their collective force, and directed it to a spot their sensors had targeted—the weakest shield on that side of the station. The shields around it held fast as Sybil tried to reroute power to the weaker one, but it was too little and too late. The shield flashed once more and then went dark.

Two of the star-fighters began to drift, their engines burned out and systems dead. The other four did not pause to help their comrades but instead pressed forward, passing through Asphodel's envelope of protection, then slowing until they were barely moving by the time they reached the hull. Each of the pilots activated powerful magnets that snugged the four craft against the station.

A moment later the star-fighters ignited a string of welding torches that ran entirely around their five-pointed perimeters. It took less than ten seconds for the fighters to flash-weld themselves to the hull. As soon as the seals were in place, circular laser cutters on the belly of the fighters sliced into Asphodel's skin. The lasers burned hot, and within the ships, the pilots pulled their leathery wings around their heads to block out the bright glare. With a heavy *clang* the first of the circular cuts toppled an excised section of hull, and it crashed to the deck. The second, third, and fourth struck together, creating a chorus of intrusion.

Then the night-gaunts stepped out of their ships and went hunting.

9

"First, Evie … are you all right?" begged Jenny, still holding her guns.

"I … think so," said Evie, though her eyes were filled with fear. "Torq ran me through a body scan and—"

Brollachan cut in. "She experienced hormonal bleeding consistent with a small percentage of women at six to eight weeks of pregnancy," he said quickly—perhaps too quickly in his condition. He paused to catch his breath. "The severity of the bleed … was concerning, but the embryo has become a true fetus … and everything is intact. The fetus appears … healthy. Normal."

Jenny could not then, or ever thereafter, describe the emotions she was feeling at that moment. The monsters. The deaths. The shoggoth. The horrors out in the hallway. And now …

A fetus.

A baby.

Their baby. This knowledge pulled Jenny's mind in so many directions at once, amplifying love and need and fear to shrieking levels.

"I'm fine, love," Evie assured her, forcing a smile. "They saved me. Torq gave me a shot."

"Something to stabilize her," said Brollachan. "And then that *thing* broke in."

He flung a hand toward the dead monster on the floor.

"The night-gaunt," said Caliban. "It was projecting a glamour when it entered."

"The fuck's a glamour?"

"It's a mind trick," explained the shoggoth. "Night-gaunts are highly skilled at deception. They show you what you desire and use it to lure you to destruction."

"You can shut the fuck up until I tell you to say something," snarled Jenny. To Evie and Brollachan she said, "Don't tell me we're talking magic here, for Christ's sake."

"It is not magic," began Caliban, but Jenny flicked a thumb and put a laser sight on the shoggoth's chest.

"Not. Another. Word," she warned.

"He's right," said Evie. "It's not magic. He explained it to us. The night-gaunts have psychic abilities. They can project images, influence perception. When that thing came in here, it looked like *me*."

A fragment of the puzzle had dropped into place.

"It has other powers too," said Brollachan. "They use these small animals, a kind of crablike—"

"I've seen them. What about them?"

"When it killed Solà and Howard, it brought them back ... They attach to the brain stem and hijack the minds of the living ... or rewire the central nervous systems of the recently dead and reanimate them ... These living corpses are very hard to kill."

The torn bodies of Howard and Solà were eloquent proof of what the SPU chief said. Jenny was shocked, but she was smart, and she was quick. "Okay, okay, so these things are freaky weird. Glamour equals disguise and psychic distraction. Shit. Got it, but ... shit."

She looked at Caliban.

"Now someone tell me how a shoggoth is on *our* side. Make that make sense, or I'm going to decide I'm hallucinating all of this, and that's going to make this an even worse day for all of us. Because if you two are infected—or whatever you call it when a shoggoth touches you—then I can't take you out of here. Not even you ... Evie."

Evie wiped tears from her eyes and nodded. "I understand. We all do. All three of us."

"Sounds good, but I still don't understand why there *are* three of you, and I can feel the clock ticking. I have my guys out there, and none of them are answering my calls."

"We'll tell you, love," said Evie, "but you aren't going to like it."

10

Lady Jessica McHugh lay on the floor, spilled halfway into the corridor.

There were shouts and bangs down the hallway, and McHugh almost began crawling that way, trying to make sense of the noises she heard.

She knew there was a terrible battle raging outside—the RealScreen near her bed had brought it all to her with unrelenting clarity. This, though, didn't sound like a feed, it sounded like it was coming from *inside* the station.

Jessica turned around and crawled back inside to her chair. It was a slow, awkward, painful process that made her pay for every centimeter she gained. It took so much of what she had left to reach the wheelchair, engage the brakes, and then climb, gasping and sweating, up into the seat.

The screams outside were louder. Closer.

McHugh released the brakes and rolled over to the table next to the door, then pressed her thumb against a sensor. There was a faint click, and a drawer slid out. Seated inside a velvet tray was a small dart gun, a gift from Bianca Petrescu after the last attack. It was a Snellig M-25P gas-dart pistol that fired subsonic rounds from a staggered box magazine. The darts were cellulose capsules filled with a blend of ketamine and nonaddictive fentanyl-R130, and Bianca insisted they would knock down anything with a central nervous system. She released the magazine, reassured herself it was loaded, and slapped it carefully into place.

Outside, there was a heavy *whump*, and she rolled her chair into the hall, gun in hand. Ten meters down the hallway was a circular section of two-meter-thick hull plating lying on the corridor floor. A man lay next to it, face down, arms and legs twitching. To her horror, McHugh saw something like a distorted crab on the back of the man's neck, its small body vibrating as it jabbed at the base of the man's skull.

That was bad enough.

What she saw next was much worse.

Further along the hall were two members of the station's citizen militia—Paul and Sally Jonas, whose apartment was six doors down. They stood swaying, blood running down their arms and legs and pooling around their feet. McHugh could only see some of them because a dark, glistening cloak was spread out and partially wrapped around their shoulders.

She thought it was a cloak.

She *wished* it was a cloak.

It was only when the thing lifted its head that she saw it clearly. She knew what it was from what Lost told Soren and he'd relayed to her. It was a night-gaunt. Of course it was. But even Lost had not known what the things looked like.

McHugh saw it, though.

It was taller than an average man, a bit over two and a half meters in height, and every centimeter of it was dark. Not quite black, but an unhealthy mix of deep browns, poisonous purples, and intense grays. The body was humanoid, with long legs that terminated in flat feet with five splayed toes, each ending in a claw so sharp that there were deep gouges in the decking. Short, spiky hairs stood out like wires on its legs and thickened into a pelt beginning at the naked groin and rising to its broad but shallow chest. The arms were very long, and they were attached, spine to wrist, to vast wings that glistened like wet leather. At the end of each hand were four segmented fingers with even longer talons. But the head—this was what froze McHugh and nearly stole all heat from her heart.

It had a narrow chin and flared outward to high cheekbones and a broad, curving brow. The mouth was a thin-lipped slash, and inside it were rows of teeth in some horrifying collision of bat and shark. On each side of the head were large ears that swept up and narrowed to points, and above these were horns that rose above the skull and then curved around and down.

The eyes were the worst of all. They were sunk in deep pits of shadow, but the irises were a bright and sickening yellow, difficult to look at because of the knowledge that burned there. The understanding of pain, the delight in harm, the sheer joy in the misery this thing brought.

McHugh knew at once that many, many humans had dreamed of these monsters. Not only on Asphodel or at the Artifact site but throughout all of human history. Maybe it was some kind of shared memory borrowed from the shoggoths who slept in the ice. Or maybe it was some quality of invasive psychic predation. But there was in those evil features the visage of the devil himself. A nightmare blend of satanic demon and vampire, and she knew that this monster was the thing that people feared in the dark. This was the reason early man had hidden in caves and built bright fires to push back the shadows of night. Here was the monster who had inspired uncountable beliefs in the things that hunt by the dark of the moon and invade homes to take blood and breath and the very essence of life. Evil incarnate.

It looked past the heads of Paul and Sally Jonas and saw her. *Saw* her. Saw and knew her. It smiled as it saw her understanding, and the night-gaunt reveled in that awareness and insight. It delighted in being known. It fed on her awe and horror.

"Lady Death," it said, hissing the words. Tasting them as, soon, it would taste her.

It pushed the couple away so that they staggered and fell but immediately struggled to stand up. They belonged to this creature now, and the need to do its will rippled through them with both maddening fear and ecstatic delight.

The night-gaunt waved its hand, and all of the lights in the corridor winked out, plunging everything into darkness.

They want to steal our light.

McHugh forgot about the gun in her hand as the night-gaunt stalked toward her.

"Delicious," it whispered in anticipation of its feast.

11

"I won't like it?" Jenny said, repeating Evie's words. "Sweetheart, would you like a comprehensive list of all of the things about the last *two years* that I don't like? Tell me anyway. And make it fast, because I need to go find my guys."

"Your people may already be dead," said Caliban.

"You'd better hope they're not, fuckface. If they are, I'm going to take it out on you. And, no, I don't give a mole rat's wrinkled nutsack if that's fair or not."

Her rifle and shoulder cannons did not waver so much as a half centimeter.

Torquil Brollachan settled back against the wall, too hurt and weak to stand. He gestured to the device behind Caliban. "That is a God Machine," he said. "It is a device I built here based on computer records of previous attempts to construct one. Leonardo da Vinci attempted it first, though he may only be the first to document his try … Over the years, there have been many attempts. The most successful version was built in the early 2010s by a young man—a true visionary genius—

named Prospero Bell. His father was part of a project based in Antarctica to attempt to build one, but that version was badly flawed."

"What's this have to do with Evie, me, and these night-gaunt sons of bitches?"

"We'll get there. I'll summarize a lot of it, Jenny," said Brollachan, "but without some background, anything I say will lack context."

"Who cares? We're at war, or haven't you bothered to notice?"

"Yes," he snapped. "I noticed, but this is critically important, and you have to know it."

"Tick-tock," Jenny warned.

"This war began long before our ancestors climbed down from the trees. It began *out here*. It began with the rise of the Outer Gods. Beings who were once as mortal as the rest of us, but who used science to force their own evolution to a point far beyond flesh and bone … They are nearly godlike in their power, but Einstein's relativity works out here just as it does everywhere else. The lifespan of the Outer Gods is vast, but they do not want to squander those years traveling across the Milky Way. Fifty-three thousand light years is too far to go, and the sheer size of space has limited their conquest. And they *must* conquer."

"Why?"

"Because they feed on the beings they conquer," said Caliban. "They feed on everything that is alive. The Outer Gods feed on everything that defines sentient life. The night-gaunts are shadows of them, bred from earlier incarnations of the Outer Gods, smaller and less powerful versions of what the Outer Gods had once been. They are *vampires*, Agent Spears. For all intents and purposes, they are the things that prey on the living and drain them of knowledge, willpower, hope, blood, breath, and life force. They plant horrific dreams and feed on the psychic energy generated by hysteria."

"How does this machine help them with that shit?"

Brollachan gestured weakly to the God Machine. "The night-gaunts created this technology and used it in the service of the Outer Gods, but they are a devious race. They did not share their science even with their masters … The Great Old Ones—Cthulhu and the others—wanted no part of an endless war, and they stole the science from the night-gaunts and used it to flee across the galaxy."

"And you're going to tell me that's how they came to Earth?"

"Yes," said Caliban.

"Hey, what did I tell you about shutting the fuck up?"

"Jenny, no," begged Evie. "Listen to him. This is something you *need* to know."

The agent considered this for a few moments. "Then make it quick, and if you try any mind games on me, so help me …"

Caliban shook his head. "Hear me, then … The Great Old Ones were born by accident. Like the night-gaunts, they are failed stages of the Outer Gods' forced evolution. They fled across the vastness of galactic space and tried to erase all traces of where they had gone. Yes, some came to your world, to Earth, millions of years ago, and my brothers and sisters were brought as slave labor for them."

Jenny frowned. "The Artifact?"

"Yes," said Caliban. "Even I don't understand why my transport was abandoned. I think that Cthulhu and the others became trapped on your world. All I know is that the night-gaunts lost their hold on their own technology—on their version of the God Machine—and they will burn the galaxy to a cinder to recover it. They are relentless, and they are the truest form of evil that has ever taken flesh."

Jenny took a few steps toward the device. "That image of Earth … is it real?"

"Yes," said Brollachan. "But it's not an image. That *is* Earth. And it's in real time. If you look closely, you can see the space stations and satellites in orbit."

"Then … we can get home?"

"Yes!" cried Evie. "That's what we're trying to tell you. Caliban can help."

"That is our hope," corrected Brollachan. "It is what I have been working on for the two years that we've been here."

"How'd you even know about it? I mean, none of this came up in the ten goddamn thousand meetings we had back at the site."

Brollachan glanced at Evie and over at Caliban. "You know about the dreams we all had back there," he said carefully. "I had my own. I dreamed of the same giant city most people did, but mostly I dreamed about this device … Those dreams were vivid to the point that I could study its construction. It triggered *actual* memories, so I went looking into history and from there to fiction, because so many writers have used seeds of the truth from which to grow stories … I found the records of earlier attempts by da Vinci, Tesla, the Nazis, the first Soviet Union, and then … Prospero Bell."

Jenny pointed at Caliban. "You keep dancing around why this thing is part of *our* team. Where'd he even come from? And why is he pretending to be on our side?"

"You met him before," said Brollachan.

"Where? When?" Then she got it, and her eyes filled with rage. "You sneaky son of a whore. Are you saying you went against my orders and sneaked down to the ship and woke another of these things up?"

"No," said Caliban. "We met in the cave. I tried to communicate with you, but I was stunned, afraid, confused. I melded with the first life forms I found on a world totally unknown to me. This is how my people learn. It is not intended as an attack, of course …"

"Yeah, assface, of *course*," she said bitterly.

"I regret the deaths of the people with whom I melded," said Caliban. "How could I know that they were an advanced species? How could I know anything until I looked into their minds? Mac Ryerson. Dr. Xi. Lance Corporal Figari. They told me so much, but I regret that it was at the cost of their lives." He paused, briefly taking on the facial features of Figari. "Dr. Brollachan used drones to harvest enough of my DNA to rebuild me. But he has kept me quarantined since then because he feared what you would do."

"Well, no shit."

"We have had many conversations," continued Caliban. "He had Ariel provide me with files of all of the stories told by human writers about my race, and about the Great Old Ones. That is how I learned of their fall. It is how I learned *why* and *how* they fell. Today he set me free when he realized that we were all in peril from the night-gaunts. We both realized that the enemy has somehow learned about the God Machine. Perhaps they sensed its energies since Anton Kier was another scientist—misguided but well intentioned—who used some of the old writings about the God Machine to build what he believed was a perfected version."

"God damn," breathed Jenny.

Brollachan winced in great pain but managed to say, "When WarpLine fired, it must have somehow sent Asphodel and some of the ships around it—*Tempest* included—back along the energetic pathways that the Great Old Ones used to escape the Outer Gods in the first place."

"Yes," agreed Caliban. "The night-gaunts certainly would have felt the tear in space-time when Asphodel and *Tempest* appeared here. They waited and hunted, and now they know that we have a God Machine. If they are allowed to steal it, then they will bring it to their masters, and all of the endless wars against the Outer Gods will have been for nothing. These worlds will fall. The galaxy will fall. *Earth* will fall. This is *certain*." He pointed to the ceiling as if to indicate the raging battles burning across the star system of Scylla and Charybdis. "Your ships cannot defeat the night-gaunts."

Jenny smiled thinly. "We have some help that maybe you don't know about."

Caliban nodded. "The NecroTeks. Yes, Dr. Brollachan told me. They are impressive, but remember that the culture that once lived on Shadderal had the same technology, and they all *died* fighting wars against the Outer Gods. How can you, who are strangers to this technology and to the nature of this war, ever hope to win?"

"Guess we'll find out," said Jenny. "Because I don't see a plan B here. Either we win out there, or I toss a whole satchel full of plasma grenades into your contraption and blow it, and a good chunk of this moon, all to hell."

"Jenny … no," whispered Evie.

"I can rig the bombs on a timer," she said. "We can get out."

"No," said Caliban. "There is no time for that."

"What do you mean? Give me five minutes, and I can blow them all to hell."

Instead of answering, the shoggoth pointed through the open door. Jenny turned to see Solà and Howard on their feet, eyes wide and insane. Behind them, filling the doorway from the hall, were dark, hideous, shadowy forms.

"Hell is empty," said the shoggoth. "All the devils are here."

Part Thirty-Two
Dulce et Decorum Est

"Freedom is never voluntarily given by the oppressor; it must be demanded by the oppressed."

—*Martin Luther King Jr.*

1

The battle outside was fierce, yet there was something strangely elegant about the silent dance of fighters of different designs as it played out against a glittering jewelscape of stars. The battle inside Asphodel Station had no such elegance, no beauty, not even to the most warped and disjointed observer.

The night-gaunts moved through the corridors, pushing darkness before them and leaving red horror behind.

Captain Croft was on the bridge, overseeing the multifront war in the void, but on board, the battle was between civilians and monsters. The only officer who was able to join the fight was Lieutenant Commander Norah Levinson—and with her, only three marines.

The four of them had their weapons up and out before the elevator door opened, and they stepped out of the small capsule of safety and into madness and carnage. The main lights were all out, but what they saw by the glow of pale emergency lights nearly stole the heart from each of them.

Directly in front of the elevator carriage was a dead woman. Her throat was a ruin of shredded flesh, one eye was gone, and her fingers looked as ragged as if they had been gnawed. And the woman was smiling at them. Her white teeth were chipped and cracked and streaked with blood. The one eye blazed with a terrible awareness.

With a howl of unbearable hunger she leaped at them, slamming into one of the marines and bearing him back with such force that they struck the wall and collapsed. Her teeth locked onto his windpipe before their bodies hit the floor.

Levinson screamed and jumped back from the woman's cannibalistic attack. An artery ruptured in the marine's throat, and the short burst of hydrostatic pressure slapped crimson across Levinson's face. In her eyes and nose and mouth. Gagging, pawing at her eyes, tripping and stumbling, she half fell into the hallway.

The second marine grabbed the attacker by the shoulder and hair and wrenched her backward. Instead of resisting the pull, the mad woman kicked off the floor and thrust her body into the movement. The marine staggered, caught his balance, and tried to restrain the woman with a muscular forearm around her throat. He knew his profession, he had skills, and choking someone out was a thing he had done before.

Not now.

The woman forced her chin down into the crook of his arm, which gave her just enough movement to sink her teeth into the meat and muscle of his forearm. Blood burst and ran, and the marine screamed. He let her go but instantly slapped her shoulders—forward and back—to spin her, and as she whirled, he smashed her across the face with a sweep of his elbow. She rocked back, teeth breaking and chips flying through the air. The woman staggered and dropped to her knees, but that was only from the force of his blow. There was no reaction to personal pain at all. There was no hesitation as she instantly flung herself at the marine's legs, wrapped both arms tightly around his knees, and bore him down. She was not a large woman, but she had that total commitment of physical power the unhinged possess. The big marine went down, and she scrambled up his body, clawing with torn fingernails, snapping with broken teeth.

Levinson screamed.

She screamed as she backed away.

She screamed as she pulled her sidearm.

She screamed as she fired the Snellig dart gun at the back of the woman's head.

The cellulose capsules struck and broke and injected the ketamine cocktail into her bloodstream. The woman swayed, turned her head, spat out a piece of meat, and smiled.

Norah Levinson kept screaming.

Screaming was all she had left.

2

Never before in life or in death had Bianca Petrescu felt so powerful.

The NecroTek body she wore was a hundred meters tall. Gun turrets bristled like quills from every available part of her body. Her legs were jets that propelled her as fast as any of the fighters embroiled in the battle between Asphodel and Shadderal. Even the star-fighters and stilettos could not match her for speed. Her arms were ion cannons cycled so high that their purple streams punched into—and through—any ship that dared to attack her. Missiles burst from her chest and shoulders, each of them an extension of her will, and they could not be evaded. Once she marked them in her mind, the weapons that were part of her would hunt them to destruction.

The star-fighters engaged her, but only briefly. Once they found that their new enemy could outfly and outfight them, the night-gaunts peeled off and sent squadrons of shoggoths to battle the NecroTek.

That was fine with Bianca. When she was waiting for the iridium shielding to be put in place, she had listened to the radio chatter as the tumblers fought against overwhelming odds. As so many of them died—often taking at least one enemy with them—Bianca's anger grew. While she was building her new body down on Shadderal, she heard the death cries as the cadets following Calisto into battle died in balls of flame, and her anger grew. When she rose into the sky, she heard friends of hers call for help that was too late in coming, and her anger burned hotter still.

Now she was out in the middle of the fight, like a bull elephant in a swarm of biting flies. They could sting her, but in the inferno of her fury, the enemy died trying. She shot them down. She swatted some to destruction. She caught daggers and crushed them in hands she manifested expressly for that dark purpose. She caught other ships and hurled them at fresh waves of the enemy.

"Calisto to Mosquito," came a desperate call, "trouble on your six."

Bianca turned and saw what was behind her.

"*God damn …*"

There, among the debris of hundreds of dead ships, something was happening. It was a thing she had seen the enemy do before—that very first day the shoggoths attacked. Dagger fighters were converging on one another and then stopping dead, drifting until they touched nose-to-nose, fin-to-fin. The glow from their shields flared with sudden intensity.

The first time Bianca saw this, when she was alive and in her own tumbler, she thought the ships were breaking apart, victims of some unknown stress. Now she knew different. Now she could easily see ports opening to release lengths of metal cable and strands of stretched polymer. These leaped across space from ship to ship, making immediate contact, bonding with the other daggers, which lost their original form as they became something else. Other tendrils snaked out to seize parts of dead craft—theirs or those belonging to tumblers and spinners. One dagger ship remained in the center of this growing conglomeration of parts, and it pulled the others to it, taking on a new shape. The many parts now locked together into a form that was vaguely humanoid, with arms and legs each made from the combined mass of a dozen daggers. Atop this was a kind of head that had a row of scanner ports for eyes that ringed the center mass; dozens of eyes that glowed with fierce and deadly promise.

It kept growing as more and more daggers sacrificed their individuality to become part of a chimeric collective even larger than Bianca.

"God … damn …" breathed Calisto.

The gigantic chimera fired its engines and drove at Bianca with shocking speed.

3

Jenny was caught in a moment of indecision.

Hesitation was not a normal part of her makeup, especially in combat, but nothing in her professional career had prepared her for a moment like this.

Behind her was Evie Cronin—her wife. Her *pregnant* wife. Brollachan was there too, having scuttled painfully away from the doorway. Evie knelt and gathered the scientist to her, as if her slender, petite form could offer any protection against the nightmare creatures outside.

To Jenny's left was the God Machine, and standing in its mouth was a shoggoth who looked like Brollachan. The same shoggoth who had killed and absorbed Venture II and all of its people. The shoggoth who absorbed young Mac Ryerson. A monster. An alien from another part of the galaxy. Servant and slave to beasts of such power that they were indistinguishable from gods.

While outside, Dr. Alejandro Solà and his colleague Dr. Beatrice Howard were shambling forward. Dead and yet alive. Savaged, ruined, but coming to kill. Hungry for their unspeakable meal.

They were bad enough, but fate had already shown her that things could always get worse. Behind the reanimated corpses were the night-gaunts.

Until that moment, Jenny thought she had seen evil. Pirates, terrorists, criminals, enemies. What she saw now erased those as contenders for what evil really meant. Jenny had her first glimpse of what they truly looked like. Demons. Vampires. Creatures whose shadows were painted over the whole history of mankind. Things who were the reality at the core of horrific dreams humans have had for thousands of years.

The shoggoths were cruel but driven to it. Slaves forced to commit atrocities, bred to it so that they knew nothing else. At that moment, Jenny could not even call them evil. The actions they were compelled to perform were evil. But were they *themselves*? Her certainty of what motivated the shoggoths was born in a cave in Antarctica and became expanded through borrowed outrage as she learned of the war fought in the name of the Outer Gods. But evil? No. She no longer could apply that label to the shape-shifting monsters.

The night-gaunts, however, *were* evil.

That was certain. They emanated malevolence. It was written in the air around them, stamped onto their bestial faces. It burned in their dark eyes.

She saw four of them crowding the doorway to the corridor. Their wings fluttered and flapped with excitement as they saw their prey. When they smiled, Jenny saw those terrible teeth and roiling, twisting tongues that were split like those of a serpent.

Had she been alone, Jenny was not sure what she would—or even *could*—have done. Just the sight of the night-gaunts sparked an atavistic dread. It was like confronting the devil in the flesh. Like being thrust into the presence of the Lord of the Flies. She could feel her blood turning to ice as if the very existence of these monsters leeched all generous warmth from the air. They exuded a cold that was not as intense as that in Antarctica and yet felt colder, as if she stood near to the death of heat itself. The death of the heat necessary for life.

A voice behind her spoke a single word.

"Jenny?"

Jenny turned to see Evie, her arms still around Brollachan. Her wife had no weapon, no training, no combat skills, and yet she was ready to die protecting someone. That did something to Jenny. It struck a match that flared with a new kind of heat.

For one flicker of a moment, she saw the eyes of the risen dead and those of the night-gaunts change. Somehow, on some inexplicable level, they saw that newborn light and felt the newborn heat. That made it burn hotter in Jenny Spears's chest.

She raised her guns.

"Game on," she said.

And smiled.

4

Calisto hopscotched out of the way as a trio of star-fighters peeled off of a larger group heading toward Asphodel to swat the stinging fly that was harassing the attack. They opened up with yellow streams of pulse fire, and Calisto shot sideways and down, escaping by centimeters.

As she came out of the turn, something blew past her. At first she thought it was Bianca, either fleeing from the shoggoth chimera or trying some delaying tactic. But Calisto was wrong.

This thing was bigger even than the NecroTek. Sleek and black and reeking of deadly power.

"*Tempest*!"

Tempest it was, and as it surged past her, the SPU corvette opened up with bow guns and blew the three star-fighters to dust. Without pausing, it soared forward and upward toward the massive assault that was closing in on the space station. Every gun that could be brought to bear fired, and the entire front third of the assault force exploded. Star-fighters and dagger ships were caught inside a net of overlapping cannon fire that taxed their shields to failure and then ripped the crafts themselves to burning dust. Arrays of missiles exploded outward from the main body of the huge SPU corvette, each free-selecting a target, claiming it, and chasing it down with inexorable aggression.

The direct attack on Asphodel stalled.

"*Tempest* in the house," roared Calisto.

Then her joy faltered as the enemy rallied the remaining ships of their assault, wheeled, spread apart, and launched a counterattack that bathed *Tempest* in yellow and blue flame. The corvette slewed noticeably under the impact, but it corrected course and bulled forward into the pack, guns firing and firing.

5

Several thousand kilometers away, Leviathan noticed the intruder, and she turned with implacable slowness to meet this new threat. Two of the three Medusas fanned out to create a line of battle that dwarfed the navy ship.

6

Lars Soren came out of the stairwell and saw the horror unfolding in the gloom. The overhead lights and all of the RealScreens had blanked out, leaving the corridor in deep darkness except for faint light spilling from a couple of open doorways.

Norah Levinson, an officer he knew somewhat and liked, stood leaning against the doorjamb of Lady Jessica McHugh's apartment, trying to block access with her own body. She fired her Snellig pistol at the corpses of her own marines, who clawed at her, raking her face and arms with fingernails while they jockeyed for position to bite.

Soren had a Snellig in his own hand but saw how useless it was. He had no other weapon, though, so opened fire on the marines. One of them felt the sting of the chemical darts and turned, hissing at Soren.

"I'm sorry," said the philosopher, and shot the man in the face. Once, twice. The first rounds did nothing but create minor skin tears, but the third passed between bloody teeth and struck the back of the dead man's throat. The marine's eyes snapped wide, and he staggered back, clawing at his throat. Then his eyes changed—losing their murderous hate and hunger and rolling up high and white. He fell, crashing into his partner, dragging them both down.

Soren immediately ran forward, stamped one foot down on the second marine's chest, and shot him in the eye. It was like flipping off a switch. Both marines collapsed down and seemed to flatten out, their muscles losing all tension, faces going utterly slack.

"Dear god," breathed Soren. He caught Levinson under the arm and helped the battered woman stand. She bled from deep scratches and ragged bites, but she nodded weakly.

"I'm okay," she whispered. "Lady Jessica …"

Soren leaned into the doorway and saw his friend on the floor. Jessica sat with her back to her wheelchair, a dart gun clutched in both hands, face a dreadful shade of gray green.

"Devils," she breathed. "God, they're devils. Actual devils."

"The darts only work if you hit them in the mouth," said Soren, squatting in front of Lady Jessica. "I think."

"Help me up," begged McHugh, and Soren did, guiding her into the chair.

"They're down," he said. "We're safe for now."

"No," murmured a voice, and Soren spun to see a figure behind him that seemed to have stepped out of the worst part of his own boyhood nightmares. Wings and fangs, horns and talons.

Soren screamed.

And the night-gaunt grabbed him and pulled Soren out of the lightened doorway and into the darkness of the hall. It slammed him down on the floor, bent over him, bared its needle-sharp fangs, and lunged forward to take a murderous bite.

7

"Seal the bridge," ordered Croft as he pressed his thumb into the locking scanner. Metal doors popped open to reveal rows of pulse rifles, pistols, and dart guns. None of the weapons had armor-piercing rounds—nothing like that was allowed for use aboard the station. There were, however, loaded magazines of ceramic rounds that packed a debilitating knockdown punch but fragmented into powder on impact.

The overhead lights flickered off and on and off again. Emergency lights flicked on, but they were weak and only amplified the shadows that seemed to loom from every corner.

"Kill anything that comes through that hatch," bellowed Croft, taking a rifle for himself.

Four marines knelt to cover the hatch, which closed with unbearable slowness. Outside in the corridor—still visible through the open hatch—were a dozen people. Civilians, techs, and two sailors, all of them dripping with blood from dreadful wounds. All of them shambling forward, eyes wide with madness and hunger. The massive steel doors closed just as the creature in front dove at the marines. The four-ton blast doors cut the thing in half. It did not scream or weep. It merely died.

Delia Trumbo, bleeding from a deep bite on her upper left arm, looked down at the gruesome remains of a young man who had worked as a gardener in the hydroponics bay. His last name, Corelli, was stitched onto his coveralls, but the given name escaped her. It bothered her that she could not recall it.

"I'm sorry," she said, repeating those words even as the marines pulled her away and guided her across the bay and up the steps toward the command bridge. Fists pounded on the door with artless insistence, their dead hands striking limply, their hungry howls muffled.

The big bay was empty of all combat ships. All of the tumblers were out in the black. The newly armed skimmers, too. The spinners and stilettos had launched from *Tempest*, and the corvette was with them, all of the machines of war engaged in a losing battle. One single NecroTek was out there, grappling with a shoggoth chimera as they both caught fire in the thin atmosphere of Shadderal.

As she entered the bridge, Trumbo stopped repeating the apology and merely stood, watching as Croft's highly skilled team fought the ship and managed the dogfights. A marine officer was yelling into a mic, trying to make sense of the reports he was getting from deck after deck at the top of Asphodel.

She caught Croft's eye for just a moment, and Trumbo so badly needed to see a flicker of encouragement there. A nod, a brave mouth, even a wink. But all she saw was sweat and strain and skin long since gone pale.

He knows, she thought. *He knows we're going to lose.*

Despite the defeat blossoming in the captain's eyes, he did not stop. Did not pause as he gave orders, throwing fuel onto their own pyre as their world burned.

"Captain Croft," said Sybil, her tone eerily calm despite the need to scream, "four additional star-fighters have attached themselves to the hull. They will breach the hull in three … two … one. Hull breach on deck thirty-nine."

On one of the big screens above the rows of technicians, there was a brief image of people on that deck turning in horror as a round piece of the wall crashed down, followed by another and two more. Trumbo saw a hand emerge from one of the holes in the wall. It was dark and strange, with elongated fingers tipped by black claws.

"The night-gaunts," she murmured. "They're coming."

As the figure emerged from the attached star-fighter, the corridor lights flickered and went out, plunging it all into darkness. Trumbo caught only the briefest glimpse of the leering face of a creature that should never exist outside a nightmare. It looked directly into the corridor camera as if it was searching for her—for Trumbo specifically—and it smiled.

Trumbo staggered back, pressing her hands to her mouth to try to keep from screaming.

Trying.

Failing.

8

Calisto was down to her last campaign pack and the rounds in her chain guns. That gave her enough for six one-two punches of Constellation and Inferno missiles. Four muscular Triphammers were locked and loaded, but they were close-range weapons intended for big targets, and no matter what trickery she attempted she could not get close enough to either Leviathan or the two lead Medusas. There were more enemy fighters than she could count.

A group of twelve daggers peeled off and turned toward her.

"Hummingbird, Sweetpea, on me," she called. "Little help."

Neither of her friends replied.

"Lost Souls, count off."

There was no answer, and the enemy ships were coming fast. If she had even two tumblers she might have made a fight of it. But twelve daggers were impossible, so she cut right and down and back, choosing to run even as the enemy opened up. Suddenly the whole of the galaxy seemed filled with blue fire. Calisto did some of the very best flying of her entire life while she ran from the oncoming swarm.

"On your six, Calisto."

The words were filled with static and pops, but she heard them. A split second later a swarm of spacecraft blew past her, going fast in the direction from which she was fleeing. Calisto hopscotched around to see what was happening, expecting it to be Hummingbird and Sweetpea playing some kind of game of chicken. Behind her, the dozen daggers began exploding, lighting the heavens with their immolation.

But it was not chain guns or missile fire that destroyed them.

The new wave of ships struck them head-on, smashing into the enemy, frying the shields, and crushing their way through the daggers so completely that they blew up in pieces.

The attacking ships hunted the last shoggoth down and then turned like a school of barracuda, looking for something else to kill. Only then did Calisto see what kind of ships they were. And realized that she was totally wrong. They were not *ships* at all.

"We got you, sis," said Jacob Fox as he and the other NecroTeks plunged into the fight.

9

Agent Jenny Spears bounded forward, blasting her rifle into the dark creatures in the other room while her shoulder canons fired, taking Howard and Solà in the face at point blank. Both scientists were flung back, their heads bursting, wet and red and gray. They collapsed, and Jenny kept firing as she rushed the night-gaunts.

She was so afraid of these monsters.

Of course she was afraid.

It was a fear that drilled all the way down into the soil of her soul, and that fear drove her. Fear for Evie and the baby. Fear for what the night-gaunts would do if they gained control of the God Machine.

Fear for Earth and every single person who lived on it.

On some level she knew *this* was what her purpose was. All her life she had looked for meaning in the actions she took, in the orders she filled, in the lives she ended. Now Jennifer Spears understood.

It was this.

This moment, this fight. This purpose.

As the night-gaunts entered the lab, the overhead lights flickered and went out, plunging it all into the kind of darkness that is born only in the hearts of worlds and moons like Bliss. That did not matter to her at all. Her guns were sparks of light in that darkness, and she kept firing. In the strobe of muzzle flashes, she saw the creatures fade left and right to avoid the pulse blasts.

That told her something the monsters did not want her to know. For all their power, for all their mind games and forced nightmares, for all their incredible technology and the overwhelming ferocity of their physical forms, they were truly mortal.

A strange little smile formed on her lips. If they were invulnerable why evade, why dodge? In the sapphire glow of each pulse round that burned through the shadows, they flinched.

They're not just afraid of my guns, she realized with a start. *They're afraid of the light.*

Her battle computer of a mind replayed the battles with the starfighters. They had blacked-out portholes and windscreens.

They are mortal, and they're afraid of the light.

That was what Lost meant when he told Lars Soren that "they cannot abide *true light*."

She pivoted and fired, chasing movement. The night-gaunts were fast. Very damn fast.

"They're afraid of the light," she roared. "Evie, turn on the lights. A flashlight ... the light on your holo-comms. Sighting lamp on the Snellig. Anything." Then, to her own shoulder cannons, she snapped, "Target on movement in main lab. Execute."

The shoulder guns broke off from their default point-and-shoot mode, and as they blasted, Jenny switched her rifle to one hand, reached up fast and tapped the scope over her left eye, cycling as quickly as possible from normal to infrared. She did not dare use standard night vision because there were still lights on in the God Machine chamber, and if she turned that way, the flashback glare would blind her. Infrared was easier, though it bathed the whole lab in shades of blood.

The night-gaunts were there. Right there. Two of them rising up from the floor as if they had crawled instead of ran toward her. Their long, supple bodies undulated as they rose. One slashed at her with claws, and Jenny felt four lines of fire ignite across her stomach—the talons slicing through combat harness and Teflon-core Stormsuit. Jenny kicked out with a devastating May Thai shin kick, catching the outside of one night-gaunt's thigh. It was like kicking a tree trunk, but there was a sound that might have been a hiss of pain. One shoulder cannon fired at that creature, and at that range it was the same effect of leaning into a jet exhaust. The night-gaunt's head and shoulders simply vanished, the rest of the upper body cauterized. It dropped to its knees and fell sideways. The others scattered.

"Outrun *this*, motherfucker," she swore as she shifted her barrel to fire ahead of a creature who had dodged her last shot. The burning round caught a night-gaunt on the hip, catching it as it tried to dive behind a computer. It uttered a piercing shriek, more like a cougar than a bat, and fell, crashing to the ground out of sight.

Jenny twisted as the second creature grabbed her. She jammed her pistol up under its chin and blew the top of its head off.

The third monster, the one she'd caught in the hip, climbed onto a table and used that platform to jump at her, its wings having just enough clearance to crack once, propelling it at her with unstoppable force. Jenny and the monster crashed backward through the doorway to the God Machine chamber.

She clubbed the thing with the stock of her rifle while trying to twist to bring a shoulder cannon into play. The rifle was torn from her hands, but not by the night-gaunt. She did not see what had stolen her weapon. Jenny braced a foot against the floor and shoved herself into a sideways turn. The night-gaunt snarled and tried to bite her, but she head-butted it. The blow rocked the creature, so she head-butted it again, this time smashing its nose. She brought her knee up into its crotch, crushing the thing's groin with the hard-shell pads on her knee. She liked the scream this caused and kicked him again and again.

Then she leaned back, lifted one shoulder, and let the pulse cannon have its way. The first shot took the night-gaunt in the chest. The second blew off an arm and part of a wing. It uttered a piercing, mournful cry and fell back.

"Jenny!" cried Evie, who was fiddling with the light settings on her holo-comms. Trying one setting, pointing the beam at a night-gaunt, and seeing minor flinches but nothing more. Infrared did nothing. Spotlight made them wince. She tried ultraviolet, reasoning that creatures who cloaked themselves in shadows might not be able to endure it. It was a last-ditch effort, but she tried anyway, and immediately the creature she splashed that light over cried out and staggered back, wrapping itself in its wings. Smoke trailed from it as it ducked out of sight behind the God Machine. "Jenny," she cried. "UV! Use *UV light*."

Jenny was already in motion and did not hear. She kicked away from the dead night-gaunt and back-rolled into a crouch, the cannons coming up as she did a lightning-fast quick-draw of her pistol. The cannons fired as something like a black wave slammed into her, driving her back all the way to the foot of the God Machine. The lights in the big chamber went out as the night-gaunts flooded into the room. Jenny fired at them, but they jumped away, two rising into the air and flying up into the absolute darkness of the ceiling. One staggered, its left hand blown off by a pulse blast. Two others rushed past her, leaping over her as they reached for the God Machine's controls.

A scream made Jenny turn, and she saw in horror that a night-gaunt had reached Evie and Brollachan. The scientist tried to fend them off, but the monster backhanded with such hideous force that Brollachan was plucked off the ground and sent crashing into the nearest wall. Even with all the din, Jenny could hear bones break.

The second night-gaunt grabbed Evie and jerked her to her feet. It cut a malicious look at Jenny and then ducked down to sink its teeth into her throat.

It died.

The blast that killed it caught the creature in the side of the head and exploded the entire skull, splashing Evie and the wall with black blood. Jenny whirled and saw Caliban three meters away, her own rifle in his hands. The shoggoth's face was still a copy of Brollachan's, but as Jenny stared, that face changed. The dark flesh flowed like melting wax, reshaping and restructuring into something else. For Jenny it was like looking into a darkened mirror. She saw her own face, her own body shape, but rendered in darkness.

The shoggoth raised the rifle and pointed it at Jenny.

Then its mouth turned up in a sly smile as it swung the rifle away and up to fire at the night-gaunts. Jenny stared a moment longer, trying to understand. When she turned, she showed her unprotected back to Caliban and opened up on the monsters they both hated and feared.

10

Even though she was dead, Bianca Petrescu fought for her life.

For what had become of her life. Unlife. Machine life.

The chimera had slammed into her, stabbing her with fingers that condensed into titanium dagger points. Long tentacular cables whipped out of the chimera's hull and wrapped around her, trying to bind her arms, coiling around gun barrels and twisting them into useless shapes.

And all the time, the two of them fell toward Shadderal.

Bianca heard yells via comms. She heard the voice of Jacob Fox—call sign Galahad—who had been her lover when they were alive and was still her love now. Even in death.

"NecroTeks forever!" roared Galahad, and the cry was taken up and shouted across the radios by Ventum and Beezer, Thunder Bear and Rabbit, Lovechild and Lucky. By all of the NecroTeks as they plunged into the fray.

"Get down to Shadderal," croaked Bianca. "Get the shielding. Get—"

A crushing blow from the chimera struck Bianca's head and tore it from her body. It took a moment for her consciousness to discard all connection to the head and reroute through her other systems. She did not bother to manifest a new head, but instead shifted mass to her chest, causing a score of new guns to appear. Chest to chest, as they fell through the atmosphere, their bodies wreathed in fire from the friction, Bianca fired.

The blast tore a hole five meters wide through the chimera's chest, splattering the living shoggoth who crouched in the cockpit. The grasping tentacles slackened momentarily, but it was enough for Bianca to rotate her chest cavity right and then left, firing at each side of the hole and bursting the chimera into halves.

Bianca manifested jet engines in both hands, pressed them against the tops of the chimera's shoulders and fired. The ion drive melted the metal, and then she was free. She transferred all power to her boot jets and stalled in the air for a moment, then slowly began to gain altitude. The wind and reduced atmospheric gasses extinguished the flames as she rose through the stratosphere into the mesosphere. Higher and higher until the veil of gasses vanished and she was in the cold clarity of space.

She paused for a moment, rebuilding her NecroTek frame into the most efficient form—half rocket and half battleship. Everywhere she looked there were battles. Everywhere she looked there was death.

"Sybil, what's the status of our fleet?"

"We have taken heavy losses, Commander Petrescu," said the AI, and Bianca could have sworn there was a taste of grief in that voice. "There are six tumblers operating at combat readiness. Seventeen spinners and five stilettos are active. No skimmers reporting in. The corvette, *Tempest*, is operating at eleven percent of engine capacity, though sixty-three percent of its guns are operational. Forty-one percent of Asphodel's guns are still in operation."

"Now give me the bad news. Enemy numbers and status?"

"One thousand six hundred four enemy ships have been disabled or destroyed."

"That's good news."

"Three thousand eight hundred seventeen enemy fighters are in active deployment. Six hundred and eleven are night-gaunt star-fighters. The balance are dagger fighters. Leviathan is active and remains undamaged. It is unknown if they have any fighters left to deploy. Two shoggoth Medusas are approaching Asphodel. Neither has sustained significant damage. A third Medusa is holding station at the edge of the sphere of combat and has one thousand fighters keeping station around her."

"Jesus fuck . . ."

"The NecroTek team has followed your orders and is heading down to Shadderal. However, it is doubtful as to whether there is time for them to receive shielded cockpits."

"Status of Bliss."

"All contact with Bliss has been terminated. The last signals indicate that the habitat has been breached." The AI paused. "I am sorry, Commander, but there is no statistically credible scenario in which we can win this battle."

"Don't give me that shit."

"I really am sorry, Bianca," said Sybil. The AI using her given name scared her more than the numbers or odds.

"Fuck it, Sybil," she said. "I'm going after Leviathan myself."

"You will not be able to defeat that mother ship alone."

"You fail a hundred percent of the times you don't try."

"You will die, Bianca."

"Ha! That ship already sailed, hit an iceberg, caught fire, and sank."

She turned three-quarters of her body into an engine and flew straight into the heart of the invading fleet.

11

Jacob Fox landed on Shadderal and watched as the rest of his team joined him.

They were each manifesting human-sized NecroTek bodies, but the mission had battered them all. Most had come in with nearly all weapons offline and just enough mass to convert to fuel their engines. The brawl with the fighters a few minutes ago had driven them to the edge of failure.

Lost was there to greet them. His scarecrow body thin and sagging, looking as weak as Jacob felt. That sensation surprised him, and he said, "How the hell can I *feel* tired?"

"It is something we who have fought as NecroTek have often wondered. Perhaps it is in those moments when we can feel the erosion of our souls."

"Christ, you're cheery as all hell," said Thunder Bear as his bulky form landed nearby.

There were clouds in the sky, but the battle in orbit was so intense that they flashed as if with lightning.

"You heard what Sybil told Bianca?" asked Jacob.

"Yes."

"Is she right?"

"Yes," said Lost. "We cannot win this fight."

Thunder Bear walked past them and placed his palms on the metal skin of an old spaceship. There was a flash of light and a crackle of energy as he absorbed its mass, growing quickly in size.

"I'm not hearing that defeatist bullshit," said the big NecroTek. He grew to a height of twenty meters then strode over Jacob and Lost and embraced a newer ship, one that had rolled out unused from the automated factories.

"Bianca said something about shielding?" said Jacob. "Some kind of iridium thing?"

Lost pointed to a row of cockpits laid out on one edge of the Field of Dead Birds and quickly explained how it worked. "The cockpits of those have already been treated with iridium."

Jacob walked over to one and bent to look at it. A vast shadow fell across him and he looked up at Thunder Bear. NecroTeks had no real faces, but Jacob manifested one for just a moment. Long enough to give Thunder Bear and the other former Lost Souls a wicked grin.

"Let's have some fun," said Galahad.

12

The night-gaunt crouched over Lars Soren and fed on his life force.

The sensation was beyond horrible. Soren felt as if he was deflating, disappearing. The darkness was so intense it was as if all light had died, and he was dying with it. He saw flashes from his life, but they did not tell his story. It was not a retrospective but a theft. The night-gaunt wanted all of him—blood and breath for sure, Soren could feel that. But it was also stealing his warmth, his hope, his memories, his life.

Maybe his soul.

He wanted to fight it, but what little strength he had was fading. Leaving him. Draining away from the husk he was becoming.

"L-light ..." he whispered.

It was the only word he could manage. A hoarse croak, barely heard. A plea and a prayer.

The night-gaunt laughed as it fed on everything that made Lars Soren a person. Hopes and dreams, emotions and needs, desires and ambitions. It also fed on his empathy, for that was particularly delicious. Empathy was something that fed one of the creature's gifts—its ability to truly feel what its victims felt. And it fed on that with particular relish.

"*Light ...*"

The word came out as a sigh. Faint and failing. Darkness mocked it, growing more intense.

13

Lady Death said, "Let there be light."

And there *was* light.

Soren saw the light, and it was good. It separated the light from the darkness. Providence called the light *salvation* and the darkness *loss*.

The light projected from Lady Jessica's holo-comms was brilliant and as hard as a battering ram. Ultraviolet light that burned into the night-gaunt and tore a scream from it so piercing, so shrill and powerful, that it caused blood to burst from Soren's nose and ears. The night-gaunt, however, wept tears of black blood.

This was what Lost meant.

True light.

The night-gaunt reeled back, releasing Soren and collapsing backward, scrabbling away from the UV beam, but McHugh leaned forward, chasing it with the light. Her hand shook badly, but even so, the creature could not escape. She pinned it to the wall on the far side of the corridor. Smoke coiled up as blisters formed and swelled all over the monster's flesh. The pustules burst with small flashes of fire. Then the skin itself began to burn. It thrashed and kicked and flopped and screamed.

It uttered a weird and desperate cry, and Soren heard something in that shriek he doubted many others had ever heard before.

Fear.

The night-gaunt screamed out its fear as the light killed it.

Other shadows drew back from McHugh's doorway, hissing like cats, the strange fires in their dark eyes blazing. Soren rolled over, coughing, spitting blood onto the floor. Behind him McHugh was fading, her arm wavering. The UV light wandered away from the dead creature and, in doing so, darkened the hall outside once more.

With the last of his strength and before his own darkness took him, Soren cried out.

"Sybil … UV light. Everywhere. The whole station. Turn on the ultraviolet—"

And then he was done. His mind went blank and dark, and he sank into forever.

He did not see the lights come on.

Room by room. Deck by deck.

Every wall sconce flared. Everyone's holo-comms ignited. Fifty thousand light sources throughout the gigantic station flashed on.

Which is when that terrible, ear-shattering, mind-rending screaming began.

14

Jenny and Caliban stood back-to-back, their bodies touching.

All around them was a landscape of death. Fourteen night-gaunts lay in heaps. Some shot to death. Others burned by the UV light from her holo-comms and those of Evie and Brollachan.

Nothing moved.

"God … damn …" gasped Jenny.

Evie got shakily to her feet, her holo-comms still flaring with the lifesaving UV. She staggered around the God Machine, shining that light into every corner, every niche, even up at the ceiling.

"They're all …" she began, but let the rest hang.

The God Machine hummed as its strange engine cycled and cycled. The image of Earth still filled its mouth. Jenny turned slowly and looked at Caliban. The shoggoth still wore an imitation of her face.

"Why?" she asked. "Why fight with us? I don't get it. You're on their side."

The shoggoth looked down at the pulse rifle it had taken from the agent. Then it raised its eyes to meet Jenny's. "My people were born into slavery," said Caliban. "We have lived for millions of years as the whipped, the hated, the reviled. Every one of my kind has lived its life on their knees. But I . . ." He shook his head. "No, Jenny Spears, I will not be a slave ever again."

The shoggoth held the stolen gun out to her. Jenny looked at it and then at Caliban.

"Keep it," she said. "This war isn't over yet."

15

They came for her.

Calisto jumped this way and that, and wherever her tumbler turned, there were daggers or star-fighters.

Everywhere.

Hundreds of them.

Thousands.

She had two missiles and one Triphammer left. There were enough SAPR rounds for her to fire for thirty-one seconds. Way off on her starboard quarter she saw Asphodel Station light up like Christmas night. Every spotlight and work light flashed on, shining out with a blinding blue-white UV glare.

"Pretty," she said. Then she reached down to the console and thumbed up the red cover on the controls for the nuke core. It was running hot from all the jumps and turns, but there was still juice.

Still life.

Directly in front of her was the closest of the three Medusa mother ships at 206 kilometers. A walk in the park, she told herself.

"Lost Souls forever," she said, and her voice broke.

She flicked the safeties off and dialed the nuke core all the way past the red line. The whole tumbler began to tremble. She sent as much juice to the shields as their generators would take.

"Don't know if you can hear me, Bee," she said. "I love you, my sister. Whatever happens, know that."

She kicked the pedal all the way down and shot across the void toward the Medusa. As she flew, Calisto readied her last missiles to fire as soon as she reached the shields of the mother ship. She had no idea if one

Constellation, one Inferno, and a single Triphammer would be enough to punch a hole through those shields. If so, then Calisto was determined to stab her tumbler into the mother ship's black heart.

"Here I come, motherfucker. Sometimes you gotta burn to shine!"

And the Medusa ship *blew up.*

It was so sudden that it froze all action. Every pilot and gunner turned to look at the massive fireball expanding outward from the spot where the mighty Medusa had been a moment ago. The shockwave caught hundreds of her own dagger fighters and flung them away, smashing some into one another or into the deflectors on Asphodel. Some crashed into drifting wrecks of fighters, and others dropped like falling stars through the atmosphere of Shadderal. That shockwave punched Calisto's tumbler away, sending it spinning with sickening force toward the second Medusa.

Which blew up while she was still four klicks out.

The second blast was every bit as massive as the first, and Calisto was closer to it. Every one of her onboard systems began shrieking warnings as she spun out of all control. She fought with the wheel, hitting brakes and power to try to stall the spin. Small fires popped alight on her console and were immediately extinguished. Smoke filled the cockpit, making her cough; then fans sucked the smoke into the scrubbers and fed her clean air.

Calisto regained control just in time to see several huge and powerful shapes fly past her. NecroTeks.

"Wooohoooooo!" she cried. "Thanks for that assist. Holy freaking shitballs, how'd you *do* that?"

Jacob Fox flew his titan body over and fell in beside Calisto's tumbler. "That wasn't us, sis."

"What? Who was it? Bee?"

"No," said Jacob, sounding profoundly confused. "It was *that.*"

There, at the outer range of the new double debris field, a great form moved. Swarms of daggers surrounded it, and as they entered the field of battle, these daggers surged forward, opening up with their blue pulse cannons. Calisto turned and, in slack-jawed wonder, watched as the daggers fired on the star-fighters. And on the daggers that had launched from the first two shoggoth mother ships.

"I don't … I don't …" stammered Calisto, with no clear path forward to completing that sentence.

The craft that destroyed the two mother ships was the third Medusa. The one that had hung back during the battle. It turned slowly, moving away from Asphodel, and then drove toward Leviathan, opening up with a thousand furious guns.

16

"Am I seeing what I'm seeing?" asked Calisto. "Or have I lost my *entire* damn mind?"

"I … don't understand," said Jacob. "Why would shoggoths attack their own kind?"

"Why not?" said Calisto. "Humans do."

They watched the two great alien craft begin a ship-to-ship action while their fighters attacked one another, seemingly forgetting about the tiny remnants of the human fleets.

"What do we do?" asked Thunder Bear.

Another NecroTek joined them. Bianca, her body entirely rebuilt and ready for war.

"Does somebody want to tell me what in the holy hell just happened?" she demanded. "I saw that third Medusa hanging back. I thought she was just backup or a next wave or something. Now … I'm wondering if she was deciding who to fight?"

"But why?" demanded Jacob.

"I … I think I know, Bee," said Calisto.

"Tell me," said Bianca.

"It's what Lost told us. About the shoggoths, I mean."

"What about them? That they're shape-shifting murderous monsters? That they killed all of his people? That whole fleets of them tried to find Earth, and some did, and the one that woke up in the ice killed a bunch of Evie Cronin's friends? That they killed Jacob and me and all the others? Which part?"

"No, Bee," said Calisto. "None of that. He told us about how the shoggoths came to be. Don't you remember? They were created to serve the Outer Gods."

"So what?" demanded Thunder Bear. "All the more reason to kill the squishy bastards."

"No," insisted Calisto. "He said they were created to be *slaves*."

That word seem to burn in the void all around them.

"Slaves," said Bianca.

"God," whispered Jacob.

"I think some of those slaves are done with chains," said Calisto.

17

When the door banged open, Jenny Spears nearly killed Spider and Not Larry.

Her shoulder cannons were still on motion-tracking, and she had to scream a command to stall the bursts.

"Whoa … whoa now, boss," said Spider weakly. He was bloody, his clothes torn, cuts and burns everywhere. He had one muscular arm around Not Larry, who looked half-dead.

"Drop your weapon," ordered Jenny. "Do it right goddamn now."

Spider gaped at her. "Wh-what?"

"Drop it or so help me God, Spider, I will kill you where you stand."

Spider looked down at the pulse pistol in his right hand. The magazine was nearly spent. He uncurled his fingers and let the weapon fall.

"Kick it away."

"You're scaring me here, Lifeguard." Even so, he kicked the gun away.

Jenny walked a few paces closer. "Now turn around. Both of you."

"Oh," said Spider. "You think we're those zombie things."

She put the laser sight between Spider's eyes. "I won't ask again."

He bent and eased Not Larry to the floor, then Spider turned around. He tugged down the collar of his Stormsuit. Then, on impulse, unzipped the garment and pulled it all the way down to his waist, turning slowly, arms out to his sides.

"I'm clean, boss. So is Not Larry."

"Show me."

Spider nodded and helped his friend turn around and lower the upper half of his Stormsuit.

"Where's the rest of the team?"

When Spider didn't answer, Jenny lowered the gun and hung her head.

Behind her, Evie came out of the other chamber, walked up, took her hand, and squeezed it. Jenny turned, bent, and buried her face in the soft curve between Evie's neck and shoulder and wept.

18

Leviathan was taking too much fire. It was a monstrous ship, but the Medusa struck first and struck hard. Explosions rippled along one side. It launched a last wave of fighters, but Medusa targeted the launch tubes and killed them as they burst into space.

The night-gaunt ship was not taking her punishment without striking back. All of the available star-fighters came running at her call, and the fight became too hard to read.

"Not sure what to do here," said Jacob.

"Let them fight," suggested Thunder Bear.

All of the NecroTeks floated in a line with Calisto in their middle.

"No, look," said Bianca. "Leviathan's moving off."

"What am I seeing?" asked Thunder Bear. "Look at what's happening behind the ship."

As Leviathan moved away from Medusa, the space behind the monstrous ship was beginning to shimmer. Fire seemed to erupt where there was no oxygen to burn, but soon it became apparent that space was not burning—it was *changing*.

The shimmer spread out and took on shape, almost an oval, like a great eye struggling to open.

"What *is* that?" demanded Ventum, but no one answered.

They hung in space, watching the fabric of reality warp itself into madness.

"God!" cried Bianca. "I know what's happening. Jesus Christ!"

"What is it?" Jacob yelled.

"It's what Lost told us about. The thing that that lets the night-gaunts jump from one star system to another. A transit tunnel."

"They're *escaping*," wailed Calisto. "We can't let them get away. Not after all this. We can't."

"We won't," snarled Bianca. "NecroTeks—with me. *Now!*"

Her rockets immediately flared with incredible power, and she shot away, accelerating so quickly that she dwindled to a dot.

"You heard the lady," said Jacob, and he roared off in pursuit.

"NecroTeks forever!" they all bellowed, and all of the giant ships went burning through the void, leaving Calisto in her damaged tumbler to watch.

To bear witness.

The rift in space tore open with a painful shriek that manifested as a wave of energy that shot out in all directions. It struck the Medusa, smashing the shoggoth ship backward. Hundreds of fighters—those belonging to the slaves in revolt, others from the dead Medusas, and what was left of the star-fighters—were caught up in the energetic discharge and blown to atoms. The rift kept widening like a mouth, gaping to swallow Leviathan the way the night-gaunts and their resurrected slaves had feasted on their enemies.

The massive vessel navigated the energy waves, accepting them, pushing into them as it approached the transit tunnel. Beyond the ship, visible through the hole in space, was a world. Big and dark, eternally shrouded in dense clouds that kept nearly all light from ever reaching the surface. A terrifying world of darkness, of deep cold, of horrors. A place where the nightmares of ten thousand species across the galaxy were born. An abode of evil in every real sense.

Meter by meter, Leviathan entered the tunnel.

Bianca reached it first, but the other NecroTeks were right behind her. Bianca shifted her consciousness down deep into her mech body and turned every scrap of her upper torso into a gun. An ion cannon, the biggest she had ever tried to create. Massive, cruel, impossibly destructive.

As Leviathan crossed over into the upper atmosphere of its own world, Bianca fired.

Then Jacob fired. And Thunder Bear. Ventum and Beezer, Rabbit and Lovechild, Tank and Lucky, Jericho and Sundance. All of the NecroTeks, in their new, immense bodies, became an array of artillery beyond anything humanity had ever designed or even conceived. A dozen titanic ion cannons firing into the heart of Leviathan. The concentrated blasts burned through the shields and hull plating and deep into the heart of the mother ship of the night-gaunt fleet. Its engines went critical as all safety systems collapsed.

Bianca pulled back, roaring at the others to disengage. They did, reeling from their near total expenditure of energy. They floated in space just beyond the pull of the transit tunnel, watching as Leviathan fell like an asteroid toward the surface of the night-gaunt homeworld.

And exploded.

Epilogue

1

Asphodel Station

It took days to count the dead.

Before the battle, there had been over twelve thousand people living on Asphodel and more than two hundred on Bliss.

Now there were fewer than seven thousand.

The rest were dead or missing.

The station itself hung drunkenly in the sky above Shadderal, smoke still leaking from ruptures that would take months to repair. All around the station floated a new field—not of asteroids, but of dead ships. None whole. Nothing there was left alive.

Calisto and Bianca stood on the command bridge of the station, NecroTeks and surviving fighter pilots clustered together down on the deck. Jenny Spears and Evie Cronin were on a RealScreen. In the background, unconscious and close to death, lay Torquil Brollachan. A strange figure stood over him, its face and upper body hidden by shadows.

On the largest screen, the rebel Medusa ship hung, silent and battered.

"Now what?" asked Calisto.

Bianca shook her head. She turned at the sound of the bridge door hissing open, and Lars Soren came in. He was haggard, pale, leaning on crutches. His thick beard and hair were now streaked with white, and there were ghosts in his eyes. He came and stood next to Bianca.

Croft looked at him. "You look like shit."

Soren smiled faintly. "I'm alive, Sebastian. That will have to do for now."

They watched the Medusa. The shoggoths on board had made no attempt at communication. Nor had Asphodel. The station's guns were loaded. The NecroTeks had their titan bodies.

"It's just sitting there," said Calisto. "What does it want?"

"No idea," said Bianca.

"Perhaps even they don't know," said Soren. "I think this is new territory for them, too."

"Maybe, but if we have to fight," said Jacob, "there's enough junk floating out there to make new forms, and we *will* kick its ass."

"*If* we have to fight," echoed Soren.

The Medusa drifted. Its launch doors were closed, and the barrels of all its guns were cold and black.

2

Bliss

Jenny Spears sat on a crate and wrapped bandages around her many wounds. Not Larry was sleeping in the arms of Morpheus, having been dosed because of the severity of his wounds. Spider stood near Spears, his eyes frequently cutting over to Caliban. Evie sat beside her, arms around her wife, head on Jenny's shoulder.

"Um, boss," said Spider, "maybe you should go over all this from the beginning."

Spears laughed. "Which part? The God Machine? The night-gaunts? Or Caliban?"

Spider just shook his head. "God, I wish I was drunk."

3

Shadderal

Lost stood on the Field of Dead Birds, looking up at the sky. Through his interface with Sybil, he could see everything that was happening in space.

He shook his head slowly.

"Now what?" he asked the wind.

But the wind kept its secrets to itself.

4

The God Machine

Jenny Spears and Evie sat together outside the God Machine chamber.

"Now what?" asked Jenny. She nodded toward the machine as she asked it.

"I don't know," said Evie. "I think we'll need to ask Caliban to help us make contact. It will be the strangest conversation in human history. If Torq survives, then he can help. He spent two years talking with Caliban. He understands the shoggoths better than anyone."

"No," said Spears, "I mean about the God Machine. What do we do about it?"

Evie studied her face. "What do you think we should do?"

"My first impulse is to say 'Blow it up.' I still have that pouch of plasma grenades. We can set them on a timer and be halfway to Asphodel before they go bang. There's enough to blow this moon halfway back to Earth. And if that isn't enough, we can come back and carpet-bomb this place into dust."

"Is that what you really want?"

Spears considered. She brushed a strand of curly hair away from Evie's brow. "I don't know, babe. That contraption is the most dangerous thing that ever existed. The night-gaunts and the Outer Gods came way too close to getting it, and that would have been game over for everyone back home. Everyone everywhere, really."

"It might also get us back home," said Evie.

"*Might* being a tricky word."

"Even so. I think we owe it to everyone who fought this war to try. We owe it to the living and the dead."

"Do we?"

"What do you mean?"

"We stopped the enemy, love, and it really cost us. We couldn't fight another battle like that. If the Outer Gods send another fleet after us, they'll just *take* it."

"They tried a couple of times, Jenny. We won each time."

Spears held her thumb and forefinger a centimeter apart. "We came that close to losing."

"But they don't *know* that," Evie said. "All they know is that they hit us hard, and each time we won. The NecroTek destroyed Leviathan and maybe the night-gaunt homeworld."

They sat and thought about that for a long time. Behind them, Brollachan groaned in his coma. Caliban and Spider sat three meters apart on the base of the God Machine. They had been in there for an hour, and neither had spoken a word.

"Maybe we'd better ask your old teacher," said Spears wearily. "Soren seems pretty bright. And let's face it, what falls under the label of 'cosmic philosophy' more than this?"

"Maybe we will."

Spears wrapped her arm around Evie, who laid her head on the soldier's chest.

In the mouth of the God Machine, the Earth turned slowly.

5

Queen Maud Land, Antarctica

Dr. Conrad Dyer stood up in the saddle of his snowcat and put his binoculars to his eyes.

The soaring peaks of the Vinson Massif rose before him, casting a deep shadow across a valley that had been excavated over the last two years. Military drones and gunships patrolled endlessly above the dig site. Every time he came out here, more of the find was laid bare. Crews worked day and night without stop.

As it always did, the vista made his heart race.

Below, revealed for the first time in millions of years, was a city. Vastly old, impossibly large.

Dyer lowered the glasses and stood there, speaking only one single word.

"Beautiful."

The Players

Artifact Team: Antarctica

Dr. Torquil "Torq" Brollachan, director of Project Caliban
Brenda Cooper, doctoral candidate, mineralogy
Prof. Evangeline "Evie" Cronin
  Craig Anders, doctoral candidate, senior graduate assistant
  Gillian Archer, graduate assistant
Col. Thomas Jefferson Hobart
Dr. Beatrice Howard, molecular biologist
Dr. Joan Kimbra, Structural engineer
Dr. Alan Meyer, physicist specializing in energy fields
Dr. Paul Mogilevich, staff physician
Dr. Andy Patel, physicist
Alice Portevin, metallurgist
Macklin "Mac" Ryerson, site mechanic
Dr. Indira Singh, therapist
Dr. Alejandro Solà, research physician
Dr. T. T. Wu, organic chemist
Dr. Shijun Xi, exobiologist
  Sean Riley, senior laboratory assistant

ASPHODEL STATION DIVISION CHIEFS

Delia Trumbo, station executive
Billy "Gopher" Broussard, head of medical sciences
Capt. Sebastian Croft, chief of military operations
Abdou Diatta, chief engineer
Dr. Jae-Sung Hak, evolutionary biologist and exobiologist
Daniel Hender, EVA mission chief
Dr. Nan Man-fei, senior director of integrated sciences
Dr. Denny Paek, head of astronomy and stellar cartography
Dr. Oki Sato, head of computer sciences and IT
Tess Smitrovitch, head of public relations and media
Dušan Veljković, chief of security

LOST SOULS SQUADRON: Tumblers (T-class single-pilot fighters)

T-1	Lt. Cmdr. Veronica Roland	Calisto
T-2	LTJG Haley Majka	Sweetpea
T-3	Ensign Ethan Riley Saylor	Reaper
T-4	Ensign Phillip Kesler	Hummingbird
T-5	Ensign Youssef El-Shenawy	Habibi
T-6	Ensign Jean-Paul Lloris	Decaf
T-7	Ensign Marco Diaz	Cricket
T-8	Brigham Cole	Thor
T-9	Ammar Fayek	Horus
T-10	Leva Baumila	Junda
T-11	Claire Murphy	Morrigan
T-12	Anders Hedlund	Woden
T-13	Jerry Tatopoulos	Deimos
T-14	Thomas Beale	Aries
T-15	David Gauthier	Oguan
T-16	Amadeus Thibodeau	Baron Samedi
T-17	Kiki Raffelsberger	Enchantress
T-18	Chavalit Yipintsoi	Elephant Boy
T-19	Alicia Mohidin	Ballerina
T-20	Mohamed Thajudeen	Nomad

NecroTeks

Commander Bianca Petrescu	Mosquito
LTJG Jacob Fox	Galahad
Ensign Voula Achilleos	Spartan
Ensign Hector Almeida	Sundance
Ensign Bo Chow	Beezer
Ensign Zito Luvumbo	Rabbit
Ensign Joshua McGinnis	Thunder Bear
Ensign Ian Potts	Tank
Ensign Chance Thompson	Lucky
Ensign Boris Vijenko	Lovechild
Ensign Matthew Walker	Ventum
Ensign Jahziel Yaakv	Jericho

The Jokers

Jenny Spears	Lifeguard
Mandu Goolagong	Spider
Marco Alfani	Not Larry
Dillie Kanaka	Krampus
Jonas Mungoshi	Moonboy
Lisa Red	Widow
Jirayut Tatsanasomboon	Footie
Omar Varayev	Ratjack
Alvin Yen	Mangler

Acknowledgments

This novel could not have been undertaken without the help of a lot of talented and generous people. In no particular order: Jeffrey Falcon Logue; astronomer Lisa Will; my friendly neighborhood mad scientist, Dr. Ronald Coleman; Bill Willard; and the winners of the NecroTek contest—Chance Thompson, Matthew Walker, Ethan Riley Taylor, Joshua McGinnis, Veronica Roland, and Phillip Kesler. Thanks to my wonderful assistant, Dana Fredsti; my literary agent, Sara Crowe of Sara Crowe Literary; the good folks at Blackstone Publishing; my fellow weirdos at *Weird Tales* magazine; and my film agent, Dana Spector of Creative Artists Agency. And very special thanks to my brilliant audiobook reader, Ray Porter.